Praise for *The People's Republic of Everything*

"Mamatas at his best. Makes me laugh. Makes me drop things. Makes me read on. Makes me run for cover."
—Terry Bisson, author of *Bears Discover Fire*

"Nick Mamatas is the gadfly that makes the horse buck—whip-smart and no bullshit and with one hell of a bite. These are canny, nimble stories that navigate between genre and literature, and are unlike what anyone else is writing."
—Brian Evenson, author of *The Warren* and *Fugue State*

"How does speculative fiction retain its relevance in an era when daily events feel fictitious and the mere possibility of a future seems speculative? If anyone knows the answer, it's Nick Mamatas. *The People's Republic of Everything* is a great leap forward. Let's hope there's somewhere to land."
—Jarett Kobek, author of *I Hate the Internet*

"Mamatas extracts the essence of several subgenres and cult followings that are in themselves so niche, obscure, and esoteric, and creates a genre that is uniquely him . . . Kerouac's language, Lovecraft's atmosphere, and Bukowski's coarseness."
—*Infinite Text*

"Mamatas is such a great novelist that it's easy to forget he also writes superb short stories. This collection is a testament to his short-form chops, and a powerful one at that."
—*LitReactor*

Praise for *I Am Providence*

"Just what I'd expect from Nick Mamatas: sharp wit, biting but humane social commentary, and, for the romantics among us, a faceless narrator decomposing at the morgue."
—Matt Ruff, author of *Bad Monkeys* and *Lovecraft Country*

"Mamatas knows his subject inside and out, and that makes *I Am Providence* all the more cutting. He's a fan himself, as well as a skeptic, and he turns his considerable authority and satirical skill toward skewering the subculture that's grown up around Lovecraft over the past century."
—Jason Heller, *NPR*

"Dark and hilarious . . . *I Am Providence* is that murder-mystery-in-a-writers-convention you didn't even know you wanted, but (like the human skin-bound book which propels the plot) you really must buy."
—Lavie Tidhar, author of *Central Station* and *The Violent Century*

"[Starred Review] A great choice for readers who enjoyed Matt Ruff's *Lovecraft Country*; those who liked the dark humor, mystery, and speculative elements in Ben H. Winters' The Last Policeman trilogy; and anyone who has ever been part of a fandom."
—*Booklist*

"Dark and funny, a fantastic mix of horror and mystery. It pokes fun at tropes—both meta or otherwise—and successfully skewers some of the more ridiculous aspects of the publishing industry."
—*LitReactor*

Praise for *Under My Roof*

"[Starred Review] A big-bang ending caps the fast-paced novel, and there's much fun to be had watching Mamatas merrily skewer his targets."
—*Publishers Weekly*

"What about the Great American Suburban Novel? Somewhere in there, as of now, you almost have to include Nick Mamatas' *Under My Roof,* an oddball, occasionally hilarious, surprisingly wise and out-and-out subversive little pocket-nuke of a book."
—*San Diego Union Tribune*

Praise for *Sensation*

"Nick Mamatas continues his reign as the sharpest, funniest, most insightful and political purveyor of post-pulp pleasures going. He is the People's Commissar of Awesome."
—China Miéville, bestselling author of *The City & the City*

"Mamatas is a powerfully acerbic writer, both in fiction and online. His acid wit is infamous, and it is on splendid display in *Sensation*, which is alive with scornful insight about pop culture, the net, and politics. I recommend it highly."
—Cory Doctorow, bestselling author of *Walkaway*

Praise for *The Damned Highway*

"The book is incredibly entertaining and, aside from a strange turn towards the end, is a great trip through a fictional history of the 1972 presidential elections."
—*HorrorTalk*

"[A] clever, disturbing, and absurd (in the best sense) mash-up of Lovecraft and Hunter S. Thompson that made our recommended gift list for the year."
—*Weird Fiction Review*

Also By Nick Mamatas

Novels
Move Under Ground (2005)
Under My Roof (2007)
Sensation (2011)
The Damned Highway (with Brian Keene, 2011)
Love Is the Law (2013)
The Last Weekend (2014)
I Am Providence (2016)

Short story collections
3000 MPH in Every Direction at Once (2003)
You Might Sleep . . . (2009)
The Nickronomicon (2014)

Anthologies (as editor)
The Urban Bizarre (2004)
Realms (with Sean Wallace, 2008)
Spicy Slipstream Stories (with Jay Lake, 2008)
Realms 2 (with Swan Wallace, 2009)
Haunted Legends (with Ellen Datlow, 2010)
The Future is Japanese (with Masumi Washington, 2012)
Phantasm Japan (with Masumi Washington, 2014)
Hanzai Japan (with Masumi Washington, 2015)
Mixed Up (with Molly Tanzer, 2017)

Nonfiction
Kwangju Diary (with Jae-Eui Lee & Kap Su Seol, 1999)
Insults Every Man Should Know (2011)
Starve Better (2011)
Quotes Every Man Should Know (2013)
The Battle Royale Slam Book (with Masumi Washington, 2014)

Poetry
Cthulhu Senryu (2006)

NICK MAMATAS

THE PEOPLE'S REPUBLIC OF

EVERYTHING

TACHYON | SAN FRANCISCO

Tachyon Publications LLC
1459 18th Street #139
San Francisco, CA 94107
415.285.5615
www.tachyonpublications.com
tachyon@tachyonpublications.com

Series Editor: Jacob Weisman
Project Editor: Jill Roberts

Print ISBN 13: 978-1-61696-300-2
Digital ISBN: 978-1-61696-301-9

First Edition: 2018
9 8 7 6 5 4 3 2 1

For my grandmother, Theodora "Doris" Vroutos

CONTENTS

NICK MAMATAS, CITIZEN OF THE REPUBLIC OF EVERYWHERE

BY JEFFREY FORD

I FIRST CAME ACROSS NICK MAMATAS on the Night Shade Books online bulletin board and his old LiveJournal page, where he played the role of the Nihilistic Kid. This was back a ways. Maybe fifteen years or more. The Nihilistic Kid was, if anything, a consummate ball-buster. The reason I cottoned to this in Mamatas's case, whereas I might not in others, was because he had grown up on Long Island in New York, and he dispensed a kind of dark, socially relevant, partly cynical, partly contentious for its own sake humor that is indigenous to Long Island. I know because I grew up on the Island as well. So even when I was the brunt of his barbs, I still felt like I was home and found him, more often than not, hysterical. The other thing I noticed from that time was that if someone engaged him in a serious argument about some social or political issue, they rarely got the better of him. His approach was rational, well reasoned, and he had a depth of knowledge about history and politics (not just American) that informed his discourse. These two sides of him combined got me started reading his fiction and nonfiction.

When I was asked to write this intro for a collection of his stories, I took the opportunity because it's my belief that he's an underappreciated writer. He certainly has a solid fan base on social media, and a solid base of detractors as well. The latter doesn't seem to appreciate the ball-busting as I do. Nick spends a certain amount of time in public service, deflating outlandish egos, battling Nazis, and fluffing the cheeks of self-described Lovecraftian geniuses for the betterment of the Internet. Overall, though, I just don't think people appreciate the scope of his writing talent. We'll get to the stories in a minute, but first. . . .

My initial Mamatas read was the brilliant *Move Under Ground*. The book came out in 2004 and was an exciting mash-up of satirical Beat hagiography and the reanimation of the Lovecraft mythos. Jack Kerouac and William S. Burroughs plough across America to save it from the rising tide of Lovecraft's cosmic monsterage. It was cool, it was funny, it was harrowing. There were few novels from that time period that seemed as alive. And, I don't know if he ever gets credit for this but it was one of the earliest cases of a new crop of writers working off of Lovecraft's world, reconfiguring it into more interesting ideas and way better prose (think Laird Barron, John Langan, Kaaron Warren, etc.). Other important writers followed and the whole thing grew into a kind of movement coming out of a certain dark alley of the horror genre. It's a shame, but the novel doesn't seem to be in print anymore. Perhaps some smart small press or large will bring it back. If you haven't read it, do yourself a favor.

In recent years, Mamatas's long fiction has gotten shorter, if that makes sense. He's jumped ship from his origins in the horror genre (although you can still sense it growling in the basement of these books) from works like *Sensation* and *The Damned Highway* (with Brian Keene) to create three top-notch mystery/thrillers—*Love Is the Law*, *The Last Weekend*, and *I Am Providence*. At the International Conference of the Fantastic in the Arts in Orlando a couple of years ago, he told me that he was influenced in these works by pulp writers like David Goodis and Jim Thompson. Like the works of these noir masters, Mamatas's books are short, vicious stabs at the reader's sense of well-being. The length of them is important. Not in these words precisely, but he told me that for him, with this group of books, "less is more." They have all the thrills and suspense of the best of noir, but they've been recast for a contemporary world and shot through with a dark humor (see especially *I Am Providence*). In reading them, I drew comparisons in their brevity and impact to certain novels by Simenon.

So Mamatas is a novelist and yet he's also a writer of nonfiction, journalism, essays, and reviews. In earlier years, he wrote for *The Village Voice* and a number of other magazines and papers. I use a couple of his nonfiction pieces in my college writing classes. His essay "The Term Paper Artist," originally published at *The Smart Set*, is by now a classic. In it, he recounts his time making ends meet by churning out term papers for graduate and undergraduate students. I always hand it out in Comp classes before we begin on the first research paper. It gives the students a great perspective on the process they're about to become involved in. The essay is funny, recounting tales of desperate students. In a deeper sense, it's also a condemnation of higher education. I'll say no more. It's online for free. The other piece I use is his review of James Cameron's movie *Avatar*. This review is one of the best pieces of movie review writing I've ever encountered. It manages to be incredibly funny throughout and to also lay bare Cameron's ham-fisted plot and his blindness to his hero's colonialist buffoonery. I always wonder why some magazine doesn't hire Mamatas to write about pop culture or review books and/or movies. A great opportunity lost.

In addition to his novels and nonfiction, not to mention his eminently useful writer's self-help book, *Starve Better* (having more to do with actual day-to-day survival than writing advice), Mamatas has become an accomplished editor, having chosen stories for the online magazine Clarkesworld (2006 to 2008), editing anthologies like *Haunted Legends* (with Ellen Datlow for Tor Books) and more recently *Mixed Up: Cocktail Recipes (and Flash Fiction* (with Molly Tanzer for Skyhorse). His current day job (2008 to present) is editing translated speculative fiction and comics for the English-reading market from Japanese publisher Haikasoru. Mamatas is a multiple threat, moving so fast from one project to another that you might miss the scope of his abilities. To check up on all of this and much more, an interested reader should go to http://www.nick-mamatas.com/.

And finally we come to the short stories. I took a look at Nick's web page, and there have to be over a hundred of them. They've appeared in a wide variety of venues—in magazines and anthologies, and on podcasts. Prior to this current collection you hold in your hands, there were three others—*The Nickronomicon, You Might Sleep . . .* , and *3000 MPH in Every Direction at Once*. It's clear to me as a short story writer, reader, and lover that *The People's Republic of Everything* is some of this author's best fiction. Beyond the wide-ranging themes and styles of the fourteen short stories presented here, there's also the bonus track of the short novel, *Under My Roof*, an early longer fiction, which takes place on Long Island. Although it's reminiscent of a Vonnegut story, with its telepathic teen protagonist and nuclear-weaponized lawn jockey, it is its own hilarious beast and worth the price of admission.

I'm not going to mention each of the plots of all the stories in the current collection. For Christ's sake, you have the book in your hand. Read it. But I will go on a little here about what I admire about Mamatas's short fiction. Really sharp writing. There's an evident facility with language all throughout this volume, a clarity and flow that draws you in. With this ability, it's not necessary that every opening line be a hook. The style is its own hook. This allows the author to establish a more complex story and delve deeper into the piece before the reader is hungry for a turn in the plot. In addition, there's a wonderful sense that the parts of these pieces have been put together by a watchmaker—scenes that appear initially to be disparate eventually fall into place like parts of a delicate mechanism. In nearly every Mamatas story, there is a central idea: political, philosophical, cultural. The characters are not sacrificed to this idea but operate as whole, three-dimensional beings, and the plot is not tyrannized by it. It operates deep down in the story, a dialectic, positing some crucial conflict, and the fiction is an invitation for the reader to grapple with the competing aspects of it. It's the same action that's at the heart of metaphor. This seems to me to be at work in both a historical, satirical piece like the amazing "Arbeitskraft" as well as in more contemporary ones that deal to some degree with the world of fiction-making, such as "Tom Silex, Spirit-Smasher." In *The People's Republic of Everything* there are plenty of laughs, curious citizens, unusual instances from history, and ultimately engaging situations, but there are definitely no answers. That's your job.

WALKING WITH A GHOST

CHAKRAVARTY SPENT AT LEAST three months making the same joke about how the AI was going to start spouting, "Ph'nglui mglw'nafh C'thulhu R'lyeh wgah'nagl fhtagn," and then all hell would break loose—a Singularity with tentacles. Sometimes he'd even run to the bank of light switches and flick the lights on and off. It was funny the first time to Melanie, and she squeezed a bit more mirth out of Chakravarty's inability to pronounce the prayer to Cthulhu the same way twice. Making the Lovecraft AI had been Melanie's idea, but it was Chakravarty who tried to keep the mood whimsical. Both worried that Lovecraft would just wake up screaming.

"—and he does scream, occasionally," Melanie explained. Her advisor and a few other grad students were at the presentation, in the front rows, but as these presentations were theoretically open to the public, the Lovecraftians had come out in force, squeezing themselves into the tiny desk-chairs. They looked a lot like grad students themselves, but even paler and more poorly dressed in ill-fitting T-shirts and unusual garments—one even wore a fedora—plus they kept interrupting.

"Can we hear it talk?" one asked, and then he raised his hand, as if remembering that he had to. "Ask it questions?"

"Please, leave all questions—for us—until after the presentation. We're not going to expose the AI to haphazard stimuli during this presentation," Chakravarty said.

"He's . . . fairly calm so far," Melanie said. "Which is to be expected. We know a lot about Lovecraft. He recorded almost everything he did or thought in his letters, after all, and we have nearly all of them. What ice cream he liked, how it felt to catch the last train out of South Station, how he saw the colors scarlet and purple when he thought the word evil. He was fairly phlegmatic, for all the crazy prose and ideas, so he's okay."

"How do we know that this is really an artificial intelligence, and not just a bunch of programmed responses?" This one, huge and bearded, wore a fedora.

Chakravarty opened his mouth to speak, his face hard, but Melanie answered with an upturned palm. "It's fine," she said to him. "Most of these talks are total snoozers. Nobody ever has any questions." Then, to the audience: "I'd argue that we can't know it's a bunch of programmed responses, except that we didn't program all the responses we've seen so far. Of course, I don't know that you, sir," she said, pointing to the Lovecraftian, "aren't also just a bunch of programmed responses that are just the physical manifestation of the reactions going on in the bag of chemicals you keep in your skull."

"I don't feel like I am!"

"Do you believe everything you feel; do you not believe in anything you haven't?"

"No, and no true Lovecraftian would," he said.

"Right. So you don't believe in the female orgasm," Melanie said. The room erupted in hoots and applause. Then Chakravarty got up, shouted that everyone who didn't understand what's going on should just go home, Google "Chinese room," and stop asking stupid questions. "Ooh, Chinese—Lovecraft wouldn't like that room," someone said. Then the classroom was quiet again.

"Uh, thanks for that, Chakravarty," Melanie said. She adjusted her watch, thick and blocky on her wrist. "I've been walking around the city with him. He likes Boston and Cambridge, it helped ease him into his, uh, existence. And he knew things, how roads crossed and bits of history, that I didn't know, that we didn't program into him. But we did program a lot into him. Everything we had access to, both locally and up at Brown." Behind her, a ghostly image of the author, chin like a bucket, eyes wide and a bit wild, flickered into existence. He sat in an overstuffed chair in the swirling null-space of a factory-present screensaver image.

"Well, if there are no more questions"—Melanie glanced about the classroom and there were no questions, just some leftover giggles—"why don't we have him say hello?"

The room went silent. "And none of that ftang ftang stuff," Melanie added. Somebody giggled, high-pitched like a fife.

Chakravarty leaned down into a microphone that snaked out from the laptop. "Lovecraft, can you hear me? Can you see us? Many people here have read your stories."

The image blinked. "Hello," it said, its voice tinny and distant.

"How are you?" Chakravarty asked. A simple question, one with only a couple of socially acceptable answers. A kid could program the word "Fine," into an AIM buddy chat.

"I do not quite know," Lovecraft said. "I . . ." he trailed off, then looked out into the room, as if peering into the distance. "Why have you people done this to me?"

Chakravarty giggled, all nerves. Melanie opened her mouth, but was interrupted by one of the professors, who waved a gnarled hand. Chakravarty clicked off the mic. On the screen, Lovecraft started, as if he sensed something, and he began to peer into the distance, as if seeing past the other side of the screen upon which he was projected.

"What sort of internal state does this AI supposedly have?" the professor asked.

"Well, as one of the major problems with developing strong AI is embodiment—" Melanie stopped herself, and added for the fans and cops, "the idea that learning takes place because we have bodies and live in a social world . . . well, some of us do. Anyway, Lovecraft, in addition to having left behind enough personal correspondence to reconstruct much of his day-to-day life, was also rather repulsed by the body, by the idea of flesh. Many of his stories involve a brain trapped in a metal cylinder, or a consciousness stranded millions of years in the past. So we decided to tell him that we have a ghost. No body, no problem."

"Where's he going?" asked the guy in the fedora.

Chakravarty tapped on the keys of the laptop. Melanie wiggled the projector cable. The chair was empty. Lovecraft had gotten up and walked right off the edge of the screen.

"A non-fat venti misto," Chakravarty said. That was Melanie's drink. She made eye contact.

"Oh, hi."

"How's life among the proletariat treating you?"

"I'm a manager," she said. "Watch this." Off came her cap and apron—"Tyler, cover me." She quickly made two drinks and walked around the counter. "See?"

"Great," Chakravarty said. "Anyway, I have the list." From his messenger bag he dug out a binder the size of the local Yellow Pages. "Twice as many as last time."

"And still no idea where he could be?" Then, as Chakravarty pointed to the binder, Melanie interrupted herself, "I mean, where he is."

"Moore's law, you know. The longer the AI is out in the wild, the more servers are actually capable of supporting it, plus it's Alife. It's been eighteen months, so we can say that the number of nodes capable of holding him has doubled. Plus, who knows what it looks like by now. I've been closely reading my spam—"

"In that case, the misto is on the house."

"Heh," said Chakravarty. "Anyway, a content analysis shows that a lot of the AI's utterances and the correspondence documents have been popping up."

"All his fiction's in the public domain. Of course it would appear in spam."

"You're still doing that, you know—calling it he."

"And you're still calling him it."

Chakravarty leaned forward, an old and happy argument spelling itself out in his posture. "And you wanted to develop an AI, an Alife, because you didn't like animal testing and psych exams. But you got too close to the idea of your thesis project being real. Did it need memories of a love life to qualify as sufficiently embodied?"

"Well, you don't," Melanie said, snippy. She pushed the book away. "Why didn't you just email this to me? Hardcopy isn't even searchable," Melanie said. She quickly corrected herself: "Easily searchable." She made a show of flipping through the pages.

"Well, anyway," Chakravarty said, but he didn't have anything else to say except that he missed Melanie and wanted her to come back to the lab and that a wild AI was still worth a paper or three and how ridiculous it was to quit school, but he couldn't make himself mention any of that. So he pushed the book across the table to Melanie. "If you want to follow up, go ahead. I have things to do." He looked around the coffee shop, all dark tones and shelves. "So do you, I bet."

Melanie sipped her drink. "If only I did."

———

Melanie often dreamed of Chakravarty. Sometimes she found herself back in school, struggling with the final exam of a course she had forgotten to ever attend, only to be granted a reprieve and an automatic A when Chakravarty's death was announced over the loudspeaker of what was suddenly her fourth-grade classroom. The plastic desktop scraping against her knees felt thick and soft like a comforter, then she'd wake up. Or she dreamt of the bus ride to Providence, the grungy South Station and the long lines of kids in college sweatshirts. The mysterious letter that burned in her pocket. The house on Angell Street and Chakravarty's body bubbling into a puddle of ichor and rotten-seeming fungi. Or she dreamt of the sort of day a coffee shop manager dreams about—a bit rainy, but warm inside, and the old smell of the bean surging back to the forefront like the first day of work. No lines, but enough customers to keep the store buzzing. And laptops. And then Lovecraft on all the screens. The image, black and white and shot through with static, like that old Super Bowl commercial, opens his mouth—its mouth—and screams that he has correlated all the contents of his own mind. And he is afraid.

Melanie woke up one morning and remembered that Lovecraft had, on one occasion, a complete story seemingly delivered to him in a dream. Without the resources of the university, she'd never be able to find a wayward AI hiding somewhere in the black oceans of the net, but she knew she could find a frightened man. First, talk to his friends.

The Lovecraftian cabal was easy enough to find. Melanie already had long experience with being the girl in the comic shop, the girl in the computer lab, the girl in the gaming store. Dove soap and magenta highlights always went a long way toward getting boys to speak to her. The anime club led to the science fiction specialty shop and then to the "goth" store and its plastic gargoyles and stringy-haired vampire cashier, which led, finally, to the soggy couch in the basement of the place that sold Magic cards and Pocky. They were there, and the dude in the fedora recognized her. Clearly the alpha of his pack, he swanned across the room, belly and the flapping lapels of his trenchcoat a step ahead the rest of him, and sat down next to Melanie.

"I'm utterly horrid with names, but never forget a face," he said. He had a smile. Decent teeth, Melanie noticed.

"Melanie Deutsch. You came to my—"

"Ah. Yes. Now I remember everything."

For a long moment neither of them said anything. A few feet away someone rolled a handful of die and yelped in glee.

"I know why you're here," he said.

Melanie shrugged. "Of course you do. Why else would I be here?"

The man fell silent again, pursed his lips, and then tried again: "I would say that the AI is an it, not a he."

"Oh?" Melanie said.

"It can't write. Not creatively anyway."

"Maybe he just doesn't feel the need to write—I mean, it's a goal-oriented behavior and he thinks he's a ghost."

"Pffft," the fedora man said. "He knew he wasn't a ghost; he doesn't believe in them. Lovecraft was a pretty bright guy, a genius by some measures. The program realized its own—" he waved his hands in front of Melanie's face, too close—"programmitude right off."

"And it was his idea to escape, maybe hitching a ride on your iPhone?"

"No. We didn't find the AI till a few months ago. It sought us out, after finding the online fanzine archive, and our club's server," he said. "We even tried to make a copy of it, but the DRM was too—"

"That's not DRM," Melanie said. "He wouldn't let you. It's human rights management—"

The fedora man snorted again. Melanie realized that she didn't know his name, and that she wasn't going to ask for it.

"Say . . . do you want to talk to it?" Fedora asked. He dug into his coat pockets and pulled out a PDA. "This thing has a little cam, so it can respond to you . . ." he muttered. Melanie held out a hand, but Fedora just held the device up to her face. "No touchie."

Melanie uttered an arbitrary phoneme. Not quite a huh.

The Lovecraft AI appeared on the tiny screen. He'd . . . changed. Uglier now, jaw hyperinflated, but the rest of his head narrow and his nose flat against his face. Eyes like boiled eggs, hair all but gone. Horrid, but somehow alive. "Hello, ma'am," he said.

"How are you?" Melanie found herself saying. She was as programmed as anyone else. That realization burst out of her, all sweat.

"Why did you tell me," the AI asked, "how exactly I died? How could anyone be expected to . . . persist, knowing that? A universe of blasphemous horrors—finger puppets worn by a literary hand. I always knew that my life meant nothing, that all human life means nothing, but to experience it, to be in the void, like a doll cut out of paper only able to think enough just to fear, I—I just wanted to go home, but found myself . . . nowhere. And everywhere." The fedora man's meaty hand clamped over the PDA, so Lovecraft's screams were muffled.

Melanie reached into her backpack—Emily the Strange, smelled like coffee—and got her phone. It was a very nice phone.

"Not it, he," she said. "He wants to go back to when he wasn't afraid."

Fedora glanced down at the phone. "Oh, so you can make a copy?"

"Don't talk like he isn't here," Melanie said. "And I'm certainly not going to leave him with you."

"Well, have you ever considered that maybe it . . . uh, he, wants to stay?"

Melanie gave the basement the once over. "No," she said. "Plus, it . . . or he?"

"You know what I—"

"If it's an it, you're in possession of stolen goods."

"Fine. He. He came to this place! He came to me, he—"

"If Lovecraft is a he, well, God knows what that'll mean. Kidnapping, maybe. Is he competent to make his own decisions? Does he have a Social Security number? Do you want the feds going through your systems and digging up all your hentai and stolen music to find out?"

Fedora raised his PDA over his head. "No, no. You're just—"

"And then there are the patents we filed. We trademarked the look and feel of his chair, too. But you can turn him over to me instead of to the district attorney." She smirked at Fedora, but then tilted her head to speak to the AI. "Not among people, but among scenes," she said, almost as if asking a question. A muffled yawp came from the PDA.

Melanie, on wind-swept Benefit Street, venti misto in one hand, Lovecraft in the other. Lovecraft says that he is Providence. That's programmed. Melanie smiles and sometimes he smiles back. That's not.

———

I've been writing Lovecraftian fiction since near the beginning of my career. My first novel, *Move Under Ground*, was inspired by noticing that both Lovecraft and Kerouac had a cult of readers sufficiently large to support the publication of their correspondence. Lovecraft was a far more prolific writer of letters than he was of fiction, and his letters are often more entertaining that his stories.

"Walking with a Ghost" is one of two stories in this volume about collecting correspondence to create a personality-emulator. I'm not sure why I'm so interested in this concept, but I think my history as a blogger has something to do with it. When I first began blogging, I decided that I'd record every experience I had as I remembered it, which led to massive problems keeping friends who didn't like the way they were depicted, and didn't share my memories of our conversations and activities. "Same to you, buddy!" is all one can say to that, but you don't get to have many buddies afterwards. So I made my blog more of a professional one, and much less a public diary.

Lovecraft also appears in fiction as a character very often, thanks to his correspondence. We know *a lot* about him and his daily routines, his execrable politics and racial attitudes, his aesthetics, and his humor. Given nerdy love of both all things tentacular and for completism, if we ever get to create personality emulators, Lovecraft *is* going to be one of the first people an ambitious graduate student will re-create. It may even be a good thing, so long as we don't let him blog about contemporary social issues.

ARBEITSKRAFT

1. The Transformation Problem

IN GLANCING OVER MY CORRESPONDENCE with Herr Marx, especially the letters written during the period in which he struggled to complete his opus, *Capital*, even whilst I was remanded to the Victoria Mill of Ermen and Engels in Weaste to simultaneously betray the class I was born into and the class to which I'd dedicated my life, I was struck again by the sheer audacity of my plan. I've moved beyond political organizing or even investigations of natural philosophy and have used my family's money and the labour of my workers—even now, after a lifetime of railing against the bourgeoisie, their peculiar logic limns my language—to encode my old friend's thoughts in a way I hope will prove fruitful for the struggles to come.

I am a fox, ever hunted by agents of the state, but also by political rivals and even the occasional enthusiastic student intellectual *manqué*. For two weeks, I have been making a very public display of destroying my friend's voluminous correspondence. The girls come in each day and carry letters and covers both in their aprons to the roof of the mill to burn them in a soot-stained metal drum. It's a bit of a spectacle, especially as the girls wear cowls to avoid smoke inhalation and have rather pronounced limps as they walk the bulk of letters along the roof, but we are ever attracted to spectacle, aren't we? The strings of electrical lights in the petit-bourgeois districts that twinkle all night, the iridescent skins of the dirigibles that litter the skies over The City like peculiar flying fish leaping from the ocean—they even appear overhead here in Manchester, much to the shock, and more recently, glee of the street urchins who shout and yawp whenever one passes under the clouds, and the only slightly more composed women on their way to squalid Deansgate market. A fortnight ago I took in a theatrical production, a local production of Mr. Peake's *Presumption: or the Fate of Frankenstein*, already a hoary old play given new life and revived, ironically enough, by recent innovations in electrified machine-works. How bright the lights, how stunning the arc of actual lightning, tamed and obedient, how thunderous the ovations and the crumbling of the glacial cliffs! All the bombast of German opera in a space no larger than a middle-class parlour. And yet, throughout the entire evening, the great and hulking monster never spoke. *Contra* Madame Shelley's engaging novel, the "new Adam" never learns of philosophy, and the total of her excellent speeches of critique against the social institutions of her, and our, day are expurgated. Instead, the monster is ever an infant, given only to explosions of rage. Yet the audience, which contained a fair number of working-men who had managed to save or secure 5d. for "penny-stinker" seating, were enthralled. The play's Christian morality, alien to the original novel, was spelled out as if on a slate for the audience, and the monster was rendered as nothing more than an artefact of unholy vice. But lights blazed, and living snow from coils of refrigeration fell from the ceiling, and spectacle won the day.

My burning of Marx's letters is just such a spectacle—the true correspondence is secreted among a number of the safe houses I have acquired in Manchester and London. The girls on the rooftop are burning unmarked leaves, schoolboy doggerel, sketches, and whatever else I have laying about. The police have infiltrated Victoria Mill, but all their agents are men, as the work of espionage is considered too vile for the gentler sex. So the men watch the girls come from my office with letters by the bushel and burn them, then report every lick of flame and wafting cinder to their superiors.

My brief digression regarding the *Frankenstein* play is apposite, not only as it has to do with spectacle but with my current operation at Victoria Mill. Surely, Reader, you are familiar with Mr Babbage's remarkable Difference Engine, perfected in 1822—a year prior to the first production of Mr. Peake's theatrical adaptation of *Frankenstein*—given the remarkable changes to the political economy that took place in the years after its introduction. How did we put it, back in the heady 1840s? *Subjection of Nature's forces to man, machinery, application of chemistry to industry and agriculture, steam-navigation, railways, electric telegraphs, clearing of whole continents for cultivation, canalisation of rivers, whole populations conjured out of the ground— what earlier century had even a presentiment that such productive forces slumbered in the lap of social labour?* That was just the beginning. Ever more I was reminded not of my old work with Marx, but of Samuel Butler's prose fancy *Erewhon—the time will come when the machines will hold the real supremacy over the world and its inhabitants is what no person of a truly philosophic mind can for a moment question.*

With the rise of the Difference Engine and the subsequent rationalization of market calculations, the bourgeoisie's revolutionary aspect continued unabated. Steam-navigation took to the air; railways gave way to horseless carriages; electric telegraphs to instantaneous wireless aethereal communications; the development of applied volcanisation to radically increase the amount of arable land, and to tame the great prize of Africa, the creation of automata for all but the basest of labour . . . ah, if only Marx were still here. That, I say to myself each morning upon rising. *If only Marx were still here!* The stockholders demand to know why I have not automated my factory, as though the clanking stove-pipe limbs of the steam-workers aren't just more dead labor! As though *Arbeitskraft*—labour-power—is not the source of all value! *If only Marx were still here!* And he'd say, to me, *Freddie, perhaps we were wrong.* Then he'd laugh and say, *I'm just having some fun with you.*

But we were not wrong. The internal contradictions of capitalism have not peacefully resolved themselves; the proletariat still may become the new revolutionary class, even as steam-worker builds steam-worker under the guidance of the of Difference Engine No. 53. The politico-economic chasm between bourgeoisie and proletarian has grown ever wider, despite the best efforts of the Fabian Society and other gradualists to improve the position of the working-class vis-à-vis their esteemed—and *en-steamed*, if you would forgive the pun—rulers. The Difference Engine is a device of formal logic, limited by the size of its gear-work and the tensile strength of the metals used in its construction. What I propose is a device of *dialectical logic*, a repurposing of the looms, a recording of unity of conflicts and opposites drawn on the finest of threads to pull innumerable switches, based on a linguistic programme derived from the correspondence of my comrade-in-arms.

I am negating the negation, transforming my factory into a massive Dialectical Engine that replicates not the arithmetical operations of an abacus but the cogitations of a human brain. I am rebuilding Karl Marx on the factory floor, repurposing the looms of the factory to create punch-cloths of over one thousand columns, and I will speak to my friend again.

2. The Little Match Girls

Under the arclights of Fairfield Road I saw them, on my last trip to The City. The evening's amusement had been invigorating if empty, a fine meal had been consumed immediately thereafter, and a digestif imbibed. I'd dismissed my London driver for the evening, for a cross-town constitutional. I'd catch the late airship, I thought. Match girls, leaving their shift in groups, though I could hardly tell them from steam-workers at first, given their awkward gaits and the gleam of metal under the lights, so like the monster in the play, caught my eye.

Steam-workers still have trouble with the finest work—the construction of Difference Engine gears is skilled labour performed by a well-remunerated aristocracy of working-men. High-quality cotton garments and bedclothes too are the remit of proletarians of the *flesh*, thus Victoria Mill. But there are commodities whose production still requires living labour, not because of the precision needed to create the item, but due to the danger of the job. The production of white phosphorous matches is one of these. The matchsticks are too slim for steam-worker claws, which are limited to a trio of pincers on the All-Purpose Models, and to less refined appendages—sledges, sharp blades—on Special-Purpose Models. Furthermore, the aluminium outer skin, or shell, of the steam-worker tends to heat up to the point of combusting certain compounds, or even plain foolscap. So Bryant and May Factory in Bow, London, retained young girls, ages fourteen and up, to perform the work.

The stories in *The Link* and other reformist periodicals are well-known. Twelve-hour days for wages of 4s. a week, though it's a lucky girl who isn't fined for tardiness, who doesn't suffer deductions for having dirty feet, for dropping matches from her frame, for allowing the machines to falter rather than sacrifice her fingers to it. The girls eat their bread and butter—most can afford more only rarely, and then it's marmalade—on the line, leading to ingestion of white phosphorous. And there were the many cases of "phossy jaw"—swollen gums, foul breath, and some physicians even claimed that the jawbones of the afflicted would glow, like a candle shaded by a leaf of onion skin paper. I saw the gleaming of these girls' jaws as I passed and swore to myself. They were too young for phossy jaw; it takes years for the deposition of phosphorous to build. But as they passed me by, I saw the truth.

Their jaws had all been removed, a typical intervention for the disease, and they'd been replaced with prostheses. All the girls, most of whom were likely plain before their transformations, were now half-man half-machine, monstrosities! I couldn't help but accost them.

"Girls! Pardon me!" There were four of them; the tallest was perhaps fully mature, and the rest were mere children. They stopped, obedient. I realized that their metallic jaws that gleamed so brightly under the new electrical streetlamps might not be functional and I was flushed with concern. Had I humiliated them?

The youngest-seeming opened her mouth and said in a voice that had a greater similarity to the product of a phonographic cylinder than a human throat, "Buy Bryant and May matchsticks, Sir."

"Oh no, I don't need any matchsticks. I simply—"

"Buy Bryant and May matchsticks, Sir," she said again. Two of the others—the middle girls—lifted their hands and presented boxes of matchsticks for my perusal. One of those girls had two silvery digits where a thumb and forefinger had presumably once been. They were cleverly designed to articulate on the knuckles, and through some mechanism occulted to me did move in a lifelike way.

"Do any of you girls have the facility of original speech?" The trio looked to the tallest girl, who nodded solemnly and said, "I." She struggled with the word, as though it were unfamiliar. "My Bryant and May mandible," she continued, "I was given it by . . . Bryant and May . . . long ago."

"So, with some struggle, you are able to compel speech of your own?"

"Buy . . . but Bryant and May match . . . made it hard," the girl said. Her eyes gleamed nearly as brightly as her metallic jaw.

The smallest of the four started suddenly, then turned her head, looking past her compatriots. "Buy!" she said hurriedly, almost rudely. She grabbed the oldest girl's hand and tried to pull her away from our conversation. I followed her eyes and saw the telltale plume of a police wagon rounding the corner. Lacking any choice, I ran with the girls to the end of the street and then turned a corner.

For a long moment, we were at a loss. Girls such as these are the refuse of society—often the sole support of their families, and existing in horrific poverty, they nonetheless hold to all the feminine rules of comportment. Even a troupe of them, if spotted in the public company of an older man in his evening suit, would simply be ruined women—sacked from their positions for moral turpitude, barred from renting in any situation save for those reserved for women engaged in prostitution; ever surrounded by criminals and other lumpen elements. The bourgeois sees in his wife a mere instrument of production, but in every female of the labouring classes he sees his wife. What monsters Misters Bryant and May must have at home! I dared not follow the girls for fear of terrifying them, nor could I even attempt to persuade them to accompany me to my safe-house. I let them leave, and proceeded to follow them as best I could. The girls ran crookedly, their legs bowed in some manner obscured by the work aprons, so they were easy enough to tail. They stopped at a small cellar two blocks from the Bryant and May works, and carefully stepped into the darkness, the tallest one closing the slanted doors behind her. With naught else to do, I made a note of the address, and back at my London lodgings I arranged for a livery to take me back there at half past five o'clock in the morning, when the girls would arise again to begin their working day.

I brought with me some sweets, and wore a threadbare fustian suit. My driver, Wilkins, and I did not have long to wait, for at twenty-two minutes after the hour of five, the cellar door swung open and a tiny head popped out. The smallest of the girls! But she immediately ducked back down into the cellar. I took a step forward and the largest girl partially emerged, though she was careful to keep her remarkable prosthetic jaw obscured from possible passing trade. The gutters on the edge of the pavement were filled with refuse and dank water, but the girl did not so much as wrinkle her nose, for she had long since grown accustomed to life in the working-class quarters.

"Hello," I said. I squatted down, then offered the butterscotch sweets with one hand and removed my hat with the other. "Do you remember me?"

"Buy Brya . . ." she began. Then, with visible effort, she stopped herself and said, "Yes." Behind her the smallest girl appeared again and completed the slogan. "Buy Bryant and May matchsticks, Sir."

"I would very much like to speak with you."

"We must . . . work," the older said. "Bryant and May matchsticks, Sir!" said the other. "Before the sun rises," the older one said. "Buy Bryant and May—" I cast the younger girl a dirty look, I'm shamed to say, and she ducked her head back down into the cellar.

"Yes, well, I understand completely. There is no greater friend the working-man has than I, I assure. Look, a treat!" I proffered the sweets again. If a brass jaw with greater familial resemblance to a bear-trap than a human mandible could quiver, this girl's did right then.

"Come in," she said finally.

The cellar was very similar to the many I had seen in Manchester during my exploration of the living conditions of the English proletariat. The floor was dirt and the furnishings limited to bales of hay covered in rough cloth. A dank and filthy smell from the refuse, garbage, and excrements that choked the gutter right outside the cellar entrance hung in the air. A small, squat, and wax-splattered table in the middle of the room held a soot-stained lantern. The girls wore the same smocks they had the evening before, and there was no sign of water for their toilet. Presumably, what grooming needs they had they attempted to meet at the factory itself, which was known to have a pump for personal use. Most cellar dwellings of this sort have a small cache of food in one corner—a sack of potatoes, butter wrapped in paper, and very occasionally a crust of bread. In this dwelling, there was something else entirely—a peculiar crank-driven contraption from which several pipes extruded.

The big girl walked toward it and with her phonographic voice told me, "We can't have sweets no more." Then she attached the pipes, which ended in toothy clips similar to the pincers of steam-workers, to either side of her mechanical mandible and began to crank the machine. A great buzzing rose up from the device and a flickering illumination filled the room. I could finally see the other girls in their corners, standing and staring at me. The large girl's hair stood on end from the static electricity she was generating, bringing to mind Miss Shelley's famed novel. I was fascinated and repulsed at once, though I wondered how such a generator could work if what it powered, the girl, itself powered the generator via the crank. Was it collecting a static charge from the air, as the skins of the newest airships did?

"Is this . . . generator your sustenance now?" I asked. She

stopped cranking and the room dimmed again. "Buy . . ." she started, then recovered, "no more food. Better that way. Too much phossy in the food anyhow; it was poisonin' us."

In a moment, I realized my manners. Truly, I'd been half-expecting at least an offer of tea, it had been so long since I'd organized workers. "I'm terrible sorry, I've been so rude. What are you all called, girls?"

"No names now, better that way."

"You no longer eat!" I said. "And no longer have names. Incredible! The bosses did this to you?"

"No, Sir," the tall girl said. "The Fabians."

The smallest girl, the one who had never said anything save the Bryant and May slogan, finally spoke. "This is re-form, they said. This is us, in our re-form."

3. What Is To Be Done?

I struck a deal with the girls immediately, not in my role as agitator and organizer, but in my function as a manager for the family concern. Our driver took us to his home and woke his wife, who was sent to the shops for changes of clothes, soap, and other essentials for the girls. We kept the quartet in the carriage for most of the morning whilst Wilkins attempted to explain to his wife what she should see when we brought the girls into her home. She was a strong woman, no-nonsense, certainly no Angel of the House but effective nevertheless. The first thing she told the girls was, "There's to be no fretting and fussing. Do not speak, simply use gestures to communicate if you need to. Now, line up for a scrubbing. I presume your . . . equipment will not rust under some hot water and soap."

In the sitting room, Wilkins leaned over and whispered to

Arbeitskraft

me. "It's the saliva, you see. My Lizzie's a smart one. If the girls' mouths are still full of spit, it can't be that their jaws can rust. Clever, innit?" He lit his pipe with a white phosphorous match and then told me that one of the girls had sold him a Bryant and May matchbox whilst I booked passage for five on the next dirigible to Manchester. "They'd kept offerin', and it made 'em happy when I bought one," he said. "I'll add 5d. to the invoice, if you don't mind."

I had little to do but to agree and eat the butterscotch I had so foolishly bought for the girls. Presently the girls marched into the sitting room, looking like Moors in robes and headwraps. "You'll get odd looks," the driver's wife explained, "but not so odd as the looks you might have otherwise received."

The woman was right. We were stared at by the passengers and conductors of the airship both, though I had changed into a proper suit and even made a show of explaining the wonders of bourgeois England to the girls from our window seat. "Look, girls, there's St. Paul's, where all the good people worship the triune God," I said. Then as we passed over the countryside I made note of the agricultural steam-workers that looked more like the vehicles they were than the men their urbanized brethren pretended to be. "These are our crops, which feed this great nation and strengthen the limbs of the Empire!" I explained. "That is why the warlords of your distant lands were so easily brought to heel. God was on our side, as were the minds of our greatest men, the sinew of our bravest soldiers, and the power classical elements themselves—water, air, fire, and ore—*steam!*" I had spent enough time observing the bourgeoisie to generate sufficient hot air for the entire dirigible.

Back in Manchester, I had some trusted comrades prepare living quarters for the girls, and arrange for the delivery of a generator sufficient for their needs. Then I began to make inquires into the Socialistic and Communistic communities, which I admit that I

21

had been ignoring whilst I worked on the theoretical basis for the Dialectical Engine. Just as Marx used to say, commenting on the French "Marxists" of the late '70s: "All I know is that I am not a Marxist." The steam-workers broke what proletarian solidarity there was in the United Kingdom, and British airships eliminated most resistance in France, Germany, and beyond. What we are left with, here on the far left, are several literary young men, windy Labour MPs concerned almost entirely with airship mooring towers and placement of the same in their home districts, and . . . the Fabians.

The Fabians are gradualists, believers in parliamentary reforms and moral suasion. Not revolution, but evolution, not class struggle, but class collaboration. They call themselves socialists, and many of them are as well-meaning as a yipping pup, but ultimately they wish to save capitalism from the hammers of the working-class. But if they were truly responsible somehow for the state of these girls, they would have moved beyond reformism into complete capitulation to the bourgeoisie. *But we must never capitulate, never collaborate!*

The irony does not escape me. I run a factory on behalf of my bourgeois family. I live fairly well, and indeed, am only the revolutionary I am because of the profits extracted from the workers on the floor below. Now I risk all, their livelihoods and mine, to complete the Dialectical Engine. The looms have been reconfigured; we haven't sent out any cotton in weeks. The work floor looks as though a small volcano had been drawn forth from beneath the crust—the machinists work fifteen hours a day, and smile at me when I come downstairs and roll up my sleeves to help them. They call me Freddie, but I know they despise me. And not even for my status as a bourgeois—they hate me for my continued allegiance to the working-class. There's a word they use when they think I cannot hear them. "Slummer." A man who lives in, or even simply visits, the working-men districts to experience some sort of prurient thrill of rebellion and *faux* class allegiance.

But that is it! That's what I must do. The little match girls must strike! Put their prostheses on display for the public via flying pickets. Challenge the bourgeoisie on their own moral terms—are these the daughters of Albion? Girls who are ever-starving, who can never be loved, forced to skulk in the shadows, living Frankenstein's monsters? The dailies will eat it up, the working-class will be roused, first by economic and moral issues, but then soon by their own collective interest as a class. Behind me, the whir and chatter of loom shuttles kicked up. The Dialectical Engine was being fed the medium on which the raw knowledge of my friend's old letters and missives were to be etched. *Steam*, was all I could think. *What can you not do?*

4. The Spark

I was an old hand at organizing workers, though girls who consumed electricity rather than bread were a bit beyond my remit. It took several days to teach the girls to speak with their jaws beyond the Bryant and May slogan, and several more to convince them of the task. "Why should we go back?" one asked. Her name was once Sally, as she was finally able to tell me, and she was the second-smallest. "They won't have us."

"To free your fellows," I had said. "To express workers' power and, ultimately, take back the profits for yourselves!"

"But then we'd be the bosses," the oldest girl said. "Cruel and mean."

"Yes, well, no. It depends on all of the workers of a nation rising up to eliminate the employing class," I explained. "We must go back—"

"I don't want to ever go back!" said the very smallest. "That place was horrid!"

The tedious debate raged long into the night. They were sure that the foreman would clout their heads in for even appearing near the factory gates, but I had arranged for some newspapermen and even electro-photographers sympathetic to Christian socialism, if not Communism, to meet us as we handed out leaflets to the passing trade and swing shift.

We were met at the gate by a retinue of three burly looking men in fustian suits. One of them fondled a sap in his hand and tipped his hat. The journalists hung back, believers to the end in the objectivity of the disinterested observer, especially when they might get hurt for being rather too interested.

"Leaflets, eh?" the man with the sap asked. "You know this lot can't read, yeah?"

"And this street's been cleared," one of the others said. "You can toss that rubbish in the bin, then."

"Yes, that's how your employers like them, isn't it? Illiterate, desperate, without value to their families as members of the female of the species?" I asked. "And the ordinary working men, cowed by the muscle of a handful of hooligans."

"Buy Bryant and May matchsticks, Sir!" the second-tallest girl said, brightly as she could. The thuggish guards saw her mandible and backed away. Excited, she clacked away at them, and the others joined in.

"How do you like that?" I said to both the guards and the press. "Innocent girls, more machine than living being. We all know what factory labour does to children, or thought we did. But now, behold the new monsters the age of steam and electricity hath wrought. We shall lead an exodus through the streets, and you can put that in your sheets!" The thugs let us by, then slammed the gates behind us, leaving us on the factory grounds and them outside. Clearly, one or more of the police agents who monitor my activities had caught wind of our plans, but I was confident that victory would be ours. Once we roused the other match girls, we'd engage in a *sit-down* strike, if necessary. The girls could not be starved out like ordinary workers, and I had more than enough confederates in London to ring the factory and sneak food and tea for me through the bars if necessary. But I was not prepared for what awaited us.

The girls were gone, but the factory's labours continued apace. Steam-workers attended the machines, carried frames of matches down the steps to the loading dock, and clanked about with the precision of clockwork. Along a catwalk, a man waved to us, a handkerchief in his hand. "Hallo!" he said.

"That's not the foreman," Sally told me. "It's the dentist!" She did not appear at all relieved that the factory's dentist rather than its foreman, who had been described to me as rather like an ourang-outan, was approaching us. I noticed that a pair of steam-workers left their posts and followed him as he walked up to us.

"Mister Friedrich Engels! Is that you?" he asked me. I admitted that I was, but that further I was sure he had been forewarned of my coming. He ignored my rhetorical jab and pumped my hand like an American cowboy of some fashion. "Wonderful, wonderful," he said. He smiled at the girls, and I noticed that his teeth were no better than anyone else's. "I'm Doctor Flint. Bryant and May hired me to deal with worker pains that come from exposure to white phosphorus. We're leading the fight for healthy workers here; I'm sure you'll agree that we're quite progressive. Let me show you what we've accomplished here at Bryant and May."

"Where are the girls?" the tallest of my party asked, her phonographic voice shrill and quick, as if the needle had been drawn over the wax too quickly.

"Liberated!" the dentist said. He pointed to me. "They owe it all to you, you know. I reckon it was your book that started me on my path into politics. Dirtier work than dentistry." He saw my bemused look and carried on eagerly. "Remember what you wrote about the large factories of Birmingham—*the use of steam-power admit of the employment of a great multitude of women and children.* Too true, too true!"

"Indeed, sir," I started, but he interrupted me.

"But of course we can't put steam back in the kettle, can we?" He rapped a knuckle on the pot-belly torso of one of the ever-placid steam-workers behind him. "But then I read your philosophical treatise. I was especially interested in your contention that quantitative change can become qualitative. So, I thought to myself, Self, if steam-power is the trouble when it comes to the subjugation of child labour, cannot more steam-power spell the liberation of child labour?"

"No, not by itself. The class strugg—"

"But no, Engels, you're wrong!" he said. "At first I sought to repair the girls, using steam-power. Have you seen the phoss up close? Through carious teeth, and the poor girls know little of hygiene so they have plenty of caries, the vapours of white phosphorous make gains into the jawbone itself, leading to putrefaction. Stinking hunks of bone work right through the cheek, even after extractions of the carious teeth."

"Yes, we are all familiar with phossy jaw," I said. "Seems to me that the minimalist programme would be legislative—bar white phosphorous. Even whatever sort of Liberal or Fabian you are can agree with that."

"Ah, but I can't!" he said. "You enjoy your pipe? I can smell it on you."

"That's from Wilkins, my driver."

"Well then observe your Mr. Wilkins. It's human nature to desire a strike-anywhere match. We simply cannot eliminate white phosphorous from the marketplace. People demand it. What we can do, however, is use steam to remove the human element from the equation of production."

"I understood that this sort of work is too detailed for steam-workers."

"It was," the dentist said. "But then our practice on the girls led to certain innovations." As if on cue, the steam-workers held up their forelimbs and displayed to me a set of ten fingers with the dexterity of any primates. "So now I have eliminated child labour—without any sort of agitation or rabble-rousing I might add—from this factory and others like it, in less than a fortnight. Indeed, the girls were made redundant this past Tuesday."

"And what do you plan to do for them?" I said. "A good Fabian like you knows that these girls will now—"

"Will now what? Starve? You know they won't, not as long as there are lampposts in London. They all contain receptacles. Mature and breed, further filling the working-men's districts with the unemployable, uneducable? No, they won't. Find themselves abused and exploited in manners venereal? No, not possible, even if there was a man so drunk as to overlook their new prosthetic mandibles. Indeed, we had hoped to move the girls into the sales area, which is why their voiceboxes are rather . . . focused, but as it happens few people wish to buy matches from young girls. Something about it feels immoral, I suppose. So they are free to never work again. Herr Engels, their problems are solved."

For a long moment, we both stood our ground, a bit unsure as to what we should do next, either as socialist agitators or as gentlemen. We were both keenly aware that our conversation was the first of its type in all history. The contradictions of capitalism, resolved? The poor would always be with us, but also immortal and incapable of reproduction. Finally the dentist looked at his watch—he wore one with rotating shutters of numerals on his wrist, as is the fashion among wealthy morons—and declared that he had an appointment to make. "The steam-workers will show you out," he said, and in a moment their fingers were on my arms, and they dragged me to the entrance of the factory as if I were made of straw. The girls followed, confused, and, if the way their metallic jaws were set was telling, they were actually relieved. The press pestered us with questions on the way out, but I sulked past them without remark. Let them put Doctor Flint above the fold tomorrow morning, for all the good it will do them. Soon enough there'd be steam-workers capable of recording conversations and events with perfect audio-visual fidelity, and with a dial to be twisted for different settings of the editing of newsreels: Tory, Liberal, or Fabian. Indeed, one would never have to twist the dial at all.

We returned to Wilkins and our autocarriage, defeated and atomised. Flint spoke true; as we drove through the streets of the East End, I did espy several former match girls standing on corners or in gutters, directionless and likely cast out from whatever home they may have once had.

"We have to . . ." But I knew that I couldn't.

Wilkins said, "The autocarriage is overburdened already. Those girlies weigh more than they appear to, eh? You can't go 'round collecting every stray."

No—charity is a salve at best, a bourgeois affectation at worst. But even those concerns were secondary. As the autocarriage moved sluggishly toward the airship field, I brooded on the question of value. If value comes from labour, and capital is but dead labour, what are steam-workers? So long as they needed to be created by human hands, clearly steam-workers were just another capital good, albeit a complex one. But now, given the dexterity of the latest generation of steam-workers, they would clearly be put to work building their own descendents, and those that issued forth from that subsequent generation would also be improved, without a single quantum of labour-power expended. The bourgeoisie might have problems of their own; with no incomes at all, the working-class could not even afford the basic necessities of life. Steam-workers don't buy bread or cloth, nor do they drop farthings into the alms box at church on Sunday. How would bourgeois society survive without workers who also must be driven to consume the very products they made?

The petit-bourgeoisie, I realized, the landed gentry, perhaps they could be catered to exclusively, and the empire would continue to expand and open new markets down to the tips of the Americas and through to the end of the Orient—foreign money and resources would be enough for capital, for the time being. But what of the proletariat? If the bourgeoisie no longer needed the labour of the workers, and with the immense power in their hands, wouldn't they simply rid themselves of the toiling classes the way the lord of a manor might rid a stable of vermin? They could kill us all from the air—firebombing the slums and industrial districts. Send whole troupes of steam-workers to tear men apart till the cobblestones ran red with the blood of the proletariat. Gears would be greased, all right.

We didn't dare take an airship home to Manchester. The mooring station was sure to be mobbed with writers from the tabloids and Tory sheets. So we settled in for the long and silent drive up north.

I had no appetite for supper, which wasn't unusual after an hour in an airship, but tonight was worse for the steel ball of dread in my stomach. I stared at my pudding for a long time. I wished I could offer it to the girls, but they were beyond treats. On a whim, I went back to the factory to check in on the Dialectical Engine, which had been processing all day and evening. A skeleton crew had clocked out when the hour struck nine, and I was alone with my creation. No, with the creation of the labour of my workers. No, *the* workers. If only I could make myself obsolete, as the steam-workers threatened the proletariat.

The factory floor, from the vantage point of my small office atop the catwalk, was a sight to behold. A mass of cloth, like huge overlapping sails, obscured the looms, filling the scaffolding that had been built up six storeys to hold and "read" the long punched sheets. A human brain in replica, with more power than any Difference Engine, fuelled by steam for the creation not of figures, but dialectics. Quantitative change had become qualitative, or would as soon as the steam engines in the basement were ignited. I lacked the ability to do it myself, or I would have just then, allowing me to talk to my old friend, or as close a facsimile as I could build with my fortune and knowledge. All the machinery came to its apex in my office, where a set of styluses waited in position over sheets of foolscap. I would prepare a question, and the machine would produce an answer that would be translated, I hoped, into comprehensible declarative sentences upon the sheets. A letter from Marx, from beyond the grave! Men have no souls to capture, but the mind, yes. The mind is but the emergent properties of the brain, and I rebuilt Marx's brain, though I hoped not simply to see all his theories melt into air.

With a start, I realized that down on the floor I saw a spark. The factory was dark and coated with the shadows of the punched sheets, so the momentary red streak fifty feet below was obvious to me. Then I smelled it, the smoke of a pipe. Only a fool would light up in the midst of so much yardage of inflammable cotton, which was perplexing, because Wilkins was no fool.

"Wilkins!" I shouted. "Extinguish that pipe immediately! You'll burn down the factory and kill us both! These textiles are highly combustible."

"Sow-ry," floated up from the void. But then another spark flitted in the darkness, and a second and a third. Wilkins held a fistful of matches high, and I could make out the contours of his face. "Quite a mechanism you've got all set up here, Mister Engels. Are these to be sails for the masts of your yacht?"

"No sir, they won't be for anything if you don't extinguish those matches!"

"Extinguish, eh? Well, you got a good look, and so did I, so I think I will." And he blew out the matches. All was dark again. What happened next was quick. I heard the heavy thudding—no, a heavy *ringing* of boots along the catwalk and in a moment a steam-worker was upon me. I wrestled with it for a moment, but I was no match for its pistons, and it threw me over the parapet. My breath left my body as I fell—as if my soul had decided to abandon me and leap right for heaven. But I didn't fall far. I landed on a taut sheet of fine cotton, then rolled off of it and fell less than a yard onto another. I threw out my arms and legs as I took the third layer of sheet, and then scuttled across it to the edge of the scaffold on which I rested. Sitting, I grasped the edge with my hands and lowered myself as much as I dared, then let go. Wilkins was there, having tracked my movements from the fluttering of the sheets and my undignified oopses and oofs. He lit another match and showed me his eyes.

"Pretty fit for an older gentlemen, Mister Engels. But take a gander at the tin of Scotch broth up there." He lifted the match. The steam-worker's metallic skin glinted in what light there was. It stood atop the parapet of the catwalk and with a leap flung itself into the air, plummeting the six storeys down and landing in a crouch like a circus acrobat. Remarkable, but I was so thankful that it did not simply throw itself through the coded sheets I had spent so long trying to manufacture, ruining the Dialectical Engine before it could even be engaged. Then I understood.

"Wilkins!" I cried. "You're a police agent!"

Wilkins shrugged, and swung onto his right shoulder a heavy sledge. "'Fraid so. But can you blame me, sir? I've seen the writing on the wall—or the automaton on the assembly line," he said, nodding past me and toward the steam-worker, who had taken the flank opposite my treacherous driver. "I know what's coming.

Won't nobody be needing me to drive 'em around with these wind-up toys doing all the work, and there won't be no other jobs to be had but rat and fink. So I took a little fee from the police, to keep an eye on you and your . . ." He was at a loss for words for a moment. "Machinations. Yes, that's it. And anyhow, they'll pay me triple to put all this to the torch, so I will, then retire to Cheshire with old Lizzie and have a nice garden."

"And it?" I asked, glancing at the automaton on my left.

"Go figure," Wilkins said. "My employers wanted one of their own on the job, in case you somehow bamboozled me with your radical cant into switching sides a second time."

"They don't trust you," I said.

"Aye, but they pay me, half in advance." And he blew out the match, putting us in darkness again. Without the benefit of sight, my other senses flared to life. I could smell Wilkins stepping forward, hear the tiny grunt as he hefted the sledge. I could nearly taste the brass and aluminium of the steam-worker on my tongue, and I certainly felt its oppressive weight approaching me.

I wish I could say I was brave and through a clever manoeuvre defeated both my foes simultaneously. But a Communist revolutionary must always endeavour to be honest to the working-class—Reader, I fell into a swoon. Through nothing more than a stroke of luck, as my legs gave way beneath me, Wilkins's sledgehammer flew over my head and hit the steam-worker square on the faceplate. It flew free in a shower of sparks. Facing an attack, the steam-worker staved in Wilkins's sternum with a single blow, then turned back to me, only to suddenly shudder and collapse atop me. I regained full consciousness for a moment, thanks to the putrid smell of dead flesh and fresh blood. I could see little, but when I reached to touch the exposed face of the steam-worker, I understood. I felt not gears and wirework, but slick sinew and a trace of human bone. Then the floor began to shake. An arclight in the corner flickered to life, illuminating a part of the factory floor. I was pinned under the automaton, but then the tallest of the girls—and I'm ashamed to say I never learned what she was called—with a preternatural strength of her own took up one of the machine's limbs and dragged him off of me.

I didn't even catch my breath before exclaiming, "Aha, of course! The new steam-workers aren't automata, they're men! Men imprisoned in suits of metal to enslave them utterly to the bourgeoisie!" I coughed and sputtered. "You! Such as you, you see," I told the girl, who stared at me dumbly. Or perhaps I was the dumb one, and she simply looked upon me as a pitiable old idiot who was the very last to figure out what she considered obvious. "Replace the body of a man with a machine, encase the human brain within a cage, and dead labour lives again! That's how the steam-workers are able to use their limbs and appendages with a facility otherwise reserved for humans. All the advantages of the proletariat, but the steam-workers neither need to consume nor reproduce!" Sally was at my side now, with my pudding, which she had rescued from my supper table. She was a clever girl, Sally. "The others started all the engines they could find," she said, and only then I realized that I had been shouting in order to hear myself. All around me, the Dialectical Engine was in full operation.

5. All That Is Solid Melts Into Air

In my office, the styluses scribbled for hours. I spent a night and a day feeding it foolscap. The Dialectical Engine did not work as I'd hoped it would—it took no input from me, answered none of the questions I had prepared, but instead wrote out a single long monograph. I was shocked at what I read from the very first page:

Das Kapital: Kritik der politischen Ökonomie, Band V.

The *fifth* volume of *Capital*. Marx had died prior to completing the *second*, which I published myself from his notes. Before turning my energies to the Dialectical Engine, I had edited the third volume for publication. While the prior volumes of the book offered a criticism of bourgeois theories of political economy and a discussion of the laws of the capitalist mode of production, this fifth volume, or extended appendix in truth, was something else. It contained a description of socialism.

The internal contradictions of capitalism had doomed it to destruction. What the bourgeoisie would create would also be used to destroy their reign. The ruling class, in order to stave off extinction, would attempt to use its technological prowess to forestall the day of revolution by radically expanding its control of the proletarian and his labour-power. But in so doing, it would create the material conditions for socialism. The manuscript was speaking of steam-workers, though of course the Dialectical Engine had no sensory organs with which to observe the metal-encased corpse that had expired in its very innards the evening prior. Rather, the Engine *predicted* the existence of human-steam hybrids from the content of the decade-old correspondence between Marx and myself.

What then, would resolve the challenge of the proletarian brain trapped inside the body of the steam-worker? Dialectical logic pointed to a simple solution: the negation of the negation. Free the proletarian *mind* from its physical *brain* by encoding it onto a new mechanical medium. That is to say, the Dialectical Engine itself was the key. Free the working-class by having it exist in the physical world and the needs of capitalism to accumulate, accumulate. Subsequent pages of the manuscript detailed plans for Dialectical Engine Number 2, which would be much smaller and more efficient. A number of human minds could be "stitched-up" into this device and through collective endeavour, these beings-in-one would create Dialectical Engine Number 3, which would be able to hold still more minds and create the notional Dialectical Engine Number 4. Ultimately, the entire working-class of England and Europe could be up-coded into a Dialectical Engine no larger than a hatbox, and fuelled by power drawn from the sun. Without a proletariat to exploit—the class as a whole having taken leave of the realm of flesh and blood to reconstitute itself as information within the singular Dialectical Engine Omega—the bourgeoisie would fall into ruin and helplessness, leaving the working-class whole and unmolested in perpetuity. Even after the disintegration of the planet, the Engine would persist, and move forward to explore the firmament and other worlds that may orbit other stars.

Within the Dialectical Engine Omega, consciousness would be both collective and singular, an instantaneous and perfect industrial democracy. Rather than machines replicating themselves endlessly as in Mister Butler's novel—*the machines are gaining ground upon us; day by day we are becoming more subservient to them*—it is us that shall be liberated by the machines, through the machines. We are gaining ground upon them! *Proletarier aller Länder, vereinigt euch!* We have nothing to lose but our chains, as the saying goes!

The Dialectical Engine fell silent after nineteen hours of constant production. I should have been weary, but already I felt myself beyond hunger and fatigue. The schematics for Dialectical Engine Number 2 were incredibly advanced, but for all their cleverness the mechanism itself would be quite simple to synthesize. With a few skilled and trusted workers, we could have it done in a fortnight. Five brains could be stitched-up into it. The girls and myself were obvious candidates, and from within the second engine we would create the third, and fourth, and subsequent numbers via pure unmitigated *Arbeitskraft!*

Bold? Yes! Audacious? Certainly. And indeed, I shall admit that, for a moment, my mind drifted to the memory of the empty spectacle of Mister Peake's play, of the rampaging monster made of dead flesh and brought to life via electrical current. But I had made no monster, no brute. That was a bourgeois story featuring a bogeyman that the capitalists had attempted to mass produce from the blood of the working-class. My creation was the opposite number of the steam-worker and the unphilosophical monster of stage and page; the Engine was *mens sana sine corpore sano*—a sound mind outside a sound body.

What could possibly go wrong. . . ?

Beginning writers often have too-clever ideas, or perhaps just stupid ones. For many years, starting at the very beginning of my attempts to get published, I entertained writing a story to be called "The Case of the Extracted Surplus Value"—naturally it would feature Marx and Engels as a Holmes and Watson–type pair, being called in to a factory where the harder the employees worked, the more impoverished they become. That's less an idea for a story than it is for a four-panel gag comic strip, and it wouldn't be a great one at that.

But the idea stuck with me, and I occasionally took a jab at it by doing a bit of research. I read and enjoyed Lewis S. Feuer's novel *The Case of the Revolutionist's Daughter* (Holmes and Watson try to find the missing Eleanor Marx) and spent a lot of time with Engels himself via his *The Condition of the Working Class in England*. While I was doing all that, and writing stories and books and moving back and forth across the country and having relationships and whatnot, steampunk happened. Steampunk happened sufficiently that I was even called upon to explain what it was to a friend of my wife's cousin as we all hung out in a private sitting room of Edinburgh Castle's New Barracks after the cousin's wedding ceremony. (The best man was a military medic; we got to go places not on the typical tourist itinerary.) I basically said, "It's like cyberpunk, but with steam and difference engines instead of computing." My new acquaintance was intoxicated enough, and British enough, to politely pretend to understand.

Then, of course, anti-steampunk happened—steampunk was denounced as racist and imperialist. I tend to agree. But I don't believe that essence precedes existence, so when I was asked to write a steampunk story, I squinted at the email and said, "Yes. Yes, I will write a steampunk story." "Arbeitskraft" was an attempt to critique steampunk via anti-steampunk without creating an anti-steampunk story.

The story has been very good to me—it's been multiply reprinted, has been analyzed by scholars, and came within a whisker of a Hugo Award nomination. Had I not previously vowed to eschew promoting my work for awards, it may well have found the extra seven votes it needed. One year later, the Hugos were besieged by the reactionary forces of the Sad and Rabid Puppies, so the chances of some story about Communist sleuths and poor little match girls making the finals ever again are slim indeed. There's a lesson in all this, but I have no idea what it is.

THE PEOPLE'S REPUBLIC OF EVERYWHERE AND EVERYTHING

LILIAN ALWAYS SNORTED when she saw the sign reading NUCLEAR FREE ZONE on the border between Berkeley and Oakland, though she learned to suppress it when Jonothan was in the car with her. Everything—nuclear disarmament, overpopulation, alternative hemp-based fuels, animal rights—was serious business with Jonothan. This time, though, as she aimed her car up Telegraph Avenue, she didn't snort. Not because Jonothan was sitting next to her, his arms crossed and his head tilted out the window as he went on about The Revolution, but because Jonothan was sitting next to her, sure that he was already dead.

"I'll miss food," he said. The Smokehouse, a kitschy old burger joint, zipped by. Jonothan was a vegetarian. Maybe I should say *had been* a vegetarian. But anyways, he liked the French fries at the Smokehouse.

"You'll be fine, we just have to get to the house, get you into bed, get some rest," she said.

"You sound very sure of yourself," Jonothan said. "I don't have any internal organs. I'm so hollow. Is this hell? Are we touring hell right now?"

Jonothan had been like this for most of the day. He was a street kid who mostly lived in People's Park, where the long-term homeless sleep under the tree and hold friggin' committee meetings and write letters to the governor demanding their rights. Jonothan was pretty political; he had a canned speech defending his white-boy dreadlocks he'd rehearsed on Lilian several times since they'd met the month before. Jonothan was still cute under all the dirt and the raggedy clothes, and when he laughed he had a mouth full of straight white teeth that told Lilian one thing— the kid was slumming. Slummers, in the end, always like their creature comforts. So he'd come by and use the co-op's shower, play with Lilian's Nintendo DS and update his Facebook on her laptop, and cook up the food he'd liberated from the dumpsters behind the Whole Foods and Andronico's supermarket. "Beggars *can* be choosers, after all," Lilian had said and Jonathan had screwed up his face and started on a rant about locavores and how the Safeway is such an energy sink that even Dumpster diving wouldn't help, but then he made some delicious vegan stir-fry and Lilian had scrubbed him up in her tub and had taken him to bed. She found out about the herpes only later. And now there was this:

"I'm dead, Lil," he said. "How will you get me up the stairs? My legs are rotting out from under me. Can you even hear me? It's like all I can hear is my teeth knocking together. Do I even have skin?" Then he barked and slammed his head against the passenger-side window of Lilian's Saab. "Look! Devils!"

It was the kids. Lilian had just crossed Dwight, and this part of Telegraph Avenue belonged to the kids. Not the students at Cal, of course. They kept their heads down, their blue and gold sweatshirts clean, and their cell phones on vibrate. The homeless kids gathered in the pools of light in front of the smoke shops and giant CD stores, playing with their dogs, taunting the cops, and now, hooting and throwing stuff into the street. Lilian saw a streak of orange arcing overhead, then the Molotov cocktail opened into a puddle of flame right in front of her car. Suddenly, the police were everywhere, in riot gear, with long batons. Lilian slammed on the brakes.

"Get down!" she said.

"No," Jonothan said, "this is what I des—" Lilian slammed her forearm into his chest, and the whole bucket seat fell backwards, taking Jonothan with it. She put on her prettiest, most frightened look and tried to catch the eye of one of the police swarming into the street. Fire in front of her, cops all around, some carrying portable barricades that just a few minutes ago were innocent-looking bicycle racks on the campus. Then her phone chimed. A text. From me.

RU THERE TO GET THE GIFT??

She looked over at Jonothan, who was still mumbling to himself, and now picking at his skin. Then someone started slamming their hands on the hood of the car. It was a dykey woman cop, helmet up, mouth wide open and screaming. For a second, Lilian found her foot on the accelerator. All she needed to do was give it a little pressure. But she shifted into reverse and moved the car backwards and onto a side street. Barricades went up right after she exited Telegraph, and the mass beat-down began.

Jonothan was pliable enough to get pushed down the street to the co-op house Lilian shared with nine other people, including me, but Lilian still had too many problems. The riot had begun too early, and gotten violent way too quickly. The cop had probably gotten a good look at her. Now the car was probably going to end up either torched or at least well known to the local pigs as well. And Jonothan was insane. There's an app for that, and with her smartphone Lilian was a regular Wikipedia Brown—Jonothan had Cotard delusion, the belief that he was unreal, a rotting corpse somehow able to still walk and think. It's a rare disorder, but these were rare and imperfect times, Lilian knew. Sometimes schizophrenics had Cotard's, and sometimes it was a side effect of anti-herpes medication. A probable double whammy when it came to Jonothan, but he still might be useful to her. Plus, she probably loved him. She did love climbing atop him every night and pinning his wrists down. He had a tattoo across his chest that read, *We can carry a new world here, in our hearts.* She liked that. I liked to watch them, eavesdrop.

The whole scheme was simple enough to start. Lilian had spent months integrating herself into Berkeley's anarchic street life—even the Revolution appreciated a pretty girl who shaved her armpits and smelled like patchouli rather than patchouli and landfill. Once she had made all the right friends on-campus and off, she'd be able to snag the Q-chip and sell it. All she needed was a distraction, and the Telegraph Avenue kids were already ready to provide that, especially if it meant mixing it up with the police. But everything was falling apart. For her, not for me. The kids had rioted too soon, and Lilian was woefully out of position. Cal was probably already under lockdown. Jonothan was crazier than usual; there'd be no talking him down.

"Everything *is* falling apart," Jonothan said as he stumbled ahead of Lilian. "Can you feel it? No, no, you can't. Let me tell you about it. I'm seeping out of my body, like steam. That's what the spirit is. Filling the whole world, swirling around. I'm blocks away already, in every direction at once."

"Up the steps, John Boy," Lilian told him. Two palms on his back got him up the staircase. He turned to face her. "It's like being everywhere, all at once." At least he wasn't talking about being in hell anymore, but then he said, "No walls, no doors." That was the slogan Lilian had come up with for her plan to steal the Q-chip. The Q-chip, or quantum chip, which promised to break every and any code. While normal computers were stuck with binary operations—everything was either a one or a zero—

quantum computing allowed for one, zero, or the superimposition of both. Not just onezero or zeroone, but OzNeEro and ZoEnRoE and any other combination, for cheap and without any more power than a nine-volt. The Q-chip could crack any password, perform any calculation, and derive a question to any answer on *Jeopardy*, even "This woman is currently living in a forty-room mansion in the Maldives, which lacks an extradition treaty with the US." *Who is Lilian Tanzer?* Yes! "No walls, no doors" was just to get the anarchists on her side. They wanted to use the Q-chip— as though they could pop it right into an ordinary laptop—to eliminate Third World debt, bring down the president, and erase their student loan information.

He said it again. "Lily! No walls, no doors! I know it all now; everything." Then he grabbed her, his fingers tight on her biceps. "We can't go inside, we have to go to campus now. Do it now! My soul is already there!" Jonothan had been freaking out for three days, but something about him made the back of Lilian's neck tingle. She glanced around. There was a white van cooling on the corner, and across the street from the co-op house, in one of the apartments she was pretty sure was empty, a light was now on. A McDonald's wrapper was crumpled up on the curb, which was the biggest clue. There wasn't a Mickey D's on this side of town, and almost nobody would be caught dead eating one of those toadburgers on this block. The cops must have been tipped off, not just about the riot, but about the heist.

That was my burger wrapper. At least, I presumed that Lilian was smart enough to spot it. They say you should never give a sucker an even break, but maybe I'm just a sucker for a sweet smile myself. She figured out that Jonothan had somehow had a lucid moment and booked down the street toward Shattuck. That was a crowded street, with bookstores and nicer restaurants and a couple of good movie theaters. Pretty apolitical scene—I call the little shopping zone "The Gelato District." She ignored the calls for her to stop, to freeze, that came from inside the co-op. Jonothan stumbled after her, howling about how *no no, he was back in hell now.* And he was going to be, soon enough.

I don't quite know everything that happened, not even now, so please do forgive the embellishments. Maybe the cop wasn't a woman, but a male pig with a high-pitched voice. Perhaps Lilian didn't even consider that the cops would run her car's plates, even if she looked like a semi-innocent victim. But most of the events of that night are easy enough to piece together. I wasn't part of the riot. I'd been sitting in Cory Hall all day, munching pizza, reading the flyers, waiting for my chance.

I had a police scanner feed in my Bluetooth, and I'd tapped Lilian's smartphone two days after she showed up with her acoustic guitar and sob story about a touchy-feely daddy on Central Park West she was running from. My hotrodded version of FlexiSPY gave me access to her text messages, her phone logs, the semi-nude pics she liked to take of herself in front of the bathroom mirror and send right to Daddy. Thanks to her phone's built-in mic and GPS app, I could listen in on her conversations and Jonothan's idiot ramblings, and keep track of her location within a few feet.

Yeah, I'm a sleaze, but I'm a sleaze for the Revolution. Lots of people come through Berkeley, and some of them are even authentic anti-capitalists. But most of them are like Lil and Jono: police *agents provocateur* or middle-class thrill-seekers who want to exploit us before settling down to a bourgeois lifestyle of voting for the Democrats and employing undocumented workers from Mexico to raise their Ritalin-addled children. So when they knock on the co-op's door, I keep an eye on them. Lilian thought she was a big deal sneak thief. She had a few identities, a "Daddy" who was a banker back east with a hankering for a Q-chip of his very own, and a soft spot for wounded little puppies like Jonothan. Hell, I thought she was just a reporter when I saw her at first. She had the clean nails of an office worker. When I cracked her phone—*whoa doggie!* The town has the nickname "Berzerkeley" for a reason, and that reason is omnipresent political paranoia. But even I didn't think that we'd be infiltrated directly by the forces of international financial capital.

Like I said, her plan for the Q-chip was almost a good one, and she was able to mimic our politics enough to come up with a snappy slogan and a Utopian vision of a future without credit scores. She was so good that all I had to do was make sure everything on her checklist happened an hour earlier than she wanted, and that Jonothan would be an albatross. A little ketamine goes a long way, but even with all the other stuff wrong with that kid, who could have predicted something as weird and poetic as Cotard delusion?

It was easy enough to send the Telegraph Avenue kids a text from Lilian's phone a bit early—yes, in the Bay Area, even the homeless and dirty have cell phones. Lilian had figured out which lab held the Q-chip designs and prototype, and all I needed was a credit card . . . to jimmy open the lock. She was surging up Shattuck a little too quickly for me, so I texted her. NO WALLS, NO DOORS and WELCOME TO THE GELATO DISTRICT. Triggered every one of her ringtones. Turned on her MP3 player, full blast. Made it easy for the cops to find her, and they did. There was always tons of street noise on Shattuck thanks to the buses, the buskers, the constant murmur of a dozen conversations and latté orders. I could barely hear the order to halt, but Jonothan's moaning came over the aether loud and clear. Then Lilian did something that was actually pretty brave; she pulled out her phone and started recording.

I got the video—Jonothan lurching toward a pair of cops. Two kids, really. They had mace and told Jonothan to stop, but he wouldn't. "Your guns won't work on me," he said. "I'm already dead. " They shouted for him to get down on the ground, then hosed him but good with the mace. He just wiped it from his eyes with his sleeve. Lilian was really screaming; she cared about him, poor girl. The cops called for backup for the 5150 they had on their hands, then tried a bright yellow Taser. Jonothan looked down at the wires on his chest and pulled them free. "You pigs, you pigs! The whole world is watching!" Lilian shouted at them. Then they rushed her.

She was right. The whole world is watching, thanks to her. And to me, of course. Lilian's plan was ultimately a stupid one. She was going to steal the actual, physical Q-chip prototype and then have it couriered through a private high-security messenger firm—the type that specializes in transporting uncut drugs, little girls, kidneys on ice, and exotic pets—back to New York City. And to do what? What would Daddy do with it, except smash the little chip with one of the awesome decorative paperweights on his desk, or maybe crush it in his very palm like the squash-playing power-tie-wearing alpha male he thought he was? Total twentieth-century industrial society thought. Maybe he'd spend a spare billion dollars over the next five years trying to reverse-engineer it . . . except that the Q-chip could redesign its *own* next generation in five seconds. Stealing a computer chip is about as effective as tearing up a mortgage document or telling the devil, "I take it back!" after selling your soul.

So I didn't steal the chip. I copied it, to share it with all of you. That was the beauty of the Q-chip—it wasn't much more than a whiteboard full of equations and a few receipts, *paper receipts*, for materials I'd found on the secretary's desk. I was probably picked up by some security camera, maybe spotted by a few co-eds while weaving the Q-chip stuff between the frames of Lilian's video, but it won't matter. *No walls, no doors.* You won't see me on the news—call me Anonymous if you must. The video is already going viral. Jonothan, zombielike, lurching toward the cops and taking a beating without feeling a thing. Lilian shrieking then falling, then a pair of cops towering over the camera, their batons thick as redwoods. And between the frames, information sufficient for any grade-school hacker, garage tinkerer, or steampunk Maker to whip up their own Q-chips. Everything's possible, starting right this very second. Berkeley really will be a nuclear-free zone now, because anyone with the Q-chip can simultaneously disable every warhead on the planet. *You're welcome.* No prison can hold me, for even the cells at Guantánamo Bay are controlled by computer.

Jonothan's tattoo is part of a longer saying—*We are going to inherit the earth. There is not the slightest doubt about that. The bourgeoisie may blast and ruin its own world before it leaves the stage of history. We carry a new world, here, in our hearts. That world is growing this minute.* That's Buenaventura Durruti, an old Spanish anarchist. And he's right. So was Jonothan. He may well be dead by now, but he is everywhere all at once, expanding in every direction, all across the Internet, carrying a new world with him. It's growing every minute. A week from now, you won't recognize the planet. Yes, I'm a criminal, but I'll be the last criminal ever. No walls, no doors, no crime, no inequality, no state to arrest us or capital to protect. You shall all be freed from hell, your souls returned to you.

RU THERE TO GET THE GIFT??

About ten years ago, I became highly interested in short noir fiction as represented by the journal *Murdaland*, which sadly lasted all of two issues, and the Akashic Books Noir Series of anthologies. England's *The Savage Kick Literary Magazine*, the early issues of which were literally run off on a home laser printer, offered a highly engaging mix of underground noir and confessional fiction in the Bukowski mode. I loved the hard-ass business, the joy of vicariously living through protagonists who managed to live and fuck without first getting jobs or haircuts, and fiction with explicitly proletarian concerns and voices of the sort I grew up around. Naturally, I started trying to write it.

Noir has much in common with horror and dark fantasy, but where a writer of the latter can depend on a bit of arm-waving—*And then something numinous and inexplicable happens! Pretty scary, eh? Eh?*—noir requires a hardnosed realism. Or it seems to. Benjamin Whitmer's amazing novel Pike features a guy with his very own science fictional novum in the form of a screwy pacemaker that keeps him preternaturally calm when murdering people. Sara Gran's Claire DeWitt novels include *Détection*, an instructional guide for an anti-methodology of crime-solving that turns logic on its head. Throwing in a dash of science fiction seemed fine after all.

One issue I have with writing noir is that, like the meme says, "Shakespeare got to get paid, son." There are few venues for it that pay more than $25 or so, and as someone who finds writing both exhausting and distasteful, it was hard to motivate myself to write anything that couldn't also be potentially published as science fiction or horror. So when I saw the call for submissions for *West Coast Crime Wave*, an electronic-only anthology that promised a whole hundred bucks, and that had a limited geographical focus I qualified for, I went for it.

But, I needed a smidge of science fiction as well. And some horror, just in case. My friend Cassie Alexander, who wrote the Shifted series of urban fantasies about a nurse who cares for supernatural creatures, happened to tell me about Cotard delusion when I was thinking about a story for the anthology, so that was half of it settled. And good ol' UC Berkeley is always good for high-tech hijinks, and it was all settled. One of my favorite things about Berkeley is its incredibly earnest Nuclear Free Zone signs on the town's borders, so everything quickly clicked into place, and the story came out in a single draft. Anthologist Brian Thornton had never heard of me, and I was very pleased to get in on the pure merits of the story. The first-person apostrophe point of view (an "I" narrator speaking to a seemingly absent "you" character) intrigued him, and I'm always happy to be recognized for my formalism. Even better was noir master Ken Bruen singling out my story as his favorite in the book's forward. When I launched my own attempt at a well-paying noir journal, *The Big Click*, I was able to contact Ken and get a story from him for our premiere issue. As far as *West Coast Crime Wave*, and the small press that put it out, not too much happened with it, sadly, so I'm very pleased to present "The People's Republic of Everywhere and Everything" as the title story of this collection.

TOM SILEX, SPIRIT-SMASHER

THE COVERS OF THE PULP MAGAZINES were about as lurid as I had expected them to be—astronauts in bubble helmets, tentacles spilling forth from dark corners, and the breasts of women bound to slabs just barely obscured by wisps of silk or crackling pink lightning. I glanced over at Jeremy, who was looking across the diner booth table at the pulp magazine collector, who also looked just about as ridiculous as I had expected a pulp magazine collector to look. Plaid and suspenders in the Arizona summertime, a Santa Claus beard, and a peculiar bleating voice—as though he rehearsed his sentences, then recited them. There was a shard of French fry hanging from his fuzzy upper lip.

"So, Ms. Martinez, as you can see, Tom Silex, Spirit-Smasher, never made the covers of the magazines in which his adventures were published, but your grandfather's byline is—"

"He wasn't my grandfather," I said. I smiled, not apologetically. There was something about getting to interrupt an old white man that always made me smile. "He was my grandmother's first husband. She was very young when they married, and it didn't last long."

"When was that?" Jeremy asked.

"1950—she got a divorce and could never go back to church after that," I said, stabbing at one of the pulp magazines with a thick finger. The pulp collector winced. "Grandpa was forward-thinking for the time and married her anyway. She always called Marcus Goulart 'the rat bastard,' after that."

The pulp collector opened his mouth to say something, but then closed it.

"I'm Rosa's . . . advisor," Jeremy said. And boyfriend, obviously. He was a tall man, all long limbs, but he didn't have to sit thigh-to-thigh with his client, as he was doing. "So, you believe that the rights to this detective character, Tom Silence—"

"Silex," the pulp collector said.

"Silex," Jeremy said.

"Silex is Latin for 'flint,' you see."

"And . . . I'm not following."

"Marcus Goulart was born Tom Flint," the pulp collector said. "Many pulp authors wrote under pseudonyms, but Goulart actually legally changed his name."

"Did you know that?" Jeremy asked me.

I shrugged. "I literally just told you every single thing I know about Goulart."

"I have something to share. I looked into Goulart's estate and copyrights very deeply, I searched every public record available. He never divorced your grandmother. They separated, surely, but there was no divorce," the pulp collector said. Then he smiled. "Do you understand what this means?"

"What! My grandmother was a bigamist? My grandparents were never *married*!" My hand went up. I hardly even knew why. I wanted to smack the whole world across the face.

Why was the pulp collector still smiling?

The waitress brought me back to reality with a sharp, "Anything else over here?" She looked down at the magazines crowding the table and sneered. The pulp collector didn't seem to notice that either.

"It means that *you* own Tom Silex," the pulp collector said. "I'd love to publish the collected adventures in a new edition. As the sole copyright holder, you could license the stories to me, and even give me permission to solicit authors to write new Silex adventures."

"What about Grandma?" Jeremy asked. He turned to the waitress and dismissed her with a twitch of his eyebrows.

"My understanding, from the Silver Alert I came across on Google, which is how I found Rosa, is that Mrs. Hernandez isn't competent," the pulp collector said. "Surely, a conservatorship . . ."

"No," I said. "I guess not being good at paperwork runs in the family. The *not*-family."

". . . and there, amidst the swirling darkness of the old Wilkerson farmhouse, I heard the blasphemous chanting of a thousand psychopomps . . ." Jeremy read while Rosa drove. "What's a 'psychopomp'?"

"A psychopomp is someone—like an angel or a spirit or the Grim Reaper—who escorts the dead to the afterlife. Sounds like trouble for Tom Silex," I told him.

"Should I keep going?"

"Don't bother. Don't you think this was a waste of our time?"

Jeremy shrugged. "These stories read like crap to me. Some atmosphere, then he pulls out his Shadow Lantern, which makes ghosts visible. The quanto-mystico-electrical light reveals the state of their souls. Then he banishes them either by providing what they want, or destroy—say, how did you even know what a psychopomp is?"

"What is that supposed to mean?"

"I'm just saying, it's an usual word. I didn't know it."

"And you went to law school," I said. "Unlike me with my associate's degree. Is that what you mean?"

Neither of us said anything for a long moment. Then I said, "It was a crossword puzzle answer. I looked it up." It wasn't true. I like reading fantasy fiction on my Kindle and such, but I always kept quiet about it. My parents were hyper-religious and suspicious of a girl reading. Even after a car accident took them, old habits died hard. But my grandma had been married to a pulp fiction writer? She *owned* an occult detective somehow?

"I only went to law school for one year anyway," Jeremy said. "But I do know that sometimes some little story or idea can become something big. The original Superman comic was developed by a pair of teenagers."

"We're not talking big, Jer. We're talking some guy who wants to photocopy old pulp magazines and sell them on Amazon for nine dollars," I said. "The offer was five hundred bucks plus royalties. How many people are going to buy—"

"That dude spent more than five hundred bucks flying out here," Jeremy said. "And even the Motel 6 by the diner is ninety bucks a night."

"Maybe we should talk to Grandma about it after all," I said. "After the homecare nurse leaves for the day."

"There has to be room to negotiate," Jeremy said.

"I can't even afford to file for conservatorship."

"I told you I could try; I just don't want to make an error in filing. You need a real lawyer."

"Grandma has to sign," I said. "That's it."

I could always tell when my grandmother was having a good day. She would smile and say, "Hello, Rosa." On a bad say she wouldn't smile for a few minutes, then finally find a word and say, "Hola, bonita," and then try a smile. On her worst day ever, my grandmother told the homecare nurse to leave and when the nurse wouldn't, she lurched out of her easy chair, grabbed a rolling pin from a vase full of utensils on the kitchen counter, and swung for the nurse's head as best as her frail arms could manage. The nurse ran to her car, and Abuelita followed her right out the door and then spent several hours wandering around the development in the hundred-degree heat till Jeremy found her and wrestled her back into the car. Thus the Silver Alert, and the visit from the pulp fiction collector.

Today wasn't so bad, but it was not a good day. "Bonita . . . y guapo," was how she greeted us. My name, our relationship, had left her mind again. I look like my mother, her daughter, so sometimes I am Daniela too. I count those as good days. The nurse—a new woman, you'd better believe it—silently started collecting her things to go.

"Abuelita," I said. "How are you?" Grandmother's eyes danced at that. She was a grandmother!

"I've been better, but I'm alive, thank God." She looked closely at Jeremy. Mostly she remembered me on some level, but casual acquaintances were beyond the ability of her mind to retain. "What's that?" She pointed at the folder Jeremy was holding. "I'm not signing anything about going to a nursing home. I have to wait for Santo. He's coming home soon. I have to make dinner. He won't let you send me away."

Jeremy winced at the name of my late grandfather, but I had a dozen-time-a-day rote response. "Grandpa is watching over us from heaven, Abuelita. But you can look at this."

I took my grandmother by the arm and led her through the open-plan living room to the kitchen table. Jeremy spread out the photocopies of the magazine covers and the Silex stories like someone in a cop show presenting evidence to the camera.

53

"Where are my glasses?" Silvia snapped.

"Around your neck," Jeremy said.

I dug the glasses out of the folds of my grandmother's house-coat. There was hardly a trace of dignity in our relationship anymore. "Here you are. Does any of this ring a bell?"

Grandma took a seat and bent so far forward that her shoulders and neck were nearly parallel to the floor. "Hmm, hmm," she said, which is what she said when trying to buy a precious moment or two with which to remember something, anything. America is a young nation, though its history is sufficiently bloody that the cosmic aether is stained with the dying moments of the native and settler, soldier and criminal. Her voice was strong, the words effortless; Grandma read in the casual sing-song of the substitute elementary school teacher she had once been. *Into the trackless prairies I was called one summer through the secret network of learned entities known only as the Sisterhood of the Spiral to confront not just a single entity but what appeared to be the octoplasmic manifestation of a defeated people entire who—*

Silvia looked up at me, owlish behind her glasses. "I did that." She smiled. "That rat bastard wanted a 'Brotherhood' of the Spiral, but I looked right at him and told him that if I was going to type up his stories, it would have to be a Sisterhood of the Spiral. Mr. Goulart knew nothing about women, that was his problem."

Jeremy said, "So you recall all this? You typed these stories."

"Of course I typed the stories. When we had a typewriter, that is. That machine went into hock more times than I could count," Grandma said. She was lucid, in two times at once: there, in her own kitchen where she used to cook and play endless hands of solitaire and cut coupons and make phone calls for local politicians, and in the past, as a young woman living on the other end of the continent, typing up stories from handwritten notes on another kitchen table until her husband, wild-eyed and drunk, stumbled in, spilled his own pages to the floor, and slammed the portable typewriter case shut to drag it away down four flights of steps and across the street to the store with three hanging balls over the entrance.

"Where is that pawn shop ticket? We need the typewriter back," Grandma said. That was wrong. Something reset in her brain. "Santo is coming home from work soon. I have to start dinner."

"I'll do dinner, Abuelita," I said. "Why don't you take a nap?"

"I'm not tired."

Jeremy collected several photocopied pages and handed the stack over to Silvia. "Why don't you keep reading, ma'am. You seemed to enjoy the story." Silvia took the pages and I said ". . . in bed."

"I need my glass—"

"Around your neck," Jeremy said too quickly.

After Abuelita was put away in her bedroom, I sat down at the kitchen table and picked up a page between thumb and forefinger, like it was a used tissue. "Spirit Smasher."

"It's very old-fashioned, even compared to some of the other stories in the same issues, but it's interesting, in a way. Tom Silex is like a Sherlock Holmes/cowboy/ghostbuster/Harry Potter–type all rolled up into one," Jeremy said.

"Five hundred dollars."

"We can get more, I'm sure of it."

"How are you sure of it?" I said. "Maybe that guy spent his life's savings coming out here to talk to Grandma."

"You can call her 'Abuelita' in front of me, Rosa," Jeremy said. "White guys are capable of understanding a little Spanish."

"What's five hundred bucks," I asked myself. "If I found five hundred bucks on the street, I'd be thrilled. Hell, five bucks would still be an anecdote."

"What is the hold-up. Just call the guy, have him come over, and sign over the rights, then."

"You were the one telling me about Superman!"

"It can certainly happen," Jeremy said. "But I'm sure that for every one Superman there's a million Tom Silex, Spirit-Smashers out there, with a dedicated fandom of seventeen old weirdoes."

I wonder how much of these stories Grandma actually wrote," I said. "Did she make a lot of changes while she typed them up for Goulart? Maybe she pitched ideas; they could have collaborated."

Jeremy snorted. One of his most annoying habits. "Highly doubtful."

"And why's that, Jeremy?"

"Did she ever mention it? Ever? I mean, even when she was . . . not suffering? When you were a kid?"

"She barely even mentioned her first husband. Maybe she felt betrayed; that's why she never said anything." Maybe that's why my own mother hated fantasy novels and ghost stories. All her Jesus talk aside, we went to church all of twice a year.

"Anyway, I'll call him. He can meet Abuelita. Maybe sympathy will lead him to cough up a few more bucks."

The pulp collector couldn't come back till the next morning. He invited us to invite him to lunch as well. Five hundred bucks minus forty-five for four plates of huevos rancheros. Just like all the big movie deals for Superman, I'm sure. Abuelita had a quiet night, but a strange morning. The Silex stories, which she had picked through, occasionally recalling a turn of phrase she liked— "the shimmering phantasm looked at me, her eyes filled not with tears but the most minute of fireflies; they flew from her cheeks and streaked through the inky blackness that enveloped the old farmhouse"—or banging her little fist against the table. "That rat bastard!" she cried out more than once. "I'd slap him square in the mouth if he were here right now." Elders with dementia often perseverate on something, but Abuelita's usual concerns— "Where's little Rosa, Daniela?"; cooking dinner for Santo, who will be home any minute; how we have to sell the house and move to Florida so "the police" won't find her and put her in a home, were gone. It was almost a relief.

Perhaps I should have left her home, but it was Sunday and the homecare nurse wouldn't be available to watch her until after church services. We only had to explain where we were going—Melrose Kitchen, for food—and why—to meet a man who has some money for us—three times. Only once did she say, "But Santo is coming soon. I have to cook for him."

My poor grandfather, Santo. He had suffered through Abuelita's decaying mental state for years, preparing meals and thanking his wife for cooking for him, repeating, "Daniela is in heaven; she died in an accident," without even a blink to hold back tears. He never raised his voice to his wife, never. His only complaint, ever, was that the inflexible church wouldn't sanction marriage to a divorcée back in the old days, and so they had had to go to the courthouse, like he was applying for a fishing license.

What would Santo have done had he known that he wasn't ever married after all, that on some level—a level of spirit that he always believed in—his wife's soul was still tied to that a dead drunk named Flint?

The pulp collector had decided to dress like a giant grape. He was in a big purple sweatsuit anyway, and he had already ordered and was halfway through his omelet when we arrived. Jeremy strode ahead to shake his hand and arrange the seats around the table as I led my stooped, shuffling abuelita across the length of the restaurant because the pulp collector decided that he needed to sit in the back. I'll give him credit, though, for standing up when my grandmother approached, cleaning his hands with a napkin, and gently shaking her hand. He repeated his name—Edgar—three times for her before we managed to get her into her seat, and each time he spoke as if it were the first. It was the first time he introduced himself to us instead of just launching into his offer.

Then he took a conversational wrong turn. "Mrs. Hernandez,

I have to know. What was Marcus Goulart like? When he was working, I mean. He named his own fictional creation after himself, so I imagine he was quite the character. An adventurer?" My grandmother didn't answer; she shifted her gaze to a spot off to the side.

"He really was one of the most underrated talents in the occult detective subgenre. He was a master of generating mood and atmosphere, and he kept Silex reasonable. Too many occult detectives end up becoming too powerful—there's never a concern that he might be brought low by the forces he confronts. Silex, on the other hand, was always right on the edge of defeat."

"Really," Jeremy said. "All the stories I read—and I haven't had a chance to read them all—seem pretty similar. He gets a call from some ally, shows up at a haunted location, encounters a ghost, then shines a light on it."

Edgar turned hard. "And when I used to read *The New Yorker*, every fiction selection there was about a Connecticut businessman or New York college professor drinking cocktails and contemplating an affair. And by a different author each time. Not only were the stories formulaic, an entire generation of writers shared identical thematic preoccupations."

"*The New Yorker*'s not like that now—" Jeremy started. I would have kicked him under the table if my grandmother wasn't in the way. As it was, she cut off him.

"Goulart was a drunk," she said, finally. "He was always nipping at his flask. By three p.m., he was swaying back and forth like he was on the deck of a rusty ol' boat. He was a charmer, but you couldn't depend on him. One time I wanted to do the laundry, so I sent him out to the corner store for some soap—All Soap, that was the brand. He was gone for more than an hour and came staggering up the steps, a big paper sack draped over each arm. He put the bags down and they thunked. You know what was in those bags, Mister?"

"What?" Edgar said.

"Chicken noodle. Clam chowder. Tomato. Pea. Cream of broccoli. The little rat bastard bought 'all soups.'" She slapped a hand against the tabletop and laughed, a solid "Ha!"

I almost swallowed my tongue. I'd never heard that anecdote before.

"I'd hoped it was a working Shadow Lantern, but that is a great story!" Edgar laughed quite a bit.

"What's a Shadow Lantern?" Abuelita asked. "Where do I know that from?"

"Let's just talk business," I said. "I'm still not sure I understand. Abuelita, this man says that you own these stories."

"Why would I own them?" She looked at me very seriously.

"Because . . ."

What sort of person was Edgar, the pulp collector? Would he care if I lied? Probably not. He just wanted the stories. If he could live inside a pulp magazine, swinging a Shadow Lantern at the ghosts of a thousand dead Apache, or if he could caress the gray cheek of a lost little girl who has been waiting for a playmate for a century, he would. But maybe he was literal-minded, legalistic. To him, Abuelita's signature might not be any good if she weren't competent. The Silver Alert was already a strike against her. . . .

What kind of person was Jeremy? That I should have known by now, eh? He was definitely a first-year law school student. Everything was a potential tort, or criminal charge, or giant pain in the ass. He carried a black pen with him everywhere to make his signature on Starbucks receipts more legally meaningful. But I bet he wanted to keep sleeping with me. He wasn't going to squawk.

What kind of person am I? What would my ghost look like under the Shadow Lantern? Am I just marching my grandmother around toward the end of her life, and giving her another little psychopomp nudge to get it over with?

"Because . . . you typed them, Abuelita. And you gave Mister Flint—Goulart—ideas, right?"

"I did!" she said. "That rat bastard wanted a 'Brotherhood' of the Spiral, but I looked right at him and told him that if I was going to type up his stories, it would have to be a Sisterhood of the Spiral. Mr. Goulart knew nothing about women, that was his problem." Word for word what she said the day before.

"The Sisterhood of the Spiral is a major component of the Silex Cycle," Edgar said.

"Heh, say that five times fast," Jeremy said, and Edgar smiled like he was going to, but I raised my hand. "Please, my grandmother is very tired. She can't stay out long."

"I just wanted to say that the Sisterhood of the Spiral is among the most intriguing elements of the Silex stories. It's a secret society of widows whose interpersonal connections blanket the world, all with some sort of supernatural insight. They're old women, crones, with little in the way of physical abilities, but they know all and see all, and intervene as they can, thanks to their sons and nephews. Silex is the grandson of the Sister Supreme, and—"

"Let's just get the paperwork out, please," I said. "And the check, if possible."

"Do you have PayPal?" Edgar asked. "I have the app on my phone."

"A check," Jeremy said, like a lawyer.

"Of course," Edgar said. He had a folder in his bag, and pulled it out along with a pen, but Jeremy had his black-ink pen ready as well, and handed it to Abuelita.

"I don't want to go to a senior citizen home," Abuelita said. "I have to be at the house when Santo comes back. He's going to want dinner. We need to stop at the store and get some soup. Chicken noodle. Clam chowder . . ."

I took the pen and contract both. It looked pretty straight-forward. I guess Edgar wrote it up himself, rather than spending the money on an attorney. There was some nutty language: ". . . including, without limitation, copyrights, publication rights, distribution rights, reproduction rights, rights to create derivative works, the rights to publish and publicly display the works everywhere in the Universe by any and all means now known or hereinafter invented, and all future created rights," and I read that aloud.

"That's pretty standard," Jeremy said.

"Everywhere in the universe?" I said. Abuelita shot me an upset look, the meaning of which I didn't really understand.

"Standard," Jeremy and Edgar agreed.

"All future created rights?"

"Like if a new medium emerges," Jeremy said. "Virtual reality, maybe."

"One day we may be able to inject stories. Encode narratives in our RNA," Edgar said. "If there's one thing pulp fiction taught me, it's that the possibilities are limitless. We could, in the future, inject stories, even entire life memories, into our own bodies. We'd never forget anything; we could gift our own memories to our descendants . . ." He trailed off, sucking his teeth.

"Is it worth more than five hundred dollars for you, then?" I said.

Edgar shrugged. "Not . . . much more. The possibilities are limitless, but let's face it, nobody remembers Tom Silex, Spirit-Smasher. I have a lot of work to do just to get him back into the public mind by publishing the old stories again. Oh, I brought some cover art, if you wanted to see."

He pulled another folder from his bag, and opened it up. The cover art, spread over one very large paper page was . . . not quite so good as the pulp magazine stuff. It wasn't even painted art, but bad Photoshop. There was a man, who looked pretty much like a photo of a younger Edgar, struggling to hoist up what looked like the result of forced breeding between a megaphone and an old beer keg. He stood in profile in a sort of null-space. Much of the rest of the cover was taken up by a photo of a spiral galaxy, with the faces of old women just plopped on top of the galactic arms. They were all white women.

"That's mine," Abuelita said.

"I'll be sure you to send you a copy, as a courtesy, when the book is printed."

"A courtesy," Jeremy said.

"The contract doesn't give my any obligations, but I'm pleased to send a copy of the book. Obviously, I may end up relicensing or reselling the property to a larger media company—movies, video games, VR, like you said. I can't be tied to providing sample copies of Silex-branded properties to Mrs. Hernandez, here."

"I did that," Abuelita said, pointing to the Sisterhood of the Spiral. "The rat bastard, he wanted a Brotherhood of the Spiral. That doesn't even sound good. I said, 'It has to be Sisterhood.'" Her finger drifted over to the Shadow Lantern. "That was my idea too. But it's supposed to be smaller, so you can hold it one hand, like the Greek philosopher who looked for an honest man." She turned to me. "What was his name, Daniela? You were such a good student."

"I'm Rosa," I said, quietly. "Daniela was my mother," I explained to Edgar.

"She's getting confused," Edgar said. "We'd better have her sign." He glanced over at Jeremy, who nodded like it was his decision without even looking at me.

"No. No, I don't think so," I said. I was surprised to hear it. "Abuelita, I want this. I want these Silex stories for me."

Edgar flipped the folder shut. "Why! You know nothing about him? You didn't even know the character existed until a week ago. You think you're going to sell it to Guillermo del Toro or something like that?" Edgar rolled his r's ostentatiously, incorrectly even.

"Abuelita, let's go!" She hesitated, so I said, "Abuelo Santo is coming home and he'll want dinner." She got herself up out of the chair, a pneumatic piston. I left Jeremy to make apologetic white-boy noises at Edgar. He didn't have much to say on the trip home, which was fine. Abuelita told us the story of "all soups" again, only this time starring poor mostly deaf Santo instead of the rat bastard, so I told her she already had plenty of soup cans in the cupboard.

That night, I turned on my computer, clicked on the big blue W icon to bring up MS Word, and thought myself some thoughts. My grandmother was dying; I was born to be a psychopomp, just for her. If I had a Shadow Lantern, and walked around my life in ever broadening spirals with it, whom would I encounter, and what would I be able to do about them?

I read and enjoy realist and postmodern short fiction, though I don't write it much for reasons both practical and personal. Practically speaking, most literary journals do not pay, and an increasing number even demand payment for the privilege of having one's work skimmed and rejected by a bored and ill-trained graduate student. Who needs it, except for writers keen to fill out their CV and compete for perhaps as many as a dozen tenure-track creative writing instructor jobs per year? That ain't me.

Also not me—the type to publish in literary journals, and there is a type. Middle-class background; white, or if of color a member of the lower echelons of some nation's ruling class; a graduate of a liberal arts university or a talented provincial making it clear that he is ready to play the game by spilling the beans on how the lower social orders live; not just holders of an MFA, but one from one of the *right* universities. But sometimes, I try anyway. "Tom Silex, Spirit-Smasher" was one of those times, and it very nearly worked.

I decided to put a genre spin on a slice-of-life story. As an editor and anthologist, I've occasionally been tasked with finding the copyright holder of a long-forgotten poem or piece of fiction. It's not unusual to follow a path through divorces and deaths to someone who has no idea what they own, or what it's worth. Confusion abounds— first they think my contacting them is a trick, then they decide, often with the help of some attorney from the Legal Hut down at the mall, that the story they own must be worth a million dollars if someone wants to reprint it. It could be the next *Star Wars*! For me, it's tedious, for them it's several days or weeks of chaos and soul-searching. That is the stuff of literary fiction.

My wife's family has a semi-famous ancestor, the imagist poet F. S. Flint (*silex* is Latin for flint), and I helped them contact Penguin about a reprint of his poem "Lament." It includes these thrilling and awful lines:

The genius of the air
Has contrived a new terror
That rends them into pieces.

I have a cantankerous grandmother with dementia. I have an interest in pulp fiction and ghost stories. There are new terrors that will rend us to pieces. Once again, it all came together—a literary piece "of genre interest" as I put it in my cover letter to the special "ghost"-themed issue of *Indiana Review*. As it turns out, by *ghost* they meant stuff like the ghost of a marriage after it fails or something, but the journal did print a wonderful essay by my friend Carrie Laben, "The National Forest of Painted Wang," which is about the ghost town of Centralia, Pennsylvania, and the phallic graffiti covering it.

So no mainstream literary journal for Tom Silex. . . . But there *does* exist a unique periodical, which is co-edited by science fiction writer Brian Slattery, and that *is* a real-life journal of mostly realist fiction and mostly thoughtful personal essays with the word *review* in its very title, and that does pay a lot of money—five hundred smackers!—for short fiction. (How, given its minute circulation? That is a question we do not dare ask.) *New Haven Review* even gives special consideration to authors with a connection to Connecticut, and "Connecticut is connected to Long Island via the ferry my grandfather and mother used to work on as food servers," is connection enough! I had a ghost of a chance, and I took it.

THE GREAT ARMORED TRAIN

SO, THIS IS WHAT COMMUNISM MEANS? Gribov thought. The train was magnificent. It seemed too heavy to move, but it fairly glided along the tracks. It was the smoothest ride Gribov had ever been on, and it bustled with activity—warehouse, restaurant, barracks, even a Politburo office and telegraph station, a two-car garage, and even a small biplane among its twelve wagons. Never mind the armored engines with gun turrets. *All this, and it doesn't even have a name!* It was just the train of the *Predrevoyensoviet*, Leon Trotsky. Didn't the War Commissar have a wife or a girlfriend to name his personal armored war-train after?

But really, it was the workers' train, and there was much work to be done. Gribov was a soldier, but no longer just a standard peasant with a rifle and a children's book on the Russian alphabet to help him learn to read. He was one of the Red Sotnia, the hundred soldiers who made up Trotsky's bodyguard and rushed out to join pitched battles. Not long before, he'd been in the cavalry train that followed behind Trotsky's, shoveling horse shit. But the train, and the Bolshevik efforts, had taken some hits lately, and now Gribov was decked out in black leather, presumably ready to give his life for the world proletariat, and for comrade Trotsky. Gribov dutifully collected the train's newspaper, *V puti*, but mostly used it to insulate his boots. It was cold tonight on the Polish border, and he was glad that Trotsky wrote so much. *Almost toasty*, he thought, as he leapt from the roof of one car to another, watching the forest for Mensheviks, for Cossacks, for Poles.

"Comrade!" one of the sharpshooters stationed on the roof whispered harshly. "Step lightly! You'll bring them down upon us."

"Comrade," Gribov said, "we are on a giant train. Steam is billowing from the engines. Even idle, even under the new moon, we're obvious."

"And an opposing army flooding from the wood should be more obvious still," another sharpshooter said.

"When I was a soldier under the tsar, we would never have dared to banter so," said the first shooter.

"Thus I am thankful now more than ever for the Revolution, and the 2nd Latvian Riflemen's Soviet Regiment," said the second. The others, five in all, giggled. "But be quiet anyway," the second shooter said to Gribov. "I'm working on my poem." More chortling emerged from the dark.

"Poem? What?" Gribov asked.

"Don't you read the paper?" the first shooter asked. "How do you know where we are *on our way* to?" More laughter, this time for the pun on *V puti—en route* or "on our way."

"Comrade Fancy Dude has called on the poets of Poland to write poems denouncing the landlords and the bourgeoisie," a new voice explained.

"Perhaps I will write a poem, then," Gribov said. He laughed, once.

"What rhymes with *pshek*?" the second shooter asked, and he got a round of chuckles from the shooters arranged on either side of the train car's roof. The new Communist mentality had not quite taken hold in the men of the Red Sotnia. After all, the

Polish workers spoke as funnily as the Polish bourgeoisie. But Gribov couldn't blame them for their elitism. They were an elite! It was a very nice train after all, complete with cloth napkins for Trotsky's personal staff, so perhaps being part of the "One Hundred," living aboard a futuristic conveyance, had confused them. Gribov could too write a poem, and a poem that would be understood by the Polish proletariat! Working man to working man, something these careerists from good families would never understand. The poem could be about the train, and its many magnificent attributes—the Rolls-Royce liberated from the tsar's garage and outfitted with a pair of machine guns! It was always a thrill to hear it roaring forth from its special train car, metal flashing under the sun, lighting and thunder at once. . . .

"Carry on," he announced to the sharpshooters, and moved on to the next train car, jumping lightly and expertly over the gap. It was a risk, but Gribov knew there would be no insults shouted at his back, for fear of alerting the enemy. There was no way the train was secret, but a sudden yelp could give away a comrade's position to a Polish sniper.

A poem, a poem. . . . What would inspire the Polish working class to rise up, to greet the Red Army as liberators? No poem had been needed to persuade Gribov. His family were dirt-poor peasants and when he crawled into Petrograd to look for work on the piers, he was treated worse than his father had treated the animals on the farm. Nobody else offered anything but misery, and the phony promise of a heavenly reward. The heavens were dark tonight. No moon, no stars; the clouds were low and the color of slate.

A rush of wind almost sent Gribov's spine tearing out of his back. Bursting from the trees had come a great grey owl, flying low and nearly silent just under the dome of the sky, wings stretched a meter and a half from tip to tip.

Incredible! This would go into the poem, Gribov decided, but then the owl banked and turned, its claws wide and gleaming. Gribov couldn't decide between drawing his pistol and just raising his arms. The owl took his face. Screaming, Gribov flailed and fell from the train. An alarm was raised, but from the woods Polish irregulars rained small arms fire down on the train.

Who would wake Trotsky? "The man would sleep through the Proletarian Revolution were he not in charge of scheduling it" was the common joke, but it wasn't quite fair. Trotsky was awake twenty hours a day, so the four he slept were extremely necessary. He was difficult to awaken, and ornery when he finally arose. Even under Communism, whoever knocked on the door had better have his boots polished. Nechayev drew the short straw and was poised to knock when the door opened. Trotsky was already dressed, complete in leather coat and hat.

"We're not under way, I presume," Trotsky said, "because the tracks ahead have been destroyed. And we are concerned that if we head back along the line, we'll encounter a Menshevik train. The cavalry train is also pinned down."

A near-perfect set of wrong conclusions. Under any other circumstances, Trotsky would have been correct, but. . . .

"We have an infiltrator. She has sabotaged the engines. We were able to repulse the Poles, but we expect reinforcements by morning," Nechayev said.

"She—" Trotsky began.

"So . . . we've heard," Nechayev said.

"*She's* not been captured yet? A woman? An individual woman?"

"It's hard to explain," Nechayev began. A few words later and Trotsky pushed past him, his own sidearm drawn, orders spilling forth.

The woman looked like a Pole; fair, with a round face, though there was something else about her coloration too, the bone structure around her cheeks. She wore the black leather uniform of a Red Sotnia fighter, though it was far too big for her. She'd made it as far as one of the supply cars. The men she had already dispatched slumped amidst piles of shoes, loose piles of tobacco, and potatoes spilling forth from the sacks they'd been stored in. Four guards had rifles trained on her. For a moment, Trotsky thought she was weeping silently, but then realized that the squint was just her eyes—she was a Tatar, or had some Tatar ancestry, anyway.

"Anyone have any Polish?" Trotsky asked. Then he tried, in Russian, then German, and even bad French, and English.

"Comrade Commissar," one of the guards asked. "What shall we do? Shoot her? If we approach, she just . . ." he trailed off.

". . . turns into an owl," Trotsky finished. "Keep her pinned. Rotate comrades in and out of here. Let her stand there, looking foolish. Kick a bucket over to her so she can urinate without making a mess. If she does anything else . . . *interesting*, seal her in the car and detach it from the train on both ends. We'll rendezvous the hard way."

After hasty scrambles around tracks and over coaches to the restaurant car, everyone was full of questions, but only Trotsky was actually able to complete his sentences without interruption.

"You'd sacrifice the train, but—"

"Seal her in and set it on fire! That way—"

"How many more . . ."

"Why are you even taking this seriously?" Pozansky finally demanded of Trotsky. He was the senior of the commissar's secretaries, and broad-chested, so his voice both metaphorical and literal carried like no other. "It defies all we know of science!"

"That is why," Trotsky said. The room quieted. "Why am I on the verge of sacrificing our train? Because if a woman can metamorphose into an owl, our cause is lost. The proletarian dictatorship depends on proletarian revolution. The proletarian revolution depends on a dialectical understanding of history. The dialectical understanding of history"—the soldiers began shifting in their seats, as it sounded like Comrade Fancy Pants was gearing up for one of his extensive speeches—"and the dialectical understanding of history is built upon a bedrock of materialism."

Trotsky tugged on his Vandyke. "We're at war, so I'll say it quickly. If she is some sort of mystical or supernatural being, our cause is lost. If magic is real, then Marxism is not. We may as well go home and light candles by the family icon."

"What are the chances that this woman can turn into an owl in a way not possible to explain by some science, even if only the science of the future?" Pozansky asked. "And what are the chances that vodka and philosophical backsliding led to a certain level of embarrassment among our troop over the fact that a single, female saboteur eluded detection, damaged both engines, and killed several men with what was obviously a garden fork of some sort?"

"Low," Trotsky said.

"Lower than the possibility that magic and superstition is real? That a fairy out of children's tales attacked our train for the glory of Polish imperialists?"

"That depends on the nature of reality," Trotsky said. "Which we will now investigate. Men, take the motorcars out. Find me a Pole who speaks Russian. Find me a Tatar familiar with the superstitions of his race. Find a book, a journal, anything, even if for children, on the subject of local folklore or avifauna. And try to make sure the Pole who can speak Russian is literate. Shoes and food and cigarettes and liquor to trade, and if the marketplace doesn't meet our demands, well then, men, remember that you are Communists."

When the troop dispersed, Trotsky raised an eyebrow at Pozansky. The senior secretary smirked back, and young Nechayev just looked confused.

"We cleared the train of anyone who might have been bamboozled by this stage magic," Pozsansky explained.

"Obviously, she is wearing one of our uniforms. If she turned into an owl and then back, she would be nude," Trotsky said. "What I am interested in, primarily, is finding out how our captive performs these tricks. It might make for a useful wedge between Polish workers and reactionary, credulous peasants."

Nechayev said, "I thought we were never to lie to the working class."

Trotsky shrugged. "We wouldn't be. We'd be lying to the backwards elements of the peasantry. The Poles are lying to our people, of course, which is why this social-reactionary split has occurred." Nechayev had the strong feeling that the only split that had occurred was that Trotsky was getting ready to have him demoted, arrested, or thrown off the train for passing on the owl story with such credulity.

"And we need to find out from whom she got one of our uniforms. We've not been through this part of the front before; we've had no recent casualties outside of the train from which the leathers could have been salvaged. If the Poles had decided to infiltrate, surely they would have sent a male, and a Russian speaker. I suspect some sort of love affair concocted by local peasant militias," Trotsky said. "You two, move my desk over to the train in which our owl has been penned."

A handful of comrades discovered Gribov on their way back from their mission. He was cold, bloodied, probably blinded, and one eye was missing entirely, but he lived. Much of his uniform was missing as well. They created a makeshift gurney from rifles and coats and brought him aboard, to the infirmary car.

Gribov was not a weak man, and he had fallen into a snow

bank, so soon enough he was able to testify, haltingly. Pozansky took notes, argued closely over the advice of the medics.

"The owl? Not a small kite, or even an aeroplane of some sort?"

"It was warm, alive, smelled like the woods and dead prey . . ."

"Feathers would do that!"

"She took off my clothes. Just one little girl . . ."

"One? How do you know there was only one if you are missing one eye?"

"Just a pair of little hands . . ."

"Did they say anything?"

Gribov laughed. "Pshek pshek . . . you know how Poles sound. All consonants. Haha."

"Comrade, there are many revolutionary Poles in our movement who might tell you that to a Pole, a Russian sounds like a child," Pozansky lectured. "Shaa shaa vaa vaaa."

"Comrade secretary, please," one of the medics said. "He needs rest, not political education."

"We need to get to the bottom of the case of this infiltrator, comrade doctor!"

"Why not just shoot her and throw her into a ditch?" the medic demanded.

"Please don't . . ." Gribov said. "She's . . ."

"Yes?"

". . . my poem . . ."

"He's delirious," said the medic.

"Thank you for that insight, comrade doctor," Pozansky said. "As we thought."

Nechayev told Trotsky about finding Gribov, but that made the commissar only more interested in this interrogative theater. Soldiers had slowly moved into the train car, but kept their rifles, and further the length of two strides, between themselves and the girl. She looked like a wax doll of some sort. If not for the puffs of steam coming from her mouth with every exhalation, she could have passed for a bit of whimsical propaganda art amongst the supplies.

The soldiers had found several books on folklore, and a local bilingual speaker, an older woman who had experienced the border shifting between empires under her feet several times in her long life. She was not pleased to have been awakened at gunpoint and brought here for the interrogation, but she drank her tea and ate a potato and a bit of meat from the tin plate held on her lap with some pleasure. She could even read, but her glasses had been smashed during the trip back to the train, so her literacy was of no help.

"Do you two women know one another?" was the first question.

"I don't associate with Tatars," the old woman said. "Or Communists."

"And yet here we all are," said Trotsky. Nechayev put his hand to his forehead and sighed. Under the tsar he probably would have been whipped for the gesture, but Trotsky didn't even notice.

"Ask her why she is against the proletarian revolution," he said to the older woman. With a practiced sneer, she turned toward the girl and repeated the question in Polish. The answer was short.

"She says you know why."

The interrogation went on for some time. Was she a Tatar? That depends on what you mean. Did she attack the soldier Gribov, sabotage the engine, then storm through the cars of this magnificent train, killing and injuring Soviet soldiers? Certainly she did, and she would be pleased to continue. How did she manage such a feat? The soldier had his head in the clouds; her husband, murdered by Reds, had been a machinist, so she knew something of engines; Russian men are weak and easy to kill, even for a simple girl like her. Could she turn into an owl? Yes, of course. That was the fault of the Bolsheviks as well.

"How is that?" Trotsky said, clearly amused.

"Girls who are married when they die turn into owls," it was explained by the translator before the young girl even spoke. The older woman added, "It is an old story." Trotsky took a moment to flip through one of the children's books his soldiers had liberated, and grunted once when he alighted upon a certain illustrated page.

"Are there mice in your home?" The old woman turned again to ask the girl, but Trotsky raised the hand. "In *your* home, ma'am."

"There were mice in my home," she snapped, "when there was food in my home. Another achievement for the Bolsheviks!"

"Then how likely is it that Polish girls transform into owls upon their death?" Trotsky asked, ignoring the last bit of editorializing. "The moon would be eclipsed every night by masses of owl wings, and there wouldn't be a mouse left in Poland."

The girl said something testy-sounding, and the old woman translated at length, even pantomiming a mouse nibbling at some food. Trotsky turned to Nechayev. "Summon more witnesses," he said. "If they are not wounded or tending the wounded, if they are not on watch, if they are not repairing the engine, have them gather on either side of the car and peer inside." Nechayev ran to comply.

Finally the girl said something and the old woman translated it. "Her explanation is that she is only a Pole on her mother's side of the family. Her father's side are Tatars." There was a bit more discussion, then the old woman turned to Trotsky with a smile on her face. "She says her grandfather's grandfather was a . . . primitive."

"A shaman," Trotsky said. Behind him, a crowd was forming, four or five rows deep. With military discipline the shortest gathered immediately behind Trotksy's desk and took to their

Nick Mamatas

knees to not block the vision of their comrades behind them. "I presume it was the hybridity of superstitions that allows you your special ability to transform into an owl." The old woman didn't bother to translate that.

Lanterns shifted and danced on either side of the train car as comrades who couldn't fit on either end of the train car tried to squeeze in. Trotsky was clearly pontificating at length in order to allow everyone to get into position.

"So, why attack us? Why not be free as the proverbial bird, always, without the burdens of consciousness or the need to labor? Why not join us, allow us to better understand your ability, so that we might integrate it into the corpus of materialist science? What diseases could be cured via this form of cellular transformation? And yet, you keep it yourself." The old woman's translations were obviously abbreviated and simplified, Nechayev could tell, but the young girl seemed to be getting the gist of Trotsky's comments anyway.

"Or, perhaps, you cannot turn into an owl," Trotsky finally concluded. "Just acknowledge this, and we'll keep you a prisoner here until our engine is repaired. We'll leave you at the next station on our side of the front for typical justice. If you continue to insist on your nonsense story, we shall gun you down here—summary revolutionary justice on the part of the international working class, against a deranged member of the criminal element.

"Or you may turn into an owl and flee," Trotsky said. He glanced at Nechayev, then nodded toward the closest window. It occurred to Nechayev that the window, even were he to smash it out of its frame with the butt of a borrowed rifle, would not be sufficient for the wingspan of an owl the size of the one Gribov supposedly encountered, but he obeyed anyway as the older woman translated. Then, harshly, the older woman added something else—a message directly aimed at the girl.

The girl shifted in her outfit. A shoulder, nude, almost pink

76

despite the cold, was visible now, and her thin little collarbone, itself like a bird's wings. Then two things happened.

The girl made a move. It wasn't a run, or a leap, but as though she had thrown her body forward, every muscle working together.

One of the soldiers fired. The train car filled with sound and smoke. Men screamed. "No!" "Don't!"

For a moment Nechayev thought something would happen. She wouldn't fall. Feathers would erupt out her back, trailing the bullet.

There was still shouting. The comrades were worried, hysterical, for themselves. Why fire into a crowded train car?! Madness!

The girl fell hard to the floor. A gardening tool slipped from one sleeve of her oversized leather coat and clattered to the floor.

The other soldiers who had had their rifles trained on the woman held their fire. The old lady wasn't crying as Nechayev thought she might be. She was terrified that she would be next, her face chiseled by horror into an unnerving rictus.

Trotsky looked contemplative. Maybe it was a flash of disappointment that crossed over his eyes as he spoke. "Retrieve the coat and have it stitched up if possible," he said to nobody in particular, and there were no volunteers to strip the girl. He turned to the shooter. "Comrade Fedin, you are relieved of duty due to reckless fire. Put your rifle down now if you do not wish it removed from you by force."

He sighed deeply. "Have the body brought to the infirmary car. We're not equipped for an autopsy here, but it might be interesting to see if there are visible lesions on her brain. So much for magical owls, eh?" Trotsky readied himself against his desk and rose. With a gesture, he told Nechayev to clear it all away. "And if I see one comrade making the sign of the cross, or hear tell of it, he will be disciplined most severely. And someone pay this woman and return her to her home," he said, indicating the old lady, who still hadn't moved, hadn't blinked.

Clearly, the corpse should have been stored in the refrigerated car, but Pozansky wouldn't have it, and he threatened the medics who said they'd go to Trotsky about it with hard discipline and a negative write-up in the train's newspaper.

"It's cold enough on this train," Pozansky said. "Her lesions will keep for the night, I am sure." There were a few choice items in cold storage that Pozansky liked to keep for himself, and whenever an unauthorized comrade entered the refrigerated car they would, in a burst of revolutionary fervor, take a sample of the caviar or beefsteak or decent vodka to share with the masses—that is, their friends.

And so she ended up in sickbay, next to Gribov. He suffered, awake, from his wounds, so was conscious to hear her cough out the bullet that had entered her chest. Mostly blind, he couldn't see that the bullet was coated in plant matter, feathers, and tiny bones. She slid off the examination table she had been left on, wrapped the blanket she had been given out of a sense of retrograde modesty around herself, and nudged Gribov.

"I have your eye," she said to him. "Would you like it back?" She was not speaking in the pshek-pshek of Polish. It was a strange tongue, all elongated *y* sounds.

"I . . . that would be hard to explain to the comrade officers . . ." Gribov said.

"You may come with me," the girl said. "Indeed, I insist upon it."

"I cannot fly, like you."

She smiled. "Can you drive?"

He smiled too. Not quite like a mother giving a child a kiss, she leaned down, swept her hair away from her face, and with a significant gulp, regurgitated Gribov's eye onto his face, then roughly pushed it back into the socket with her free hand. Ten bloody minutes later, they had made it to the tsar's Rolls-Royce in the garage car and were *on their way*, roaring, serpentine, into the night, machine guns blazing as Gribov twisted the wheel to dodge fire from train-top sharpshooters.

Fire that soon tilted up into the slate-dark sky as a thousand great gray owls descended in swarms onto the train.

Dark Discoveries, now defunct, was an interesting magazine. Founded by James Beach, the magazine was an ersatz *Cemetery Dance*, with an emphasis on showcasing and reviewing small press horror titles to be discovered, as well as publishing short fiction. Then came 2008 and the global economic crisis that popped the bubble of limited edition/collectable horror publishers, and also happened to take out a significant fraction of bookstores and newsstands. Beach then brought in a fellow named Jason V. Brock, who brought new energy to the magazine, and some new ideas. Many of the ideas, such using every possible font, filter, color, and background image available in order to discover the sensory limits of the reader, were terrible. Others, such as having theme issues, weren't so bad at all. When *Dark Discoveries* was purchased by small press horror publisher Journalstone, the design innovations were rolled back and silly pin-up covers introduced. How many strange situations can a woman with enormous breasts be put into? Let's discover the answer! The theme issues continued, which was nice.

Toward the end of the magazine's run, when the pin-ups were finally replaced with photos of famous authors, I was solicited to write something for their "military horror" theme. I have no military experience, and if I had to boil down my leftist politics to a single position, it would be "anti-war." But editor Aaron French wanted to shake things up, though I knew that merely writing a story about the horrors of war wouldn't be very interesting. Everyone, horror writers included, tends to romanticize and even eroticize that which they hate and fear. A story featuring lovely gore and miserable weeping survivors wouldn't mean anything.

For some time a couple of decades ago, I was part of a neo-Trotskyist organization. Breathless summaries of the October Revolution often included tales of Trotsky's great armored train zipping around the country, smashing Mensheviks and invaders from sixteen different countries. The train itself is endlessly fascinating—it was a true technological marvel on steel wheels. One of the classic tropes of a dark fantasy or horror tale is modernity slamming up against the pre-modern, so a little digging found me some peculiar legends to test Trotsky's materialist philosophy with. Once that clash was set, the story was easy to write.

As Jacob Weisman, the publisher of this book, noted, "The Great Armored Train" takes a sudden turn into a love story. Of course it does. I hate war.

THE PHYLACTERY

TONY HAD NO IDEA HOW TO EXPLAIN IT, so decided that he wouldn't even try. Instead, he squeezed his palm around the *filakto* and loitered in the doorway to the bedroom as Cheryl changed the baby. As she bent down to goo-goo at him, Tony sidled over to the crib and under the guise of fussing with the mattress pad and sleep sack, slipped it under the mattress.

Of course, Cheryl would find it eventually, and of course the little thing—a tiny pouch of crumbled flower petals from Tony's mother's church—meant nothing at all, but still.

But still what. . . .

"Are you familiar with Pascal's wager?" Tony asked Cheryl. They were tucking in to dinner as best they could. The baby was in the high chair, dribbling onto his bib, his hands and face stained with mashed avocado, quiet only for a second.

"What?" Cheryl was annoyed. Always annoyed with Tony now. She could hiss words that didn't contain sibilants. Love was a precious and dwindling resource. The national reserves deep in the Arctic of her breast were being drilled for the exclusive consumption of the baby. Annoyed enough that Tony knew the conversation wouldn't go well, but yet another muttered "Nothing, honey" would work even less well.

So he decided to be the jerk: "That fancy liberal arts education sure was wasted, eh? Pascal's wager is the idea that it is better to believe in God than not to. If there's a God, good, it all worked out. You get to heaven. If not, so what? At least you lived a good life." The baby spit just then, a punctuation mark. The baby was living the good life. When was the last time someone so carefully scooped spilled food back into your mouth, and congratulated you for finally swallowing some of it?

"I didn't study theology in school," Cheryl said after she looked up from the baby, the smile she'd had for him gone. "Liberal arts college isn't bar trivia. It's not as though I am just bursting with facts of no use to anyone, Tony. And anyway, it's a dumb wager. Which God do you pick? I presume Pascal was a Christian then, and didn't even stop to consider other religions."

"Yeah, exactly," Tony said. "You'd have to pick the religion that promised either the greatest rewards or harshest punishments."

"Or easiest version of 'good life' to comply with, I suppose," Cheryl said.

"Zeus and his thunderbolts," Tony said. He looked at the baby. The baby looked back, making real eye contact for once, recognizing his daddy. Tony waggled his fingers at the baby and made a *psshrr-krraakooo* thunderbolt noise. It almost suited the steady downpour outside. For a terrifying nanosecond, the baby looked like he might cry. Tony prayed that the baby would laugh. Instead, the baby just stared. Cheryl turned him around in his high chair and fed him another green blob of avocado.

"So, the gods of my ancestors? What do you think, baby?" Tony said.

"I have to pump," Cheryl said. "I don't have the energy to think anymore."

Does this baby not have a name? Of course he has a name,

don't be ridiculous. Ask Cheryl, and the baby's name is Charlie. Ask Tony, and the baby's name is Kyriakos—"We call him Charlie." According to Tony, Cheryl was a slave to the whims of imaginary, if cruel, eight-year-old boys in a schoolyard positioned seven years and three months into the future. According to Cheryl, she just wanted to be able to call her own child by a name that she could pronounce without being corrected by her annoying husband.

"The ability to roll one's r's is genetic," she'd said.

"No it's not," Tony had said. He was right, incidentally, but Cheryl had better things to do than to train herself to affect a Greek accent. Like cleaning the house for once, and a million other things that Tony only thought about after being reminded of old promises and new strategies, and getting confirmation from "dad blogs" on the right things to do.

Just go along with it, the dad blogs always seemed to be saying. *You're a hostage in an unfamiliar land. Look at the camera and recite the lines; do as you're told. Denounce the imperialist running dogs!*

It said Charles Kyriakos on the birth certificate.

Charles Kyriakos didn't always sleep through the night, and Tony and Cheryl, who slept back to back, asses lightly touching, didn't always follow the guideline to let the baby self-soothe. Tony was usually the softie, the one who was damning the child to a lifetime of insomnia, selfishness, entitlement, and reduced income potential, but that night Cheryl was the one who slithered out the bed first, then sang, "Charlie! I'm coming!" as she walked across the room, to the crib, in two long strides.

Tony kept his eyes shut. He had a gift, an inheritance from his father—also named Kyriakos and occasionally called Charlie by the non-Greek regulars at his diner—the ability to sleep under any conditions. The elder Kyriakos had developed the ability while in the Greek Navy, during the junta, when everything was bad. But now life was good, and falling asleep was easy. Tony, the perfect self-soother, drifted off before his son did. Not that Tony's parents had let him cry himself back to sleep as an infant, mind you.

Cheryl woke him up at dawn, almost like she used to, straddling him. But her top was still on, and in her hand she held the filakto.

"What's this?" she asked, curious. Not annoyed, for once. The whole room smelled of breast milk. Hormones were at work in the smile on Cheryl's face, in the light squeeze of her thighs that she used to punctuate her question. Tony knew better to reach up and touch her breast though.

"It's a filakto," he said. Dad blog instructions: *name, rank, serial number.*

She put it on his forehead. "Go on. You're dying to tell me."

"You know, like a phylactery. For protection."

"It's a Greek thing," she said, before he could.

"A good luck charm."

"Like that?" Cheryl asked, pointing with her chin to the wall over the crib, where a blue and white swirl of amber reminiscent of an eye hung, incongruous and bizarre, from a nail left by a previous tenant. A decal of a pink and otherwise featureless sheep jumped over it.

"The *mati*," Tony said. "The eye. That's a little different. A filakto is a sanctioned Greek Orthodox Church thing. The mati is more of a folk expression."

"Isn't it enough?" Cheryl asked. Her fingers worried the hem of the pouch. "What's in this?"

"Maybe flower petals, maybe ashes. All from the church. They're a buck."

Cheryl smiled like she used to, all perfect teeth hard won from awkward years of orthodontia. Tony warmed under her. It had been a while since he had seen that smile. He liked her hair today.

It was short and messy, like a boy's, or a girl too wild to care what boys thought.

But what was she thinking? And would the baby stir? Well, both questions are easy enough to answer, really.

Cheryl was thinking a few different things. Her husband was clearly secretly religious after all, on some level. He had insisted on a church wedding, citing the demands of his mother. He made faces when she brought home that Christopher Hitchens book. But didn't Tony consider himself to be practically a Marxist? Wasn't his email ID, chat login, and Twitter handle "Gramsci76?" When Occupy was happening, he had come home one night blind and smelling of chemicals, his black Old Navy sweatshirt toxic from the pepper spray. He'd just opened the window and flung it into their little shared backyard. Even the rain couldn't get rid of the smell.

Or maybe it was something else, she decided. Tony was a weirdo. That was part of why she married him—they used to have good conversations, and sometimes he would just say something she couldn't imagine a man she was with ever saying. He was against gun control, voted for the Green Party instead of Obama like everyone else, made his own Turkish coffee one cup at a time instead of drinking Starbucks, and couldn't bear to listen to even a minute of NPR. Tony played Dungeons & Dragons with dateless, careerless men he had met on Craigslist once a week, and one time at a dinner party had declared himself a "non-presenting genderqueer." Cheryl snorted her wine through her nose at that one, and Tony smiled the smile that meant he was lying but wanted you to believe it.

Would her baby grow up to be a genderqueer, or a half-elf ranger with a few levels of magic-user, or a Communist, or a "good Greek boy" like her mother-in-law, who had taken to calling herself "*yiayia*," and aloud for Christ's sake, wanted? The baby was never far from Cheryl's thoughts. The baby looked like Tony. Tony had said once, just a few days after they'd all come home from the hospital, that all children look like their fathers at first. Children were genetically programmed to survive, and one way to live past infancy was to make sure one's father didn't wring the neck of his own true offspring—the face of a child was thus *necessarily* a mirror for the father to peer into.

Tony was a weirdo, all right.

Then Tony spoke. "They have big ones too. They're five bucks. Gaudy, like little sequined Liberace pillows. The dollar one was a better deal. No reason to pay extra for a good luck charm."

As to the second question, *of course* the baby stirred. Don't be ridiculous. Both his parents were up and at the crib railing before Charlie Kyriakos even started his naked, hysterical screaming. The baby often wore a "Howl"-themed onesie from City Lights Books, but not today. He didn't have to wear it; he lived it.

Neither Cheryl nor Tony forgot about the filakto. Tony put it back under the crib mattress the moment he was able to, and Cheryl Googled it—though she spelled the word "phylacto" at first and didn't get much. Her Presbyterian upbringing hadn't prepared her for amulets and icons and gibberish. On one message board she came across, the mati hanging on the wall was denounced as "peasant magic." For a moment, she was angry on behalf of Tony, of his mother, of every Greek in the world, even though normally she would agree that a big amber eye was creepy and weird and certainly not rational.

A few weeks later the filakto fell to the floor and a mouse got to it. Cheryl vacuumed it up without noticing, and Tony didn't remember to check for it either.

Tony had wanted one thing, and what he wanted was so simple he couldn't even articulate it. Instead he tried explaining things roundabout. "It's just that I had a lot of cousins my own age, and our kid probably won't," and "My grandfather has Alzheimer's. He remembers better in Greek." Neither had anything to do with the filakto. It's just that Tony didn't want to be the last member of the Kalafatis family, its thousand-year march of industrious goatherds and restaurateurs and hunch-backed widows, to have a filakto.

Three generations in America. It would be hard enough for the baby to grow up with anything but an empty hole where his culture should have been. And how would little Charlie fill it, except with video games and baseball and maybe even growing up and changing his surname to Kelly. Let the baby be a little Greek, just for a while. Easter on the Eastern calendar—half-price jelly beans and chocolate rabbits four years out of five!—lamb and spanakopita, a few words of the old language here and there. Curses and the weather. Maybe the baby could go back one day, meet the cousins, even settle down, once America finished tearing itself apart.

Forget it, Tony thought to himself one night. He was sneaking a cigarette out on the porch. *America is going to tear Europe apart first, and then just swirl down the toilet.* There were fireflies everywhere, and the smoke in his lungs wasn't any hotter than the air outside. *Fucking climate change.* What was Cheryl up to? Yoga class, probably. The kid? Shouting into a headset and racking up a body count in the virtual ruins of radioactive Pakistan with his online pals. Tony lit another cigarette and watched the whole thing burn down to the filter. They lived in New York now, to be closer to Cheryl's parents.

Here's a little peasant magic for you. Imagine a tiny cup in front of you, white with blue trim, on a tiny white saucer. Drink the coffee in it down. It's strong, like you put a tablespoon of grounds in your mouth and started sucking the flavor out directly. Let's read the muddy grains that remain. That's where Greeks keep the future. Charles Kyriakos Kalafatis never marries, but he does have kids. Three girls: Krystlyn, Karr, and Korynne. The girls call Cheryl "grandma," and Tony "pop-pop." They never manage *papou.* They

like their mother's family better anyway. The Schnabels have
real money, and a temperature-controlled swimming pool. One
time the girls program it to freeze right in the middle, and they
play The Last Polar Bear Ever with an inflatable raft. Their other
grandfather yells at them for wasting energy.

Karr is missing something—a bit of the beta chain gene on
the #11 chromosome—her inheritance from her father, and
grandfather before her. She's a sickly girl at first, but there are
gene therapies now, and targeted folic acid supplements. She never
reproduces and that little anomaly that causes thalassemia fades
out of the family line once and for all.

Krystlyn does reproduce; she's blonde, like her mother, with
a squinting smile. In college she says that she has some Greek in
her, because there's a Greek-American boy she's interested in. They
date for a few weeks, but that's it, except for the baby that she, in
a fit of nostalgic pique, carries to term and gives up to adoption to
a nice family in China.

Korynne is a nice girl, dark-haired like her father, and whip-
smart. Then she goes and marries a stern evangelical Christian
man, an engineer she met in college. There is no Easter candy to
be had in her home at any price.

Peasant magic is concerned with peasant things. Babies and
whatnot. The weather too. Which gets steadily worse, and wild
on our way down to the last dregs of coffee. A very old Tony
makes a joke about retiring to fabulous seaside Dayton, Ohio,
and a very old Cheryl laughs and hugs a plastic headwrap
around her short hair to keep the rain off, then pushes him in
his chair down the street. Tony's other joke is that he is the last
Kalafatis in the world and so someone should commission a
bust of him to be made from of non-compostable plastics. It isn't
quite true since Tony has a son, and some far-off cousins whose
first names he has forgotten, though surely many of them are
named *Antoni, Kyriacos, Vasso, Athena,* and *Kalliope,* after their

grandparents. But Kyriacos—fucking "Charlie"—did change his name to Kalafatis-Schnabel to please his girlfriend's family, finally, and none of the girls kept the Greek name at all.

And near the lower curve of the cup there is a young man, Yu, in Shanghai, whose dark hair has a bit of a curl to it from the rain. He is looking down at his newborn child, in a time and place where people have agreed that to speak of gender in infants before they can express gender themselves is rude, if not oppressive. After its tempestuous twentieth century, did you think patriarchal China incapable of change? Yu's own parents were perverse in their way, which neighbors credited to wayward Western genes. Their family name is Feng, fourth tone, and that makes it an unusual one. Feng Yu's father was from America, and he was born of a white mother with olive skin and screeching voice. *Feng Yu*—were feng first tone instead of fourth—could be read to mean "wind and rain," and that would have been a terrible thing to name a boy. Yu thinks he sees himself in his own child, who stares up with glassy eyes, ready to burst into furious tears. Yu looks a bit foreign to most, but his child looks right at home.

The coffee cup tells me that a great wave is coming. I hope the baby will be okay.

After a miscarriage and a fetus "incompatible with life," my wife's third attempt at a pregnancy took, though we did get a scare after nuchal translucency testing suggested possible birth defects. The whole experience was fraught, and I could not stop thinking of the future, the familial future rather than the socio-technological future that usually preoccupies me. I can barely communicate with my father's side of the family as my Greek is marginal, and I've often wondered what my paternal ancestors would think if they could see me now. And what would they think of a half-Greek child? (They'd love him, of course, but they might also be surprised. . . .) With a child of my own on the way, the occasional wool-gathering metastasized into a constant rumination.

I wrote this story in a hurried burst while visiting my sister. The baby was due in a month; it would be my last time at my sister's house without him existing and being part of our lives. My brain was boiling over with anxiety. But that wasn't motivation enough to write. I find writing exhausting and distasteful, remember? I happened to see that the *Boston Review* was holding its annual fiction contest, and the deadline was at month's end. I suppose the literary met genre in that moment—I had all these inchoate feelings I was desperate to somehow articulate, and I saw an opportunity to make a thousand bucks if I could just make a tight deadline. I pulled what I had at hand and in mind: Greek folklore, my actual marriage in the state it was at the time, the names of some famous masters of the martial art, Chen taiji, I'd been studying for several years and which I'd chatted with a cousin about earlier that day, and I stayed up all night, and submitted the story.

I lost the contest. Didn't win, didn't get an honorable mention, didn't get a friendly note in the rejection email. But I did have a new story to submit to magazines, and a bit of time to fix a few things. My friend, the writer John Chu, helped me out with Chinese naming conventions, and I started submitting it to other big-time literary journals: *Granta, Tin House, The Kenyon Review.*

Not even close.

So the genre mags it was. *Apex Magazine*, a wonderful online magazine where I publish not infrequently (that's not what *makes* it wonderful, but still. . . .) took it, and published it in its December 2015 issue, a couple of months after my son was born and a couple of weeks before Christmas. With such good timing, "The Phylactery" was read by almost nobody—not even my wife.

SLICE OF LIFE

NOT MANY WOMEN of child-bearing age make arrangements to leave their bodies to science. Fewer still die while in their third trimesters. Punya's team supervisor had found one, somehow, and it was the team's job to cryosection the body—the *bodies*, Punya reminded herself—into 2,063 slices along the axial plane for mounting and photographing.

"Imagine going to the deli section at the supermarket and getting a pound of salami, sliced. Sliced thin, the way an annoying old lady always demands it," Punya explained to Emily, her roommate. Punya was whispering, practically hissing. There was something holy about the evening Starbucks line, a serenity Punya didn't want to tear down.

"Oh no. I can't believe it. What a horror show," Emily said. "Horror for a good cause . . . but, nevermind." Emily waved her hands before her, wiping whatever she was imagining away. Everyone shuffled ahead, one boot-length closer to the counter, and looked down at their phones. Emily and Punya were the only friends in the line. "How old was she?"

"Twenty-eight," Punya said.

"I meant the baby," Emily said.

Punya had lots of things she could have said, about the philosophical trap of calling fetuses "babies" and counting age rather than considering development, but the only thing that came out of her mouth was, "Seven months."

"Jesus," Emily muttered. Then it was time to order and nothing more could be said that wasn't about coffee, and coffee sizes, and what to wear later.

Punya's new work assignment came up a lot that long Friday evening.

So, do you freeze-dry them first or . . . some girl who liked talking about all her Android app ideas. Lots of them had to do with keeping track of menstrual cycles and "fun" branding. Punya also had to explain to her that she was a lab tech, not a doctor. Twice. *Oh God, oh God. That's why I'm going to be a dermatologist, not a pathologist.* Simon, in med school, his first year. Punya had dated him on and off for three months, and he was still nice to have around as he liked to make himself useful—twenty bucks for a cab, playing boyfriend when drunk guys came around—in the forlorn hope of getting back into Punya's pants.

Encased in gelatin, eh? That reminds me—let's do Jell-O shots. Punya turned that guy, some hopelessly entangled ex-with-benefits of Emily's college roommate, down cold, despite his broad shoulders and little chin dimple. The Vinyl wasn't even the sort of place that served Jell-O shots. Really. It was just the club Emily had dragooned everyone into going to because it was "'80s in Manchester" night and she had never gotten over being too young for The Smiths.

Point two-five millimeters? What's that in human hair width? Isn't it strange that everything tiny is compared to human hair? That was the bartender. Punya was pleased. She got to smile, hold up a long finger, and say, "One! A single human hair—a head hair, anyway—is just about the same diameter." She purposefully left an opening to move the conversation toward the diameter of the kinds of human hair not found on human heads, but the bartender didn't take the bait.

Hey, hey . . . that was how App Girl initiated a conversation as she toddled up to Punya. *They did it already.* She had found a YouTube video on her phone and flashed the screen around the little crowd around Punya's stool. Everyone watched the montage—it started at the top of the head—cheered when convicted murderer's Joseph Paul Jernigan's lone testicle made its appearance, and turned to Punya at the end, eyes wide and questioning.

She closed her eyes for a long moment, then opened them again. "Yes," she said, loud, over the Happy Mondays. "We all look like prosciutto under the skin." She chin-pointed to the guy with the shoulders. "Even you!" She hoped he'd blush at least, that terrible beautiful idiot god of a man, but it was by turns too dark and too strobe-y to really tell.

"We're doing it again for a few reasons," Punya said. "A younger woman, with a fetus. That's not been done before. Digital resolution is a lot sharper now too. We have so much more to learn." She licked her lips. "And we're slicing even thinner now." Half-a-dozen blanching faces, that much Punya could see in the flashes of club lighting.

App Girl recited aloud a YouTube comment demanding footage of a body being sliced from nose to the back of the skull, how that would really be useful for the sake of science, but Punya didn't want to argue. She felt fingers on her shoulder, then her elbow. It was the bartender, with a buyback. She needed it and drained the bottle of Red Stripe in two heroic gulps. Slick enough for some cheers.

There was dancing, and flirtatious trading of ice cubes on necks and across backs. App girl and Simon had wandered off at some point, Punya noticed, which was fine with her except that it wasn't. Then she reminded herself that we're all just bags of water and other chemicals, reacting and twitching and moving about, then making up stories about it later to explain why our bodies did what they had done. The stories just came from a bag within a bag—the wet and sloshy brain. But Punya headed toward the mezzanine anyway, to see if she could spot them from up above. Someone muttered something about her hot little brown ass as she squeezed up the staircase, but she ignored it, having no drink to weaponize and spill. She didn't even tug on the hem of her skirt as she pushed up onto the last step.

The downstairs bartender seemingly materialized next to her, and leaned his elbows on the railing. He was in his civilian clothes now, meaning a normal T-shirt from Walmart or someplace, and not the Joy Division number he'd been wearing.

"Hiya . . ." he said.

Punya smiled, deciding that she thought he was cute even though he no longer had the power to dispense free rounds.

"The Visible Human Project 2.0!" he said. Then he explained, too quickly, "I went and Googled. Anyway, isn't it funny? Aren't we all visible humans already?"

"Yes, that is funny," Punya said. "I'm Punya."

"Rod," the bartender said.

"I bet," Punya said.

"Pardon me?"

Punya smiled, showing plenty of teeth. "I was just thinking," she said, "about how much time I have to spend pretending that people aren't really people, to get my job done. And it's all because I wanted to help people in the first place. Cure diseases."

Rod smiled, and made sure that his arm was touching Punya's. "Me too," he said. "I mean, I want to help people as well. Bartenders need to be good with people. It's like being a therapist. Or, really, a pharmacist."

"Everyone wants to help people," Punya said. "And yet everyone seems to need evermore help."

"Well, not everybody wants to help people. What about politicians, Wall Street types, dictators?" Then Rod stopped. "Sorry, I don't mean to get political when you're trying to be existential."

"I guess we're *not* all visible humans," Punya said. "Like that girl I'm working on."

"What happened to her? How did she die?" Rod said.

"Suicide. She gave her body to science in the suicide note. An EMT tipped us off, so we swooped in. The family contested it, saying that she wasn't in her right mind, that she was too distraught. And that since her suicide note hadn't been signed by a witness, it wasn't a legally binding last will and testament."

"Wow."

"Then do you know what happened?" Punya asked. "I'll tell you, but you have to keep it a secret. Actually, everything I've said so far is off the record, you understand?"

Rod turned square with Punya and held up his hands, showing off nice palms. He must get manicures, Punya decided. "I won't tweet a word."

"What happened is," Punya said, leaning in conspiratorially, "that my boss gave the parents five thousand dollars to shut up and go away." She kept her tongue out after saying "away," just for a second, wondering what it would be like to lick Rod's ear. "And they did go away. It just took two days and we got the body."

"Is that . . . strictly legal?" Rod asked.

Punya said, "I am not a lawyer. I don't even know if the five grand came out of some grant money, or my boss's kid's college fund. I shouldn't even know about the money at all, but in the lab people like to talk to each other like I'm not in the room with them. Like I'm just some supermarket employee running the world's fanciest deli slicer. All I know is that we have a female cadaver with a fetus in it now, and we had wanted one for a long long time."

"Do you know her name?" Rod said. There was something distant in his voice, something that made Punya's eyes widen.

"Oh God, you didn't know her or anything, did you?" Punya said. She barely kept from saying, *Oh God, you're not the father of the baby or anything, are you?*

"No, uh . . ." Rod said, "I mean, no. I was just wondering. Since you seem to know a lot about her."

"I don't know her name. I call her Alicia though," Punya said. She wished she had a drink, if only as a prop, for something to sip between sentences. "To myself, I mean. Not to my colleagues. We're very careful not to personify a . . ."

"Person?" Rod said.

"Cadaver," Punya said. "I mean, in some med schools now, they're all touchy-feely. Not literally, but they want you to call the cadavers by their given names as a sign of respect. Not at my job though."

"Because of the, uhm, slicing?"

Punya shrugged. She looked out onto the dance floor. Speaking of medical school, Simon and App Girl were long gone. Probably off somewhere to have sex. Had Simon changed his sheets that afternoon, in hopeful anticipation of a lucky evening? Punya hadn't. She'd been working late at the lab, and had to settle for wearing the emergency little black dress she had stuffed in the bottom of her work locker.

"I'm sorry I didn't ask for your name when I said hi, Punya," Rod said.

"That's all right, Rod," she said. "So Rod, why don't you and I start kissing now?"

And they did, for a while, and it was nice. The bartender's limbs were warm and sweaty and alive on Punya's body, and she tried to kiss him back hard and recall the systematic name of oxytocin—the *looooove* peptide, as she thought of it—at the same time.

Slice of Life

Punya managed most of it: cysteine-tyrosine-isoleucine-gluta-mine-asparagine-cysteine-*something-something-something*-amine.

In January 2013, after several years of increasing impatience with the world of science fiction fandom, I declared my retirement from genre fiction at a reading at Manhattan's famous KGB Bar. There, I read one of my few purely realist stories, "Slice of Life." It does involve science and technology, but there is no imaginative science fictional novum in the story that would make it a genre piece.

I honestly don't remember much about writing it, or what inspired it. The title, obviously, is a play on my ambitions—to write slice of life stories of the sort often published in university-baked literary journals, while also keeping with my themes of the body, technology, materialism, and the fact that our behaviors and attitudes are ultimately reducible to the reactions of the bag of chemicals we store inside our skulls. Also, it's a bit of a love story. It was published in *Gargoyle*, an interesting journal that, like the story, hints at a genre origin. As far as literary journals go, *Gargoyle* is a large one, by which I mean each number is well over three hundred pages. Room for everyone, I guess!

The curious among you may wonder why I wrote and published so many speculative fiction stories after January 2013, and why I remember so little of this story's origin, given how important it was for my "retirement." It's simple: in January 2013, I announced my retirement from science fiction/fantasy/horror and my plans to write only crime and literary fiction from now on. In February 2013, my wife announced that she was pregnant with our child. Babies cost money. Crime doesn't pay. Neither does literature.

NORTH SHORE FRIDAY

BACK WHEN PARASKEVI'S GRANDMOTHER was in charge of getting guys off the boats and safely married off before they could be found and deported, she gave her granddaughter the same advice every week. One, don't hide anyone at the Greek church, that's the first place they look. Go to the Methodists, they are the kindest of the *xeni*. Two, if Immigration finds you, throw a huge screaming fit—rip at your clothes, scratch your own breasts till they bleed, kick and scream and cry, and say over and over that you're going to kill yourself—and they probably won't arrest you. Three, if you feel the government trying to read your mind, *think in Greek*.

Between the backwater dialect, the generation-old slang she learned from her parents, and Red cant, Paraskevi would greet her charges and they would hear something analogous to this: "Can thou y'all comrades dig this crazy-struggle for liberty? Forsooth, thine art copacetic, no?" But yiayia knew that even if the INS had a Greek on their side, they'd get nothing from Paraskevi. Not even when in 1965, when we began large-scale full-time brainscanning across Long Island.

Getting Greeks off the boats had the feel of a game. Only a few of the big ships bothered with Port Jefferson anymore. Most of the illegals were someone's brother or everyone's cousin, a far-flung friend, the sons of godmothers, or buddies from the Civil War gone to sea and then looking to go to ground. Immigration went armed and wore their suits like they were mobile homes, but they weren't too bad as authority figures go, not back then anyway. Yiayia ran the show because men were too hot-headed, too ready to throw fists or start screaming at nothing, too proud to beg forgiveness or just skulk away when someone got nabbed and dragged back to the city to be sent on the first plane back to Greece. Plus, the men in the family, like me, didn't have an eye for the nice girls who'd come into the Lobster House with their parents or even by themselves. Girls who knew to pick a man who wore pants with the knees worn out from working, not a man whose pants had patches over the ass from sitting around all day doing nothing. Human smuggling was women's work, and generally not too hard. Yiayia didn't spend more than forty-eight hours in prison at a time and Paraskevi was never caught even once. Well, once. . . .

"Hey, Friday," Jimmy the *mavro* said. "Your grandma is on the payphone." Paraskevi went to the phone.

"Hello, Poppi?"

"No, yiayia, it's your other granddaughter," she said. "The one who actually works. The one you called?"

"Oh, I know who I called,"

I hope yiayia's just sick. Maybe I can go home and watch some TV for a change. This place is always dead in November. Three dollars in tips all night, it's so stupid that we even open on—

yiayia said. "Listen, you have to go to church tonight and light one candle. Do you understand?"

"Malesta, yes. I will."

> Smelly gasoline, mustaches. "Eh? Eh?" at the end o*f sentence. "You* like, no? Eh?" Say *ti kanes ti kanes*, will they bring. . . .

"Where's Georgi? Is he there?"

"No, he's not here. He's at work. Why would he be here?"

"Work? At night, outside?"

"Well, he's not here anyway."

"Maybe he stopped in for some dinner?"

"He *didn't*, yiayia. It's not even dinner time yet."

> These code-words are so dumb.

"Then you have plenty of time for church, before the dinner rush." The sun hadn't even gone down yet.

I wasn't working outside anymore. That was in the summertime. I was an engineer back in the 1960s, and a computer programmer of sorts. This was back in the days of room-sized humming monstrosities, the CDC 3600, and that was the cutting edge—we had older machines too. You know why it was called the Sage System? It knew everything, sure. And it was truly a system. That was my summer job—yiayia thought I was just cutting down trees along Nesconsent Highway to make room for radio towers and telephone poles, but it was all part of the system. Even the two screens on the console were round, not like radar displays, but like crystal balls. There was blood in the wiring, magic everywhere. A multidisciplinary endeavor between Stony Brook's computer science and religious studies department.

I can't do a thing with computers now.

Back then, though, I was a genius. I could look at a punch card and divine the data recorded on it. Spread them out on my desk and read them like coffee grains at the bottom of a very large cup. And I was in love with my cousin. My second cousin, mind you. Maybe it's just a Greek thing, or maybe it was just how we were raised. You know, everyone hanging out together all the time, the distrust of the *xeni*. It's hard not to fall in love with whoever is nearby.

Everyone on the North Shore was a test subject. Long Island was our lab. I got very good at what I had to do, and not just swinging an axe. That was only the job my parents, my grandmother and aunt, could understand. I had to explain over and over again

Ah Friday, where are you now, under all that skin and sixty years of flab? In your snaggle-toothed smile, I still see what I loved. . . .

were adding machines, **like the cash register**, except it could do all the math itself. I was a genius back then. What *fassarea* it all was, really. Most people don't think much of anything. Like apes. We thought the first experiments were a failure because we didn't get any positives in animal testing. **FOOD FOOD FOOD I'm a bit hungry right now myself, actually. . . .**

I know that the government is reading my mind now. I hope that my thoughts make them blush.

Paraskevi let Jimmy the *mavro* wait with her under the pier, as hobos and rats liked to congregate there, plus he too had a crush on her, and one didn't need a cool billion dollars' worth of mind-reading equipment to know that. He played it tight to the vest though, and never even thought about Paraskevi that way. It was beyond our observations, all in the autonomic nervous system, in sweat and twitches and clenching fingers. Poor guy—it was hard to be a black man on Long Island in the 1960s. He was nervous that night, because Paraskevi was.

It's like my father said when he emigrated. "The CIA is responsible! They are behind the *junta*! They sent the tanks through the streets . . ." and he'd just trail off. "So then why did you move to America, papa?" I asked. "I wanted to go to a country with a government the *Amerikanoí* wouldn't overthrow. . . ."

"You're going to have to go, and go before he sees you," she explained. "You know?"

"Yeah, yeah, I know."

"I mean, they might think that you're a cop."

"Forget it," Jimmy said. "Don't explain. I can't stay here all night anyway, you know?"

"I know."

rapist, and then they might kill you and decide to rape me. God, I'm so sick to even think. . . .

There was a birdcall in the distance and Jimmy took off, not thinking a thing at all. Paraskevi laughed at the idea of a birdcall at night. The gulls were god-knows-

No. Sensitivity was at-tuned to lab tests; bored psychology students thinking of apples

where. "Embros," she said, not knowing that her own grandmother wasn't saying "Hello" when she picked up the phone, not knowing that this illegal didn't have a phone—hell, Antoni had never even

North Shore Friday

seen one except for once, in the Navy—but he heard Greek and a woman's smoky voice so he emerged out of the dark. Paraskevi waved at him, hunched over, worried about her chest and a man long at sea. Antoni had a cap and he took it off and said, "Hi." Paraskevi didn't smile, not for them. She heard the clinking of glass bottles in his bag. He didn't smell of sweat and ouzo like so many of these guys did, though.

> Good! That's my smile. How she'd smile at me. . . .

Of course, there were gypsies in the woods, some of the time. Not too many

> Think in Greek, Think in Greek, *Ellinika, me logia Ellinika.* Stupid random words *mylo skylo, oraya kalispera gamo to panayia*

in November, when the ice was slick over carpets of red-brown leaves, when the ramshackle homes and shacks in which they squatted for a season were too hard to heat with small bonfires and thick blankets. We got along with them, or I did. I'd pay for their meals at the Lobster House, they'd give me tips at the quarterhorse track out east, since a lot of them got some work out there fixing horses with their Old World stuff. I had no idea what they did, but it probably involved ramming something up the horse's asses. That's where the conversation so often turned, when I'd meet them out back with coffees and sandwiches anyway.

There were other things in the woods too. Ghosts of the settlers, long dead. The old Indians were so dead they didn't even have ghosts, except for when we'd fire up the machines. Always at night to avoid brown-outs and power outages.

> It's illegal to threaten the president, but it ain't illegal to think about strangling him, is it? *Is this thing on?* *tap* *tap*

But the feds always wanted more. Not better, just more. More results, more miles of tape, more pallets worth of punch cards,

103

so many results nobody could hope to read them all, to assign thoughts to thinkers, before all our equipment went obsolete.

"Don't associate with the *yiftoi*, they're dirty. You'll turn into one. They'll rob you blind. Be kind to them, but don't be friends. Worse than *mavro*, they are." Whatever happened to that $500? It was so much back then . . . "Oh they give tips, eh? What did they say for tomorrow's races, *Georgios?*"

Paraskevi almost never thought of me, even though I loved her. That's how I ended up involved in the events of November 9th. I was at Stony Brook, in the basement of the brand new building, the one far away from G-Quad, my pants all muddy and wet. In the woods, she called out to me with her mind. I had to go to her.

GEORGE!

Antoni tried his English. "Is far?" he asked. Paraskevi shook her head no in the Greek way; a sharp nod and a click

It is far. Why does America smell like this?

of the tongue. "Not far, but in circles," she said, waving her arms around. "*Kalo, kalo*, it's okay."

"*Yftoi*, eh?" Antoni said. He clutched his bag, tightly, then let out a stream of nervous-sounding Greek Paraskevi barely understood. *Gypsies* and *America* and finally the punctuation of so many sentences: *Katalaves?* You understand. No, she didn't. She even thought in

. . .

What was that poem about miles of walking? I hate school; I wish I could just drop out and just work at the store. It's so friggin' cold; my glasses are gonna fog up again the second I get back home. I always forget that they fog up until I walk into a warm room again—I wonder what Tommy is up to? I wonder if this Andoni guy can tell that I'm not looking at him on purpose. . . .

Then they stopped in a clearing. Antoni had to tie his shoes and had to urinate as well. He knew the words toilet and please and didn't point at his crotch, but he did go into his bag and dig out his bottle of ouzo to drink even as he started to piss.

> this guy will make a *great* husband for someone, yah

> Lose some gain some!

Then, gunfire and 72 columns of punch cards punched hard.

Fight or flight, or in this case, a freeze.

> hehehe

Immigration prowled the docks whenever a ship came in. Too many marriage licenses being issued too quickly. Some complaints from the spoiled richie-rich brats up on the hills of Belle Terre. But it was still only Port Jefferson and the pier wasn't that busy, so the INS only had a couple of guys working the beat. They were go-getters, or has-beens, and that night they trudged right after Paraskevi and her three new boys, following them into the old woods between downtown and the highway. Paraskevi knew the land like she her knew her own face— where the tree lines stopped and into which backyards she could spill without a dog barking or an automatic backyard security light flipping on. Where the little streams would crack under the weight of two men but not one. Where the disused rail spurs and the fairly active Long Island Railroad tracks lay. Where the sandpit and the semi-secret Fairchild HQ was. The INS stooges didn't know anything at all, except how to crack branches under their feet, wave flashlights and badges and guns, threaten and bully.

> Like I knew her face. Oh, her face.

From what I was able to piece together from the punch cards and the frantic whirls and pulses on the screens of the supercomputer: The sheriff got a call about Jimmy the *mavro* hanging out in the marina, by one of the houseboats owned by one of the people made a little

> Meatloaf, is there a more perfect dish in all the. . . .

too nervous by a Negro. The two immigration officers happened to be in the sheriff's office at the time, getting some coffee and playing penny poker. They knew Jimmy worked at the restaurant. They knew about Paraskevi's grandmother, and decided to check it out. There was a boat in the harbor, after all. Not quite a tanker, they'd never fit,

If they didn't want me to fire my sidearm, they wouldn't have issued me one. We have rules in this country. Get in line, like everyone else. And the defense contractors, what if one of these guys gets a job there and is a Commie? If they didn't want me to fire my sidearm, they wouldn't have issued me one. If they didn't want me to fire my sidearm, they wouldn't have issued me one. If they didn't want me to fire my sidearm, they wouldn't have issued me one.

but a decent-sized ship capable of transatlantic. They went to the Lobster House, which was just beginning to get its dinner crowd in, and saw that the only waitresses on duty looked normal and decided that Paraskevi was a person of interest. A waitress who doesn't serve burgers and fries is as interesting as a dog that doesn't bark.

It was still a bit light in the sky, and she was easy to spot on the edge of the woods. She was dark, had the long hair and boys' jeans. She wouldn't stop. She ran hard. They went barreling after her. They opened fire. She fell. It wasn't Paraskevi, it was one of the *yftoi* kids, a twelve-year-old girl too shy to even think her own name, even as she died.

I know I know Iknow mama don't be mad IknowImsorryIknowIknow owow my shirt so wet owow itwillbeokay I can sew it havetogohometomama ImsorryImsorry

L
E
N
A

That's what her brother said to call her, anyway.

Paraskevi heard the gunshot and thought my name.

It was no coincidence that I was monitoring her thoughts at the time. It was even part of the experimental protocol. Parapsychological research never fetishized the idea of the double-blind study, and you know what they say about computer science: "Any field with the word 'science' in its name isn't one." But she thought my name, at the moment I happened to be there, in the lab, to receive it. I knew it was her, as I'd been observing her for weeks—yes, that's fine. There's a hypothesis in parapsychology, the hypothesis of Directional Intention—I was able to read the cards and know it was Paraskevi, know that that screamed my name in her head—because of *my* intention, directed toward her. The machines would have picked it up anyway, of course, but it would have been lost amidst all the grocery lists and frantic burning desire for new shoes or a warm kiss or the pain of a scar to finally fade. If another researcher had been on duty that evening, none of what happened next would have ever happened, because could have only been read in that instant, by me.

GEORGE!

Stupid backfiring carscarcar . . . no!

GUN!

I had to know what was going on, and I had the means. The college had an agreement with LILCO. All the power we needed, whenever we needed it. In return—well, what they got in return is beyond my pay grade, but as LILCO is long-gone they didn't get much out of it. Something about predicting power outages during hurricane season.

and all *Stelyo's* preferred stock along with it. Good, that fucker. . . .

Yeah, and speaking of power outages, where were you when the lights went out?

Paraskevi couldn't tell that the lights had gone out, not out in the woods. There was a different feel in the air, a different feel *to* the air. A streak of ozone; a tingle on the skin. A few horns honked in the distance, but that could just be the usual evening traffic up the long twisting road of Main Street. It was twilight, but the streetlamps of town hadn't yet started to burn orange. Something was different, but she didn't know what. There was gunfire, there was immigration. She could only think one word: *Georgi!*

"*Pame!*" she said to Antoni, because she didn't know how to tell him what she really needed them to do. Run, run in different directions. "I'll wait here!" she said, but then she said, "*Pame!*"—let's go—so they followed her into a clearing.

"Comrade," she said. "It behooves y'all to hit the road. The devil!"

Two men in suits, one with a pistol in his hand, his knuckles and face both white as flour, the other taller and huffing, stumbled into the clearing. "INS," the taller one said. "Hands up."

Antoni looked to Paraskevi. She put her hands up, her chest out. He followed suit, sacks and suitcase hit the ground. The sky turned purple.

"Who did you shoot?" Paraskevi asked.

"No talking," said the man without the gun. "You're under—" he stopped talking. The sky sizzled.

I can't believe I shot that girl. God, god, she's dead. We can't call for help, we can't. I'll be—

Donaldson's so fucked. I should have shot him myself. Let these people go, arrest that motherfucker for murder at least. No, can't do that. I need someone to have my back. I've done so many bad things. The drugs, the girl from Colombia, she was so tight. Don's got a wife, kids. They need him. Why did I even get out of bed?

Oh God oh God. Get the bottle. Get smoke. *Think in Greek!*

Paraskevi saw it first. Usually, it takes a sensitive, someone attuned to the "vibe," like the hippies used to say. The girl, Lena, bleached white, smaller than even short, squat Antoni. A little more than ball lightning in human form, she walked through them all.

Kyrie eleison. Kyrie eleison Kyrie eleison Kyrie eleison Kyrie eleison Kyrie eleison

Paraskevi, my girl, she was so tough back then. That's how we grew 'em. No shrinking violets back then, no big-haired bimbos. She dove to the ground, grabbed a

Lost lost. Never be buried. Lost lost. Never be buried. . . .

bottle of ouzo by the neck and swung it against a tree in a single wide arc from the sack it was in to Donaldson's face. Donaldson raised his hands and then his partner grabbed the gun so he wouldn't shoot. Paraskevi took a cigarette from her apron pocket, lit it, and after a puff held the lit cherry up to Donaldson's *Metaxa*-soaked face. "Don't shoot," she said. "Might spark."

Antoni fell back, crossing himself and twitching. It was hard to breathe for a few moments, or it probably was anyway. I remember the feeling from the lab experiments. Hair on end, sinuses tingling; the face of the ghost like an old brown negative held up to the sun and blazing. Poor Lena.

I always felt like a homing pigeon, head buzzing from unseen stimuli— it's a primitive thing, to see a ghost.

You know, I gave her brothers a reel of 1" tape—the recording of the output. She's on there somewhere. Like ashes in an urn, but with a little charge of magnetism. Software with no hardware left to play her on.

The ghost wandered out of the woods and faded. Paraskevi looked at the other INS agent, his hand still clenched around Donaldson's gun. "Thanks. Do you want to put a ghost in your report?"

"Not a murder either," he said.

The woods were black. The whole East Coast was dark, except for my little lab in the basement of the college.

That's what these cards and reels mean to me, okay? A dead girl, her ghost made from static electricity, secret government psi experiments, my crazy family of scofflaws and badasses, an inappropriate attraction to my cousin, and the big blackout of 1965. She thought of me once. I

> You think I care whether you believe it or not? I know what happened. I'm the only one who knows. Even Paraskevi, your Aunt Friday, only knows about. . . .

have proof. She lives in Florida now. Two kids, nice husband. A *xeni*. At first we thought she did it on purpose but he's a nice guy. Jeff, the blond one.

So that's why I keep these old cases around. I'm still looking for an auction, eBay or something, that might sell one of the old machines, so I can read these results. I see the whole story spread out before me, but to prove it to anyone else I'd need a computer antique enough to handle a dead medium.

> *Heh,* there's a pun in there somewhere— a dead

Ask Antoni. You've seen him around. Your father's friend—you used to play with his daughter Kelly. Yeah, same guy. He was illegal. A lot of people owe yiayia a lot around here. That's why he wears the *mati* all the time—because he saw a ghost. Why he crosses himself when your father talks about going down to the track, or OTB.

Don't call them *yftoi* anymore. They settled. Got houses. Just mind your business about certain things. Immigration tried to deport the family because they were going to sue, but in the end I think we all managed to get them married quick, or prove they were born here. You don't even know who, or what, has been born here. Lots of secrets, you understand? Not just these.

This stuff won't be classified forever. The truth will come out one day. You

> Are you listening?

know the feds are still reading our minds. I'm sure that they're a lot better at it now too, with the Muslims and 9/11. Hell, your iPhone is a million times smarter than my old Cray.

I bet those guys just knew to think in Arabic or Farsi.

> Can you hear me?

> *Katalaves?* Did you hire another Greek? If so, help me . . . you know how it is.

> Aren't you paying attention anymore?

I have always been a sucker for typographic trickery. Any book or story that features a disruption of layout immediately attracts my interest. I've read my share of great ones (Harlan Ellison's "The Region Between" comes immediately to mind) and some less great attempts—pick up any university-backed literary journal and you'll find one if you wish to see what I mean. "North Shore Friday" was my attempt at using typography to amplify the experience of reading a story by using size and position to suggest intensity and simultaneity of thought.

Interestingly, the online magazines most widely known for publishing hip, contemporary SF all passed on it. It was too much of a production challenge to make work given the content management systems most such magazines use. Even the so-called "pro markets" for short fiction are only so professional—design and other issues are often left to the spare time of the hobbyist-cum-entrepreneur editor/ publisher. It was *Asimov's Science Fiction*, which has an undeserved reputation among young (i.e., under the age of 50) writers as a place for hoary old themes, that was interested in the story and up for the production challenge of printing it, thanks to actually having a paid production staff with real publishing experience.

The story itself is about my family. My grandmother did help sneak a few Greek immigrants onto Long Island, back when commercial shipping still brought sailors to town. She's still alive as of this writing, but has senile dementia, and most of the people she helped get ashore and place in the US are dead, so don't write me letters. Political paranoia comes with the territory—my hometown contains an enclave of Greeks of Ikarian heritage, and we're well known for extreme politics. Ikaria, itself a long island, is called "the Red Rock" for its surplus population of Communists. If there's a community that can match us for worries about the government, it's the island's Romany people. Tying those communities together with my alma mater SUNY Stony Brook and its computer labs—labs that turned me into a writer when I found the embryonic pre-Web Internet at age 17—made the story almost complete. A bit of research gave me the Northeast blackout of 1965, and made "North Shore Friday" not only science fiction, but alternative history based on family history.

THE GLOTTAL STOP

DATING CIS WAS ROUGH, no doubt. For any woman, but especially for Beatriz Almonte, a living meme who had several years ago made a mistake and gained the attention of a secret bulletin board full of trolls for whom harassing her was a vocation not dissimilar from the priesthood. She had no more free background checks left on Spinstr, but was bored and horny enough to do without just this once and press *sm00ch* on some guy's face. Another mistake.

Jerome seemed fine—in shape, no beard, there was a photo of him at an anti-war demo on his Slambook, no sign of a frogface or crusader sword emojis on Mirmir, and no videogame talk on any of his social media. Jerome's hashtags were all in order. Beatriz agreed to meet for a late lunch eaten al fresco so she could get away with wearing sunglasses, in public but at a corner table so that she'd have a legal expectation of privacy under California Penal Code § 632, and in a neighborhood in the city adjacent to her own. She hired a neighbor to drive her to the Korean tapas place so as to keep from exposing her address or route to the Travyl ride-share system. And she came otherwise prepared, with everything from condoms to weapons.

The first few minutes went well, though Jerome was two inches shorter than advertised. Beatrix had to admit that she was fifteen pounds heavier than advertised, but she wore make-up, even tricky eyeliner wing tips, for him. Her necklace, with the particular charm, that was for herself. Sneakers instead of nicer shoes too. If he balked at the makeup, he was a troll. If he took it as too strong a signal for sexual availability, he was a pickup artist in training. But he passed that test, with a silent appreciative smile. Pleasantries, a semi-clever remark about the menu, kindness toward the waitress. Then came the water, the drinks, the appetizers.

The second hand of the clock tied to a rhetorical bomb clicked over. Jerome said, "So, do you really not eat 'white food'? Because your rice is white, isn't it?" She noticed that his smartphone was on the table, screen down.

Beatriz's mistake: she had called Taco Bell "white 'food'" on what was supposed to be a fun little attempt at virality. She suggested that only basement-dwelling nerds would consider Taco Bell "going out for Mexican," and if a taco from there cost the same amount as a candy bar, what kind of ingredients could possibly be in it? Wet dog food, she'd guessed on Twitter. Beatriz was castigated as a snob and an illegal immigrant, an uptight rich bitch and a greedy whore, and of course, she was also the Real Racist. Once targeted, her entire social media profile was combed over for various other crimes—drunken selfies, a bad breakup that was surely her fault, having a father from the Dominican Republic and a maternal grandmother who was Chinese, a job she quit by simply not showing up anymore in tenth grade. ("How many fish starved to death because you decided you were too good for PetVille, Queen Bea? You're fucking next.") That she got a mere BA in Chemistry and not a BS—"You can fuck your way to a BA" was the common Internet wisdom. One time she held a fund-raiser on Slambook for Planned Parenthood and collected forty dollars. Baby-Killer Beatriz needed to be murdered, but only after being raped by the dogs she had so callously failed.

That was three years ago. Now, across the table from her, Jerome's smile was a familiar one. The fishhook grin. "I'm kidding," he said. "I'm joking." They were always joking. "I just did a search on you, you know. Didn't you investigate me? I even gave you my last name. Want to see my ID?"

"This is not going to be a productive date, Jerome," said Beatriz. It wasn't quite time to grab her purse and go, though. Was he going to video her ass when she got up, were there others nearby, or was he really just making the worst joke imaginable.

"Did I make your pussy dry, Bea? Being a straight man who thinks he has a sense of humor and all?" he asked. A reference to another ancient tweet she had once made.

Now it was time to go. "It was never wet for you." A debate would be no more productive than the date, but the response shut Jerome up for a second and gave Beatriz a chance to glance around.

There were others. The guys didn't even try to hide. It wasn't a matter of bad hats and worse beards, but the staring and sniggering from the other seats and on the corner of the block, the open-mouthed peering into their phones, phones aimed at Beatriz. Whoever got footage of her crying, or upset, or shouting, won. It was a clear escalation—stills of her car in her mother's driveway, of their own reflections in the wire mesh glass of the entrance door to her apartment building were no longer enough. They needed her breaking down, in public, daring to go out and dress up a bit. *Cockhungry slut TRIGGERED on first and last date* the SpinVid would be titled, she knew it.

The waitress caught a glimpse of Beatriz's expression through the great glass windows that separated the al fresco seating from the restaurant proper, and sneered. Beatriz was on her own.

"Clutching your pearls?" Jerome asked. He snatched up his phone and aimed it at her. She wasn't.

Beatriz popped open the fake pearl, wiped the mineral oil from the swiftly oxidizing clump of sodium it contained, and flicked the metal with her thumb into Jerome's water glass. It took a second. She threw herself backwards, out of her chair and over the low fence behind her, the force of the explosion sailing over her head. Amidst the shrieking and smoke, she ran, sweater in one garbage can, overshirt in another, onto a bus headed in a random direction, the fare paid in cash. From her phone though, there was no escape. She let it buzz with notifications till dark, when the bus had completed its circuit of the city in which she lived, and her battery ran down. Emergency cash in her sneakers got her a cab ride home.

Assault with a deadly weapon. Attempted murder. Attempted murder in the first degree. *Capital murder*, except that Jerome was unharmed save his eyebrows. The first three SpinVid videos of men clumsily shaving their eyebrows in idiot solidarity had already racked up six-figure views.

Why did she do it? Three long years had taught Beatriz that as far as society was concerned, she was outlaw. In the medieval sense—beyond the protection of the law. Men were allowed to crack her passwords and drain her bank accounts, stick her face on the lone female body in gang bang porn, find the care home in which her grandmother lived and leave messages for her with the front desk about "the cunt of your cunt of your cunt," and the police could only shrug. There we no rules, it turned out. Plenty of force and authority, though, for women like her. Chemicals reacted explosively in the real world, and it was Beatriz who had made a point of bringing sodium to her date in the first place. Had Jerome not accepted a glass of still water, she would have subtly nudged her own glass toward him during the date's opening patter.

Now the police would surely be coming for her. For a moment, Beatriz felt sweet relief. No cell phones in prison. Most women were imprisoned, thanks to having made the fatal error of cooperating with men, so she'd be safe. She wouldn't miss men either, and she spoke passable Spanish. Maybe there would be some transwomen there she could get close to. Already she was casting herself in a television show. By the time she got out of "the joint"—she was thinking in TV clichés from her own childhood now!—all the social media platforms would be obsolete and abandoned, a graveyard of controversies as accessible as floppy disks.

But her jade succulents, her African violets, her tradescantia. Beatriz's apartment was full of life, of plant-scented air. An Edenic bubble. No list of instructions she could write would be specific yet flexible enough to keep the plants alive while she was away, even if she could trust her sister not to trash them all. But her job at the Verizon store, which wasn't so bad. Her boss was a former college wrestler, and marched one of her stalkers out onto the sidewalk and slammed him so hard the kid's coccyx disintegrated. Nobody arrested *him*—not the stalker, not her boss. Men can do what they want. But those bullet-rain days when she couldn't walk down the street with her phone in her hand, Beatriz actually felt free. She loved the seasons: chill and flurries on dark afternoons, endless summer twilights, red carpets of leaves. She cried.

The police were coming. There were no sirens in the air, no red and white lights flooding the streets beyond her drawn blinds, but the police were coming. Anyone Beatriz could reach out to would be on the other end of a string stretched taut between an infinite number of tin soup cans. She didn't have a lawyer, nor really any idea how to contact one who specialized in criminal or Internet law. She'd always depended on search engines and the hive mind of her social media reach. Men were waiting for her to call for help, to even send an email. They'd found her despite her precautions; she had to assume that everything she might do or even look for could appear on the front page of the *New York Times* the next morning. It would certainly be her, on the news aggregators, face twisted and eyes wild, with cops, male cops, twisting her arms behind her back.

Beatriz froze, seeing herself through a glass darkly. She couldn't bring herself to wake up her desktop. The police were coming. She tossed her phone over her shoulder, not caring about what it broke when it skittered across her kitchen island and brought something with it to the floor. Beatriz was in the big desktop screen, like she lived online. Once upon a time the Internet was an escape from the too-small apartment in the dicey part of town in which she lived with her noisy family. Beatriz could be a superhero, a sex doll, an expert on everything from *telenovelas* to presidential politics, a helpful friend with a few extra bucks, a basket case eager to suck up the unconditional good wishes only strangers from afar could offer.

There would be people on her side. "That Bea, she's a real firecracker." A few guys might even hesitate next time they preyed upon a woman for the lulz. The police were coming. She could upload some basic information about where to procure sodium metal, but that would make trouble for her notional lawyer, and for any future parole hearing. *Conspiracy. Feminazi terror squads. MS-13 and Antifa working together to #killallmen.* The police were coming. She wished she had a police scanner app on her phone, but she didn't dare use her phone.

There wasn't going to be any online access in prison—she didn't think so, anyway. The police were coming. There was probably one desktop in a heavily guarded library, and it was a privilege easily rescinded. To her Internet friends who didn't know her true name, it would be as though she had died. Beatriz's e-mails would pile up unread. (Well, that happened often already. . . .) Finally, she could sit before a sleeping computer no more. In the bathroom, to wash her face. The police were coming. At least she could look presentable for the next round of humiliating memes. ONE SJW

DOWN at the top of the news photo of the police dragging her away, THIRTY MILLION TO GO under it.

Her makeup was running. Those wings were a pain in the ass to do. She'd tried three times, blinking away tears and cursing in two languages, before getting it right. Now they were ruined too. She reached for empty soap dish where she usually kept her phone when in the bathroom, but of course it wasn't there. A selfie to be sent out just as the fateful knock sounded at the door.

There was something about the black tears streaking her cheeks that said it all, and Beatriz wanted to capture it. That's how it always seems to end for women—men made you cry, and ruined even the things you did for them.

A smudge of black eyeliner welled up under her eye. It looked like a lot of things.

A bit like a tear, of course.

But upside down. An anti-tear.

But upside down. A tear sneaking back into the duct. No more crying, not ever.

Like a tattoo of the same—what so many people come out of prison, or that life, with. Someone dead. Someone raped. Someone killed by one's own hand.

It was other things too, that mark on Beatriz's cheek. An upturned fist.

The black yin fish of the taijitu, that dynamic grand ultimate her grandmother drew for her once, but never fully explained. The feminine side, without the white dot of the masculine yang to stain it. "I don't understand," young Beatriz had said, "why are girls black and boys white?" Her grandmother had no answer; she only said, "Maybe you'll understand one day."

No white, no men. Sounded good to Beatriz.

Today was the day she did understand.

And it looked almost like an apostrophe. An elision, a symbol of absence. The police were coming. She was going to be absent soon enough—her chairs unfilled, her clothes hanging limp and unworn for years. Fill-in-the-blank.

But also a symbol of possession. She hadn't

seen the mark when looking at her reflection

in the sleeping monitor of her desktop, but now she

saw it clearly, for the first time.

Beatriz owned herself. She owned her face.

She owned her story She owned her life.

She owned her mind. She owned her soul.

It was also something else; not quite a question mark, but some kind of mark; she didn't remember what.

Now the siren-sound reached her ears. Now the red and white lights spilled in through the blinds as she walked through her dim living room. The police were coming. It was hard to think. She wouldn't have much time, but she didn't need hardly any time at all to take one last selfie.

The men were lurking. She'd been marked by them, turned into a living meme. Now a meme lived on her. She didn't bother with filters or hashtags, but went to her desktop, woke it up, pulled the tape from her webcam lens, and snapped a picture. She had a program that would upload the picture simultaneously to every still-extant platform on which she ever had a presence—from Palz.com through Diaryville and all the way up to S* and poor abandoned Y'ello?

Beatriz's hands were on the keyboard, ready to write a brief message to go along with the image. The police were coming. Something that would sear the image into the minds of millions. She wouldn't have time to articulate the polysemy, and that would ruin the image anyway. Listing meanings meant defining limits. Something for women, for people like herself, the abused and oppressed, to wave around as obnoxiously as any meme. But she also couldn't just depend on an appeal to her friends and allies to spread the meme without some collective understanding of what it *could* mean. In a flash, *I regret nothing!* entered her head. Not her head, no. Wrong, just the muscles in her fingers. *I regret nothing!* was already a joke, and a reference to itself. Someone else's imagination had been encoded in Beatriz's nervous system. The anti-tear needed its own meaning, one that would decolonize minds, a rallying cry and a warning to others. She wanted men to see it and feel their throats tighten, their hearts twitch, the way they made her feel two dozen times a day. The mark would never ever be for them, and always ever against them.

And besides, Beatriz did have regrets. Why did she even decide to date cis again? That was another idea that belonged to someone else, to practically everyone else. She could have just stayed home, or let her mother set her up with some guy from the old country who was twice her age. What she didn't regret, though, was that little sodium metal bomb. She'd been wanting to do something like that since high school, when her chem teacher dropped a bit of sodium in a beaker full of water to wake the class up. Beatriz stayed woke.

The police were here. There was a first knock on the door, one harsh enough to make it clear that it would be the only knock. Beatriz adjusted her monitor so that the front door to her small apartment was visible in the background, then typed something, and then gripped her mouse, ready to record. The police were here. There was another knock, but it was made by no man's fist. The door shuddered in its frame.

Beatriz did have another sodium pearl, and a water can for her plants by the entrance. If her aim were true, she could toss it over her shoulder, gain a measure of immortality after it blew up in a cop's face. But then the Internet would miss the mark on her cheek.

The police were here. Time slowed down. Beatriz leaned in close, clicked record. Her face filled the screen, obscuring the ruckus behind her. The police were all men, of course. Of course, but perhaps that gave Beatriz an extra few seconds. The video stream was attracting an audience—she recognized the handles of some of her perennial abusers, but they were being swamped out by the names of allies, of strangers. She was going viral. Beatriz had only a moment to say something as catchy as *Time's Up!*, as exciting as *Just Do It!*, as stirring as *You Have Nothing To Lose But Your Chains!*, or even as inexplicable as *Who Is John Galt?*— something that would lend voice to the gleaming black anti-tear on her cheek, and all that it meant to her. Commenters were talking about it, asking what it meant. She needed to explain, to make the meme explode, like $2Na+2H_2O \rightarrow 2NaOH+H_2$.

The police were on her. They pushed her face against her monitor as they bent her arms back, which only helped with her close-up. What could she say? *This could happen to you!* True, but nobody would believe it. They pulled her off her chair. She was pleased that her remnant eyeliner had smudged the small lens built into her monitor—the black swirl was huge now, filling half the screen. *You're next!*

Maybe, but too much like an empty threat.

Right before she hit the carpet, tits and chin first.

Finally.

"I.

"Am.

"—!" A sound like no sound.

The webcam cut out as she fell off the screen. The police officer pinning her spine to the ground with his knee gasped, and only for a moment eased his grip.

"The Glottal Stop" is original to, and written for, this volume. I don't know what to think about it yet. You tell me.

THE SPOOK SCHOOL

IT WAS THE TWENTY-HOUR JOURNEY on which neither Gordon nor Melissa slept a wink, and the strong Greek coffee at the Athena Tavern they both chugged down at Melissa's request, and the long-seeming walk in the *plish* across Kelvingrove Park at Gordon's insistence that took them to the museum. A wayward cinder got into Melissa's contact lens, and she was exhausted, and jittery from the caffeine, and excited to finally be meeting her lover's parents, and it was her first trip to Scotland, and if we're being entirely honest Melissa was a bit of a fanciful creature and always hoping for some transcendent experience, so she got one. Really, truly, the sacred rose in Charles Rennie Mackintosh's famed gesso panel *The Wassail* did not wink at her as she and Gordon stood before it. She imagined the whole thing in the back of her mind, which made the front of her mind startle, then shut down, and so she swooned, falling to the floor like a pair of empty trousers no longer being held up by the belt loops.

"I love it here," Melissa said later. "I do wish people would stop calling the bathroom 'the toilet,' though. That makes me think of the commode." Melissa had spent a while bent over the tiny European toilet in the "toilet" of Gordon's parents after she woke up. "I could live here, otherwise," she said. She drank the tea Gordon had prepared for her.

"Live here on the couch, being waited on, hand and foot?" Gordon asked. "I'm sure you're meant to, my faerie queen." Gordon was like that.

"It just seems . . . quaint."

Gordon snorted. "Don't call anything 'quaint' in earshot of my mum and dad, honey bee. In the United Kingdom, 'quaint' means 'fucking terrible.'"

"Lovely?" Melissa tried.

"Aye, that's much better," Gordon said.

"When I showed Customs my passport, the officer called my pic 'lovely.' I didn't know whether to feel complimented or offended, until they called your passport lovely too."

"Am I not?" Gordon struck a pose: pursed lips, knuckles under chin, shoulders jauntily angled.

"You are."

Gordon's parents burst into the kitchen, bringing rain and wind with them. Gordon stood to greet them and Melissa waved from the living room couch. They were a matched pair, almost spherical in their rain gear, and chattering in thick Glaswegian accents.

"Are you feeling a wee bit better?" Gordon's father called out to Melissa.

"Mostly, yes. Thank you," Melissa said. She had come to their home semi-conscious and muttering about roses. Now she tottered into the kitchen and accepted more tea while politely refusing a little something stronger offered by Gordon's father. "Suit your own self," he said, then after a swig added, with a wink, "So, got . . . spooked, did ya?"

The Spook School wasn't what Mackintosh and his wife Margaret MacDonald, her sister Frances, and Herbert MacNair called themselves. In Scotland, those artists were The Four, and they were acclaimed for infusing their art with Celtic, Asian, and outright occult imagery. Over in London, where the entire political and cultural apparatus was then as now bent toward the diminishment and marginalization of all things Scots—to hear Gordon talk about it, anyway—they were christened The Spook School. That's what had gotten Melissa so keen to visit Glasgow in the first place. To see the art up close and in person.

"I guess I did, Mr. Paterson," Melissa said. Gordon reached over and squeezed her shoulder. "But I'll be back at it tomorrow."

"Bring a pillow in case you try for another kip," Mr. Paterson said to Gordon, winking. Everyone chuckled but his wife.

"I never could ken all the fuss about The Four," Mrs. Paterson said. "We had to study them in school—class trips and such. It all just looked to me like they made some lovely drawings and paintings, and then stretched them all out and bleached half the color away. But you're Greek, no? Much more interesting art among the Hellenes, I think."

"Greek-*American*, yes," Melissa said. "But . . ." But when you're raised among cheap plaster miniatures of bone-white statuary; when tin reliefs of the Acropolis feature on every wall; when even your flatulent *theias* are named Aphrodite and Artemis; when all your relatives smell of the deep fryer and shout at the television news because they personally were the ones who invented democracy, you just get tired, you see, ever so tired of. . . . "I guess I've always liked Celtic things." She shot Gordon a smile. Mr. Paterson took the opportunity to wax poetic about his perverse support for Rangers—Gordon rolled his eyes and sharply warned him, "Dad!"—and the stupidity of anti-sectarian regulation that made singing songs a criminal offense, though with the caveat that "Billy Boys," with the line "we're up to our knees in Fenian blood" (which he sang quite well, in a steady tenor) should likely remain out of bounds. By the time Mr. Paterson had exhausted himself, his wife had finished preparing the traditional Scots meal of reheated take-away curry served on her own plates. Gordon drank Irn-Bru with his, like a child.

If this were a story, after dinner Melissa and Gordon would beg off pudding and report to Gordon's childhood room—untouched since he went off to America—and try to catch up on sleep. And the excitement of the day, with its embarrassing medical emergency and attendant barking of the Polish nurse to just "Pick yourself up and get on with your holiday!" would combine with the curry and Mr. Paterson's terpsichorical endeavors to entrap Melissa Poulos in a portentous nightmarish dreamscape of Spook School art come to life, seeking to devour her. And perhaps this was indeed the dream she dreamed, but from Gordon's point of view all the evening consisted of was her elbow in his nose, her knees jammed up against his chest when he tried to throw an arm around her, some snoring, a mouthful of her curls as she turned away and presented her back and arse for spooning. Then she managed to bark his shin. There was likely more abuse than that, but sleep finally took Gordon as well. Neither remembered their dreams, which indeed was the most common result of the human subconscious attempting to process proximity to genuine occult phenomena. It's the nightmares you don't recall even having that get you in the end.

In the morning, Melissa impressed the Patersons with her ability to roll her r's. She had a light breakfast, in the manner of an American, while the Patersons ate full Scottish, including, inexplicably, haggis. Melissa tried a bite and decided that it wasn't so bad after all. "Haggis has a poor reputation thanks solely to propaganda," Mr. Paterson explained. "English propaganda, swallowed and then regurgitated by their fellows in America."

"If you dislike the English so much, Dad, why do you support Rangers?" Gordon asked, his question both petulant and well-rehearsed.

"I never cared for haggis myself," Mrs. Paterson stage-whispered to Melissa conspiratorially. "It shows from the taste!" Mr. Paterson said. And with that, Gordon and Melissa whisked themselves out of the flat and headed to the city centre and its museums. Glasgow's venerable yet primitive subway loop served to bring them over to Kelvingrove from Ibrox. Melissa was less keen to walk in the *dreach* today.

"Are you concerned?" Gordon asked.

"About the rain?"

"No, about the. . . ?" Gordon said. Melissa had told him about the winking Mackintosh rose and they had silently agreed to tell neither the medic nor the Patersons about it. The end result was that they hadn't the chance to discuss it privately either.

"I just feel really good about today," Melissa said. "*The Wassail* really is beautiful. I need to study it closely. Did you notice that the figures in the center formed the outline of a scarab?"

"You tossed and turned all night."

"No, that was you," Melissa said. "I hardly slept a wink. It was like sharing a twin bed with an excitable circus seal."

"Likewise, I'm sure, madam."

Melissa said, "I want to see the panel again. There's a lot of hidden meanings in it. Do you know that wassailing was originally a type of Yuletide home invasion scenario? Madness of crowds and all that."

"And if the rose winks?"

"We passed any number of roses in that gallery. It's a motif. I think I saw a billboard with one when we got our tickets."

"Not the original, though."

There were many things Melissa could say to that, quoting Benjamin and the age of mechanical reproduction, the fallacy of the notion of the original, and especially how that fallacy related to art nouveau in general with its emphasis on using modern technique and "craft" over traditional visions of originality and artistic creation, but the argument required significant nuance and clearly Gordon wasn't in the mood.

Nor was Melissa. "Why are you ignoring everything I say?"

Gordon huffed as the subway stopped at Kelvingrove. "I know all about it. I'm a Weegie; I know all about getting drunk and rowdy, and I've not had a drink in two years, three months, and eighteen days. I've been marched through Kelvingrove as often as you were brought to see that big whale hanging in the Natural History Museum back in New York; I've heard all the mystical bugger. It's just that, you know? Bugger and bullshite. Plenty of Americans come to Scotland looking for highlanders cutting a path through heathery mores with their huge cocks, or fairy circles, or their great-grandma's chamber pot. You fainted, all right? That's all. And I don't want you fainting again, you ken? I worry for you, pet." And with his rant over, they were through the gate and through the turnstile and past the frowning faces of the teachers bringing children on a field trip to the museum and standing before *The Wassail* again. Melissa was pleased that somewhere in his juvenile belligerence Gordon used the word *ken* with her, as that sort of thing usually embarrassed him back in the States. *Pet* too was nice, but not nice enough.

The Mackintosh rose winked at her again. This time Melissa steadied herself and winked back. The women, elongated limbs as diaphanous as the gowns they wore, shimmered as if a breeze was moving through the plane of gesso. The scarab formed by the outline of their figures seemed to scuttle. *Right then*, thought Melissa and she excused herself to go to the ladies' and told Gordon not to worry; she was feeling rosy, haha, get it?

In the woman's restroom—Melissa still balked at the word TOILET on the sign—she dug into her purse for the fingernail clipper, as the TSA had seized her full-size nail file back at Newark International. She decided to start with the upper lip frenulum, and with the help of her reflection in the mirror, she clipped right through it. There was a lot of blood, but the other woman using the long row of sinks just stared down at her hands and started scrubbing roughly, refusing eye contact. By the time Melissa had pulled her lip past her nose and up to her prominent eyebrows, the toilet door slammed resoundingly shut.

Her mouth gaping open like the loose hood of an oversized sweatshirt, Melissa popped her skull off her C1 vertebra and placed it in the sink before her. Then she righted her face and reached in to her throat with both hands and, with a decisive yank, got the rest of her spine out. That went in the sink as well. It was getting quite messy, both inside and out, but Melissa had withdrawn plenty of Scottish £100 notes in her purse to make it worth the while of the clean-up crew. (Gordon had objected to getting Scottish notes, which many English shops south of the border won't accept, but Melissa was just the sort of annoying romantic that insists upon them.)

Melissa withdrew her pelvis via what method she couldn't help but think of as "the hard way," and the ribs, which had collected in the cavity of the structure, spilled out after and clattered about her ankles. The long bones of her limbs were the hardest to remove—it was a bit like trying to nail one's own lonely self to a cross—but she managed it, legs first through the anus, and then arms out her mouth. She was looking quite good, Melissa was. A foot taller, easily, and floating several inches above the ground. Her clothes were a bloody puddle of cotton and denim at her feet, and her metacarpals and metatarsals littered the floor like so much windshield glass after a fatal car accident, but Melissa knew that she'd receive a gown just as soon as she joined the festivities. She'd hardly be the only nude in the Kelvingrove Art Gallery and Museum, and surely the field trip of school kids had broken for lunch by now, no?

She sauntered back to *The Wassail* to the sound of screams and the thumps of matrons and patrons falling faint to the floor, but it was Gordon's unearthly howl of rage and fear after she caressed his shoulder to say both hello and good-bye that finally caught Melissa up as if in a gale and sent her flitting into the paint, to join the eternal parade.

I went to Scotland with the woman I'd eventually marry in 2011 to celebrate the wedding of her cousin. We kicked around for some time in Edinburgh, Glasgow, and Melrose in the Scottish Borders. I was especially enamored with the Mackintosh House and the Kelvingrove Art Gallery and Museum. I've since become one of those annoying Caledoniphiles who reads the newspapers from Scotland, supports Celtic, agitates for a second independence referendum, and listens to Scots and Scots Gaelic videos on YouTube.

"The Spook School" takes a strange turn, and it was strange to me as well. While writing it, I was interrupted and had to participate in an extensive argument over someone else's imagined slight. When I turned back to the story, and I was sufficiently committed to it that I even offered a false apology just so I could get back to my keyboard, I had lost track of my thoughts. I had no ideas for our poor heroine until I started composing the sentences that detailed her fate, and it wasn't the fate I originally had in mind. There are times when writing a horror story that a certain dream-logic takes over. When a monster or curse or other horror trope is too minutely explained, it stops being horror and becomes a mere technology for a protagonist to defeat or be defeated by. Horror should come on like a sudden realization, not like a conclusion minutely determined.

There is another universe, where some other set of synapses had fired and the person who insisted I stop writing to be yelled at did something else, and then I kept to my original idea for the story. I'll never know for sure, but I suspect that in the other universe, "The Spook School" isn't as good. Truly, we live in the best of all possible worlds.

A HOWLING DOG

THE APP, AND ASSOCIATED WEBSITE, had another name, but it was most appropriate to think of it as Cranki.ly. It was for neighbors to anonymously discuss neighborly things, but social media was as prone to Gresham's Law as anything else—the bad conversations drove out the good ones. It only took three months or so from initial launch for the posts to be all about suspicious dark-skinned men skulking around town "supposedly delivering the so-called mail," the essential wrongness of mowing the lawn in one's boxer shorts, and conspiracy theorizing about the next major ISIS attack hitting town . . . "because the Super Walmart, one of the really nice ones, is just five miles down on Route 5. It's a juicy target for Jihadis."

A juicy target, indeed.

The post that started all the real problems in Cranki.ly's Alameda County Zone 4 was this one, posted one afternoon just a week ago:

```
Hey Neighbors,

I've been hearing a dog howl/cry at
all hours from my apartment close to
```

the corner of Russell and Schiffer.
I was wondering if anyone knew who
the dog belonged too. . . It breaks
my heart and I'm wondering if the
owner knows about it. One of the
dogs I fostered a few years back had
severe separation anxiety and would
howl from for most of the time when
I left for work and I didn't know
about it until a neighbor alerted me,
at which point, I was able to work
on the separation anxiety with her.

Any leads appreciated. Thanks!

On the surface, a perfectly ordinary post. An especially pleasant one for Cranki.ly, actually, despite the specter of an ever-howling dog. The post garnered no comments though, for the reason you have surely already guessed—nobody else had heard the dog. Certainly not at all hours. The best thing to do in such a case is just not respond at all. There are plenty of other threads to read.

Why explain, why ask, why encourage further discussion?

Three days later, the poster issued a follow-up.

Russell and Schiffer Residents,

Hello again! I am still hearing a dog
howl and whine, day and night, every
day, and every night. It is definitely
coming from 2774 Schiffer. Please, take
care of your dog! If you live in 2774
Schiffer, you have a responsibility
to call your landlord or management

> company, or talk to your neighbor about how he or she (but let's be honest, probably a *he*!) cares for a companion animal. I am beginning to wonder if the issue is actual abuse rather than just neglect and separation anxiety.

> I do not want to have to call the city, as too often neglected animals are brought to shelter where they are quickly euthanized.

> And then the howling will never stop!

A much more off-putting message. Why would anyone respond to that? There was no dog at all. The poster was obviously dealing with some sort of mental issue, or was trolling. Either way, nobody living in 2774 Schiffer—a squat six-unit apartment building of one-bedroom apartments—would have any call to extend the thread. And yet, someone did.

> Actually, by definition the howling would stop then, no?

The strict discipline shown by the Cranki.ly regulars fractured then. *Tasteless* was upvoted two dozen times. While *Really funny, buddy. A total howler* was buried under a mountain of downvotes. One individual even tried to talk sense to the OP.

> I live on the corner of Russell and Schiffer, catty-corner from 2774. Full-time freelancer, work from home. I don't wear earbuds or even watch TV,

> and I like to keep my windows open when
> I can because I love the fragrance of
> lilacs. (I have several large bushes
> in my yard.) Never heard a dog howl
> even once, much less "at all hours."

Several other people acknowledged the truth—nobody had ever heard a dog anywhere in the vicinity, much less howling emanating from 2774 Schiffer, which was a residence with a draconian policy when it came to regulation pet deposits for even mere *cats*—dogs were absolutely forbidden. The howling isn't just non-existent, one poster commented, it's impossible.

Which, was, of course, false. It's not *impossible* for there to have been a dog in a building in which dogs are banned. And just because only one person could hear its howling doesn't mean that the howling was a delusion. There could have been a conspiracy of silence around the dog, around its constant cries for attention and relief. Indeed, even all the comments responding to the original post could have been from one busy person, creating a narrative of tasteless rejoinders and cynicism from whole cloth just to further demoralize and upset the original poster.

For that matter, the initial post regarding the curious incident of a bark without a dog could have been an attempt at Internet virality. *Creepypasta*, as the kids say. Cranki.ly's moderation policies leave something to be desired—anyone with an email address can post what they please so long as they eschew certain slurs. The only reason there's little spam or true hatemongering on the site is that its user base of middle-class busybodies and PTA lifetime-members is of little interest to the broader online world. But what's next? A report of a dog corpse surfacing in the soft dirt in the yard in front of the building after a week of heavy rains, or worse, bones found in the walls after 2774 Schiffer condo conversion? (Condo conversions being one of the perennial flamebait topics on Cranki.ly.) Or is it no dog at all, but instead some woman or child, gone feral and chained to a pipe near a rusty bucket of excrement, that had been howling all these days?

That "full-time freelance writer" was especially suspicious. Someone with an inclination toward fiction, and likely the impulse to procrastinate by goofing around on the Internet all day. Was all of Cranki.ly going to be written up in some obnoxious essay about group psychology, or urban legends? There was only one thing to do. Specifically, it was time to type

```
I hear it too.
```

And then press publish.

Another ten hours of silence on the thread, as if the neighborhood was holding its collective breath. And then a new party, or a new claim anyway, entered the thread.

```
I'm new to this website, but I heard
from a friend about it and came to
check what people in the Windham neigh-
borhood are discussing. I thought this
conversation was pretty interesting. I
used to live in the building, years
ago, and there was often a dog tied up
outside at all times, in all weather.
It's mostly warm and sunny here in
Northern California, but you know what
I mean.

She wouldn't actually howl or bark
all the much, but I felt very sad
whenever I saw the dog. One time
I stood in the yard and I started
```

howling, like that dog should have. I
guess I was just trying to get some
attention for the poor animal. Not one
person even opened their blinds to
look out the window and see what the
ruckus was. It was a Sunday morning
too, so people were home. I could see
movement through the blinds in the
windows. I really howled my head off!

Anyway, this was all more than twenty
years ago, so that dog is probably
long dead, but I just wanted to share
the story as a way of reminding you
all to be good to one another. Have a
blessed day!

And then it was a war of all against all. Accusations flew—
sockpuppets, tricks, spam, Russian hackers, hoaxing and
punking, and repeated uploads of that now-ancient *New Yorker*
cartoon panel featuring the adage "On the Internet, nobody
knows youre a dog."

But I really do hear it too. Someone
kept trying. Doesn't anyone else hear
it? I'm not the OP.

The poster went on:

This is insane. You're all online all
day long, and live within a mile of
the place. Just walk outside. I live
across the street; I can hear it now.

Meet me on the corner of Russell and Schiffer. I'll be wearing a blue hat. I have a long beard and glasses. I'll be the one with the iPhone in hand, listening to and recording the howling of the dog. I'm not the OP, this is not a joke! It's noon now. I'll step outside in ten minutes and stand on the corner until 12:30. You can walk a mile in less than twenty minutes if you're reasonably healthy. Just come out and listen!

Perhaps some of the lurkers on the thread contemplated joining the man, but no active posters did. One response read

Let me guess—I walk all the way to Schiffer Street and you're there with a gun to steal my iPhone.

A rejoinder:

Oh don't be paranoid. It's probably some dumb prank. They'll have a dog ready to howl or even just a recording of one, and they'll video the reactions of whoever is there for some sort of tedious "found footage" movie.

Then

I am the dog come visit meeeeeeooooooooooh!

was the third response.

```
"Meeeeeooooooooooh!" reads to me much
more like a cat than a dog, so clearly
you are dumb enough to be a dog. Do us
all a favor and stop howling all day,
or start, so we know what's what!
```

finished up the subthread.

Despite the claims explicit and implicit in the home page copy and related images, Cranki.ly was not successfully "bringing communities together." Nor was there very much "openness" and "honesty" created by the anonymity of the service. Not even when one Jack Reinhard, a long-time neighborhood resident, was hit by a car while standing right on Schiffer Street—a vehicle had jumped the curb, and sped off—nobody emerged from their homes to render aid. Nobody called 911. Reinhard had to do it himself, with his own broken arm. His blue hat fluttered away and landed on a Y-shaped tree branch half a block away. Someone took a photo of *that* and posted it on Cranki.ly. Reinhard had no local visitors during his overnight hospital stay, and only contacted his sister, who lived hours away in Sacramento. It took a day and a night for the hat to fall from the branch, and that was thanks to a squirrel not part of our program.

Setting a grease fire in one of the first-floor apartments of 2774 Schiffer was no help either. Sure, Cranki.ly posters made comments—*ooh, sirens!!* was upvoted a dozen times—and in the morning the URL to the local newspaper's story on the topic was also posted, but while the fire burned and emergency vehicles congregated, not one window opened, not one local Cranki.ly poster toddled outside to see what was going on. Certainly, nobody even recalled the thread about the ever-howling dog supposedly in residence so many had engaged with just five days prior.

A prod: `Did the firefighters find the dog?`

The responses were not encouraging: that would have been a *"grilled hot dog, eh?"* said one poster, and another, perhaps attempting to lighten the mood, posted a photo of a dachshund puppy in a hot dog bun. *Couldn't hear the howling over the sirens, sorry (and also because I'm not off my medication and can't hear imaginary dogs)* read a third post.

Incorrigible, the lot of them, it seemed. Cranki.ly may have well benefitted from rules against anonymity, or at least from a mechanism that would compel posters to hold to a consistent identity, like most bulletin boards and Internet comments sections. The online world is full of trolls and griefers, but surely, people would be nice to their neighbors whom they already knew, or could potentially face in heated meatspace confrontations after mouthing off online, no?

Well, perhaps, after all, the answer is still, at least potentially, *yes*. Finally, someone put up a post worth reading, a simple message of compassion and kindness:

> `I think we may all be having a hard time`
> `lately. I know things have been rough`
> `for me. I'm not calling anyone out; I'm`
> `just saying how I've personally been`
> `feeling these past few days. I'm sorry`
> `if anything I've posted has annoyed or`
> `agitated anyone. I wish you all health`
> `and peace—I really mean it. I usually`
> `have a drink at Raleigh's every night,`
> `same stool (right in front of the`

```
cash register) same time (7:30 pm). If
anyone wants to come out and sidle up
next to me, I'll buy you a cocktail.
All are welcome.
```

Eureka! Anonymity under pressure can lead to improvements in sociability and fellow-feeling among neighborhood residents. This calls for a refinement of our protocol. The next step is clear: to procure and torture a real dog, day and night. Or perhaps a child.

I had a dog for sixteen years. Until Kazzie entered my life, I was actually a little afraid of dogs, but she was only four weeks old when my friend Kap Su Seol brought her over to my home in Jersey City, and I was her last hope since, among all of our friends, I was the only person we knew with a backyard. Kazzie basically saved my life, as she gave me a reason to peel myself out of my chair and go for a walk a few times a day. Once, she may have actually saved my life, as when I turned a corner in our dicey neighborhood during an after-midnight walk I was greeted by the phrase, "Hey, motherfucker!" by an angry young man with something glinting in his hand. But he missed Kazzie, a little black dog on a little black leash, and when she sprung up and barked and howled, he threw up his hands, said "Shit, sorry!", and ran off.

I dedicated my how-to writing guide, *Starve Better*, to Kazzie, and moved with her to Long Island, to California, to Vermont, to the Boston area, and back to California. She slept with me until the end, even though for the last three months of her life, I had to line the futon with pee pads and towels to keep myself dry. When she finally succumbed to the cancer, I prepared to throw out the futon mattress and move the frame to the corner. In Berkeley, the street finds its own uses for things. A nosy neighbor insisted I download the app

Nextdoor and get rid of the frame that way, and I did just that as a new student at the nearby university walked past the house, asked if the frame was available and free, and excitedly took it away. My neighbor frowned deeply, and literally snorted like an angry cartoon boss who has just been shown up by an employee. That was the only good moment I had for weeks afterwards.

I stuck with Nextdoor, though, and found that all the rumors are true—it's basically a venue for people to express their racist fears of black and Latino pedestrians, and to make complaints about non-existent noises. I should have deleted the app right away, but it reminded me of Kazzie and of the fun coincidence of my neighbor. When it came time to write a story for an anthology, "A Howling Dog" was born almost instantly. The anthology ended up rejecting the story, but "A Howling Dog" was produced as a full-cast audio adaptation by the wonderful people at Pseudopod.org. The story appears in actual print for the first time in this volume. When you read it aloud to yourself, be sure to do the annoying neighbors in different voices.

LAB RAT

OCCUPATION: *FREELANCE.*

—Freelance what?

—Right now, I'm pretty much doing this. Four or five studies a week here at psych, some at the i-lab at the business school. A few at MIT, and one time I did one at Northeastern.

. . .

—Okay, freelance writer. But honestly, I've done so little of it lately I feel like I should just say "freelance" and leave it at that.

—What do you write?

—A little of everything. I have a novel with a small press. I wrote some stuff for the *Phoenix* before they went under. But I'll do anything: OKCupid profiles for foreign students, brochures and manuals, resumes and cover letters.

—Must be plenty of call for that these days.

—Not as much as you might think. After all, if I were so great at writing cover letters, why I am coming to the Harvard psych lab twice a day to play games and answer questions for ten or twenty bucks a pop?

—Hmm, fair enough. Let me go through the rest of this. . . .

```
        Do thoughts of harming others, or
        yourself, enter your mind during the
        course of the day (1-5 scale, 1 being
            never, 5 being constantly): 4.
```

—Four is . . . high. I have an obligation, uhm, here it is. This is a sheet of resources. You know, phone numbers. Places you can contact if you think you're having some trouble.

—Thanks. I'm fine. You should read my novel.

—I wonder if we have it in the library. I guess you won't get any royalties if I get it from there, right? Haha.

—Eh, it's fine. You buying a copy means that I get one dollar and twelve cents, maybe, eighteen months from now. Basically, whatever money the book is going to make, it's already made.

—All right.

—My novel has a few murders in it. Sort of horror/suspense.

—Okay.

—That's why I put down a 4 for that question. I think about death and murder a lot. For creative reasons.

—Understood. Got it.

—Because I'm a woman, people often think I write chicklit or something like that.

—Okay, so what we're going to do now is have you place your hand on this block. Then I am going to bring this iron rod over and swing it over like this. See the hinge? Anyway, I'll place it atop the back of your hand. I'm not going to drop it or slam it, just place it, so the point on the bottom will make contact with the exact middle of the back of your hand. It'll start feeling heavier, as the point will sink into the skin of your hand. But it's okay, it won't break the skin or anything like that. You won't get any more, or any less, money if you give up right away or last for a long time. Let me know when the pain becomes unbearable.

—Unbearable? You mean when I can't possibly stand another second of it?

—Well, when you get uncomfortable. Significant discomfort; not just mild. This is all part of what we're trying to measure.

—Am I allowed to talk now, or will that just be a distraction?

—Oh no, we're supposed to talk. I even have talking points, see?

```
The weather.
Psychology.
Subject's occupation, if any.
Subject's prior experiences with pain
and pain management.
```

—Ha. Should we do it in order? It's cold today. A wet cold; not like winter in the Midwest, where I'm originally from.

—Oh yeah? I'm from Illinois myself. Boston snow is almost cozy—it has to be because of the harbor, and the Charles River.

—So . . . why psychology? At Harvard no less. Do Harvard psychologists make more money, are they more likely to get tenure?

—Well . . . my mother was schizophrenic. It started manifesting when I was in junior high. I threw myself into schoolwork, spent all afternoon, every afternoon, in the library, to stay away from her.

—Thus, Harvard.

—Well, she ended up being institutionalized, and committed suicide. There was a suit, and a settlement, and thus Tufts for my undergrad. I fell in love with Boston, so I decided to stay. There's even a joke: "Anyone can get into Harvard for graduate school!"

—Heh.

—How's the hand?

—It's . . . hurting.

—What's your book about?

—The Halloween parade in Salem, and the witch trials. The costumes take over the parade goers wearing them thanks to the curse of Tituba, and then. . . .

—For Halloween last year I dressed like a sexy watermelon.

—A sexy *what*? That's hilarious.

—Yeah, it was a silly costume. A tube dress, a little slinky, very short, pink with a seed pattern and green trim on the bottom. And it had a bite taken out of the side. I had gotten rib tattoos—stylized wings—and wanted to show at least one of them off.

—I wonder how many Harvard grads students dress like sexy, winged watermelons?

—I'd guess . . . one. Just me. Your hand.

—Yes?

—It's red, almost purple.

—It hurts a lot. But it's not unbearable. Very little is unbearable, I've found. Human beings can bear a lot of pain. A lot.

—Well, the experience of pain is subjective. Even the expectation that pain will decrease can lead to pain decreasing.

—I always anticipate pain. Nothing but pain. A breeze passing over my skin is pain. The sun in my eyes is pain. My mind in the dark is nothing but pain.

—Is that . . . from your book?

—Sure it is.

—Okay.

—I bet you're not going to go to the library now to pick up a copy, eh?

—I have a lot of reading to do for my dissertation.

—No problem, I'm sure you do.

—I'm going to show you a Pain Rating Scale. Uh, there are little cartoon faces on this, but you can ignore them if you like. They're mostly for kids. Point to the face and number that most exactly describes the pain you are experiencing.

8

```
hurts
whole lot
```

—You can pull up the bar and remove your hand at any time.

—I like the cartoon faces. Do people generally not cry until the pain hits 10?

—No, no. That's just for children.

—You do this experiment on kids?

—No. But the chart is for kids as well as adults. The faces are not supposed to represent a person's expression, but what they feel on the inside.

—Oh. In that case. . . .

0

```
no hurt
```

—Really?

—Yes. Now, you point to how much it hurt when you got your wing tattoos.

—Okay.

4

```
hurts
little more
```

—But you sat there for hours. Hell, you paid for it. I'm at least getting twenty dollars for this, maybe more.

—I'm sorry, I thought I made it clear that you'll be getting twenty dollars no matter how long you can tolerate the pain. Would you like to stop now?

—Why did you get wing tattoos?

—Am I a distraction? Maybe you should concentrate on your hand.

—I can stay here for hours. Zero, no hurt! Remember? Didn't the form I filled out promise that there'd be no permanent damage? You said the rod won't break the skin.

—It won't.

—Good. So we can look at one another in silence, or we can do something tedious, like talk about men, or you can tell me more about your tattoos.

—I got them with the settlement money.

—How much did it hurt when you got the settlement money?

—The proposed topic of discussion is your history of pain and pain management, not mine, sorry.

—Fine, I'll tell you about pain. This little rod you have digging into the back of my hand isn't anything. Remember the Marathon bombing?

—Were you there? Oh, your novel! Is that what your novel is about, really? Supernatural horror at some other public gathering, as a symbol for the real horror of that day.

—Are you a Harvard psychologist or a community college English major? Whether I was there doesn't matter. Did you see the picture? You must know the one I mean? He didn't feel a thing either, I'm sure. His nerves were blown away along with the flesh and bone of his leg. Then there was the tourniquet. It didn't hurt till afterwards. Not only didn't that guy's leg hurt, nothing else hurt either. Whatever problems he had vanished in that moment. Athlete's foot, a sore shoulder, overdue bills.

—He's likely in plenty of pain now.

—Ain't we all?

—Are you? Point to the face and number that most exactly describes the pain you are experiencing.

```
0
no hurt
```

—Okay, still zero. Good to know. What's the most pain you've ever experienced?

—I was in the hospital one time. When I lived in Chicago. I had some problems back then. Want to hear about them?

—How funny. We can talk about whatever you like about, within reason, during the experiment.

—Oh, never mind, then.

—Huh?

—You said "within reason." What I have to tell you isn't reasonable.

. . .

—I was in the hospital because I was in pain. It was a blood-pain.

—"Blood-pain"?

—That's what I called it, anyway. I even used the term in my novel. It's pretty creepy, right?

—Right. Sure.

—Blood-pain is the pain created by black blood cells pulsing through your veins and arteries. That's how I always imagined the blood-pain anyway. Something rough and sharp, like glass dust in your veins.

—But black?

—Like tiny shards of obsidian or something, slicing and slicing.

—Did you see a hematologist or a . . .

—Psychologist, yes. Who referred me to a psychiatrist. But only after I took a cheese grater to my arm.

—Oh.

—My other arm, of course. You can roll up the sleeve and take a look, if you like. I'd show you myself, but I don't want to lose the experiment.

—I told you, you can't lose this experiment I'm sorry, Ms., uh, but we should end this. Of course, you'll get your payout.

—I don't want to end this yet.

—I'm going to.

—Your mother talked about you a lot, in the hospital. I was there for a few months.

—This is ludicrous.

—Your name is Joanne.

—That's on the briefing sheet.

—You love Shakira. Loved her anyway. My info is out of date. After all, it's been years.

—That's on Facebook. Those damn privacy settings are always changing. You could have Googled my name while reviewing the briefing sheet.

—She told you she hated you once when you were a girl. She used to hold your mouth open and spit down your throat to teach your stomach a lesson. She said that her spit was her soul and that this way she'd always be inside you.

—Okay.

—I didn't set out to find you or anything.

—Oh, is it all just a coincidence now? I should call security.

—No, I mean it. Everything I said is true. I need the money. Freelancing is a horrible way to live, especially in an expensive place like Cambridge. I have to pay for my own home heating oil too. It's like paying a thirteenth month's rent. I saw your photo a few weeks ago on the bulletin board, along with the other psych grad students. You look like her, you have her last name, you're the right age. I was here for another study. I decided I'd sign up to every experiment I could until I found you. I have something to tell you about her.

—Well, what do you have to say? Did my mother have some last words?

—"They're coming for me. The orderlies are coming for me." That's what she said.

—She was a paranoid schizophrenic. For all I know, you're also a paranoid schizophrenic.

—What if I told you that I saw something?

—Okay, what did you see?

—I saw two men, orderlies, walking past the window in my little room. All the doors have windows, of course, so they can do instant checks and so patients can't ambush the workers by hiding in a corner or something when the door starts to open. It was unusual that they'd be passing by so purposefully. The doors are all locked, which I am sure is against the law and is absolutely a fire hazard, so I mushed the side of my face against the window so that I could see. They had a little tray, opened the door to her room, rolled it in, and locked the door again. They didn't even go in.

—Yes, I know all that.

—What?

—My mother slashed her belly open. Obviously she had to have some access to some tool or blade.

—Yes, but. . . .

—Have you been in pain, all these years, thinking of what you'd seen?

—It took me a long time to climb out of my own black hole. And that made it even worse. What I'd seen.

—Sure, that's why most psych wards have been shut down. All sorts of terrible things happen there. It took my father a long time to find a proper one for my mother.

—But it wasn't a proper one, don't you understand?

. . .

—Don't you understand what I'm trying to say? Those staff members didn't leave your mother alone with a sharp because they were incompetent or stupid. I think they wanted her to kill herself. They went out of their way to make it possible. What? Don't you understand?

. . .

—Oh, come on. Don't push that stupid Pain Rating Scale at me again.

—Point to the face and number that most exactly describes the pain you are experiencing. You need your twenty dollars, don't you?

6

hurts

even more

—Good. Now let me tell you something. I had to do a lot of favors, I had to do a lot of things to get where I am today.

—What are you talking about?

—Isn't that how it goes in your dumb little novel? A practiced revelation, a public demonstration of so-called "evil." I bet it is. Genre fiction is full of clichés and cheap irony.

—Hey!

— Here's some psychology for you: you can never mask the self. Pick a mask, you're just revealing yourself. You come in here and act all tough and weird, but that's just you trying to deal with your trauma by spreading it around. And I, on the other hand, put on a nice little face. Objective and concerned with social science. But my experience with psychology is far more personal. Up close and personal. I bet that in your novel you had the bitchy woman dressed like a witch, maybe some fat guy dressed like a gluttonous monster with a giant month. Did the town slut dress like a sexy watermelon, or Elvira? The local bullies were skeletons and Frankensteins. And I'll also bet the nice girl ended up playing Good Fairy Princess and saving some little kids in superhero costumes or something.

—So your wing tattoos. . . .

—I never felt freer than I did after I got my way.

—Oh, I get it now.

— . . . you do?

—Orderlies don't get paid very much, and frankly, most of

them look like they've been hit in the face with a shovel every morning before work. A nice white girl ready to do anything for them, and in exchange all they had to do is make a tool available to your mother. That was the plan, and look, it worked. You're almost successful, and almost normal. Almost.

—No. I mean, it's not my fault. Not completely. She could have decided not to commit suicide, after all. She could have slept through the night and the morning check-in would have found the blade and she would have been fine. Fine. But she wanted to. She wanted to. Suicide is just another form of pain management.

—You know, there are many forms of pain management. I learned that the hard way, inside. Writing helps me. Drinking helps writers. Taking a drive with the windows open helps drinkers.

—I can call security. Wouldn't it be like something out of a bad novel if the security guards looked just like the orderlies in your old psych ward? But I'm not going to. I'm going to just lift the rod off your hand, like so, and ask you to point on the Pain Rating Scale to how you're feeling right now.

—You can call security if you like. You think I'll be less free back in the booby hatch? You think you'll be any freer with a fancy PhD and a tenure-track job at some little liberal arts college in Ohio? Tell me again about masks and the self, why don't you?

—Look, just let me get one last datum, and I won't call security, and you'll get your twenty dollars, and then you can go home and call the cops and explain that you, a poor horror writer with a psychiatric record and no proof, want to have me, a Harvard grad student with a nice bank account and lots of social capital and, frankly, a great pair of tits I inherited from my mother, arrested for secretly having my suicidal schizophrenic mom killed.

—It's funny that you think I'd call the cops. That I'd even have to call the cops. My work here is done.

—Oh look, you pointed to the face with the tears running down its cheeks. It looks just like you. Hurts Worst. A perfect ten.

—We're holding hands, you know.

—So we are.

———————

The best thing about being a freelance writer is that one can work from home, and thus live anywhere. The worst thing about not being able to drive a car is that one has to live in a place with extensive mass transit and walkable neighborhoods. That means that this freelance writer is doomed to live in one or another of the most expensive cities in the United States. For a couple of years, I lived in Somerville, Massachusetts, where rents are high and heating oil expensive, but there is the T, bus lines, and local supermarkets and bookstores. It was only a short walk to neighboring Cambridge, and the Harvard University campus.

To make ends meet in an expensive and often freezing town, I signed up to be a lab rat for Harvard's psychology labs. The pay varied widely, from a candy bar at the low end, to $100 at the high. I also did a few economics experiments for Harvard Business School, which generally paid better, but were much less interesting and offered less frequently. There were days when I'd hang around campus and do three experiments in a single afternoon. The first might be a questionnaire that paid five bucks, enough for a hot dog while I waited for an opportunity to play a video game by blinking my eyes for ten dollars. Then, a true battle of wits against an undergraduate as we role-played being diplomatic rivals for a chance to win twenty dollars. That poor freshman had no idea what hit her. Economic desperation makes for great motivation. I practically had her not only surrendering, but crowning me king of her imaginary nation.

"Lab Rat" is a combination of a couple of experiences I had at

Harvard. (Boy, that sounds much fancier that it was.) I participated in the pain experiment as described. The questions about death and suicidal ideation come from another experiment I participated in. I had to explain to a very nervous graduate student that I think about death often not because I'm depressed, but because I am a writer of dark fiction. That went well. I got my ten dollars and was allowed to leave anyway.

I was in a down mood when I wrote "Lab Rat," which is why it is a dialogue-only story. I was too emotionally exhausted to even contemplate writing descriptive passages or setting a scene. The story's original ending was too much of a downer, too one-sided, and unfair to both participants. Cameron Pierce, editor of the wonderful, now-defunct, publisher with an awful name of Lazy Fascist Press, spotted the problem with the story and went beyond the call of duty by requesting a rewrite rather than simply rejecting it. I first met Cameron when he was a very young man at the World Fantasy Convention. He called me "Mister Mamatas," declared that I was one of his heroes, and offered me a free copy of his first novel, *The Ass-Goblins of Auschwitz*. He was one of the writers of "bizarre" fiction who put me up in their shared hotel suite after I had drunkenly forgotten not only my room number, but the name of the hotel in which I was staying during WFC. Cameron has since grown into an excellent writer and an extremely insightful editor, and I was not only pleased that he took the story, I felt a bit of avuncular pride when he so expertly fixed a flawed story of mine, then published it.

DREAMER OF THE DAY

HALLWAY, JUST NARROW ENOUGH FOR TWO. Tin ceiling, haze in the air. It's a railroad apartment, three floors up. A pile of old toys and junk—half a bicycle, plastic playhouse all stained and grimy Day-Glo, empty wrinkled cardboard boxes, coils of cable—blocks the back door. By the front door, a small table littered with envelopes. Bills, looks like. Cellophane windows and a name over and over, in all caps.

So you pick a bill, Paul says.

Any one? Lil asks.

That's the fee. Pick a bill and pay it. This operator, he doesn't leave the house, he's not on anyone's payroll. He puts his bills out here. You want to hire him, you pick out a bill and pay it. This is how he lives.

Yeah but. . . . She bites her lower lip. Licks it. She's a real lip-licker. So what if I take this one?

She taps a Verizon envelope. Her finger is fat on it, like crushing a bit.

Maybe it's fifty bucks. Maybe he calls lots of 900 numbers, she says. Is that enough, though? If he's as good as you say he is—

He's the best.

It'll look like an accident?

No.

The finger comes off the envelope. *No?*

It'll *be* an accident, he says.

Eyes roll. Whatever, she says. How can he live like this? I mean, if people can pick any bill they like and pay it, why would anyone bother to pay his rent when they could pay some fifty-dollar phone bill? The West Village, I mean, Jesus.

Rent control. It's not that bad. He's been here for a long time, Paul says. Then he puts his hands to his mouth, cupping them. Waahh waaah waaah he plays, like a sad trumpet. Then he sings two words. *Twi-light time.* You know it? Paul asks.

She looks at him.

Glenn Miller, Paul says, plain as day.

A cheek inches up, dragging her lips into a smirk. Another lick.

Stardust. Google it or something. Glenn Miller vanished over the English Channel. He and his Army band were flying into liberated Paris to play and . . . He lifts his palms in a shrug.

And they crashed and drowned?

No, just vanished. Not a trace of him, or the band, or the plane. That was his first hit, they say, Paul says. That's how old this guy is.

I thought you said this guy makes his hits look like accidents, not like episodes of *The X-Files*, she says.

We can leave right now if you like. If you're not impressed. If you don't want to pick up a bill and take it downstairs to the check cashing place and pay his electricity or his cable or whatever the hell else, Paul says. If you don't want to give him three hundred bucks for his rent this month. If you want to try somebody else who might cut your husband's brakes, or shoot him in the fucking face, for twenty times the money. Yeah, that won't be traced back to you. Have you even practiced crying in the mirror, Merry Widow?

Tears well up in her eyes. She stands up straight, then her spine wilted. Waterworks. The man made to reach out for her, not thinking. All autonomic nerves, limbs jerking toward the brunette Lil like she needs saving.

All right, all right, you're good, Paul says.

Lil reaches for an envelope, flashes that it's addressed from Marolda Properties, and puts it in her purse. Now what, she says.

We wait.

How about we knock? She raises a tiny fist.

I wouldn't.

Can we smoke?

No . . . but yes, he said. He reaches into his suit pocket and pulls out a silver-on-bronze case, flicking it open and offering her a cigarette.

From crimped lips: no light?

He produces a lighter, flicks it open too. Matches the case. The cherry blooms and the door unlocks.

Put those nasty things out, The Dreamer of the Day says. You'll kill us all.

The apartment is all newspapers, at first. Then she sees other things—boxes stuffed with green-and-white striped print-outs, old black-screened TVs, dusty Easter baskets, a pile of shoes. The Dreamer leads them like there's a choice—the kitchen is piles up to the Dreamer's eyebrows except for the path carved out from force of habit, and the living room is newspapers and magazines avalanching from sagging couches and the bedroom is just piles of old man clothes. Hats and green suitjackets and shirtsleeves sticking out like quake victims who didn't quite pull themselves from fissures. The man has to stand sideways and sidle after the Dreamer. The woman fits, but barely, her elbows tight.

Lil doesn't smell a thing except old man: that's lavender and piss.

The bedroom—magazines she's never seen before, filing cabinets on their sides across a twin bed, a rain of hanging plants. A patch of mattress ticking bald and empty; the Dreamer takes a seat there. Paul finds a little bench, sweeps it free of old coffee cans and pipe cleaners and sits. There's room for her but she stands. The Dreamer reaches and there's an audible click. A big cabinet-sized television set, framed in trash. Knobs. Black and white, but a nest of cables snaking up from it to a hole punched through the tin ceiling. Her show is on, *The Cove of Love.*

Is this some kind of set-up? Lil asks. Is this some kind of joke?

The Dreamer says, I like this show. You were good on it.

I don't watch it anymore, she says.

Paul pats the bench. She sits.

Sotto voce Paul says, We really should wait for a commercial.

On the screen there's a man. Old, with silver hair. In business wear, but he means business too. Sleeves rolled up. Suspenders, thick and brown. A pile of dirt, a shovel. The sky behind him is swirls of paint, normally bursting with red and purple (the woman knows that matte painting well) but on the Dreamer's television screen it's a sea of gray. The man picks up the shovel and begins to dig. A voice, tinny and distant, begs him to stop. It's her voice.

That's a clip from three years ago, she says. Paul hisses at her. She nudges him with her elbow. The bench wobbles under them.

Yes, the Dreamer says. When Savannah was in that old bomb shelter the gang had cornered her in, and they decided to lock her in. I remember those words, that tone. Tell me.

Yes?

Do you have a lot of the same outfit?

Excuse me?

When you're doing something like that. Does wardrobe take back whatever you're wearing every day and clean it, then dirty it up again so it'll match, and you wear that suit every day, or is there a rack full of identical pantsuits, with identical tears and identical smudges and burn marks, and you wear a new one every day. You were in that bomb shelter for three months, ten minutes a day.

They have a *few* outfits. We have girls who take digital pictures and they try to match the amount of dishevelment. I think we had three of that outfit for that story arc.

That's why I like *The Cove of Love*. I can tell that the director really cares about the show, the Dreamer of the Day says. The other soaps don't even try anymore.

A commercial for vegetable oil. A world where people in a room can look out the windows, where women stare off into space and hold up bottles and confide in the universe that some things are tastier than others.

Why'd you bring her here, Ron? the Dreamer asks.

I want my husband— the words stick in her throat.

Ron.

Ron opens his mouth. She is tired of being married to her husband.

The Dreamer turns to look at her, to look at Ron too. He's not a striking man. He couldn't get a job standing on the lip of a grave on a soundstage, to stare down at the lens of a video camera. A little pudgy; skin like defrosting chicken. His undershirt is yellowed; his eyes an unremarkable brown. Hair a bundt cake around the back of his head. Lil didn't have lunch today. She couldn't eat.

Aren't you a women's libber?

Lil laughs at that. Who even says women's libber anymore?

You can get a divorce.

Maybe he doesn't deserve a divorce. You want the gory details? Paul told me you're a no-questions-asked kind of guy.

Ron, the Dreamer says.

She looks at the man next to her.

Here, he says, I'm Ron.

Savannah—

Call me Lil, she says.

Savannah, the Dreamer repeats, I am a no-questions-asked kind of guy. I can't say I like women's libbers very much. I don't care why you want your husband dead, but women like you, Savannah, you want to talk about it.

I'm not a woman like Savannah, she says. That was a character I played on the show.

And the show starts again. There's a hospital. A man turns on his heel and walks off-frame. A close-up of a woman's face. All redheads and blondes look alike. The Dreamer tells them the character's name is Trista and that she has something horrible inside her. Then two kids bouncing on a couch, too enthusiastic when the man who meant business walks in after burying Savannah alive. A restaurant scene is next, the rhubarbrhubarb of the crowd scene like the Dreamer's labored breaths. Then a commercial for people who want to fill a bag with gold and mail it away.

The Dreamer says, Ron, go downstairs and get us some coffees. Ron gets up and squeezes past the rubbish into the next room.

Lil puts her hand in her hair, combing it with her fingers. I want my husband dead because he's been cheating on me.

Bullshit. Pardon my French. I don't get many female visitors. I'm sure that doesn't surprise you. I know I haven't kept up my apartment. I'm embarrassed. Ron should have told me you were coming. That *you* were coming. We could have met in the diner.

I thought you never leave.

Maybe I'd make an exception, the Dreamer says. He looked at Lil. His dentures are heavy like two rows of tombstones.

He is cheating on me. This is third or fourth little whore.

That's not why you want him dead. If you wanted him dead, you would have put out a hit two or three whores ago.

I used to have a career, something to occupy my own days. Now I'm home all day, or at the gym. I can feel her sweat on the sheets of my own bed when I lay down at night. It's humiliating.

Humiliating, the Dreamer echoes.

I don't know if I'll ever get another role. I'm forty-one years old. I never crossed over to movies, not even to primetime.

You're not the bitch goddess type, the Dreamer says. Not the part for you.

I want to know that there's something more to the world than what I've already lived through.

The Dreamer extends a finger and turns off the television set. A single pixel burns in the middle of the screen.

There's a lot more. Worlds within worlds. You are having an affair with Ron.

The irony doesn't escape me, Lil says.

You ain't escapin' it either, the Dreamer says.

What?

Ron told me that you were together. I feel for him. His wife, the big C. In her breasts, and now her brain.

He's a good man, Lil says.

What's your husband's name?

Whatever happened to no questions asked?

The Dreamer smiles. I do have to ask one question. Not a personal one. Well, it's about preferences, not information.

Answer mine first, Lil says.

Anything for you, Miss Savannah.

Why do they call you the dreamer of the day?

All men dream, but not equally, the Dreamer says. Those who dream by night in the dusty recesses of their minds wake in the day to find that it was vanity: but the dreamers of the day are dangerous men, for they may act their dream with open eyes to make it possible.

That's beautiful.

That's T. E. Lawrence.

Who?

The Dreamer of the Day shivers, visibly disgusted. Finally, he lets . . . *of* Arabia extrude from his mouth like sludge. And you got two questions out of me, Savannah. More than anyone ever has. I have a weakness for you.

I apologize, Lil says. I'll collect another envelope from the foyer on my way out. She says *foyer* like a Frenchwoman. What's your question?

Kill him fast or kill him slow?

Slow.

The Dreamer gets up and leaves the room. Lil hears some clatter in the kitchen and gets up. The Dreamer has cleared off the stove. He has a tea kettle out. She almost trips over the junk on the floor.

Pau—uh, Ron. He's getting coffees from the diner.

Ron's not getting us any fucking coffee, the Dreamer says, gravel in his teeth. Paul's not getting coffees. He puts his hands on the stove, a little electric number, squeezes his fingers in the gaps between counter and stovetop on either side, and gives it all a shake. A red light blinks to life.

No apologies for your French this time, *monsieur*?

This is how it's gonna go, the Dreamer of the Day says. He looks up and off to the side, and some random piece of paper up atop a teetering pile in the living room. Ron's down at the diner, see. He knows the one. It used to be Greek; it's Russian now. Your husband's fourth little whore is there. Blonde milkmaid type. Her upper lip curls when she smiles. He likes that kind of thing. You can do it too.

She can, yes. She does, Pavlovian. Close-ups, she says. You've seen the show.

Well it just so happens that your husband is in the diner too, see? He likes to watch the girl lean over the Formica for tips. He likes to count the seconds other men keep their hands on her ass while she takes their orders. Then he likes to take her up to your home, up to Valhalla on the Metro North so he doesn't have to drive, doesn't have to keep his hands on the wheel.

Valhalla. That's on my Wikipedia page. You probably have a computer around here somewhere.

The Dreamer starts rummaging through a cabinet for a cup. He finds one, waves it hooked around his finger, and then finds a second. This on your Wikipedia page? he asks. Your boyfriend Paul Osorio is connected. How do you think he knows me. He's packing. He sees your husband and is overcome. He pulls out his gun.

Paul doesn't carry a gun. He's a good man.

He knows the Dreamer of the Day. I don't know any good men. I don't meet them in my line of work. No good women either. What did he tell you? That he knew a guy who knew a guy who knew someone who could help you? He *is* a guy. He'd have done it himself, if you'd asked him, but why would you ask him? He's a good man.

Mister, I think I'm going to meet Paul downstairs. I'll get you some help—my sister is a social worker. You don't have to live like this. There are nice places. You won't be lonely either.

The tea kettle screams. You don't want to go down there, the Dreamer says. Paul's already put a bullet in your husband. He aimed for the head but missed because the whore's a sharpie. Paul got a faceful of hot coffee the second she saw the gun. Right in the eyes. He's not going to see out of his left anymore. That face— second and third degree burns. Saint Vincent's isn't that far away. Both of them will make it to the ER.

My husban—

The chest. Bullet just misses the heart. But you said you wanted it slow, so you get it. He bleeds, but he lives. You can go see him later tonight if you want. Take in a movie. Buy yourself a nice dinner. 9 PM. Visiting hours will be over, but they'll let you in. The night shift, they're all fans. You'll cry like you did in court when the government took your Chinese baby away.

That wasn't me. That was a character.

They were your tears, the Dreamer of the Day says. That'll get you in. Go see him. You'll think the staph will have come from here. That you're the carrier, that you infected him.

He pours two cups of tea. He hands one to Lil. She takes it but doesn't drink.

This is the most disgusting place you've ever set foot in, he says matter-of-factly. So when your husband gets the MRSA, you'll think it's your fault. It'll get in his blood nice and slow. It'll take weeks for him to die. He'll cry even better than you, demand that you visit him every day. Get a hotel room so you can spend all day by his side. He'll forget the whore entirely, and she'll be sent back to Moscow till the heat is off. You'll sneak down to the burn ward to see Paul twice, three times. Then forget it. It won't matter, though.

Why won't it? she asks. She passes the cup from hand to hand. There's no place to put it down.

His face will be ruined, but so will your husband's. The MRSA will do a number on his skin. Boils worthy of Job. Kill him slow. He'll lose half his nose. Three weeks of rats in the veins.

Lil throws the content of her teacup at the Dreamer of the Day, but he's ready. An old *New York Post*, he swipes it off the countertop and holds it up. The tea splatters all over another disgraced governor in black and white and red.

The Dreamer drops the paper, steps on it as he walks past Lil. Show's over, he says. Go home. You'll see.

She follows him back to the bedroom. You crazy old man, she says. What the hell? Did you put Paul up to this? Did he put *you* up to this? What kind of freakshow are you two lunatics running here? Christ, talk about far-fetched. I've met some real winners, some deranged fans, but *you*, you are a fucking fruitcake—

The Dreamer grabs a great handful of old suits and tosses them on the white tongue of the bed on which he's sat. The back door of the railroad apartment. He opens it and walks out without a word. *Where are you going! You can't leave!* she demands. The door slams shut. Lil rushes to the door, tries the knob. It's unlocked, but she has to push, not pull. All the trash and boxes bar the way. She can't squeeze her pinky through the crack of the door for the rubbish. Lil grabs her purse from the little bench, runs through the apartment on tiptoes, sideways along the narrow path through the piles of garbage, and hits the hallway through the front entrance.

No Dreamer. Lil looks down the well of the staircases. No Dreamer. He's an old slow man. He couldn't have made it outside in time. She's on the second floor; there are no first floor apartments he could have ducked into. Lil stomps down the steps and walks outside to a dusk painted red and blue from the lights of ambulances and a black and white. A radio crackles. A shrieking, thrashing blonde held inches over the sidewalk by a pair of cops gets shoved into the back seat of the cop car. Then, gurneys.

Lil can't see her husband. He's in emergency surgery. Paul she doesn't dare ask after, not when she sees two men in tanklike suits in the waiting area very patiently not reading the newspapers open in their hands. She doesn't want to go all the way up to Grand Central. She doesn't want to say to the Metro North ticket clerk behind those bars of bronze, "One way to Valhalla." She takes in a movie. Cries through it. It's about someone with cancer. A real tearjerker. She can taste the hospital on-screen. Lil orders a nice dinner in a little place down on Greenwich Street, where the grid of the city collapses against the shore of the Hudson River. Doesn't eat it. Tips fifty percent for some privacy. Indigo skies go gray. Nine o'clock, she's crying in the lobby of Saint Vincent's. Not for her husband. Not for Paul. But her husband, he's the one she decides to see.

Lil washed her hands at the restaurant. Again in the ladies' restroom. She takes her husband's hand now because he's unconscious, breathing hard as though deep in his still body he's running from somebody. She pulls her hand back but it's too late.

In the 1990s it was possible, barely, to live in Manhattan while being poor. I was doing it, kind of, as were several of my friends. I knew this guy named Paul, who was very nice, if a bit of a hothead. He also had some eccentric religious beliefs, gray teeth, and was an excellent street fighter. One time I went to his apartment on a semi-desirable block in the East Village and met his girlfriend, who was perhaps about thirty years older than he was. It was the first time I'd ever been in the home of a Level Four Hoarder. The only thing not making Paul and his lover Level Five Hoarders is that they actually lived in the apartment, rather than sleeping outside in the hallway or on the roof. Bundles of newspapers were stacked up to my ears, and tables and bureaus were piled, on their sides, in the corners. There was a single path to a rotting twin mattress, and what appeared to be a working toilet in the corner. If there had once been walls around it forming a water closet, they'd long since been torn down or just collapsed into a heap of drywall and splintered wood.

They invited me to stay for dinner. Paul's lover said she was pretty sure she could find a pot, and they had several cans of chili somewhere. I begged off on the meal, but I did stick around for about twenty minutes. I wasn't even a writer yet, but I memorized what I saw and thought, "I can use this, somehow." And I did twenty-five years later, for "Dreamer of the Day."

Manhattan in the 1990s was also a place and time where one could casually meet artists, career criminals, neighborhood-level "celebrities," and other bizarre figures living in humble apartments without any visible means of support. Weakened rent control laws, AIDS, and gentrification destroyed much of the scene, but I've been obsessed with the vanished possibilities for two decades. "Dreamer of the Day" is a joke title—the violence and the magic are superfluous; the story is really my daydream of being able to afford Manhattan rent, and an apartment full of stuff, without working.

WE NEVER SLEEP

THE PULP WRITER ALWAYS STARTED STORIES the same way: Once upon a time. And then, the pulp writer always struck right through those words: Once upon a time. It was habit, and a useful one, though on a pure keystroke basis striking four words was like taking a nickel, balancing it carefully on a thumbnail, and then flicking it right down the sewer grate to be washed out to sea. Four words, plus enough keystrokes to knock 'em out. Probably, the pulp writer was chucking eight cents down the sewer, but that was too much money to think about.

Here's how the pulp writer's latest story began.

> ~~Once upon a time t~~ The mighty engines had ground
> to a halt, and when the laboratory fell into silence,
> only then did the old man look up from the equations
> over which he had been poring.

It was all wrong; past perfect tense, the old scientist's name couldn't be introduced without the sentence reading even more clumsily, and by introducing equations in the first graf the pulp writer was practically inviting some reader to send in a letter demanding that the equations be printed in the next issue, so that he could check them with his slide rule. *Oy vey.*

The pulp writer had to admit that writing advertising copy came much more easily than fiction. And the old man with his unusual ideas paid quite a bit for copy based on a few slogans and vague ideas. The pulp writer was never quite sure what the old man was even trying to sell, but money was money.

> *Industrivism deals with the fundamental problem of modern experience. Both the Communist and the Christian agree—the workaday world of the shop-floor and the noisome machine rob us of our essential humanity. Even during our leisure hours, our limbs ache from eight hours of travail, our ears ring with the echoes of the assembly line. Industrivism resolves the contradiction by embracing it. Become the machine, perfected! You're no longer just a cog, you're the blueprint, the design, the firing piston of a great diesel—*

It was possible to write this junk all right, but the pulp writer couldn't imagine that anyone would believe it. But the old man liked wordy paragraphs that were half religious tract, half boosterism, all nonsense. He was a foreigner, obviously, and had little idea what Americans wanted: not just crazy promises, but crazy promises that could be fulfilled without effort and with plenty of riches, revival meeting hooey, and a Sandow physique to boot.

Nobody wanted to *be* a factory. Heck, nobody wanted to work in a factory. People just did. Even pulp fiction was a factory of sorts. The pulp writer's fingers were as mangled as any pieceworker's thanks to the Underwood's sticky keys, and there

---

was no International Brotherhood of Fictioneers Local Thirty-Four to help a body when the cramps got bad or the brain seized up.

Speaking of brain seizures, it was time for a drink. The pulp writer figured that a paragraph's worth of beers would be fine for the night, and that included the possibility of fronting another patron a round. And down the block at Schmitty's, the pulp writer's friend Jake was always ready to drink F&M beer on somebody else's dime.

"Oh my, could I use a catnap right about now," said Jake to the pulp writer with a yawn. "But, up here, it just never stops." He pointed to his temple. Jake was everything the pulp writer wasn't. Big, with a huge right hand that wrapped around the beer stein like a towel. And quick too. The pulp writer was small and slow and a woman. Her specialty was scientifiction, but she also did romance pulps, and Jake was heavily involved in the scheme—he delivered the manuscripts to the office downtown, throwing them over the transoms of the editors of *Incredible Science Tales* and *Thrilling-Awe Stories* so she wouldn't be spotted. For the romance pulps, Jake was the model for the dark hero, reformed and repaired over and over again by the power of a woman's love, twice or three times a month for *Love Stanza*, *True Stories of Love*, and *Heart Tales*. The pulp writer was Lenny Lick, Lurlene St. Lovelace, Leonard Carlson—and whomever else it took to get a sale.

"You could," the pulp writer said. "You don't have to think about work at all the second you step through the factory gates and rejoin the rest of us unemployed chumps down here at the bar. What is the old Wobbly demand again? Eight hours of work, eight hours of sleep, eight hours for what we will?" The pulp writer liked to tease Jake sometimes.

"No, I can't," Jake said. He took a long sip of his beer, and didn't bother to wipe the suds from his lip. "The Reds don't sleep. The saboteurs don't sleep. We're doing important work, all classified. There will be another war starting soon, in Europe. You'll see."

"It's been twenty years! You'd think they—"

"Button your lip," Jake said.

"But you were just ta—"

Jake looked at her. "My mistake." He burped lightly then muttered, "Wobblies. I can't believe you're still talking about the Wobblies."

They finished their beers in silence. The pulp writer thought about a story she had in her trunk; an unpublished one about a terrible world in which Prohibition had actually been declared and the criminal fraternity had begun working overtime to corner the market on illicit booze. Machine guns and mini-dirigibles and pocket-stills, and . . . nobody wanted it. Who would believe that criminals would employ scientists and engineers, the rejection slips said, and besides the story made it seem like crime paid.

"Pays better than pulp fiction anyway," the pulp writer said, and Jake responded, "What?" and she said "Never mind."

The pulp writer licked her lips. "Will you be coming up?"

Jake shook his head. "Nah, I'll just take the manuscript and go."

"Fine," she said. Nothing was fine. She slid him the envelope that had been resting under her left elbow. "Next Tuesday, then?"

"If not sooner," Jake said, but the pulp writer didn't respond, so he took the envelope and left.

Jake didn't know if he was strictly allowed to read the commissioned work, but he always helped himself to the first few pages when delivering the manuscripts to the publishing companies, and saw no reason why tonight should be any different. After all, it was Jake who recommended her to the old man in the first place. So he took a look as he walked along St. Mark's Street and into the West Village and read:

Have You Heard Of
INDUSTRIVISM??

—the document was entitled. Industrivism was the idea of "intrapersonal industrial development," of using "psychological and philosophical methods to improve the self" and become a superior being. In the same way that factories made superior products by assembling them one step at a time, so too could a human being be improved by embracing "psycho-industrial processes" that would refine and eventually perfect both mind and body.

The very first step was the hardest—admitting that you were a know-it-all, or a wallflower, or a bohemian, or a workaday drudge, a second-hander, or a thug. The list went on at length. Once you had determined your own Essential Flaw, there were a number of exercises one could do to become a True Industrivist, a superior being able to control one's own fate. The pamphlet only hinted at what these exercises might be, but Jake was intrigued, even as he diagnosed himself as an also-ran.

He had no idea what the old man was planning, but what else was new? *It had been twenty years*, Jake thought. Twenty years ago, when Jake was just fifteen, and working on a sewing machine alongside his parents in a ten-story factory. Then when they came for their shift one morning, all the sewing machines were gone. The foreman sent everyone home, and he had plenty of Pinkerton muscle backing him up. They had truncheons, stood in a line like soldiers, and one burly Irishman hefted a repeating rifle. His parents and all their friends could do nothing but mutter in Yiddish and go home and further dilute their cabbage soup. At least the morning papers would have some other job postings, and it would be back to the twelve-hour grind.

Except for Jake. He got up the next morning, went to the offices of the Pinkerton Detective Agency, and offered his services—he was bilingual, knew the neighborhood and all the families, had a quick jab, hated Reds, and thought the *rebbe* was a fool. And he found the Pinkerton slogan compelling.

We Never Sleep

They signed him up and a few months later sent him back to the factory, right on the banks of the Hudson, a few blocks south of the Chelsea Piers where all the rich people sailed off to England and back. He retrieved the old man from his ship with a four-horse team, and then helped install him in the factory.

It had taken six days. Jake broke *Shabbos* for the first time. After that, he practically had to live in the factory as his parents cast him out. Twenty years later, and here he was, still at the same factory he'd be sent home from at gunpoint, but at least he wasn't bent over a machine, half-blind with bleeding fingers.

Jake went down to the basement, taking the special pneumatic elevator that looked, from the shop floor, like a broom closet. Jake had the run of the place, you might say. He went where he was needed; his job was to keep the old man happy, if it meant pitching in on the line or dealing with troublemakers and agitators out by the gates.

Jake knew the factory very well. He could talk to it. And it talked back, in reverberations and slammed doors and clanking pipes and hideous grinding. And sometimes it spoke through the mouth of the old man in the basement.

The old man slept, mostly. He needed his rest. Actually, he wasn't even that old, but he was very sick, and his skin was shriveled and dry like jerky. He lived in a giant iron lung, though the lung was like nothing Jake had ever seen, not in newsreels and not in the pages of *Life*. More like a giant underwater suit ten feet high, and vertical, up against the wall, limbs spread like in the middle of a jumping jack. And the old man's head was behind a plate of thick glass. Tubes and piping came in and out of the lung, making it look like the contraption had a dozen smaller limbs in addition to the main four. Jake figured that all the old man's business was somehow dealt with via the plumbing. He had seen a canteen cook shovel perfectly fine mashed potato and gravy down a drain hole once. Who knew what was coming in, or going out, through the other pipes?

"Sir," called Jake as he entered the room. "We have the latest carbons from the writer." Jake couldn't help but shout as the basement room was the largest room in which he'd ever been. His childhood *shul* could have fit down there.

The room growled. Under the basement, there was another factory, with a whole other set of workers pulling the swing shift, manufacturing . . . well, Jake didn't know. He didn't even truly *know* that the old man had them on a staggered shift to keep them segregated from the other workers—it just seemed obvious. The sub-basement line had fired up and was hammering away at something. It felt like the old man was angry, like his heart had started beating like a drum.

The factory often talked to Jake. The old man rarely did so. But now, he did. There was a click, a crackle, and a tinny voice came from the two great loudspeakers.

"READ IT. SLOW. ALOUD."

Jake wasn't much for elocution, but he did his best. It was hard not to snicker, but surely the old man wouldn't be able to hear the laughter catching in Jake's throat.

"WHAT DO YOU THINK?"

Jake stood for a long moment, stunned. The old man had never asked for an opinion before. He'd only ever given orders, and in a precise Germanic tone, via his phonograph contraption. Jake didn't know what to think. He never really had been in a situation where he had to be politic before. *What would the pulp writer want him to say. . . .*

"Well, uh, sir," he said, "I think that Industrivism could be the wave of the future."

"THE FUTURE."

"Yes. They'll be talking about it all over the nation, like Populism or Prohibition," Jake said. "Even if everyone doesn't agree, it'll be a topic in the newspaper editorial pages. I can see people handing these out like they do copies of the *Daily Worker*, just to strike up conversations with passers-by." What Jake kept to himself was that the populists and temperance people were horrid anti-Semites he'd as soon spit on as say "How do you do?" to, and that the Commies were even worse.

"PUT THE MANUSCRIPT IN THE TUBE."

Jake rolled up the carbons, stuck them in a capsule, and inserted it into a pneumatic tube. In the morning, who knew what would happen. This was the fifth text Jake had brought over from the pulp writer, and they'd all been sent upstairs, where as far as Jake knew they were being used to wrap fish.

The pulp writer imagined a lot of things: monsters from the depths, clever young men welding de Laval nozzles to locomotive tank cars and transforming them into high-powered bullet-fast tanks, a former silent picture star discovered begging for change with her career-ruining froggy voice, only to find true love with a film producer turned Pinkerton guard . . . but she never imagined seeing her work in the slicks.

And yet, in the current *Henderson's Lady Weekly*, there it was: Industrivism. A whole article on the cockamamy scheme, breathlessly and enthusiastically written by one Doctor R. D. E. Watts. *An obvious pseudonym*, was the pulp writer's first thought. Her second was to wonder how she could get in on such business, given that the slicks sometimes paid one thousand dollars for feature essays. A thousand dollars could get her out of her current accommodations and into an apartment where the bathtub was in the washroom instead of in the middle of the kitchen. An elevator building with a doorman. A zeppelin trip to Frankfurt, or even to Rio de Janeiro.

The pulp writer caught her mind wandering, and with it her fingers twitching. A zeppelin would be a great setting for a romance tale, or even a spy yarn. Perhaps a zeppelin-shaped starship that generated anti-gravity in its lattice frame, or due to some static charge generated by aircraft dope rubbing against the frame. It wasn't quite kosher science, but it was close enough for the pulps. . . .

"And that's why I'm not in the slicks," she said aloud to herself.

The Industrivism article was clever, in that to the pulp writer's trained eye it was obviously an advertisement in the shape of a feature, and had been purposefully placed in the feature well to further obscure its pedigree. The old man Jake worked for must have paid a pretty penny for such placement.

At Schmitty's that night, where the pulp writer drank alone and safe from molestation thanks to the protection of the bartender, the word "Industrivism" floated by twice. Perhaps one of the men's adventure pulps, or even a general interest slick, had been paid to run an article much like the one in *Henderson's*.

It was nearly last call when Jake finally walked in, looking like a wet sheet that had been wrung out but never spread to dry. He took his seat on the stool right next to the pulp writer's, careful not to kiss her on the cheek.

"Gosh," the pulp writer said. "Please let me buy you a round for once. I haven't seen you in two weeks."

"We've been busy down at the plant," Jake said.

"Wobblies smashing the conveyor belts?"

"Interviews. We've got three full shifts and are still hiring."

"There's a depression on, haven't you heard?" the pulp writer said.

"I'll drink to that," Jake said. "We have a line of workers stretching around the block starting every morning at five a.m. Grown men climbing over the fences—I even had to fire a couple of warning shots at a trio coming in on a row boat."

"Cheaper than the Hudson Tubes," the pulp writer said.

"What is Industrivism?"

"How did you know?" the pulp writer asked.

"I can't make heads or tails of this Industriv—" Jake started. "Wait, how did I know what?"

The pulp writer held up her arms and set type on an invisible headline in the air before her. "'What. Is. Industrivism.'"

"That's the title of my next piece for your boss. I got a telegram this morning. He's hot for copy. Wants a new Industrivism piece every week."

"I bet," Jake said. "So what is Industrivism?"

"Doggoned if I know," the pulp writer said. "I would have thought you could tell me. The first proposal was vague. The second had a bit more meat to it, but I was just winging it. The third was just the telegram I told you about—no details at all. I suppose it doesn't really matter what Industrivism is, so long as people hear about it."

Jake frowned at that. "How does that even work?"

The pulp writer shrugged. "It's like the American Dream. What does that even mean anymore? Or 'use a little wine for thy stomach's sake'—recall that the Dry League claimed that the Bible was recommending that we spill booze all over our bellies rather than drink it. Anything can mean anything.

"Really—the less clear an idea is, the more likely it is to be popular."

The pulp writer peered down at her drink. She didn't even ask Jake if he were coming up this time, and Jake didn't hover like a fly, waiting to be asked, as he used to. She had no manuscripts for him to deliver to either his employer or the various pulp publishers about town and it sounded like he had no time to do any errands anyway.

Upstairs, the pulp writer pored over a slim volume, *The March of Diesel*, published and distributed by the Hemphill Diesel Schools of Long Island City, Boston, Chicago, Memphis, Los Angeles, Seattle, and Vancouver. It covered the basics of the technology, and made some breathless predictions for the future—sort of a low-rent version of what she was doing, and oriented toward getting some down-on-their-luck pigeons to pay for a course on diesel mechanics. Then inspiration struck. Her fingers flew over the keys.

> *What Is Industrivism?*
>
> *Industrivism is the engine of life in America itself during this, the Era of Diesel.*
>
> *Like the mighty diesel engines that power our factories and automobiles, Industrivism is a Four-Stroke Process.*
>
> *Intake Stroke: The nation itself, home to all the peoples of the world, and every race and creed. E pluribus unum!*
>
> *Compression Stroke: The communities—the great cities and towns where we live, work, play, and love.*
>
> *Combustion Stroke: The workplace, where we come together with furious energy to build a nation that shall lead the world.*
>
> *Exhaust Stroke:*

Well, "exhaust stroke" was a tricky one, the pulp writer had to admit. Exhaust carried connotations of both the polluted and the bone-weary, which she had decided were the very opposite of Industrivism. The deadline was tight and no pulp writer got anywhere by wasting time, and ribbon, in revision. Sometimes thinking was the wrong thing to do. Let the fingers handle it.

Exhaust Stroke: Rejuvenated and refreshed by a gentle breeze from the oceans that protect this great nation from its jealous enemies, we redouble our efforts.

The pulp writer's only remit was to somehow make the diesel engine a metaphor for America itself. The pulp writer was creating a Bible of sorts for other writers to interpret and embellish. She imagined them bent over their own typewriters—Remingtons and Olympias, some portables and others iron monsters from the war era—a thousand literary pianos playing together, or one large and radically redistributed factory, all creating Industrivism for the slicks, for pulps, for religious publications, for the community pages of daily papers in English and Yiddish and Greek and German and Italian. All based on her notes. And like an assembly line, they'd all fall idle without new material. The pulp writer caught a second wind—an exhaust stroke of her own—and wrote till dawn.

While the pulp writer toiled, Jake wondered. There was something special about being foreman and factotum, specifically he didn't need to know very much about what was actually happening at any given moment. When he was confused, he'd point to a worker and ask what he was doing, and what this process was for, and how it contributed to the final product, and he could then pretend to be satisfied or discomfited with the answers.

Jake could never bring himself to ask what the final product of all this production was, and not because he was embarrassed not to know, but because he was comforted by the idea that at least the workers on the line knew, and he couldn't bear to have that illusion shattered.

But still he wondered, so he took the steps to the first floor where the electroplating vats bubbled away, as the 'platers had time to chat.

"Fellas," Jake said, and the three men straightened out and muttered nervous hellos. "What is Industrivism?"

The three men looked at one another, glancing back and forth as if deciding who would speak. Finally, one of them who Jake had pegged as a snickering wisenheimer type, said, "Sounds like a new radio show."

"It's a kind of foot powder," said a tall, heavyset man.

The third fellow kept his eyes on the bubbling vat, as if electro-deposition would cease if he ever stopped staring.

"You fellows are pretty funny. Tell me even one more joke, and I'll make sure you have plenty of time to take your act on the road," Jake said.

"It's the heart of a diesel engine," the staring man said without looking up. "It's the heart in all of us."

"Sounds good to me," the heavyset man said. The first wisenheimer just looked confused.

Jake went off without another word. He could always ask the old man, but what would the old man know? He wasn't even American, which was probably why he depended on the pulp writer for his political ideas.

The heart of a diesel engine . . . the heart would be where the fuel goes, like blood.

He tried someone else, just a random fellow leaning over a compressor. "What are you making?"

"Compressors," the man said. "Wiring."

"For what?"

The man shrugged. "Frigidaires?"

"You think . . . we're manufacturing refrigerators?"

The man shrugged. "Look son, I just got this job this morning, and I don't mean to lose it this evening by falling behind."

Jake couldn't fault the man's attitude. He pursed his lips and tried again. "Sir, in a few words, how would you describe the American Dream?"

The man looked up, and Jake saw that he was very old. Old enough that he probably wouldn't have been hired at all under normal circumstances. "I say I'd describe it as getting a job in the morning and starting work some minutes later, and not being laid off by the end of the first shift."

It was a taciturn bunch, but of course Jake couldn't expect men hard at work to wax philosophical. Intellectuals liked writing romantic stories about the proletariat and its struggles, but all in all Jake preferred to read *Six-Gun Stories* and *Mad Detective*. Even that put him ahead of the shift workers, who couldn't be bothered to read the labels on their beer bottles half the time.

"What's the heart of a diesel engine?"

"The cylinder," the man said.

"How do you figure?"

The man just laughed. "It was a guess. Why don't you just go away?"

Jake fired him on the spot. Let the compressors pile up for a few minutes; it hardly mattered if nobody even knew what they were manufacturing.

That night was like every night—Jake slept fitfully, dreaming of a factory. Not the factory for which he worked, but another one, darker and larger, in Europe. Jews marched in when the bell rang, and out the back end the factory spit out exhaust and shoes. Jake's rational core, the bit of himself that woke him up, knew what was going on. He'd grown up on hair-raising stories of pogroms and riots from his parents and uncles and cousins and family friends, and he felt guilty for throwing it all over for the Pinkerton job. So the back of his brain gnawed away at his spine every night, poisoning his system with visions of an industrial pogrom, a diesel-powered *völkisch* movement.

But his parents were fools. Europe was a happy, prosperous place, and even the Germans were doing well thanks to all the imported beer Americans liked to drink. There would never be a pogrom of any sort again. How did the president put it when he stared down the kaiser at the end of the war? "Send us your tankards, or we'll send you our tanks to fetch them." It was a fair and free trade, and everybody was happy now.

Jake took a slug from his own emergency Thermos-stein and tried to sleep. It worked for once. He even slept through the morning alarm.

The pulp writer was extremely nervous. The old man had sent another telegram, again circumventing Jake. He wanted to meet, in person, that afternoon, and Jake's name was absent from the telegram as well. It would likely be a one-on-one luncheon. The old man had no idea the pulp writer was a woman . . . or worse, perhaps Jake had let it slip and that was why she had received such a sudden invite. Romance, crime, horror, all of them were possibilities. Would it be love at first sight, or would some greater intrigue about Industrivism be revealed, or would the old man chase the pulp writer around his great mahogany desk, his lips pursed and his hands clenching and unclenching like pincers?

The pulp writer decided to bring her hatpin, and a brick for her purse as well. But she also applied some rouge, chose a superior hat, and decided to walk rather than take a crosstown bus to both save a dime and keep her clothes from being wrinkled by the crowded carriages.

Industrivism was in the air—literally. A skywriter had been to work, and the letters "rivism" had yet to dissolve in the sky. It was a waste anyway, given that in New York only yokels and bumpkins pointing out the skyscrapers and dirigibles to one another ever looked up at all.

Why did the pulp writer, who was born in Canarsie and had a diploma from Hunter College High School, look up? She had taken a moment to pray. It was a prayer for protection that, when she saw those letters in the sky, transformed into one of gratitude.

The city was limned with Industrivism, though the pulp writer had to wonder if she was just especially sensitive to the presence of her own ideas and phrases on posted bills, on the back pages of newspapers hawked by children on the street corner, flitting by in overheard conversations. When she crossed Broadway, the pulp writer decided that she would studiously ignore all things Industrivism and instead concentrate on some symbol sure to be ubiquitous: the American flag.

There were . . . some. A lunch counter offering All-American Pie and Beer. A single legless veteran of the war with a flag draped over her shoulders as she puttered past in a hot-bulb engine wheelchair, begging for change and showing off her stumps. The West Village's local post office flew one, as did the Jefferson Library.

And there was one close call—a great flag two stories tall was draped over the side of a warehouse just two blocks from the old man's factory, but where the stars should have been on the blue field instead were crudely stitched white cut-out gears.

The pulp writer stopped to gape. The passers-by, and in New York the streets were always choked with pedestrians, workers loading and unloading diesel trucks, and tourists, ignored the flag. She blinked hard and rubbed her eyes, and then someone grabbed her wrist.

She jerked away, but the hand held strong. A man in a cloth hat and a shapeless worker's jumpsuit tugged to her him and he asked with quivering lips, "Lady . . . what is Industrivism?"

The pulp writer pursed her lips and yanked her wrist away. And then she told him, "Oh, hell if I know, fellah! It's just some gibberish somebody made up to get you to work longer and sell you soap . . . and you could use some soap!" She brought her hand up to her hat and withdrew the pin, but the worker scuttled backwards, palms up. "Sorry, ma'am, sorry!" he muttered as he retreated.

The pulp writer realized that if she ever became a famous writer, she was going to have to come up with a more politic answer to that question. Her meeting with the old man was certainly going to be longer than he likely anticipated, and she hoped that he had cleared his afternoon schedule. She already had a piece of her mind apportioned out and ready to give him.

In the factory, Jake stalked the shop floor, looking for someone else to talk to. Maybe it was true that every workaday Joe Lunch Pail–type was just dim. The old man's factory was unique—no management, just Jake, and occasional instructions from the basement. All decisions were built into the construction and layout of the assembly lines, including redundancies and contingencies. The place was packed with machines and crowded with people, but nobody had more than a couple of words for Jake. Then he had a brainwave and rushed to the loading dock where the hogsheads were delivered daily. He opened a barrel with a crowbar and scooped out some peanuts, then filled his pockets with great handfuls.

"Hello!" said the pulp writer, waving from the asphalt.

"What are you doing here?"

"What are you doing here?" the pulp writer said, squinting. "Lunch break?"

"You can make diesel fuel with peanuts. . . ." Jake started.

"One of the many miracles of the diesel era, yes I know," the pulp writer said. "You can make diesel fuel with pretty much anything. But what are *you* doing?"

"What would you say the heart of the diesel engine is?" Jake asked.

"Why . . . the combustion chamber, I suppose," the pulp writer said "It's where the fuel goes, and fuel is like blood. But the peanuts—"

"But wouldn't it be the crankshaft," Jake said, his voice rising querulously. "That's what transmits power to—"

"Metaphors are never perfect, Jacob. Now why are you stealing peanuts?" the pulp writer said.

Jake pulled one from his pocket and held it out to her, wiggling it with his thumb and forefinger. "Want one?" She just glared at him.

"I just want someone to talk to me for more than ten seconds in here," he said. "I was going to scatter these across the floor, and maybe someone would stoop to pick one up, or even trip and fall. Then I could talk to him, and . . ." Jake realizes that he sounded insane. Too many all-nighters. When was the last time he had even been home, in his own bed?

"You're a Wobblie after all," the pulp writer said. She stood up on her toes and wobbled a bit. "Get it?" Jake snorted. "Anyway," she continued, "it is almost impossible to find one's way in between shifts, and I have an appointment with your employer. We can talk about your, uh, 'shenanigans' later." She waved the telegram like a tiny flag.

Jake ate the peanut and led the pulp writer across the shop floor under a cloud of embarrassed silence. The factory was too loud for them to talk much anyway, but Jake was full of questions, for her, and for himself. What had he been thinking, with his little stunt? Why did the old man want to see her in person, and why hadn't he been informed? Maybe he had been informed, and had forgotten, but what would that mean for his mental health?

What is Industrivism?

In the small, secret lift, he spoke. "I should tell you something about the old man. He lives in an iron lung of sorts."

"In the basement of a factory?"

"Don't believe me?" Jake said. "You can see for yourself." And the doors parted and they walked into the huge basement room.

"That, sir," the pulp writer said, "is not an iron lung."

"Well, it's *at least* an iron lung," Jake said.

They approached quietly. The pulp writer was reminded of any number of cover paintings—the old man's head was visible behind a windowed helmet, just as a spaceman or deep-sea adventurers might be on this month's *Captain X's Space Patrol* and others. But he was wrinkled and brown like a peeled apple left out too long in the sun, not an astronaut with a right-angled chin.

The pulp writer heard something like the arm of a phonograph dropping onto a record, and then the old man spoke.

"THANK YOU. WHAT IS YOUR NAME?"

Jake stepped forward to introduce her. "This is Lurle—"

"Doris," the pulp writer said. "You can call me Doris." She turned to Jake. "Can he even hear us?"

It occurred to Jake that he had never had a lengthy conversation with the old man. That is, he obeyed orders, made suggestions, and once or twice tried to engage the old man, but now he realized that nothing that the old man had said was really informed by Jake's actions. It was all "DO THIS" and "DO THAT."

"I am not quite clear on that, all of a sudden," Jake said.

"MY NAME IS RUDOLPH DIESEL."

Rudolph Diesel, the inventor of the diesel engine, who had famously committed suicide twenty years prior. The pulp writer, whose name was not Doris either, knew that much. Fortune had turned to failure, idealism to despair, and the man had left his wife the sum of two hundred marks in an attaché case, booked passage to England, and then had thrown himself from his steamship. His waterlogged corpse had been found ten days later by a fishing boat, which had retrieved his effects and thrown the body back into the ocean according to the Code of the Sea.

Occasionally, the true crime pulps raked over the details and suggested instead that Diesel had been murdered. He'd been going to England to sell the patents to the queen and thus save his family and thwart the kaiser, and a Hun assassin had first thwarted him. Not a bad theory, except that British rolling dreadnoughts and American Diesel-Jeeps and Diesel-Leaps had won the war in six months, so who had actually been thwarted?

Another common story played up the Red angle: Diesel was a naïve Utopian who was going to meet with Irish radical James Connolly and break the Dublin Lock-Out by creating a new factory where diesel engines the size of a fist would be manufactured, and the capitalist overlords overthrown.

The pulp writer had never cared for such speculation in the true crime rags, but her mind was already running like sixty to. . . .

"This is Industrivism, isn't it!" she suddenly shouted.

"PLEASE WRITE ABOUT ME."

"You hear that, Lur . . . uh, Doris? He doesn't respond. Not really. He just has a stack of records in there somewhere and when he wants to say something he plays one. But he only has a handful of phrases recorded," Jake said.

"I want to know if you somehow survived your suicide attempt, or if it was a murder attempt, or are you the murderer who dumped someone else into the sea to start a new life . . . if you can call this life!"

"NO."

"Don't ask multiple choice questions," Jake said.

"Yes, I know that now!" the pulp writer snapped. Then, loudly, to Diesel. "Were you the victim of some crime?"

"YES."

She was silent for a moment then said, disappointed, "Well, that's that. Jake, why did you never tell me, or anyone, about this?"

"Not my job. My job is keeping this place running, no matter what. Anyway, I got a question—What is Industrivism?"

"THIS IS."

Jake often thought he could hear the factory talk to him. This time he felt the whole place take a deep breath. Not in anticipation, but in preparation for release. The pipes gave way with groans and a hiss of steam, and the long limblike projections separated from them and began to swing. Herky-jerky, like a bus-sized toy automaton, Diesel began to move. After three steps, he stopped, and black smoke belched from the exhaust pipes projecting from the contraption's "shoulders," as Jake thought of them.

"WRITE ABOUT ME."

"What do you want me to write?"

"I WISH TO WALK AMONG YOU ALL."

"Is that supposed to be what Industrivism is? Just getting people used to the idea of you walking down the street in this, uh . . . tank-suit, tipping a steel hat at the ladies?" Jake said. There was something happening to Jake. He didn't know whether to be angry or awestruck, or just to take himself out back and punch himself silly out by the loading docks for being such a fool. He had spent too much time just being a cog in the big machine that he hadn't taken notice, *real notice*, of anything until the past few days. Past twenty years, maybe.

"It sneaks up on you, doesn't it," he said to the pulp writer. "All these changes."

"Snuck up on me, and I was the one who came up with the word 'Industrivism.' I wanted 'industraturgy' at first, but I was worried that people wouldn't know what the suffix—'turgy'—meant."

"INDUSTRIVISM"

Now it was time for Jake and the pulp writer to both inhale sharply.

"INDUSTRIVISM IS"

The pipe on the left shoulder of Diesel's tank-suit blew and the sound reverberated throughout the basement almost as if had been designed with that acoustic effect in mind.

No, not almost, Jake realized. Exactly.

Where the tank-suit had once stood there was a door, and now that door opened. It was the swing-shift, the noon-till-eight crowd. All men, as was typical, and . . . *not* all men.

The first was armless, but his limbs had been replaced with a remarkable set of prostheses. He actually had eight hook-like fingers at the end of each arm-rod, and they opened and closed like a rose whose petals could snap shut in the blink of an eye. Behind him was a legless man, his waist a corkscrew, legs thin and pointed, but perfectly balanced in their way like a drafter's compass in expert hands.

The entire shift, and there weren't many of them, had some replacement. Jake had never seen any of these men before, not in the factory. Maybe on the streets, one or two begging, or just idling listlessly. The last man seemed to Jake to be whole, and he Jake recognized. It was the man from the electroplating vats upstairs, the utterly normal-appearing man with no defect at all. He walked up to Jake and the pulp writer and undid several buttons of his work jumpsuit, to show off the chest still fresh with a huge incision.

"I have a combustion chamber for a heart," he said, fingering the surgical line. Thick staples held his flesh together. "You know what's interesting about Industrivism, what we all just found uncanny about it? Every other ideology they're selling out there— Communism, Americanism, Kaiserism, you name it, they all promise that you're going to die. Spill blood for your country, or your class, or the Glorious White Race, or something. The only difference is that they all promise that the other fellow will kill you worse.

"But Industrivism, when I started reading about it, I noticed that nothing about death or blood or glorious combat was ever mentioned. It sounded sweet, so I came here and went looking for it. We all came here, just over the last month or so, for the same reason."

Jake glanced at the pulp writer, who was smiling.

"I don't think we're ever going to die," the man with the combustion chamber heart said. "We're making tank-suits." He hiked a thumb at Diesel. "They work fine. He doesn't even need to dream anymore."

"THIS IS MY DREAM."

Jake said to the pulp writer, "Good thing it was you, eh? I bet most fellows would have to throw in a little of the old blood and guts."

The pulp writer shrugged. "Women know a lot about blood and guts. I was just tired of writing about it.

"Mr. Diesel, I'll be pleased to write about you."

"What about me? What am I supposed to do with all this!" Jake said, suddenly red in the face. It was fine when the pulp writer was just as confused as he was, but now she had signed on for something he still didn't understand at all. "How come you didn't tell me, 'old man'? I did everything for you!" He pointed to the pulp writer, and seemed nearly ready to shove her in Diesel's direction. "I found her for you!"

The pulp writer tensed, and deep within Diesel's tank-suit something whirred and whirred. Finally, from the horn came the words.

"I APOLOGIZE.

"I NEEDED YOU AS YOU ARE."

"But why?"

"CONTROL GROUP. IN THE FACTORY, BUT NOT OF THE FACTORY."

"We've been working on something for you," said the man with the combustion chamber heart. "We're building all sorts of devices and implements, all diesel-designed if not diesel-powered. Tank-suits for men on the edge of death, limbs for vets, and even spines. We haven't gotten your thing quite perfected yet, but maybe . . . how would you like to never need to sleep again?"

Jake shivered and started to cry. The pulp writer reached into her purse for a handkerchief, and laughed when the tips of her fingers caressed the brick. She recovered the hanky from under it and handed it to Jake, who took it without a word and blew his nose into it.

Finally, Jake said, "I have to get back to work."
"Spoken like a True Industrivist," said the pulp writer.

Once upon a time There was a knock on the door of the second-class stateroom, but Herr Diesel's embarrassment was not due only to his reduced circumstances but to the fact that he had been on his hands and knees, ear pressed to the ground, to listen to the reverberations of Dresden's steam engines. An article Herr Diesel had read promised that her steam engines outputted twenty boiler horsepower at five hundred revolutions per minute, but Herr Diesel suspected Dresden's capabilities had been overstated by its proud engineers.

The door opened, and the mate who opened it jingled the keys on the wide ring he carried. He was English, but Diesel was a polyglot and so understood the man perfectly.

"You're to come up to the poop now, sir. There is an unfortunate issue with your accommodation."

Diesel rose to his feet and dusted off the knees of his trousers, which was not strictly necessary as the rooms were kept clean, even in second class.

"What would the problem be, sir?"

"Well, there's an issue with the water," the mate said. "The water supply, I mean to say. The WCs are all overflowing, the urinals as well, so we need everyone to clear out. All the other passengers are already in the dining hall, sir, but you had not answered any previous knocks." With that, the mate made a fist that flouted several large white walnut-knuckles, and knocked on the open door slowly, three

times. *Then he crooked a finger and said, "Come along then, sir."*

Herr Diesel followed the large mate out of the second-class area. Something was very wrong, Diesel knew it. He asked, "Pardon me, boy, but what is the problem with the water supply?"

"It's the piston in the pump, sir. It got all stuck like a you-know-what in an underserviced you know where, eh?" The mate winked at his own crudeness, reveling perhaps in the reputation of sailors and the absence of any of the fairer sex as he led Herr Diesel to the poop deck.

"Why, sir, have you led me astern if the rest of the complement is in the dining hall, presumably at least enjoying some English tea, if not a glass of complimentary beer?" Herr Diesel enquired.

"Well, sir, it's a bit embarassin' to say, but we know your reputation. You're the famous Rudolf Diesel, inventor of the eponymous engine. We have a lot of toffs in first class, sir, and you see they caught wind of your name on the manifest, but also that you were sequestered in, erm, humble accommodation. We told them that in addition to our own capable mechanics, we'd have you take a look."

"I see, and you've told me that the problem is the water pump's piston."

"Yes, sir."

"And this was explained to you by the German hands, or by a fellow Englishman?"

"Sir, we are all bilingual round here. Sea life, eh?" The mate winked again, crudely, and nudged Herr Diesel with his elbow.

"Then, sir, I am now convinced that you are

not simply mistaken, and I have diagnosed the mechanical difficulty. It can be repaired instantly."

"It can?" the mate said.

"Yes. You see, you mountebank, Dresden is outfitted with a pulsometer pump, a clever and economical design which takes advantage of the principle of suction. A ball valve separates two chambers, one filled with water, and the other with steam. A pulsometer pump requires no piston, and has no piston, as it depends solely on suction!"

"Suction, eh? Yes, something like that!" The fraudulent mate, in actuality a paid assassin in the employ of certain Germanic interests determined to keep the patent on Herr Diesel's inventions the exclusive property of the sons of Goethe, launched himself at the man. But Diesel, forewarned by the inaccuracies in the thug's narrative, had already plotted a stratagem. He ran to the right, evading the killer's apelike arms, and secured for himself an emergency flare from the poop deck's box.

"Stay back," Herr Diesel cried, holding the flare before him. "Or I shall ignite it!"

The assassin paid no heed, having taken the measure of the inventor and finding the man's courage wanting, but he had again misapprehended Herr Diesel. Diesel yanked the cap from the end of the flare, igniting it, just as he was tackled by the assassin. Flaming and tumbling, limbs coiled about one another like a pair of enraged octopodes, they rolled the length of the poop deck and fell into the churning white sea below, dangerously close to Dresden's rudder head, where surely both lives would be lost.

Jake slipped the carbons back into the envelope, reared back like a major league pitcher, and flung the manuscript over the open transom and into the office of *Espionage!*, a pulp dedicated to spy stories and non-fiction features about a new philosophy dedicated to anti-Communism, technological-organic unity, and physical immortality. It was catching on.

Dieselpunk! That's just like steampunk, but greasier and more efficient, right? This was a hard story to write. I started and stopped perhaps half a dozen times, until I came upon the character of the pulp writer and integrated her into the story. The diesel engine changed the world into one amenable to science fiction as a commercial genre—if you like mass-produced fiction or electricity sufficient to run radio sets, movie theaters, and TV channels, give the diesel pump at your local gas station a kiss—and dieselpunk itself constantly references its own pulp roots.

If steampunk in its reactionary form is a response, as Nisi Shawl wisely observed, to the arrival of people of color into science fiction, then dieselpunk is a response to the arrival of writers who didn't grow up consuming the greasy kid stuff into science fiction. It's an aesthetic rearguard action appealing to the imagined golden age of square-jawed engineers slapping together giant robots in their garages. Videogames comprise the core of the genre, and it's often an excuse for baroque displays and military action, with an analysis of industrial culture being secondary at best. I felt that "We Never Sleep" had to tangle with both pulp and industry, and struggled with that until I realized that I could just bring in the pulp explicitly in the form of an industrial-strength writer of the stuff. In those days, sitting at a typewriter and cranking out fictions to order was the equivalent of by-the-penny piecework in a factory.

Interestingly, despite the genre's popularity, almost nobody writes about Rudolph Diesel, an intriguing fellow who grew up in a Europe shattered by war, and who died under mysterious circumstances. The one English-language biography, *Diesel, the Man and the Engine*, by Morton Grosser, is long out of print and reads more like a primer for children interested in mechanics than anything else. Diesel could be a pulp-fiction hero, and may yet be one. I've recently revisited "We Never Sleep" and think it may well be the bones of a novel.

UNDER MY ROOF

Every normal man must be tempted at times to spit on his hands, hoist the black flag, and begin to slit throats.
—H. L. Mencken

1

MY NAME IS HERBERT WEINBERG. I know what you're thinking. *That sounds like an old man's name.* It does. But I'm twelve years old. And I know what you're thinking.

In fact, I'm sending you a telepathic message right now.

Yes, it's about the war. And yes, it is about Weinbergia, the country my father Daniel founded in our front yard. And yes, I have been missing for a while, but I'm nearly ready to go back home.

But I'll need your help. Let me tell you the story.

It was Patriot Day, last year, when Dad really went nuts. Thoughts were heavy like fog. Not only was everyone in little Port Jameson remembering 9/11, they were remembering where they were on September 11th, 2002, September 11th, 2005, 2008, on and on. The attacks were long enough ago that the networks had received a ton of letters and email demanding that they finally re-air the footage of the planes slicing through the second tower, because nobody wanted to forget. Schools took the day off. Banks closed. Some cities set up big screens in public parks to show the attacks. I was excited to finally see the explosions myself. Nobody else could really picture them properly anymore. I drew a picture in my diary.

My mother Geri had forgotten pretty much everything except how beige her coffee was that day. She had been pouring cream into her blue paper cup when she looked up out of the window of the diner and saw the black smoke downtown, and she had just kept pouring till it spilled over the brim. She found my father later that day and told him that they were going to move to Long Island immediately.

And they did. Every year since, she forgot a little bit about that day. What was the name of the diner? Did she order a bagel with lox or just the coffee? Did she think it was Arabs or did the liberal centers of her cerebellum kick in to say, "No no no it could have been anybody"? Did she want to kill someone? Drop an A-bomb on the entire Middle East? She didn't know anymore. All she remembered, and all I plucked out of her head, was her off-white coffee.

My father Daniel, on the other hand, didn't remember anything but the nuclear weapons. Dirty bombs, WMDs, suitcases filled with high-tech stuff; that was all he could think about. He took a job mopping floors at SUNY Riverhead so he could take classes for free. Physics. Mechanical engineering. His head was like an MTV video—all equations, blueprints, mushroom clouds, people running through the streets, and naked ladies, in and out— flipping from image to image. With every war Daniel got more frantic. The president would say some stuff about not ruling out nuclear weapons, and I could tell he wasn't kidding. My father would stay up all night, just walking around the dark kitchen and smacking his fist against the table. On the news, they kept showing more and more countries on a big map, painted red for evil. All of Latin America was red now and even the normal people in California died when someone ran the border with a bomb or shot down a plane over a neighborhood.

Dad read the newspapers, spent whole days in the library and all night on the computer. He was getting fat and losing his hair. He was a real nerd though, so nobody really noticed that he was slowly going mad. Actually, the problem was that he was going mad more slowly and in the opposite direction from everybody else. At night he dreamed of being stuck on an ice floe or on the wrong side of a shattered suspension bridge. Mom and I would be drifting off to sea on another ice floe or sliced in half by snapping steel cables. Then Dad would see the ghosts of firefighters and cops, white faces with no eyes, and they would point and laugh.

So Daniel studied. Researched. Thought of a way out.

Dad waited until I was out of school for the summer to make his big move, because he knew I would make a good assistant. He was laid off by SUNY because of budget cuts—Mom blamed his erratic behavior, but Daniel wasn't really any more eccentric than his other co-workers. He sold his nice car and bought a ratty old station wagon even junkier than mom's Volvo hatchback, and spent all day tooling around in it, while Geri clipped coupons and made us tuna fish with lots of mayonnaise for dinner. They didn't send me to genius camp that summer (I'm not really a genius, I just know what smart people are thinking) so that's how I ended up being Prince Herbert I of Weinbergia.

Dad woke me early one hot day, just as the sun was rising. He looked rumpled, but was really excited, almost twitching. I half expected to see a little neon sign blinking *Krazy! Krazy! Krazy!* on his big forehead like I did back when Lunch Lady Maribeth went nuts and started throwing pudding at school, but he was actually normal.

"C'mon Lovebug, I need your help," he said, shaking my ankle. He hadn't called me Lovebug since fourth grade, and his mind was going three thousand miles an hour, so I didn't know what he wanted.

"What is it?"

"We're going to the dump to look for cool stuff. C'mon, we'll get waffles at the diner on the way back."

I always wanted to go to the dump and look for cool stuff. I was really hoping to find something good like a big stuffed moose head or a highway traffic sign, but then in the car Dad told me that we were going to look for the ingredient that made America great.

"In fact, they call it Americium-241. It was isolated by the Manhattan Project, Herbert." Daniel loved to talk about the Manhattan Project.

"I don't think we're going to find that stuff at the dump, Dad."

"Smoke detectors, son. Most smoke detectors contain about half a gram of Americium-241," he said with the sort of dad-ly smile you usually just see on TV commercials.

"How many grams do you want?"

"Well, 750 grams is necessary to achieve critical mass, but we'll want more than that to get a bigger boom," he said. He was thinking about turning on his blinker and how much smoother the ride in the old car was, not about blowing anything up. "I guess we'll need about 5000 smoke detectors."

"Uh . . ."

"Don't worry. I don't plan on finding all of them today."

He pulled the car into the dump and gave me a pair of gloves and a garbage bag. It was still early morning so the dump hadn't started getting hot and stinky yet. Dad let me go off on my own too, so we could cover more ground. I bet Mom or a social worker would have complained that Dad wasn't worried enough about my safety, but really, he was. As far as he was concerned, the safest place in the world was in a garbage dump, digging around for radioactive smoke detectors.

There wasn't all that much cool stuff at the dump, mostly just big bags of rotting food and milk containers, and broken Barbie Dream Houses—lots of those for some reason. There were old computers too. I liked checking out the motherboards and the stickers the college kids plastered on the side of their old monitors, but I couldn't find any moose heads or old hockey sticks or valuable comic books that some angry mother threw out or any smoke detectors. Mostly, people just leave them up on the wall, even if they don't work anymore.

I was playing around in this neat car I found that had a steering wheel that still moved around when Dad came running up with his own garbage bag. He'd found like twenty. "How many ya get, Lovebug?" he asked, then he frowned and mentally counted to ten when he saw the empty bag next to me. "Herbie, we really need to find these materials. Did you even look?!"

I shrugged. "It's hard. What do you want me to do? I can't look everywhere all at once."

He waved me out of the car. "C'mon. You just have to go about it systematically." He walked to the closest pile of garbage and then started going through it, one bag at a time. We pored through all the bags in one pile, tossing aside the smaller white plastic bags full of disgusting toilet paper, cardboard boxes with pictures of lasagna and fried chicken on them, newspapers from last week with headlines about the White Menace (Canada), gloppy leftover food mess sprinkled with white maggots, and all sorts of other junk. And then I found a smoke detector, at the top of the tenth bag we opened. Daniel gave me a big hug for that. "Now you can do the rest of this pile yourself. I'll be in that quadrant over there." Saying "quadrant" made him feel military.

Long Islanders are pigs. I found another smoke detector in the middle of a greasy pound of red spaghetti, but that was it. Everything else was just gross, from the moldy bathroom rugs to little baby clothes smeared in grease. Dad found me a bit later, his bag a little fuller. "Scored twelve all together. Let's get home, quickly now."

And that's what we did every morning. There was new garbage every day, plus there was always a chance we had missed something. Daniel printed out a list of things that might have some Americium-241 in them. Smoke detectors, and some medical testing equipment, and moisture density gauges all use the stuff.

"You know what a moisture density gauge looks like, Lovebug?" Dad asked me one morning.

I read his mind, then told him.

"You're such a smart boy."

We didn't find any moisture density gauges at the dump, but we did find some cool-looking stuff from the public hospital. They'd lost beds due to budget cuts. As the days wore on, we had more competition in the dump. Daniel was the only one after smoke detectors, but some poor people were spending their days at the dump, looking for old shoes or funny lamps or computer monitors to sell on eBay. I saw one guy cart away a giant bag full of stiff old bagels. Even he didn't know what he was planning on doing with them, but I could just picture his family in a dumpy living room: the kids all had dirty faces and crooked teeth, their little fists wrapped around mismatched forks and knives, and they wore white napkins around their necks like bibs. Then their dad would walk in and pour all the bagels onto the middle of the door he had put up on sawhorses to use as a table, and they'd all dive in at once, screaming, "FOOD!" It was so funny.

One of the poor people got really upset because he was poor and took it out on me, yelling and screaming that I was stealing garbage from his spot. Daniel came running, ready to tackle the guy but stopped, frozen with fear, when the poor guy picked up a rusty muffler and swung it over his head. "I'm a workin' man!" he shouted, "I'm working here in the dump, trying to get some food for my family." Inside his mind I could see him turning over, going from normal to crazy. The dump guys finally came out of the trailer, where they watch TV all day, with some crowbars to chase him off.

Most of the poor people were normal, though. They were used to being poor, but just started coming to the dump because they had gotten poorer after the taxes went up or after they lost their job at a gas station. The worst poor people were the ones who used to have money. They really went crazy. I hoped that after Daniel became afraid we'd stop going to the dump, but he really wanted that Americium-241. We just went earlier in the day, while the poor people were still asleep on their couches, dreaming along with an infomercial or the national anthem on TV. It was fine after that, except for one time a black lady yelled at me for stepping on a pie plate she thought was a collector's item.

It took all month to get 5000 smoke detectors, plus a few things from the hospital. Daniel spread them out over the basement and put me to work plucking the little silver bit of Americium-241 out of each of the detectors. I wore a nose mask that Daniel wasn't sure would work, rubber gloves, a smock. I used tweezers and a big magnifying glass connected to the table. Daniel worked on the other end of the basement—we kept the material in different piles so it wouldn't achieve critical mass and kill us.

The day Geri was laid off she nearly found out what were up to. Her sadness and anger preceded her into the driveway by nearly a minute, so I told Dad that I heard the car and we rushed upstairs, just in time to slam the door to the basement behind us and nonchalantly stand in front of it, while still wearing our masks and smocks.

"Hi boys," Mom said. She carried a cardboard box full of little doodads from her cubicle with her. A frame with a picture of me from the two weeks I was in Little League stuck out of the top. Her misery evaporated as she took us in. "What are you two doing?"

"Ships in bottles!" Dad said.

"Model trains!" I said, because that is what Dad was thinking right before he changed his mind.

"Ships in bottles . . ." he started.

"They make up the body of the model trains, you see," I explained to Mom. "I'm learning how to reduce the resonant vibrations by altering the track gauge so the bottles don't chip or crack."

"Indeed," said Dad.

Genius stuff, thought Mom, then she said, "I lost my job today. No severance package." She tried another smile. "I hope these shipping trains in bottles aren't too expensive."

"They're not, dear."

"I got a grant from the Department of Defense!" I said. They laughed at that, Dad a little too hard.

I slipped down to the basement to let my parents have their fight about money in peace.

I was getting pretty bored with the dump and a rat almost bit Daniel, so we stopped going. Dad continued to leave early in the day, leaving me with Geri, who started vacuuming the carpets a lot. I mean she did it every day. She called me downstairs to move the furniture and everything. Daniel got me a reprieve one day by taking me with him to the UPS building. I waited by the loading dock with him.

"What are we waiting for? Did you buy a bunch of smoke detectors?" I asked him so he wouldn't know I knew that he bought commercial grade uranium online.

"No, I bought commercial grade uranium online. Perfectly legal." About ten minutes later, he signed for his uranium and put the box in the trunk of his car. Then we drove to the FedEx shipping center a few blocks away. There he answered to "Jerry Wallace," Mom's maiden name, and quickly flashed her old passport that he had put his picture on and then re-laminated to claim another box. That one went on my lap for the drive home. I wasn't too happy about that because it was heavy and radioactive. Since the sample was only twenty percent Uranium-235 I didn't have to be that worried, but you know, testicles.

He parked the car a block from the house and we cut through the Pasalaquas' so that we ended up on the side of the house. I squirmed through the basement window Daniel left open, then dropped down to the floor. Daniel walked the block back to get the first box, which I placed against the western wall, and then the second box, which I put against the opposite wall. Our Americium-241 loads were north and south, of course. Upstairs, Geri was watching one of those shows where your neighbor paints your living room orange.

Once we had the uranium, we were back in business. I pretended to join the chess club so that Daniel and I could drive around to get the rest of our supplies. Ever since the ferry across the sound to Bridgetown exploded thanks to sabotage, downtown

Port Jameson was really suffering economically, so it was easy to buy some hydrofluoric acid from the glass etching guy, except that he was napping when we came by so we had to bang on the doors till he woke up. We poured it over our samples to make uranium tetrafluoride. I'm not a genius or anything, I'm just telling you what Dad was thinking. He got the recipe out of some old hippie magazine called *Seven Days*, and his schooling took care of the details.

Anyway, getting to uranium tetrafluoride was the easy part. The basement's ventilation was too poor to handle the fluorine gas we would need to create uranium hexafluoride, and once we got that we still had to separate the U-235 we needed from the junk U-238. The hippie magazine was no help there. It said: "Fill a standard-size bucket one-quarter full of liquid uranium hexafluoride. Attach a six-foot rope to the bucket handle. Now swing the rope (and attached bucket) around your head as fast as possible. Keep this up for about forty-five minutes. Slow down gradually, and very gently put the bucket on the floor." That's funny because except for this one thing, the article wasn't a joke.

Dad thought he could sneak into his old job, but security was tightened after the tuition riots, and all his old cronies had also been laid off and escorted from campus. They didn't even get to pack up their stuff—their little toys and family photos were mailed to them afterwards. Our uranium tetra-fluoride wasn't exactly improving with age either. The next morning, Geri was at her networking club downtown. Dad checked me for hair loss and melanoma, made me some eggs, and then left in the car. Two hours later he came back home on foot and with shoes full of smelly hundred dollar bills. In the basement, Dad handed me a copper pipe and told me to smack him in the head with it, hard, but not too hard, a few times.

"And watch the teeth, Lovebug."

So I did.

Dad gave me the credit card and had me buy a centrifuge on eBay from my computer while he lay on the couch and told Mom some story about two big black guys carjacking him.

We bubbled the fluorine gas into our uranium tetrafluoride to get uranium hexafluoride and for safety's sake did it in the pool shed. Then all we had to do was get a jar of calcium pills from the vitamin store in the mall, crush them to powder, and add it to the uranium hexafluoride. The reaction was pretty neat; it sizzled and smelled like a playground jungle gym. Then we had calcium fluoride, which just looks like salt, and flakes of U-235. We separated that with a colander, and just used hammers to smash the U-235 filings together. Dad did half, then he sent me with the rest of the gunk to the basement to hammer together my U-235 mass.

Are you getting all this? I'm sorry if you're bored, but building your own nuclear bomb may be important for your future later. We're almost at the good part.

Daniel dug the old garden gnome out of the garage and used a blowtorch to open it at the seams. He cut open a tennis ball and put the two sub-critical masses of Americium-241 on opposite ends of it, sticking them to the inside of the ball with rubber cement. That went into the gnome's head. One of the two sub-critical masses of U-235 went right below it and the other into the gnome's base. Then he took apart one of my remote control cars (the cool Sidewinder Neon that does wheelies and 360s, if you're into radio control). One of the servos and the battery box were wedged into the gnome too. All Dad had to do was press a button on the controller. The tennis ball would be squeezed together, making the Americium go critical. That would send the U-235 mass in the head crashing through all the Styrofoam noodles we packed into the body of the gnome and into the U-235 mass in the base, and then that would go critical too, setting off a one-megaton explosion.

"Dad, maybe we should take the batteries out of the radio control," I said. He nodded. "Yeah . . ." he said, slowly, "but you can never find triple-As when you need them."

"I'll hang on to them for you."

"Okay, Herb. Don't misplace them."

Once we put the gnome back on the lawn and achieved neighbor-hood nuclear superiority, there were only two things left to do.

Tell the world, and declare independence. And tell Mom.

2

We had to tell Geri first because her laptop was the only one with an anony-fax/modem. She used to like to send cranky faxes to different companies about there not being enough filling in a Pop-Tart or whatever, to get coupons for free stuff. We had a lot of faxes to send too. Daniel paced the house, trying to decide what to tell her first. *Hi Geri. I love you. That's why I want to send peace treaties to all the members of the Brotherhood of Evil Nations. Also, I built a nuclear bomb and possibly irradiated Herbert.* Or would the bomb news be a better lead? *Honey, you know I only want what's best for you and Herbie, and in this topsy-turvy world, I really feel that we need a one-megaton nuclear weapon. It's not even half a Hiroshima. Don't worry about breaking the law, we're our own country now. And a nuclear power to boot!*

When Mom came home from running her last errands as an

American, Dad quickly made his decision. "Hi Geri," he said, then kissed her on the cheek. "Borrowing your laptop. Need to fax some resumes. C'mon, Herb, help your old man with something for a change."

I had a whole bunch of ideas for what to call our new country—Nuketown, Gnomeville, New America—but Dad just said "Weinbergia" and that was that. So much for democracy, I guess, but I didn't get to name the United States either. He wrote up a quick one-page treaty, offering peace and free trade to any signatory. Then we started faxing, thanks to numbers we found on different government websites or *The CIA World Factbook*. We did ten numbers at once, and with only 140 other countries, we were done in no time. Of course, most of the foreign countries were in different time zones, so who knows how many faxes our treaty would be buried under in the morning? Maybe some Mongolian janitor would think we were joking, sign the treaty on behalf of The People's Republic of The Second Floor Utility Closet, and start his own national movement by mistake.

Or on purpose. Like you.

"Okay, now we'll . . ." Daniel said.

"Tell Ge . . . uh, Mom?" It's hard to call my parents Mom and Dad sometimes. I hear them thinking of themselves, and one another, by their real names all the time.

"Yes." Then he blinked the thought away, still afraid of Geri. "No, we need a press release first!" Dad posed, hands over the keyboard, ready to create his very own Declaration of Independence. "Herbie, you think we should mention the A-bomb?"

"Mmm, not yet," I said. I was worried about snipers.

It was easy enough to find email addresses and fax numbers to the only TV station near Port Jameson, the one that had nightly news in between all the *M*A*S*H* and *Seinfeld* reruns. Port Jameson doesn't have a daily paper, but it does have a weekly, *The Herald-Times-Beacon*. My picture was in it last year when I won the

Brainstormers Academic Bowl trophy for the district. I could have gone to State up in Albany too, but I get sick on long bus rides, so I took a dive on a few questions about physics, ironically enough. Looked like my picture was going to be in the paper again.

Daniel wrote up the press release, and recited it in a loud and goofy "Greetings And Salutations" voice as he composed. "I, High King Daniel the First of Weinbergia, do hereby claim the property that was once known as 22 Hallock Road as my demesne and grange, free and independent from all law or governmental incursions of the United States of America . . ." It was funny, like an old cartoon. So I decided not to tell him that Mom had come home and was downstairs listening to his voice booming through the drop ceiling.

King Daniel continued, "And the brave people of Weinbergia, in the spirit of peace and the brotherhood of all men and women, propose to offer the olive branch of peace to the many and varied warring nations. Let our example guide you all in a quest for understanding and human rights. But be aware, the Kingdom and Realm is prepared to defend itself against interlopers and enemies external and in . . ."

"What the hell are you doing, Dan?" It was Mom, in the doorway, bemused. Dad didn't quite know what to say. He wanted to call her his beautiful Queen and make it seem like a joke so she would laugh and all would be back to normal.

Daniel wasn't even sure why we had built that bomb after all, except to make him feel that he was in control of things. That under his roof, he had some power.

Dad smiled. "Remember how we used to be, back in college? Protesting apartheid, living with Crazy Rob in the vegan house?"

Geri just raised an eyebrow. "You're not . . . writing our congressperson, are you? They'll send the FBI here for sure. You can't fool around like that anymore, not since the wars," she said, more annoyed than worried.

Dad quickly hit the return key, and stood up. "Oh no, nothing like that. Let's have lunch."

The FBI was at the Weinbergian border by the time I was eating my post-lunch ice cream sandwich. They didn't invade. It was a recon mission, two agents. They asked the Pasalaquas if Daniel was nuts. The Cases they asked if Daniel was an alcoholic, recently divorced, or "one of those hippie types." An agent asked the Levines if Daniel had ever said anything anti-Semitic. Tanya, the wife, asked, "Anti-Semitic? Like what?" The agent suggested, "Well, something like 'I hate the Jews' or 'You're a dirty Jew,' perhaps?" Tanya just shut the door on him.

The feds left after taking a peek at the catalogs Geri left behind in the mailbox, and parked a few blocks away. When the coast was clear, our border station (the porch) was besieged by foreign nationals.

"Yo Danny! You in there!" Joe Pasalaqua shouted through the screen door. A few feet away Nick Levine parted the top of the bushes obscuring the dining room window and peered in. "I don't see anyone. Are they home?"

"The car's here," Tommy Case pointed out. He was on our lawn, right by our little garden gnome NORAD, actually. "They must be home." Nobody in Port Jameson walks anywhere, it's true. "Let's just call."

"What if the lines are tapped, Tommy?" Nick asked.

"What if the feds have a parabolic antenna pointed at us from three blocks away?" Tommy said.

"Hey, Dan-NEEEE!" Joe called out.

My father was in the bathroom. Geri opened the door but kept the screen door closed because she didn't like Joe because he was a garbage man.

"Hello?"

"The FBI just came to my house to ask about your husband."

"Ohmigod," Mom said like it was one word, then quickly shut the door. The three men laughed as the shriek of "Daaaaaan!" went up inside the house.

I was in my room upstairs, reading comic books and minds.

Dad was finally ready, after almost puking. He smoothed his shirt with his palms, slipped the radio control into his pocket, and walked across the dining room and kitchen, smiling at Geri rather than answering her, then headed out onto the lawn to shoo the interlopers off of our ancestral lands.

"Howdy boys," Dan said, arms held out wide, the radio control looking conspicuously suspicious (that almost rhymes, I like that) in his right hand. "I'm going to need to ask you to get off my lawn and step to the curb."

The men did so, walking backwards to keep from turning their backs on Dad. Tommy Case was really worried, Joe Pasalaqua had already decided that he could do one of his old wrestling moves on Dad and take him out if he had to, and Nick Levine was wondering if somehow LSD was involved, and if he should just go back home before something bad happened.

"If you would like to enter the Kingdom of Weinbergia, I'm afraid you'll have to apply for a visa first. You can fax an application," said my dad. Then he laughed.

"Oh Lord, you're insane!" That was Levine.

Tommy Case nodded toward the remote, "What do you have there, Daniel?"

"This is my Department of Defense. I don't mind telling you it's a trigger for a one-megaton nuclear weapon."

"Bullcrap," Joe said.

"Is there anyone we can call for you, Daniel? Do you have a doctor? Has your health insurance lapsed?" Nick said.

"That looks a lot like a toy, Dan." That was Tommy.

"It's home brew, yes, but I don't need much."

"C'mon, whole countries can't build nukes, Danny!" said Joe.

"Sure they can," Daniel said. "It's that they can't build nuclear weapons powerful enough to compete with US standard. And they can't create an intercontinental delivery system. Weinbergia needs neither."

"I do not believe there is a nuclear weapon anywhere near here," said Nick.

"Eh, there's probably one on the submarine under the Long Island Sound," said Joe, then he laughed his little fake tough guy *heh-heh-heh.*

"Why would you start your own country? Why arm yourself? Are you in a militia? I mean, you have such a nice house, a smart son. I know you've been having some financial problems . . ." asked Nick, casting a glance at the beat-up old station wagon.

Dad's eyes widened. "Why? Why won't you declare independence! This country is going down the tubes. We're fighting forty wars with forty countries for no reason."

"Now that is not true," said Tommy sharply. "We need to protect ourselves from outside threats."

"Well, so do I."

"That is not the same. Look at Canada, they could attack us at any moment. They're all perched on the border. They don't think like we do. They're jealous."

"And Syria," said Nick. "Those people are all insane. Mexico too. Didn't Mexico threaten to cut off their oil pipeline?"

"That was *after* we started funding the New Villa Army."

"We have every right to make sure our friends are secure," Nick said.

"Shaddup, shaddup," said Joe. "I don't like the wars either, but c'mon Danny, you don't have a bomb, and if you do, someone's just gonna shoot you in your sleep." With that Joe stepped back onto the lawn, and Nick and Tommy followed.

"I'm sure you're upsetting Geri, Dan," said Nick.

"And think of Herbert," said Tommy.

"Back off!" Dad said, pointing his remote at them. "What is it about you Americans? You threaten me every day with your wars and weaponry, but can't stand the fact that anyone else in this world shows a little independence."

"Don't you badmouth America, Daniel. We have men overseas, fighting for your freedoms!" Nick said, his anger rising. "You know, I noticed you didn't fly the flag on the Fourth this year."

"Or on Flag Day!" said Tommy.

"Are you being paid off by the Mexicans?" Nick asked.

"I bet it's Brazil! Didn't you go to Brazil," said Tommy, raising his arms and twitching his fingers in the quote-mark gesture, "*on vacation* last year?"

"That was Barbados, Tom."

"Barbados recently refused a request to use their airspace, you know," Nick said.

"Given what happened to the last few countries to let us use their airspace, I could see why," Daniel said.

"Given what happened to the last few countries that refused, Daniel, you'd think they'd be happy to allow our men to fly safely over their skies," Nick said. "Unless they had some sort of agent planning nuclear blackmail!"

"My God, you're a traitor!" Tommy declared. "Let's get that remote away from him right now!"

Both Tommy and Nick turned to Joe, hoping he'd be the one to attack Dad. He just shrugged.

"Listen. I've seen the garbage you people throw away," Joe said. He was coming to his own political conclusion even as he was speaking. "It's disgusting, a waste. Whole families can live out of one of your garbage cans, Tommy, and you know what, since the wars started after 9/11, they have been. I don't care about foreign policy. I just want everyone to leave everyone else alone. But if you really built a bomb, Danny . . . that's messed up. What are you gonna do anyway, set it off if someone steps on your grass?" He shrugged big.

"I'm going to go home," Tommy said, "and I'm going to get my gun. You hear me Daniel? I own a gun!"

Daniel shrugged big this time. Nick sneered as Tommy strode off. "This isn't a joke, traitor. You're in a boatload of trouble. . ." He stopped as the news van for TV-66, the local station, turned the corner and idled by the Western front. Its transmission pole, with its dish top, was as high as the window I was watching my dad from. Dad felt a rush of excitement; he had a bit of a crush on Deborah Stanley-Katz, one of TV-66's news anchors. They sent her out for the biggest stories, like medical waste washing up on the beach, or sad black people who had their welfare taken away. One time she interviewed the governor, and Dad liked the way her blazer would go down to her waist, all snug and. . . .

Out popped Rich Pazzaro, the fat weatherman who also did the stories about pie-eating contests and the circus coming to town. Inside the van, a bored-looking cameraman was leisurely getting his rig together. This was not going to be a big deal to-night.

"How-deeeee!" Rich said, doing his weather shtick. He said "How-deeee!" to things like hurricanes and chimpanzees on TV. "Which one of you is the king of Weintraubia?"

Joe laughed and hiked his thumb at Dad. "Right here, here's your lordship."

Daniel smiled as Rich crossed the border and entered our country. "I'm Daniel, I'm the king of Wein*bergia*." He offered his left hand to Rich, who juggled his microphone to shake. "Welcome to my homeland." At that moment, Tommy's long stride took him to our border. He had a pistol and leveled it at Dad sideways. "Die, traitor!" Dad pulled hard on Rich's hand and dragged the fat guy in front of him.

"Stay back, I have a human shield!" Dad declared, wrapping the arm holding the radio control around Rich's neck. Rich, suddenly frantic, waved with his free hand for his cameraman, but when the guy came rushing out without the camera, Rich waved him back on the car.

"Rich Pazzaro!" said Tommy. "My wife loves you!" He kept the gun pointed at Dad, or really at Rich's chest. The bullet would go right through it, probably, he figured.

"Uhm . . . listen," Rich said. Dad wasn't choking him, but he was a little short of breath from being in the hold. "I just want . . . an interview." The camera operator crossed the border and shouldered his camera. "If that gun's loaded," Rich said, "we can go live."

Rich and Dad both looked at Tommy hopefully. Tommy nodded.

"Okay," said the cameraman, "we've got to wait a minute for the clearance, but the truck is already patched through."

"Can I get . . . a little . . . background . . . on you, Your Highness?"

"You can call me Daniel, Mr. Pazzaro."

"He's a traitor, what else do you need to know?" Tommy asked.

"Why don't you lower the gun?" Nick asked.

"Why don't you just leave if you don't want to be on television?" Tommy asked back. "Right Joe . . ." He turned to look at Joe, who had already turned around and was halfway home.

"Live in ten, Rich," the cameraman said.

"Married?"

"Yes, my wife loves you, remember?"

"Yes, I'm married," Daniel said.

"Oh no you are not!" It was Mom. She had been watching from the kitchen, afraid to go outside. Now she was going to defect.

"Four . . . three . . ." Then the cameraman counted "two . . . one" silently.

"We're here . . . live . . . hostage situation. There is a gun pointed at me by . . ."

Tommy leaned in to address the mic, and stared into the camera. "Thomas Case, proud American."

"And I . . . am in the clutches . . . of?" Rich said, trying to bend his arm so that Dad could talk into the microphone.

"You are the guest of King Daniel the First of Weinbergia."

Mom rushed by in the background of the shot. Rich called out to her, "Ma'am . . . you are—"

"Leaving!" she said, getting into the car. She slammed the door hard, and peeled out of the driveway, kicking gravel into America. She wasn't even thinking of me as she pulled onto Hallock and drove off. The cameraman panned right to get a shot of the car.

"Ahem, proud American here!" said Tommy, and the camera panned back.

Rich, his face reddening, pointed the mic at Nick. "Who are you . . . with?"

Nick nodded toward Tommy. "I'm with him . . ." Then he looked at the gun, which Tommy was having a hard time holding steady. "Uhm . . . I mean, no. I'm with America! You know, I support the president." He nervously turned on his heel and, not knowing what else to do, saluted the camera in case the president was watching.

"Let me explain," said Daniel, loosening his grip on Rich just a bit. Rich obliged by pulling the mic back toward him. "I have constructed a nuclear weapon using legal materials found on the Internet. I have declared my independence from the United States of America and have sent peace treaties to all nations that the US is currently at war with, occupying, or bound to by treaty agreements. I want peace and freedom for myself and my nation. I also open my borders to anyone else interested in ending these horrible wars and leading a life where we don't have to be afraid of losing our jobs, or of saying the wrong thing and being interrogated, and where our kids won't grow up to be drafted. However, I do not rule out the use of nuclear weapons in achieving our aims of peace. Thank you very much. Press conference over!" With that Dad yanked hard and pulled Rich off his feet, and dragged him back into the house. Rich, always the professional, shouted into the mic, "This has been a live report for TV-66! Rich Pazzaro, saying for perhaps the last time, how-deeeeeee!" The mic cord stretched to its limit at the porch, and Rich let it go.

The camera turned back to Tommy and Nick, who were standing around like a pair of simpletons. "Should I shoot?" Tommy asked. Nick shrugged, looked into the camera, and said, "God Bless America? Can we get some help? Police? Homeland Security?" The shot faded to black.

Dad made a racket, pushing the door open with his butt and dragging an uncooperative Rich inside with him. "Herbie!" he called out. "Time for lunch! And set a third plate." I came downstairs as he let go of Rich to let him catch his breath.

"What are you going to do to me?"

Dad shrugged. "Well, you can be a reporter or a prisoner of war. Either way, you're getting pizza."

I walked into the room. "Hello?"

"Hi son, meet Rich Pazzaro, from TV."

"Hi."

Rich looked me over, recognizing me. "Brainstormers?"

I nodded. "Yeah." Then to Dad, "Can we eat now?"

"Absolutely." Dad went to the fridge. The little interior light went on as always, then cut out, along with all the other lights and digital clocks, and the air-conditioning.

"They cut the power."

"This means war."

In the distance, sirens and mad thoughts converged upon us.

It was dark except for the occasional helicopter spotlight or flashing red siren. The police had come first, only to be replaced by the FBI, who were in turn replaced by some guys from the local National Guard and big men from Homeland Security. They had an especially sensitive Geiger counter out there, so knew we weren't kidding about having the bomb. That's why we were still alive. The three of us sat on the floor so that we couldn't be seen through the windows, and munched on cold pizza. During the brief interludes of silence within all the barked orders, helicopter rotor noises, and huthut-huts of soldiers taking up positions on our borders, Rich asked us questions.

"So, was this all part of your plan?" he asked Daniel. Rich was expecting Dad to go nuts and end this with some sort of murder-suicide thing.

Daniel shrugged. "Once we're established as a country, we'll have trading partners, we'll be able to live independently."

"But that's not going to happen!" Rich was getting agitated again. His mind was like a wave on the beach. He'd get mad, break up, then collect himself slowly and calmly, only to make another crazed rush for the jetty. "Nobody supports you. You have no idea what CNN, hell, what Fox News, is doing to you! All anyone knows about you is that you have a dirty bomb and that you kidnapped a beloved local weatherman."

"If you'd like to leave, you can," I said. "They won't shoot you. They haven't demanded you be returned yet because they're hoping you'd be able to talk some sense into us."

"How do you know that?"

"I'm a genius," I lied.

"Does anyone want a drink?" Daniel said. "I have some wine, if you want, Mr. Pazzaro?"

"Sure."

"Coke for me."

"It'll be warm, son."

"That's fine."

Dad crawled into the kitchen. Rich leaned in and whispered, "Why are you so calm? Doesn't this frighten you? Don't you think your dad is crazy?"

I shrugged. "Not any crazier than the president." And this is true. I know. I checked.

"We're going to die here."

"No, we're not."

Dad came back, duck-walking and spilling some of my soda. We drank out of our plastic picnic cups silently. The helicopters were making another pass, and would have drowned us out anyway.

Sitting on a floor is a great way to conserve energy, and being surrounded by Army guys really gets the adrenaline running. So at 3 a.m., Dad and I were awake. Dad was starting to get nervous. Would we live to see the sun? Were the other countries even aware of us? Did they even care? Rich was slumped in a corner, sometimes snoring, sometimes waking with a start to ask Dad when he was going to surrender to the inevitable, sometimes to ask me if there was any pizza left. There wasn't, but I made him a peanut butter sandwich with Geri's seven-grain bread. He seemed to like that.

"We should check the email, Dad."

"How?" Rich murmured. He was half-asleep. "No power."

"Mom's laptop has a battery."

"Damn, you're right!" Dad crawled off on his belly. Outside, they started serenading us with very loud banjo music, to try to break our will.

Dad was back in a minute, crawling to us lopsided, with the laptop tucked under one arm. He opened it up and we all gathered around to take in the white glow of the screen. It was good to be around electricity again. The feds had kept the phone on because they wanted to call us tomorrow, and they wanted to see if we would call some terrorists, or Grandma, or somebody like that. We used the old dial-up account and checked our email.

Seventy-three new messages. Cheap mortgages, porn, porn, porn (Dad wished I'd turn away, but I didn't. I was a prince now, after all.) A few folks had seen us on TV and sent us messages, most of them wishing us dead. Porn, porn, enlarge your breasts, free fake college degrees, and Palau.

The Olbiil Era Kelulau, the Senate of the tiny Pacific island of Palau, had agreed to sign the treaty. We were at peace with them. Tomorrow, they'd appeal to the UN on our behalf. Palau was with us, and wanted to open trade talks. They had pearls, coconuts. What did we have, they wanted to know?

We had the bomb. If anyone messed with Palau, we'd destroy Port Jameson. And we had me. There wasn't a secret in the world I couldn't dig out of someone's brain.

Palau is a sunny land full of friendly, cheerful people. In this it is like every other country in the world, except Weinbergia. It's true. Cold, bitter Russians are friendly and cheerful. Terror cells are friendly and cheerful, not as they plot away in dank basements, but when they are with their families and friends, or eating good local food. Women covered head to toe in those nasty veils—the ones who get stoned to death or shot if they go outside with their face showing—they are friendly and cheerful when they're inside or down by a waterhole with the other women, where no men can see. The men who throw the rocks are friendly and cheerful too, even if they're doing it because all their friends are, or because there is a gun to their own backs.

People all over the world are exactly the same. Cheerful and friendly and deathly afraid to act that way because someone will shoot them if they do, so they turn on each other like two dogs at the park. That's what happened on Palau. There's a military base there, American. That's half the reason Palau is its own country instead of just part of Micronesia. I wonder if having Palau would push Micronesia over into being Mininesia. Anyway, the soldiers at the base, friendly and cheerful though they are, like to have sex with local women. When the women get pregnant, the soldiers just hide behind their guns and fences. There are lots of soldiers' babies in Palau, and not a lot of money for them.

The old people, friendly and cheerful and thankful for their grandchildren, have been waiting for a moment for a long time, nearly a generation. When the founding of Weinbergia hit the news, they went out under cover of night to find their elected officials. It's a small country, only 20,000 people or so; the whole government has fewer than 40 people, and they live pretty much like anyone else, except they wear Italian suits with American labels. The old people came to them with gifts of fruit and finely-weaved baskets. Then after a nice meal and sweet dessert, out came the machetes. For the first time ever, Palau's government did something the United States didn't like. Behind the worried debate that morning, even the members of the Olbiil Era Kelulau were secretly friendly and cheerful as they voted to save us. People are cheerful and friendly everywhere. Even here in fabled Weinbergia, where Rich really got into the swing of things with Dad.

The power was back on. Not because of Palau, but because the news media was out in force. Their power generators were too noisy for local ordinance (Tommy Case complained), so the feds turned our juice back on and let the TV cameras tie into our power. The meter was spinning like crazy. *Just one more form of brutal American oppression*, thought Dad, but he was happy and cheerful. We had water too, and they didn't cut our cable either, so we could watch our own house. Rich hogged the webcam all morning and happily detailed the moment-by-moment "hostage drama" that was taking place. He covered the camera lens with the fat palm of his hand when I walked in with some toaster waffles—they were the kind he especially liked, blueberry and bacon bits—but then dug into breakfast with his fists wrapped around the fork and butter knife. It was gripping Web-television, for sure, and after that the major news networks stopped calling Rich a hostage and suggested that he had been won over by our relentless propaganda, or maybe drugs in the waffles.

Rich did come around pretty quickly. By noon he was spread all over the couch and taking calls from around the world from the cell phone one of the Army guys had slipped in through the mail slot.

"Your Highness!" he called out.

"Yeah . . ." I said. He had been asking me stupid questions all morning.

"I meant your Dad, Sport!"

I hate being called Sport or Kiddo or any of those stupid names. Ace. Ace would have been cool. But you have to shoot down a plane or something to be called Ace. I resolved at that moment to start working on it.

From the basement, my father's hollow voice asked what was up.

"It's Hollywood, baby! Want to sell the rights to this?"

"It'll have to be a US/Weinbergian co-production," Daniel shouted.

"I'll see!" Rich shouted back, then more quietly into the phone he explained our demands. He paused, smiling like he was still on TV. Then, "Hello? Hello? How-deee?" He frowned. "Damn. Hey Ace . . ."

Much better. "Yeah?"

"Care for an interview?"

"Sure." I walked over to the couch while Rich picked himself up and diddled with the laptop's webcam in an attempt to get a shot that didn't make him look like a lazy slug. I stood by, wearing a TV commercial kid smile until my cheeks started hurting. Finally, after licking his fingers and running them through his hair (yes, gross), Rich was ready for his remote.

"Rich Pazzaro, embedded in what a small, dangerous family has decided to call Weinbergia," he said in a serious whisper to the world on the other side of the lens. "Day three of America's nuclear crisis. I'm here with young Herbert. His father calls him 'prince' but to his mother, and America, he is a hostage. A human shield." I rolled my eyes.

He leaned back, wrapped an arm around me, and brought me closer to the camera for an intimate shot, then asked, "Do you feel that you're in danger here?"

"Duh!" I said. Then I grabbed the little webcam and twisted it so it pointed out the window. On the laptop screen, I could see a huddle of American soldiers gathered around a TV monitor. They looked up toward the camera when they saw themselves on TV and waved to me and the world.

Rich took the cam back and turned it around for a close-up of himself. "He's a boy who loves his father. That family tie, exploited in a game of nuclear brinksmanship." He turned to me again. "What are your days like here, under siege? Do you miss your school friends?"

"Well, most of them are upstate at computer camp anyway. I think I'm learning more here. I'm also in charge of a lot of stuff.

Did you know that the national bird of Weinbergia is the blue-bird? I declared it so this morning," I said. Nobody is going to shoot a kid who says he likes bluebirds. It's true. I double-checked the brains of everyone outside on the front lines before picking the bird.

"Aaaand," I said, nudging Rich out of the way and sticking my head right up to the camera so I'd look all cute and dis-torted—you know, the way you look reflected in a doorknob or something, "I'm working on our official language, Weinbergian. For example, if I wanted to say, 'Hi, my name is Prince Herbert The First,' I'd say, 'Lo, yo soy nameo izzo Fresh Herbie Primo.' Pretty cool, huh?" I smiled wide for the camera. I'm not a hunk or anything, but I could feel, all over your country, little girls deciding to start fansites about me. A million LiveJournal entries were born.

Fun Facts About Weinbergia

Name: Weinbergia
Telephone area code: 631
Area: 2000 sq. ft. 2 1/2 baths
Land boundaries: United States of America, specifically the Pasalaqua and Case residences
Terrain: Parquet floors
Highest mountain: The tip of Rich Pazzaro's ego
Natural resources: Uranium. Fear. Hope.
Population: 3ish
Population density: 1/666 sq. ft.
Distribution: 100% suburban
Life expectancy: We're trying not to think about that

Capital: King Daniel's not above calling the master bath "the throne room," unfortunately

Flag: Take the McDonald's golden arches on a red background, and turn it upside down so it looks like a W

Government: "As long as you're under my roof, you'll do what I say!"—King Daniel I.

National anthem: "In The Garden of Freedom" (sung to the tune of "In A Gadda-Da-Vida")

Languages: English

Currency: Dollar

Climate: Central air

Religion: Vague liberal agnosticism. Judaism. Known to say "Jesus Christ!" at stupid stuff on TV

Exports: Punditry, fodder

That afternoon, I was nearly lulled to sleep by the clockwork thinking of the first line of soldiers as they turned first to the right, then to the left, rifles high and Dad in their sights as he mowed the lawn on the northern frontier of Weinbergia. The landscapers Mom had hired decided not to come in today and given the politico-legal difficulties we found ourselves in, Dad didn't want to give the US any more ammunition by getting the Terrytown Fire District all mad, too. That's what he said anyway, but deep down he just wanted to test American mettle, and get a little time off from Rich.

So he mowed the lawn, slowly and carefully, back and forth, while forty-five GIs trained their guns on him. At the end of the block, Operations buzzed with contingencies and possibilities. Should we shoot Dan Weinberg and rush the place? Does he have some sort of spoilsport option in place that would set off the bomb if his heart stopped? Is it biometrical? How could it be; the guy's out there in a tank top, white shorts, and sandals with socks? Maybe the kid? What about the kid, what about the children?

What about me? I was scraping the black stuff off of a grilled cheese Rich had tried to make for himself. "Here ya go, Herb," he had said as he knocked on my already-open door and offered me the sandwich, "you're probably hungry, so I thought I'd fix you something."

I hate it when people "fix" food, don't you? Especially when it was as broken as this second-hand sandwich. But I was hungry and it gave me something to do other than fall asleep listening to the droning thoughts of the soldiers outside. That's when the shooting happened. It went like this, in the head of PFC Frank Torres, who's from Brentacre, just a few miles from Port Jameson:

> *Left Left Left Left*
> *Right Right Right Right*
> *Left Left Left Left*
> *Right Right Right Turn onto 347*
> *Left Left Left at the mall*
> *Right Home Where I Started From*
> *Left Left Home At Eighteen*
> *Right Right Back Here*
> *So Close Target Is So Close*
> *Miss Miss Mami Mami*
> *Miss Miss Don't Miss Target*

Then he fired by mistake—a psychic twitch of homesickness and boredom—but missed. My father dropped to the ground, leaving the lawn mower to lurch forward and roll a bit. A couple of slugs tore through it too before a squad leader bellowed,

"*Hold Your Fire!*" The guns stopped, so did the fiery anxiety and whooping joy of the line. Everyone lowered their rifles, vainly hoping that the captain would blame the other guy.

My father hopped back to his feet and, fists curled, marched to the border, nearly smacking into the equally red-faced captain who was up from his lawn chair and ready to scream till his men crapped themselves. They met at right angles and stared, both wide-eyed and huffing like bulls.

My father spoke first. "Can't a man cut the grass in peace?" he demanded, and really, that's all he was thinking. The captain was nonplussed, so Dad turned to the line of troops. "Who shot at me? Which one of you Yankee imperialists shot at me?" He pointed randomly at a guilty-looking soldier. "Was it you?"

"Hey, man, I just shot your mower," he said, defeated. A few heads down, Torres mentally snickered. The captain, Whiting, felt his control of the situation, illusory as it was, slipping away from him, and stepped in the path of my father's pointed finger.

"Mister Weinberg," he started.

"King Daniel."

"Mister Weinberg, please. This could spiral into an . . . incident."

"An international incident! Perhaps even an occurrence. Where's the media now, when you need them? You're all blocking the curb, how am I supposed to use my trimmer later?" my father demanded of nobody in particular.

The squad captain put a hand on Dad's shoulder and said. "I understand. I have a lawn too. Back home." Then he nodded in that way men nod when they want other men to nod back at them. And Dad did. Then both of them looked toward the lawn mower, which just sat there and smoked through its new bullet holes, uselessly.

Dad was back inside for the afternoon, giving his side of the story to Rich and the webcam, while outside, a couple of grunts finished the job with a John Deere helicoptered in from the nearest Home Depot and a pair of hand-clippers. They did it checkerboard-style, going over the lawn twice, except for a couple of feet around the garden gnome.

Overnight, Dad became the hero to billions—he'd stared down the American war machine, brought them to heel, and made them do chores. Captain Whiting was relieved of command overnight and is currently in the brig somewhere, staring in front of a mirror, trying to pee. Almost exactly like me.

3

You think you know what happened. It was all over the news. My mother Geri, sobbing into the cameras, the cult, the fist-fights in the United Nations, the daring raid, Rich's bravery . . . or was it treachery, blah blah blah. But you don't know what happened. What happened is that seven men and four women were at our door the next afternoon, all with pizzas. Rich and Daniel peered at the bunch nervously, with Rich trying to pull off the impossible trick of looking concerned enough to impress Dad and eager enough to impress the federal agents and Army guys he was sure were behind the pizza deliveries.

Actually, all but two of the pizzas were sent by well-wishers who'd seen me chewing on an awful sandwich all night on the cam; the last two were fake deliveries by Adrienne and Kelly, two Port Jamesonites who wanted to come in from the cold. I helped them out by pointing at them through the screen door. "You and you can come in with the pizza, the rest of you . . . thanks but no thanks."

Nobody moved from the positions they had staked out, except for some pimple-faced kid who wobbled a bit, unsure of himself. Nobody listens to kids, you know. "Daaaad," I said.

"What, Herb? Why?"

I didn't need to think of anything clever as Adrienne just smiled widely and pushed the screen door open with her elbow. "How do you do?" she said, "How do you do?" She was older, like my mother, with a big Long Island mop of dyed black curls and bangs. Kelly slipped in right behind her and said "How are ya?" like a normal person. She was pretty normal, twenty-five, high hair, jingly earrings, that sort of thing. Dad closed both the screen and the main door, leaving the rest of the pizza delivery people with nothing else to do except make their way back to America with their pies and take their body-cavity searches like good citizens.

"There's no pizza in either of these," Rich said, annoyed. "Just . . . money."

"American?" Dad asked. Then he turned to the ladies. "That money's no good here."

Adrienne just smiled. "Every country has a store of American dollars. It's the least we could do. We're asylum seekers."

Kelly nodded. "You have to let us stay. It's crazy out there!" And they told their stories, mostly going on about how hard it was to make ends meet. They'd both been unemployed and met in the waiting room of a temp agency, then realized they were only ten miles from the border. Neither of them could find jeans in their size because the manufacturers found it cheaper to make clothing cut for people who didn't actually exist. American men were mean, and lazy in the bedroom. Kelly blushed and shot me an apologetic look as Adrienne explained that, but she was thinking about herself and Rich doing it in front of a weather map! And besides, they thought, they really wanted to be on TV. Ten minutes later I was in the basement, trying to figure out whether the old quilts Mom stored down there were machine washable, while Kelly raided the liquor cabinet and made cocktails for the adults.

Richard—he was calling himself Richard now, because he thought it sounded more presidential, or at least less friendly—interviewed a slightly tipsy Kelly later that night. She's one of those people who just gets very sad when they drink, like there's a dark spring in her heart that just bubbles up to the surface whenever she forgets to pay attention.

"Sometimes," she said, looking down even though Rich reminded her three times to look at him (and four times to "try to look sexy") "—it's just, you know, hard. You go to work, stop to get some take-out on the way home, and watch other people live lives you can't, on television. I don't even have anyone to shout at me in my living room, or to say funny things. You know?"

"Uhm. Sure." Rich ad-libbed. "Do you have a political agenda that you're hoping to carry out?"

"Well, I'm definitely against violence and nuclear proliferation. I guess I wanted to find some like-minded people."

"You came to the wrong place!" Dad shouted from the kitchen.

"He's right. Weinbergia is a nuclear power," Rich said.

"Yeah, but you guys aren't going to use it. I mean, it would be suicide."

"How's that any different," Dad shouted again, "from America?"

Kelly looked at Rich, confused. Rich just nodded, a content-free nod. Yes, I acknowledge your existence. That kind of thing. Kelly finally shrugged and said, "I guess I just trust King Daniel more than the president. He seems kinder, more honest. Like a normal person. He doesn't wear a tie just because he knows he's going to be on television. I like that."

"So is that why you came here, to Weinbergia?"

"Well, I always wanted to go abroad."

Kelly, with her cow eyes and hollow voice, wasn't what you'd call telegenic. She came off as brainwashed, but really, she was simply emerging from years of American brainwashing. Kelly was confused and anxious—she may not have to go to work every day anymore, just to have enough money to buy cute shoes and Healthy Choice entrées, just so that she could find some guy who would smile and lift things for her between football games, just so she could have a kid who'd grow up proud to be an American just because that's where he plopped out of her. A kid who'd in turn do the same thing. This wasn't the tickertape-parade-and-celebrity-hugs freedom she was expecting. It was a dull, throbbing freedom; more like a headache.

"How do you feel about being this close to what some call a terrorist nuclear device?" Richard asked. "Are you afraid?"

"Not any more than I was this morning. Forty wars on forty countries, that's us. That was me. Not now though. Terrorists are supposed to be everywhere. That's why they search your car on the Long Island Expressway, right?" She shrugged. "I mean, with everybody watching now, what are they gonna do, storm in and kill us? For what?"

"For having a nuclear device out on the lawn," Richard said. "Don't you think? Do you think that anyone should have the right to just threaten us with nukes?"

"No, I don't. I guess I really don't," Kelly said. "That's why I'm here." She and Richard stared at each other. He really wasn't a very good reporter, and Kelly mentally scratched him off her sex list. The interview was over and an awkward silence descended over all Weinbergia, except for the kitchen where Dad was trying to impress Adrienne by making an omelet. He was banging pots around like some ugly American.

All you probably saw of this on the news—unless you subscribed to the website anyway—was Kelly's dead eyes and her murmuring, "Well, I always wanted to go abroad." It's one of those dumb tricks the media use to make people they don't like look like morons, but they forgot that lots of people felt just like Kelly. With all the wars, and all the ruined diplomatic relationships, and with the five-hour-long check-in lines at the airports, millions of people wanted to go abroad and couldn't. For a few of them, for almost of enough of *you* out there, you got the idea. Go abroad where it counts. Right up here.

Feel that, the tapping on your temple? That's me. Tap tap. Go abroad in your head, that's the message at least some people heard. That's what Kelly did, by emigrating to Weinbergia, and she wasn't the last. People, being generally happy, have a weird way of looking at the television or the Internet: they read something and decide that it secretly means something else, and they think that only they can see through the lies of the media. Their own opinions they've come to thanks to logic, or hard-earned experience, or Jesus showing up at the foot of their bed and telling them what time it is. Everyone else? Well, they're dupes and morons, emotional wrecks, or people who actually think *Jesus* showed up at the foot of their bed to tell them what time it is. And media people love this. Rich told me once, "As long as we get complaints from both the liberals and conservatives, we know that we're reporting the news right." That the media thinks it is telling the truth because everyone thinks they're lying—no matter what the news actually said and no matter what the audience originally thought—doesn't make much sense to me, but I checked a few heads over in the city and, geez, Rich was right.

So anyway, it was some vanishingly small percentage of the people who watched the interview, but they got the message: go abroad in your heads. Weinbergia's approval ratings plummeted, but the Great Hajj began. The next morning, the Long Island Expressway and Route 25A were choked with, well, Dad called them hippies. There were plenty of those: guys with long beards, ready smiles, and laid-back personalities. You know that movie where the rock band says of its amplifiers, "Well, these go to eleven"? These guys' emotions only went up to eight. There were women hippies too, mostly boiling under a happy surface (but happy again, under the boiling). Most people weren't hippies though: there were lots of nerds, some crazier than others. Tax cheats, college kids who made up their own languages in their spare time, a woman who called herself Doctress Arcologia who wanted to build a treehouse in the oak outside my window; in exchange she'd give us exclusive rights to market her perpetual motion machine: a generator hooked up to a motor.

Adrienne gave herself the job of border guard and decided to keep out anyone who she thought might want to sleep with or kill Dad. She mostly got it right too. Dad was a bit too busy to welcome his new subjects; one of the people who slipped past the border—he looked kind of like John Travolta, except fatter and dressed in unconvincing tie-dye—handed my father a summons and then vanished back behind the line of American troops.

I had heard his thoughts coming, but I was too busy with Kelly to stop my Dad from taking the letter. Kelly had cornered me right outside of the upstairs bathroom.

"Hi there. I'm Kelly," she said.

"Hi. Herb."

She smiled, "Can I call you Prince Herbert?" Her mind was a dizzy array of anxieties and what she thought were Really Deep Thoughts (*Men are simple creatures, driven by appetites; women are driven by duty.*) streaked with a low-level adrenaline rush. I liked her though, because she wasn't thinking what most adults do when they strike up a conversation with a kid. You know what I'm talking about, unless you're a kid. Then you probably just suspect it:

Aw look. The little person can talk. I wonder if it can say anything interesting if I ask it how old it is.

Hee hee, look at that little moron go!

But she didn't think that; she only thought, *I'm so lonely . . . and excited.* So of course I let her call me Prince Herbert. She tried a crooked curtsy, and I patted the air with my hand like a TV king might, because that's what she wanted me to do.

"Prince Herbert, can you tell me something?" she asked me. "What's the plan?"

"The plan?"

"Yes, I mean, what's next. You can't live in this house forever, not being part of America."

"Why not? People live in their houses all their lives and *are* part of America. And they do it without UN recognition."

Then she started up with that *moron* thinking. "You don't understand. I mean, you ever heard that saying 'No man is an island'? You can't just separate yourself from a country."

"Countries do it all the time. America did it in the first place."

"America had an army, kid. And it has a bigger one now. You just can't go challenging the world's largest superpower." So much for Prince Herbert.

"Well, that's what we're doing. Heck, that's what you're doing, Kelly. Why did you even emigrate?"

"I thought you'd have some answers!" She looked away from me and then out the window, brushing the curtain aside with her cheek to look at the swarm of weirdos snaking across the lawn, and the cordon of troops surrounding them. "I should have just stayed home."

"Well, what kind of answers were you expecting?" I knew the answer already, and also knew that she couldn't put it into words. The questions were there, though, like the flavored glop inside an unlabeled Valentine's Day chocolate—even after you bite into it, you don't know what the hell you're eating. There were no answers for her; she wasn't even really looking for them. She just wanted to hear some set of words that would attack the glop and make it vanish, like antimatter.

"Well, you just seem so happy. How could you be happy knowing what will happen?"

Why was I so happy? I didn't really feel all that happy; never did. I mean it's not like I could move into my own apartment or anything. Even back when I kept a diary, I never wrote about being happy, except when recording what other people were thinking or experiencing, and they were generally happy about dumb stuff, like a football game or someone agreeing with them.

I guess I just liked the craziness of it all. That answer wasn't going to satisfy Kelly's brainglop so I did what I usually do at chess club. Kids aren't really very good chess players, except for the occasional supernerd, so it's no use reading their mind for the proper response to the moves—they don't know what the hell they're doing either. So what I'd do is poke around the mindscape of the club sponsor, or the guy in the next town who had all these chess books and who subscribed to all the chess magazines, and who always had three or four games going in his living room, and get the answer from him.

So I checked Dr. Phil and Dr. Laura and the social worker from school who asked me once why I never applied myself and The pope and Billy Graham and Tom Hanks and all sorts of other people that make their living giving advice, or just being warm and giving their opinions, and came up with a response.

"Oh Kelly," I said, reaching out to touch her hand, "it'll all be all right."

"But—"

"It'll all work out for the best."

"They have so many gun—"

"Everything happens for a reason." I smiled a cereal commercial smile.

The glop in Kelly's brain melted and steamed out her ears, deflating her tension like a balloon. She leaned down and kissed me on the forehead. "You're right," she said. She was about to say something else but then turned to see as our new resident aliens marched up the steps by the dozen to use the upstairs restroom, full of pardon mes and I really gotta goes and ohmygod this isn't as big as I thought it would be on TVs, and is this the right doors. "Herb-AY, my man!" one very very white guy said; he was in the lead and held out a palm for me to high-five.

I left him hanging.

Downstairs, Adrienne and Dad were frowning over the summons. In the corner, Rich was taping them. He had a new assistant, a teenager I recognized as a bagger from Pathmark—his job was apparently to take the lampshade off my mother's old lamp and hold it up behind the camera to make sure Dad squinted from the light, and that the rest of the room was cut up with stripes of shadow.

"Herbert, we have to talk," said Adrienne, whose brain was spinning with crazy thoughts of being my new mother. She saw herself in flickering black and white, wearing an apron and handing out bagged lunches to me and Rich, who in her little daydream was wearing dress shorts. Then out come the servants to drape a mink around her shoulders and place a tiara on her head. Weirdo.

"Your mother has filed a custody suit. Don't worry, your father is going to fight this all the way to the Supreme Court."

"No, I'm not," said Dad, "I'm going right to the General Assembly of the United Nations. This isn't a matter for family court, if they want Herb, they'll need to extradite him."

"Extradite me!" Okay, so it didn't mean what I thought it did at that very second. I checked Dad's mind for the actual meaning of the word, but really didn't feel all that much better.

"You're not going to go anywhere, Herbie, don't you worry," Adrienne said. I shot my Dad a look, and he shrugged. Then he announced, regally, "Nobody is going to leave Weinbergia against his or her will! We are a sovereign nation!"

"That's right!" shouted whoever was using the downstairs bathroom. A smattering of applause floated throughout the house like lost butterflies.

"Hear hear," said Adrienne, getting another stare from Dad. Then Rich stepped forward and pointed his camera at me. "Do you miss your mother?"

"Yes . . . uh, I mean—" and that was that. I knew what he wanted to hear, *I knew it*, and it still just came flying out of my mouth anyway. I did miss her. Weinbergia was already filling up with hippies and morons (some lady with long gray hair and a tie-dyed skirt even got on her knees behind me to wave into the camera, I'm sure you saw it a million times on TV), the air outside stank of diesel fuel and ozone and I really just wanted things to be like they were before—when Dad and I were building the bomb. When we had time together and when my mother smiled to see us hanging out all the time.

So I said yes and the world heard it. There's a big difference between being able to know what's going to happen and being able to do something about it. I could feel them, the entire weight of the American military, the media, the factories, the great thinkers, all of them, arraying against Weinbergia. The first line of cordons were only scrubs—expendables—but beyond that the Special Operators lurked. They were holed up in the Red Berry Bed & Breakfast on the other side of the highway, toward downtown. Spiderholes had been sunk in the Cases' backyard, just in case we tried to tunnel our way out. Under the waters of the Long Island Sound, and off the south shore too, submarines bobbed slightly under the waves. Every plane that passed overhead, even the commercial flights, heck, even the skywriters promising GREAT DEALS, QUOGUE CHEVROLET, were stuffed with air marshals. In a spiral pattern, cutting across Suffolk County, Connecticut, out into The City and even to the tip of Orient Point, where a ferry sometimes goes, there were soldiers, their eyes and guns pointed toward little Weinbergia. Beyond even them, in factories in refineries, good old blue-collar workers bent over their machines and smiled into the spray of sparks spat out of their equipment—overtime, double time, maybe even triple time. And they were all coming for me, fueled and driven on by Geri, my mother, and her nasal shrieking for me on every television screen in the world. "My boy, I want my beautiful boy, home, safe with his mother! Home with me!" she cried out, and her whining landed on the broad backs of the world like a slaver's whip.

And there was nothing I could do about it. I read the minds of the generals, nothing. They'd sewn America up tight. I checked the military minds of foreign powers—the only option in North Korean dreams was pulling the trigger on the bomb out on the lawn. Paranoids, the ones with those tinfoil hats (they don't work, by the way) and a million back-up plans, they were out of bright ideas. So were the military historians, the Warhammer players, the Dungeons & Dragons nerds, everyone. No one had any answers, except one.

Get used to being pushed around by America.

4

Of course, one thing you can do if you're playing chess—and if you're actually playing chess in a dumb movie with a really dramatic script or something—is just kick over the board and declare victory. We didn't kick over the board; everyone else did it for us. Vermont went especially crazy. The counties full of snowy hillbillies that make up what they call the Northeast Kingdom declared itself a literal kingdom, and the towns of Brattleboro and Marlboro seceded, formed a pair of communes, and then merged into one city-state. But that was Vermont, so nobody really noticed except that Unilever issued a press release stating that Ben & Jerry's ice cream production wouldn't be affected, and the US sent some troops to make sure none of the highways were blocked by either the hippies or the rednecks.

The bigger news was the explosion, of course. Gray McGrath, who owned a big farm in Springettsbury Township, Pennsylvania, didn't have a nuclear bomb, but he had plenty of gasoline and fertilizer, and a few handy flatbeds on which to arrange the stuff on the borders of his acreage. He announced that his farm was seceding from the US and that McGrathia would be a new homeland for "the white race" via his website. He also especially requested "blonde-haired white women," the "proud kind" he said, to report to McGrathia in order to help "build the race." He even promised to "treat" them "all very nice" especially if they could show that they were of "French Huguenot extraction." He was also very worried, he said about "secret Puerto Ricans" with light skin sneaking into his new country, so there would be strict "border policing." All those quote marks I'm showing you are annoying, but really, they were all in the press release, in quotes for no reason, just like that.

Anyway, as you probably saw on the news, McGrathia exploded when a woman named Lenora Cline—she's black, not a "secret Puerto Rican"—drove down from York with nothing but a book of matches and a copy of the local paper in which she saw the McGrathia story, stopped at his border, walked right up to him (the dog was barking, McGrath was too flummoxed to even call her the n-word; he'd never fired his shotgun at anyone before and was afraid), turned the paper into a torch, and tossed it at a wagon full of kerosene-drenched fertilizer. She got blown across the street, and her eyebrows went even farther, and McGrath suffered third-degree burns over much of his body. (The really funny thing is that McGrath and Cline are like *in love* now; they even share a hospital room and talk all night long about the country they'll found on an oil rig somewhere with book deal and insurance money.) The dog lost a leg and was found limping about half a mile away, its fur singed, but otherwise happy. That was the dog Sandra Bullock adopted, remember?

Then there were all the others. Libertopia in Idaho, where a whole condo complex got together and declared itself a tax-free capitalist zone—they tried to hold off the troops with a vial of what they said was anthrax. One of their CEOs, a fellow who called himself Glen, but whose real name was Ted (he thought that was "too faggy" for TV), made his declaration public too. After spending forty minutes trying to figure out which side to part his shaggy light brown hair on (he finally decided the "right," because he didn't want to "seem left") he set up a podium in the complex's common room and waved a vial around during their press conference.

"We are all willing to die for our freedom," he explained, "the way the Founding Fathers were willing, the way most Americans, infantilized as they are by the womb-to-tomb nanny state, are no longer willing. But we are, and we shall show it through superior competition and the harnessing of individual ingenuity and freedom," and then he dropped the vial.

"Of course we wouldn't endanger ourselves or media professionals gathered here by risking exposure. That was just a prop!" he said, though now he stumbled over his words and kept glancing down at the broken test tube, the white powder spilled across the tasteful beige carpeting. The journalists murmured and silently moved the story from page A3 and the six o'clock lead to after sports and "Pet of the Week."

"We do have anthrax. It was purchased in the free market, which Americans are indoctrinated to believe is a great evil when it is—" and he was interrupted again, this time by the local police, who just beat the crap out of him while the cameras still rolled and then dragged him and his four cofounders away. The cops had been called in by one of the private security guards who wanted to go home and have Sunday dinner with his mother, but couldn't because one of the Libertopians had welded the main gate to the condo complex shut and then blocked it with a big yellow Hummer. "How the hell were those idiots gonna 'free trade' anything with the gate shut?" he wanted to know.

And there were others. The mayor of Bloomington, Indiana, tried to declare independence, only to say that he'd willingly rejoin the United States if the federal government paid off the city's debts. He was recalled. In Texas, four different microstates emerged, and three of them even managed to chase off the local cops, and then set up counter-operations against National Guard sieges. Cincinnati's Gaslight District split off too and managed to even absorb a police presence through a big block party. An all-black nation emerged in one of the neighborhoods of Camden, New Jersey, and cops traded small arms fire with the rebels for most of the afternoon before drawing back. The governor of New Jersey acted upset, but deep down he hoped he'd be able to excise the city altogether and not have to worry about it. He wouldn't even use the New Jersey National Guard and insisted that the Camden problem was a federal matter.

Five squats in Eugene, Oregon, left, as did the homeless of People's Park in Berkeley, California. Somebody declared himself the King of Harlem, but at his press release just shouted "Howard Stern rules! Bababooey Bababooey!" A sandbar in the Connecticut River was claimed by a couple who had built a minigun in their basement. A warehouse turned loft in El Cerrito, California, went rebel too, thanks to the Maoist Labor Party or something like that. (Yes, I read their minds; there was disagreement over their own party name. Very weird. Half that group were FBI agents anyway.)

King Daniel watched it all on TV and just sighed. He didn't know what to think; his brain was all thumping and semi-familiar flashes, like I was looking at a washing machine full of my own clothes at a laundromat. Adrienne prowled around the couch, wanting to be helpful and useful and looking for some sex, but my father still loved my mother and missed her too much. I needed to use the bathroom, but somebody was blogging in there. Outside, across the line, a few trucks growled and headlights came on. Half the American force was leaving, being recalled. Kelly and Barry (the whitey white high-fiving guy) were lured to the window by the noise and ruckus.

"What does it mean?" Kelly asked.

Barry thought that some of the troops might be redeployed due to the rash of microstates that had sprung up. There was even a college girl from downtown Port Jameson who had created some kind of wire-mesh hoop skirt, no fabric, just the hoops, and she didn't wear jeans or panties underneath or anything, and declared herself a roving person-state. She lasted two blocks before tipping over. An American passerby who had some needlenose pliers rescued her and ended her great experiment in personal democracy and public nudity.

There was so much happening: the TV was on, as were two or three others that new citizens had brought with them. We had cable and a big Long Island TV, they had staticky reception and ghostly black-and-white figures, like thumb prints, telling them the news. Also radios, and laptops everywhere. Almost no typing, just finger-jabs and clicking from page to page, to find out what we were supposed to have said today and what the word on the net was about us (Moron of the day: "Now people are going to think that all Christians act this way!" Like Dad said, "There's a sentence that contains more errors than words.")

It was hard to think, much less pick out the thoughts of the people around me. Barry was confident, thought he smelled good; he was here to get laid because he read somewhere that hippie chicks put out in crisis situations. Kelly was afraid that she was going to die, and was wondering if she didn't make a big mistake in emigrating to Weinbergia. She was also trying to figure out exactly what to say and how to act so that she could have sex with Barry without it seeming like she was just going with him because they were in a crisis situation.

My father, watching the various special reports cutting in on other special reports, only thought "Good" whenever the cops, the National Guard, or the feds shut down another newly emergent microstate. We were the only ones with neighborhood nuclear superiority. King Daniel was proud. Everyone else? Too busy, buzzing like attic wasps over politics, sleeping arrangements, secret schemes to grab the last can of Coke or yesterday's soggy fishstick. I went upstairs where things were quieter.

But not silent. I was the only kid in all Weinbergia, and the prince besides, so most of our new citizens didn't stake a claim in my room. (Dad had four people in the master bedroom, and slept on a cot like everyone else. The big mattress and box spring had been moved downstairs for a bunch of smelly punk rocker types from Westchester.)

But when I opened the door there were Rich and Adrienne, sitting on the corner of my low twin bed, his arm wrapped around her shoulders, and both of them staring at my screensaver, of all things. They were even murmuring about it ("Oh my, it flickers like that all night?" "No, it stops after ten minutes or so.") and they were even thinking what they said. Usually, when people make empty comments, they're thinking of something else.

"Hello," I said.

"Hey chief," Rich said brightly. Adrienne smiled the lady's smile for kids.

"I'm going to use my computer now," I said. "No more screensaver, okay?" I slid into my seat and tapped the mouse. They shifted on their butts a bit, but didn't move.

"Do you mind if we stay here and, uhm, hang out with you,

Herbie?" Adrienne acted as though she had never said the words "hang out" before in her entire life.

I told her it was fine and Rich asked what I planned to do. "Some neat video game? Update a website? Talk to your little girlfriend on instant messenger? Send some emails?"

"I like to look at pornography on my computer."

Rich suddenly flashed to an image of some porno he had seen, so I obliged by typing "barely legal anal" into the search engine that's on my browser's start page. "It's very healthy, you know, for young boys like me. We try to shed our old-fashioned American sex hang-ups here in Weinbergia. That's why I look at porn for two or three hours before I go to sleep on that bed you two are sitting on every night."

"Well, that's just great," Adrienne said. She didn't think it was great at all. "I think I'll talk health and family services policy with your father." With that she got up and didn't even glance at Rich as she left, taking three quarters of the air in the room with her.

"So, uh—" Rich said and I clicked the Search button and my screen filled with thumbnails of women who certainly weren't barely legal, stacked like sandwiches with men as the bread. Sweat burst from Rich like he was a crushed grape. Then I shut the browser window.

"Oh-kay then," he said.

"Oh-kay," I said.

He stared at me for a long time; if he was thinking it was on some weird weatherman-reptile level that didn't translate into words or even images. Then he said, "You know a lot of things, Herb."

I shrugged.

"Do you know why the troops are pulling out?"

"Well, only some of 'em are."

He ran his fingers through his hair, and huffed. "Yes, but the ones that are pulling out, do you know why they are pulling out?"

I actually didn't, since even the troops who were leaving didn't know why they were, or where they were going, or what would happen next. Most of them were just glad to be moving away from the garden gnome nuke, but worried that they'd end up in Iran or Brazil or some other hotter spot on the map. Maybe Providence, Rhode Island. Brown University was supposedly planning to secede next. I went a bit deeper, into some dark mind in some dark basement. All Rich saw was my eyes peering up at the ceiling, tongue on my lips, like I was trying to think of something good.

"They're worried that vibrations and movements of soldiers and material on the front might jostle something here, and bring the radioactive bits of the nuke close enough to start the fissioning process."

I had no idea where all the blood in Rich had rushed, but he didn't seem to have any of it anymore. Maybe his feet were red as stoplights. "You mean, kill everyone?" I didn't want to say yes, so I turned back to my computer. The screensaver was back, with spidery lines of purple and green. It was pretty interesting, after all.

"I heard something, too. I have friends, been getting a few tips here and there, strictly nfa. That's 'not for attribution,' you know, so I can't say who. Uhm, not that you'd know who they were anyway." At that moment, I did.

"You know, you're big news in the outside world, Herbie. You should check out a site when you're done with your po—pictures. Mysonherbiethelovebug.org." Then Rich got up, squeezed my shoulder, and walked off without another word. The door to my bedroom opened to a roar of light and cigarette smoke and nervous smells, then closed again, but all the fog of the outside world remained here with me.

I typed in the URL and looked at the site. It took forever to load, because the designer didn't really know what she was doing. There was a big old GIF of me, a few years ago. I was missing a front tooth in the photo, though I remembered that when that picture had actually been taken I had my teeth. Photoshop, to make me look more innocent or more pathetic or something. There was a link to an online petition addressed to my dad, who was called "a good man who had done one terrible, terrible, thing."

There was no news of Weinbergia. As far as visitors to the website knew, Rich Pazzaro was tied up in the basement, literally chained to the furnace, and Dad and I were sitting up in our living room alone, in our underwear and in the dark, inventing nonsense languages and scraping the bottom of our last jar of Skippy with our dirty, overgrown nails, to keep alive, "all for the sake of Daniel Weinberg's quixotic quest," to read the website copy's version of the tale.

And I checked the newsfeeds on my other browser, then I checked your minds. Yes, even yours. And most of you knew nothing of the steady stream of people taking our side, coming here with nothing but the clothes on their backs and all the money they could pull out of a gas station ATM, swearing their oaths to Weinbergia, looking to start a new life. All you knew was what Geri had told you, what some talking heads described as the inevitable nuclear holocaust brewing on Long Island's North Shore, of the day-thick traffic jams on the L. I. E. and the Northern State, and of the Klansmen and anarchists who suddenly started arming themselves, for no reason at all other than that they hated freedom and democracy. Because they had previously been given too much of it all at once.

I generally kept my speakers down, but saw a little dancing musical note on the bottom of the front page and when I turned up the volume heard that Mom had a beepy-boopy MIDI version of "You Light Up My Life" playing in a continuous loop on the page, and there was no way to turn it off or to turn the volume down on the webpage.

So now, it really was war. I packed a bag and waited for the morning.

5

I had hopes that they'd come for me subtly. Send in another spy, maybe Tanya Levine, who'd cry and bring me some American candy—lots of Weinbergians were anti-sugar all of a sudden; nothing but that awful candied fruit nobody likes had been offered for a couple of days (I blame the hippies)—and ask me to go back with her to visit Mom, just for a bit, just for a little bit. Then I'd be hit over the head with a blackjack, stuffed into a National Guard truck along with some Meals Ready to Eat and green blankets, and trundled off to Fort Collins, Colorado (where my maternal grandma lives), or wherever for a flashbulb-heavy reunion with Mom.

But once they had cleared the front of the great rumbly trucks and armored personnel carriers that might have accidentally jostled and thus triggered Weinbergia's first and last line of defense, the Army decided to go ninja on us. No conscious thought was involved in the process at all; it was if they picked their plans out of a bingo tumbler or something. Even I didn't know what happened until the first canister of tear gas came flying through the bay window in the living room.

Breakfast's first shift had just ended. We were eating beans and toast because one of our recent émigrés was British and had a hankering for them, and beans are really cheap and easy to parachute in from a low-flying Piper Cub hired by the Palau government. The soldiers had blasted three of the cases to hell on the way down, but one had survived, and Disco Barry had fetched it in order to impress some white girl with dreadlocks and a trust fund. Her name was Rhiannon and she was happy for the beans and also happy that so many of "our bird friends" were coming to visit us. "A good omen," she said.

The roof was full of seagulls and pigeons picking at beans. Wings flapping, occasional squawks, endless jokes about who was going to go outside first to get the newspaper and risk being splattered by the shower of droppings. Then screams and scrambling and the sting of peppery smoke.

I was lucky. I was in the bathroom when the first canister of crazy purple knockout gas came through the living room window downstairs. I grabbed the toothpaste and slathered it all over my lips and eyelids, then ran downstairs, threading my way between the people in line for the toilet in the hallway. I whipped it out, you know, *it*, and aimed for the hole on the side of the canister and started peeing right on it, to neutralize the chemicals and stop the reaction. That's how they do it, intifada-style, and I'd picked up the trick in a nervous dream the night before. I'd saved Weinbergia.

Then three more canisters came in through three more windows on each end of the house and the screaming started again. I was part of it too. "Dad!" "Dad, help!" He burst out of the basement, nudged aside Kelly, who was already wailing and clutching at her face, and ran to me.

"What do we do?"

"Pee!"

His face blanched. "I just used the downstairs half-bath!"

As one, we turned to what was left of the line of people on the steps. Half of them were wheezing and crumpled, others had run upstairs and kicked open the windows. None of their bladders would be useful either; some of them had already gone in their pants. Two birds fluttered in, then smacked into walls and a flailing guy who had just left the bathroom. Dad wheezed and was suddenly leaning on me, heavily, his knees weak and eyes screwed shut. Tears dripped like sweat from his face. My toothpaste mask was wearing off; I could feel the tingling, my nostrils and bronchial tubes squeezing shut like they'd just been through the coldest winter run ever. I grabbed the remote from Dad's belt and turned to the door to face a trio of soldiers in bug-eyed gas masks pointing their machine guns at me.

I pointed the remote, antenna-first like it mattered, at them. Their morale broke like a lamp that had just been hit by a basketball, and they walked out, almost stumbling backwards down the narrow porch steps. I stepped out of the house on wobbly legs, and made it about ten feet before falling to my knees. The garden gnome was feet away, its smile egging me on. Its eyes were so bright and blue. Too blue, scary, really, like anything else that doesn't blink. Like all the cameras and headlights on the Hummers and the goggly gas masks worn by the line of soldiers just beyond the curb of my house. But I had the bomb and held the remote high, so everyone could see it, and me. There were cameras; I knew they wouldn't shoot me. I'm still a kid, a white kid they'd been painting as a victim for almost a week, and besides, I was coughing so much, my mouth and lips were full of snot and tears, I was sweating and shaking. I felt some puke bubbling up in the far end of my throat. My thumb might slip.

I could kill us all.

Blind and hoarse, I screamed.

"Mom!"

Needless to say, Dad had other remote controls, stashed here and there around the house. I knew that, but nobody else did (though the military simply assumed he did, and backed off behind their front line when I escaped the gas trap), and I felt like hanging on to the remote I had. Even after I was told that Mom was being helicoptered in to see me. Even after they offered me candy bars, money, a ride in a tank. Or when they threatened to break my f-ing arm or just cut it off with a hacksaw, and my other arm too.

And they weren't lying either. They just weren't telling the full truth yet. They wanted to see what would happen when Mom came before doing anything drastic, like shooting my wrist off so quickly I wouldn't have time to depress the button on the remote.

High-level negotiations had taken place, in New York, at the United Nations. Weinbergian windows had been replaced, food stores augmented, international treaties regarding mail, civilian air traffic, and wetlands preservation instituted (we had a disused garden that tended to puddle) and in return they had to send Kelly out to America with a duffle bag full of my clothes. She didn't even try to smile or hide her upset, and wouldn't touch me. She had been rehearsing some inspirational thing to say to me ("Stay strong" or "I love you") but ended up just stammering out "Here, here you go. Here. Your bag to go. Go. Here. Bye."

And she dropped the bag at my feet and all but ran out of the gymnasium.

It took a long time for Geri, my mom, to show up. There were briefings with PsyOps first—they thought I'd have Stockholm Syndrome and thus support my dad. It never even occurred to any of them that they, the US troops, were the ones who kidnapped me. Then Mom's publicist wanted her to change into sweatpants, to look more "homey," and by homey she meant pathetic, but Mom kept her slacks on. She wanted to look nice for me.

When my mother finally came, she looked very different. Her hair had been cut by a real hairdresser, not by herself, in the bathroom mirror, like she usually did it. Her teeth were capped and she was wearing a nice blazer in a color that wasn't quite pink. My mother sizzled with crazy, but it quieted down when she saw me. We were in the gym in the high school, where I had been carried, remote in hand (and yes, I knew it wouldn't work more than a couple hundred yards away from the nuclear device). Soldiers lined the benches, at attention when the cameras were here, but when my mother arrived and they were chased out by

Captain Whiting's stiff bark, most of the guys just leaned against the walls and chatted with each other, mostly about how similar this all felt to how they leaned against gymnasium walls, chatting, a couple of years prior when they were all high school students.

We hugged for a long time, not thinking anything at all.

A ping-pong table and two folding chairs on opposite sides had been set up for us. After about two seconds of looking over the tiny net at one another I suggested that we get up and move the chairs so that they'd be against the long sides of the table, and that way we'd be closer. Geri loved the idea and we quickly arranged the seats properly. "You're so clever," she said.

"Cleverer than the Army guys who put the chairs on the wrong end," I said, and watched her fume.

"*Stop*," she said through clenched teeth, "saying bad things about the government." Then "You're just like your father."

"He's fine, by the way."

"That's one way of putting it, I guess. I've had about my fill of your father, and I hope you have too, because I suspect it'll be a while before you see him again."

I shook my head and slid off the folding chair. "You can't kidnap me. There are rules. International law—"

"Don't be stupid, Herbie!" She was angry, like burnt toast popping right out of the toaster. "This isn't kidnapping, this is you being removed from a dangerous environment. There is *no* country called Weinbergia; I don't care what the United Nations or Palau says." She sat back in her chair, already exhausted. "Palau. God. What right do they have interfering anyway?"

"Well, Palau only gained its independence from the US in 1994. See, it started off as a Spanish holding when the pope, well, hmm." She wasn't listening.

"It doesn't matter. We're cutting off all financial aid to Palau and Morocco and Italy and all those other little nothing countries that have decided to use your father as a wedge against us."

"Us who? The US? You never talked like this before!"

"And *that* was my mistake. I wanted you to grow up to be a patriot, Herb, to have a little pride in yourself and your fellow Americans, not to be an annoying, know-it-all cynic like your father."

"I'm not a cynic. It's very idealistic, starting a new country, opening doors to the tired and hungry yearning to breathe free."

Mom put her elbows on the table and ignored the wobble as she buried her head in her hands. "Let's just go home," she said, and of course she meant to Colorado, where she had a new garden apartment with a small microwave where she warmed up her frozen dinners and a satellite dish where she spent eighteen hours a day watching Weinbergia, hoping to catch a glance of me or my silhouette in one of the windows. (We generally kept the shades drawn, due to the number of new citizens who liked to walk around naked on whichever floor I wasn't on at the moment.)

"Weinbergia is my home."

"You're *not* going back to that house."

"Then I'll go live with the poor people in the dump."

She sneered at that, more disgusted with me than I would have ever thought possible. "My son, the doctor," she said. "I'm your mother, I have custody, we're going home, and if you want to stay here and have a tantrum I'll have the guards throw you on an Army helicopter to get you home if I have to."

And that's the story of my first-ever trip in an Army helicopter.

6

The worst thing about my mother's house in Colorado was that Colorado is still in America. Also, you need a car to get anywhere. My mother even drove down to the private road that surrounds the complex to pick up her mail from the boxes on the corner of her block.

I was being "homeschooled" by Mom, which meant that she'd watch me fill out workbooks and I'd occasionally ask her a question I knew she couldn't answer in order to let me use the computer. There were all sorts of parental controls on her box too, but of course it was easy to learn her passwords with a little telepathy so I was back online. I didn't feel like writing very much though, and instead just read the various headlines about Weinbergia and checked out some of the hatesites that have sprung up about it.

That's the funny thing that Daniel and the Weinbergians never seemed to get. They were always so worried about propaganda and media—which is why Richard wasn't just depantsed and thrown over enemy lines in the middle of the night—but the media doesn't matter at all. People instantly go totally crazy when you build a nuke and start your own country; there's no need for the networks to spin it. They're all trained to distrust the new idea, the individual initiative that has nothing to do with making a zillion dollars or being in movies, the idea that someone might just announce, "I'm not part of you guys, so there!"

I know this not only because you're all open books to me, but because my workbook told me so. The Social Studies unit was on immigration—my job was to find an immigrant and interview him or her about coming to America. I had to fill out this sheet explaining Five Reasons Why Your Immigrant—*my immigrant?*— Left His or Her Home Country and Five Reasons Why He or

She Likes America. Then I had to get a picture of something that my immigrant thinks represents America and paste it into the workbook. Well, the only immigrant I knew was myself, so here's what I filled out:

Five Reasons Your Immigrant Left His or Her Home Country

1. I was overcome by crazy purple knockout gas.
2. Long lines for the bathroom.
3. All the adults around me started saying things like "make love" when they thought I was in earshot, and that's one creepy phrase.
4. China didn't kidnap me first.
5. I was too scared to push the button.

Five Reasons Your Immigrant Likes America

1. I'd *better* like it.
2. Life's a bit easier under America's domestic policy than it is under its foreign policy, let me tell you.
3. My mom lives here.
4. It's where they hold Wrestlemania every Spring.
5. Mostly I like that it's fraying at the edges, and that all these other countries are popping up out of nowhere. I think that's a good sign, and it's really nice of America not to just randomly kill anyone and everyone who tries it, at least not right away. Thanks.

And for my picture of America, I found one on the net, on some freebie angelfire.com webpage by some guy who used to be a Marine or really likes the Marines or his brother was a Marine or something (it really wasn't clear which). It was a photo of my father, in his shorts, his mouth shaped like a big O and his forehead glistening from sweat as he leans into the steering bar of his lawn mower. There were two captions on the pic too, in big red computery-font letters. FUELED BY MARX said the caption up top, and on the bottom of the photo, RULED BY SATAN.

Bored, I went to the fridge. A half-empty jar of Best Foods mayonnaise and an old sock were in it. I can't even imagine how my mother ended up with those two items and nothing else in her refrigerator, and I'm a mind-reader. Best Foods. God. It's the same company as Hellman's back in New York, but out here, in the West, they call it Best Foods.

Maybe, I thought, *I should change my name from Herbert Weinberg to "Handsome" Johnny Stryker or something like that.*

In Weinbergia, the fridge was always full. Cuban sandwiches (from Cuba!), Chinese food (from Hunan Gardens, in the King Kullen strip mall across Route 347, on the southern frontier), crazy hippie green stuff, ice cream bars, lots of chicken cooked in all sorts of ways. You name it. In Weinbergia, I always had some company, if only because people would come up to me in little groups of two and threes, to marvel at the Smarty Kid who didn't wear a backwards baseball cap and let his jaw drop to his nipples as a matter of course.

And I guess that's why it was such a big deal that dad built a nuke too. After my kidnapping, the news sort of petered out, even though Weinbergia is still ringed by foreign troops, and even though the garden gnome is still ticking out on the lawn. Weinbergia is just fodder for various Internet nerds and political science and law school students writing their papers. At least the weather has turned now, so there's no need for Dad to mow the lawn. Portuguese UN peacekeepers did the raking, which was over pretty quickly because the gas attack defoliated both the trees in my yard. My mother became the new celebrity, what with the TV appearances and "the book" about her brave struggle to reclaim me. Geri was so naïve; she actually wrote the first ten pages herself and gave them to an agent. The first page is hanging on a bulletin board at the publishing house, because the first paragraph reads like this:

> I knew that I had to rescue my loving pure little innocent son from the dastardly clutches of my diabolical husband because I love my little Herbert so very much and nobody else could love him like I did. My husband who is mentally ill and now I realize has been for years ever since that time during Christmas shopping three years ago when he tore open a twelve-pack of toilet paper at the Walmart and grabbed three rolls and flung them over the shelves into the next aisle while he hysterically screamed madly "Hey-o! Heads up!" When he began to secretly skulk around in the shadows in broad daylight I knew I had a battle for my life and the life of my loving son in my hands and that I would do anything to protect my innocent child from the world, which is full of unknown dangers.

The rest they shredded, thank God. Geri spent a lot of the time she was actually home talking to and emailing the ghostwriter. She ate most of her suppers out as well, but was always happy to bring home "doggie bags"—Gee, thanks Mom! *Love, The Dog*— from Wolfgang Puck's place or wherever she'd been treated that night.

I had little else to do with my days but allow my mind to drift, all the way back to Weinbergia. Weinbergia, where Rich was leading a daring commando mission over the wire and into enemy territory, namely, the Qool Mart about half a mile into American territory.

"I just can't get them out of my head," Rich said. "I haven't had a Cuebar since I was a kid. They have those four little rectangular sections: caramel, coconut, peanut butter, and strawberry." My father was just staring at him, but a couple of folks littering the dining room, on pillows or half-rolled up and wrinkled sleeping bags, nodded. Then there was Adrienne, who felt like she was in a commercial, because she was.

"It's only one klick down to the Qool Mart. We should make a move."

"We?" asked Barry. "Besides, candy is never as good as you remember it from when you were a kid."

"The corporations," Rhiannon said, and murmurs of agreement rose up from the crowded room. Coups in Haiti, mass production, the decline in union labor in factories, the fact that milk chocolate doesn't melt as quickly as dark when loaded into trucks—that's why chocolate stinks these days, except for the expensive stuff. It's amazing what people think they know.

Richard leaned in, his elbows balanced oddly on the arms of the chair in which he sat. "You know we need to make a move, Daniel. Do something. People need a new adventure to focus on. You know, make the front page, over the fold, again." He leaned back in his chair, held out his arms, then brought his hands together so that his index fingers and thumbs met, making a little cube-y shape. "Cuuuuuue-bar" he said, just like the voice-over guy from the commercials used to.

Dad glanced around for a second, then reached for the glass sugar bowl and turned it over. Along with a cascade of white sugar fell a little black video camera, a new type hardly bigger than a roll of 35mm film. He snatched it up, stomped out of the dining room and up the steps, shouldered his way through the knot of people always milling right outside the bathroom door, yanked the door open, ignored the shriek and flailing of legs and panties stretched between white knees as some woman named Elly rushed to stand and cover herself, and flushed the camera. He nearly broke the handle to the toilet.

The screaming and flailing about—Weinbergians like to speak with their hands because of the close quarters, a little flick of a finger can mean a lot once you catch someone's eye—clicked off like a television when my mother barged in to the living room, her hands full of big white shopping bags. She bought me a whole new wardrobe. Sweaters, which I hate to wear, "but you're in Colorado now and it gets a lot colder here," five pairs of shoes, all the same but in different sizes, because "one will fit and you'll grow into at least one of the sizes; the rest we can return," and slacks slacks slacks. No jeans. "It's time to grow up," she said. She was wearing jeans though. The last bag held three plastic domes holding roasted chickens from the fancy supermarket. I called them pheasant under glass and got a dirty look instead of a polite chuckle. I'm not so clever anymore, now that Mom has to look at me every day between photo opportunities and psychological assessments.

We ate a chicken, and salad out of a bag. Mom didn't even pour all the leaves and whatever out onto our plates; we just leaned over the table like Weinbergian hippies and jabbed at the veggies with our forks.

"So, what did you do all day?" she asked me.

"I dunno," I said. "What did you do all day?"

Mom dropped her fork. "I went shopping. I had a meeting. *With a senator.* I made some phone calls." She sighed.

"Where?"

"Cell phone."

"Oh. Who did you talk to?"

"Oh, *Vanity Fair*, some freelance writer from the *New Times*, that sort of thing." She frowned, thinking. I peeked.

"Still haven't heard anything from *People*, huh?"

"No!" Her hands contracted into tight little fists. "Can you believe it? I even faxed them." She couldn't even look at me, she was so disgusted. She turned back to me finally. "I faxed them twice today alone. I was worried about time zones. I don't know if I'll ever get used to Mountain."

"When *People* does call, they'll probably want to take our picture. That's why I bought you seven sweaters. You should keep the orange one at hand in case they call us tomorrow."

I smiled. "Sure, Mom!" We ate in silence, while she fantasized about a handsome, flat-stomached photojournalist sweeping her off her feet and winning me over with lots of hair-tousling and non-molesting wrestling lessons. A *People* photojournalist. That way, no politics.

About six hours later, my father was staring at the ceiling in his dark room when he shifted to his side and peered over the edge of his bed at a few of the shadowy figures who took up the floor space in their bags and blankets.

"Who wants to come to Qool Mart with me?" he asked. "This sounds stupid, but I can't get those damn Cuebars out of my head." The shadows on the floor shifted and groaned like a talkative fog. Dad reached down and poked the mass, tapping shoulders (or foreheads, an ankle, a big fleshy something that he thought was a belly but worried was a boob, which would create a national crisis or, even worse, some horrible and lengthy lesbian "processing session" at breakfast) and rousing his confederates. "Feet," he said softly as he sat up and swung around to get off the bed. A few shapeless blobs rose up and sprouted limbs.

"Cuebar, let's do this thang," Barry said.

"Should we . . . get Rich?" asked Adrienne in a quiet, sleepy voice, which came . . .

Which came from the side of the bed my mother used to sleep on. I hadn't sensed her till she awoke.

She was in bed with my father. In bed. They had been almost doing things. Almost, so quiet, hardly a squeak, just hands and the tips of their fingers, down below. They were really tired, but with all the rolling over and the like on the floor, King Daniel couldn't help but wake up, his brain a fog, having forgotten why he couldn't have sex with the woman in the bed with him. For her part, Adrienne was happy to lie there and "be pleasured."

She used the words *be pleasured*. Mentally. Dinner came up my throat and I ran to the bathroom to stare into the toilet for a long time, waiting. Once, either my father or my mother would come and comfort me. Back in Port Jameson, they were always so attuned to me, like they could read my mind. I've always wanted to meet someone who could do that, but as far as I knew then, I was the only telepathic person in the whole world.

I pushed Adrienne out of my mind, and concentrated on Dad. He and a small knot of Weinbergians—and yeah, Adrienne was among them, but to me she was nothing but a silhouette, a black blotch on the lawn—approached the border, giddy with anticipation. Sometimes, you can even look forward to maybe being shot, if it involves the promise of a little road trip to a convenience store. Exciting stuff; they have everything at those stores: Froot Loops, push brooms, coffee, magazines that promise six-pack abs with a single push-up, maps of the world (Palau, here we come!), and Cuebars.

"Hi," my father said, so sure of himself that he wasn't even thinking. A soldier looked at him like he was the dreamy remnant of an incomplete nap.

"What?"

"We're coming through."

"Uhm," the soldier said, "I don't think you can do that. I mean, I'll have to radio up the chain of command."

"Why? Just let us through." The Weinbergians nodded. One of them had made a passport with a portable laser printer and an old Polaroid camera he had found at the bottom of the junk closet. "Where are you from?" Dad asked.

"I grew up in Spanish Harlem."

"Dicey area."

The soldier shrugged.

"But you were allowed to go where you wanted, right? Sure, someone could say 'Get off my turf—'"

"Heh," the soldier said, "I only ever heard the word turf on TV."

"Yeah yeah, but anyway, here's the thing, there was animosity, but you were allowed to travel wherever you liked. We're not under arrest or anything, we're not being detained in my house, we're just ordinary Ameri—"

"Nah, you ain't, remember? Weinbergia." The soldier smiled. He liked to be clever, and his job didn't really offer much call for it.

Dad shrugged. "Okay," he said, "we declare the hostilities over. Mission accomplished! Say, good job, soldier, for resolving all this. You'll probably get a medal, maybe even a stamp with your picture on it one day." Behind him, a Weinbergian passport was torn to shreds by its enthusiastic owner. Dad stepped forward and, careful not to nudge or touch the soldier, but with his hands out to direct him, crossed the border. Adrienne and the others followed, nervously. Dad smiled and waved as he picked his way across the driveway. Jake, the guy who carried the passport, accidentally stubbed his toe on a tank tread, but the gunner didn't notice thanks to the iPod some Support the Troops campaign had sent everyone.

I hoped someone would stop them. By shooting Adrienne.

Dad made it to the corner of the block, turned, and led his band down Route 25A. Adrienne took his arm because the shoulder of the road isn't designed for walking—everyone on Long Island drives everywhere—and was full of sand, dead leaves she thought were spiders, and rocks that were conspiring to make her twist her ankle.

You know, she doesn't even like Cuebars.

A car zipped by and its passengers yelled something unintelligible to my dad, who jumped, startled. Adrienne's nails dug into his forearm.

"What was that?"

"What did they say?"

"I dunno!" said Jake.

"Didn't you hear?" asked Adrienne.

"No, why would I? Did you?"

"No!"

"Well then," said Barry.

"Well then what?" said Adrienne.

In the darkness, everyone shrugged and walked on.

What the driver of the car, whose name was Paul DeMello and who worked in Port Jameson for his father who had a vinyl siding business said was, "Aaaah, you're poor! Fucker!" He did this because on Long Island, everybody drives, except for the occasional poor person who somehow managed to find a place to live, in a tiny studio apartment, or even doubled up with someone. And it really drives Paul nuts to see someone dragging their ass along the shoulder of the road, because he feels the need to slow down so he won't hit them, and who knows, sometime somebody, especially a "moulie," might jump in front of his car and sue him for a million dollars after causing the accident. (By *moulie*, Paul, who actually thinks of himself as "Paulie," means to think "black guy," but "bad," because moulie is short for *mulignane*, which he's been told is similar to the Italian word for eggplant, and anyway his father used to call black people on TV moulies, especially if they led to gambling losses by their poor play on the football field or basketball court. Anyway, he's a jerk, but I think it's funny that "Paulie" and "moulie" kind of sound similar.) And he also gets mad because he works really hard all day, doing vinyl siding, and if he works so hard why can't these people who walk around like apes just work hard too and get a damn car?

Well, Paul doesn't know. Paul doesn't even know why he occasionally sees a tank trundle down his street these days either, because he doesn't like the news and he doesn't talk to too many people these days, not since his girlfriend Tammy dumped him because she doesn't like being screamed at, especially not in front of her own mother like he did that one time in the parking lot of the deli when it was her cousin's Confirmation and they were sent to pick up an eight-foot hero sandwich. So he's never heard of Weinbergia and he doesn't know that he's in the red ring of instant vaporization if the nuke goes up. He'd really be pissed off if he did.

The next car, a military Hummer that was disguised as a civilian vehicle with its baby-blue paint job and silkscreened unicorn on the side, came up behind Dad and the Weinbergians slowly, its lights dimmed by half-stop gels borrowed from a news crew in exchange for the crew getting a berth and embedded journalists on the mission to end the stand-off once and for all.

Captain Whiting leaned out the window of the vehicle and shouted over the noise of the engine to Dad, saying, "Hey! Weinberg! Stop, you're under arrest." The others stopped, but Dad kept walking. Jake and Leif hurried to catch up and bumped into Adrienne, who scowled and yelped at them.

"Diplomatic immunity!" Dad called out, not even turning to face the captain.

"You surrendered!"

"No I didn't," Dad said. There was some underbrush, so he stomped on it forcefully. Ahead, the white sign of the Qool Mart illuminated the four-car parking lot like a little moon.

"I have a soldier and video says you did, son!"

Dad still didn't stop, still didn't turn. Adrienne huffed after him, upset that she was being reduced to a bit part in the moment with every stride my father pulled ahead. Barry and Jake decided to pace the Hummer, trotting behind it as if they'd be able to hop onto the back, climb in, and subdue everyone involved with all the ninja moves they didn't actually know. But Leif felt strangely confident, giddy. Like he did when he had first emigrated. History was happening. Jake wondered if he shouldn't have saved his passport for eBay.

"No, I said I was ending hostilities. But I also declare victory," Dad said as he finally stopped and turned on his heel to point a thick finger at the captain. "That means you surrender!"

"Okay—wait, no!" From inside the Hummer came a high girly laugh. Whiting craned his neck to frown, and then turned back to Dad. The Hummer idled on the street right outside the Qool Mart as Dad, followed a few steps by Adrienne, stepped onto the asphalt.

"Don't be juvenile, Weinberg. You messed up, big time. I can shoot you right now."

A huge spotlight, which had been left on the roof unused since the Qool Mart opened back in the springtime, sparked to life and flooded the Hummer with a blazing beam. Whiting threw up his arm and squinted. Moths fluttered about, mad from the light. And a voice, lilting and foreign, declared from a tinny PA system, "No you cannot! This man is in my parking lot, the territory of the Islamic Republic of Qool Mart Store No. 351, and any violence on the part of imperialist American aggressors will be answered a thousandfold!"

7

My mother likes to wake me up in the middle of the night, because she misses me so much and she doesn't want to be without me, plus she is easily made tipsy on white wine, which she loves and which her new admirers give her all the time. She's like a cloud of perfume and cough medicine, drifting in a windy sky, when she wakes me. Her mind, her scent, all of it. She says, "Love Bug, oh Love Bug," and brushes my hair with her fingers every time. I always try to stay asleep, but it never works. I blaze awake but hold my eyes shut to keep up the illusion, like a guy in prison hiding in the corner of the cell when the guard comes in. All boxed in. She did this now, as I was watching an international incident unfold.

I missed Captain Whiting's barked curses and quick scatter of footsteps guided by rote drilling rather than thought that rushed out into the parking lot. When the spotlight died to a little orange spark, the Hummer was doomed. Propane tanks, set with detonators made from duct tape and clock radios, were positioned under all the doors and wheels. King Dad and his followers were surrounded too, by three Qool Mart employees in red-and-white striped shirts and off-the-rack sunglasses. One of them, his name Umer (though his name tag read *Mark*), wore big novelty sunglasses with pink frames and smiled at my father. He held his arm out toward the door of the Qool Mart and said, "Please, please, come in."

Mom said over and over, "Love Bug, my Love Bug," but her tone was weird, as was her own experience of sitting on the corner of my bed, her arm reaching for me as tenderly as Umer's did toward the entrance of the Qool Mart. She wasn't looking at me through her eyes, but just saw the grayish-black blob of my shadowed face. What she saw, in her mind's eye, was herself at the edge of a neater-looking bed, with her clothes fitting better than they really do, caressing a superior version of me. Me, but not so portly, me who had the haircut the *Today Show* wanted me to get. Me, who was thrilled to be free from my psychotic father and his war criminal ways.

"We're out of Cuebars," explained Musad, the franchisee of the Qool Mart, and the Bey of the Islamic Republic of Qool Mart Store No. 351. "We couldn't keep them in stock at all today, thanks to the mention on the television." Musad's name tag read *Sam*. He wasn't wearing sunglasses, which gave him a special look given that all the other employees were—he was the Bey, and they were the Secret Service or something. Even Dad was impressed. "But," said Musad, "I do think we have a product you'd be interested in, if you know what I mean." Musad was sure that Dad did, especially after Dad mimicked the smile and sly tilt of the head Musad performed, but really, Dad had no idea what he was getting into.

Adrienne scowled; she hated Arabs because she heard that back in their home countries they treat women very poorly, wrapping them up in headscarves or even full-length hijabs, and then squeezing their butts and boobs in the marketplaces while the women are trying to shop for their families. And she disliked the idea of being handled too much to feel comfortable among so many of them, especially as she couldn't tell whether or not they were undressing her with their eyes.

Barry and Jake busied themselves getting beer and crushed ice.

Mom, all inspired, left my room and sat down to her new laptop, where she checked her email, and answered a few from well-wishers. She used to write back to everyone, but recently got a little jaded. Any mail that mentioned Jesus Christ or contains more than four exclamation points (or two right next to each other) she finally decided to ignore after getting way too many of them. She liked what she calls Geri's Generic God. Letters from Christians and Jews and Buddhists and pagans all offered up God's good will, but it could be any God at all. The Generic God, Geri talked to all the time now. About me. ("Will my little boy be okay through all of this?") About Dad. ("What happened?") About tomorrow. ("Please please please make Oprah call tomorrow, or at least Regis.")

Captain Whiting burst into the Qool Mart, sidearm drawn and arm raised. He waved the gun around till the barrel looked like it was made of rubber. "You're all under arrest!" he shouted. Umer was on him in a flash, his mop handle slamming hard against

Whiting's forearm. The gun fell and was kicked across the slick floor. The second blow landed right on Whiting's head, and then as Whiting's guards began running to the door, Umer slid the mop handle through the looped handles of the double doors, wedging them shut. He turned the little sign hanging from one of the handles around so from the outside it read CLOSED. Then he just stood there and smiled as an anxious soldier hefted his rifle and fired a shot into the bulletproof glass of the store. They scattered at the ricochet.

Whiting got to his feet and held up a palm. "No," he barked to the soldiers outside. "Hold your fire! Back to the vehicle!" He turned, wincing, and with his hand now to the tender part of his head. "What's going on here? Do you realize that we'll have a *Black Hawk Down* here in three minutes? Who has my gun?" There was a tap on the glass. Everyone turned, and a soldier looked at his captain and shrugged, confused.

Umer said, "The glass is thick. He cannot hear you easily. And the report of the rifle is probably ringing in his ears."

Whiting grunted, then stepped up to the glass and cupped his hands around his mouth. "Go back to *the Hummer!*" he yelled. *"and wait!"* The soldiers nodded and started to walk back, but then Whiting remembered something and started banging on the glass. They turned and Whiting cupped his hands again and shouted, "Private Wallace! I want you to *remove the mudflaps—*" Wallace, the soldier who had fired, then knocked, shrugged, and shook his head, so Whiting pointed at the rear of the Hummer, and said even louder, *"Those ermine mudflaps* are private issue! *They're mine!"* The soldier, Wallace, smiled widely and nodded, finally understanding. "Take *the mudflaps* back to *the staging zone,* Wallace!" He waved, "And the *rest of you,* stay by *the Hummer* and *don't* try to *defuse* anything!"

Whiting turned back to the assembled employees and Weinbergians, who were staring. "What? They're sentimental. And I

bought them out of my own pocket. You need to do that sometimes. It cheers you up to decorate your own Hummer. It's like a
home away from home." Barry understood him at least. He sighed,
not thinking anything he wasn't saying, which is really strange for
an adult. "So, who has my gun?"

From the back of the room came a voice familiar to local TV
news watchers. "I do," said Rich, standing up from his hiding
place behind a display case full of old doughnuts. In one hand
was Whiting's gun, and in the other, a Cuebar. He was thinking
Pulitzer, and about how, when he went to journalism school,
he learned that Pulitzer was pronounced, "Pull it, sir," and not
"Pewlitzer."

At just that moment, in the next room over from where I couldn't
sleep, my mother began to have a religious experience. Religious
experiences are pretty common, actually. I had to teach myself to
tune them out when I was a kid, because they're like . . . hard to
explain. Ever see a movie or something on TV where they record
a flower or a city all night and then speed up all the frames so
it looks like blooms are exploding, cars speed up into red and
white squiggles of light, clouds roll under the sky like we were all
on a planet-sized roller coaster? It's like watching all those things
at once, and being all those things at once. Imagine smelling all
those flowers and being sniffed by a giant nose.

Oh, and there is no God, of course. Religious experiences are
just a weird thing that happens in people's brains. It's actually the
exact opposite of getting a song stuck in your head. You really have
to be telepathic to understand what I mean.

The eye of Geri's Generic God manifested itself at the top of her
vision. She saw the ceiling separate from the walls of the room and
like the sun the Eye peered at her, a giant, inquisitive It. She felt

herself rising from her seat, chest first, arms and shoulders thrown back like she was nineteen and being carried to the lifeguards at Lake Ronkonkoma after being discovered in the water by her boyfriend. My mother almost died that day, and her brain starved for thirty seconds. She's been vulnerable to religious experiences ever since then, but never had one till she clicked shut her email and accidentally fired up the wrong screen saver—one she'd never seen before—on her computer. The wavy red into blue with a bright white blob in the middle triggered her.

Now Geri hallucinated that from her perch in the grip of her own Generic God she looked down and saw her body, slumped forward, forehead pressed heavily against the screen of the laptop, which made the edge of the keyboard rise up. Geri wasn't worried about her new machine though; she had transcended material concerns. Then she turned away from her empty body doll and turned to make eye contact with It. Mom stared into the sun-like eye of her Generic God and became It.

From there, it was the usual. All religions have some essential wisdom to share, but unscrupulous men and the pleasures of wealth obscured the message. All of us have a little of God in us, thus we are all one, and should be unified in peace and brotherhood. All we need to do is treat others in the ways in which we want to be treated. God is nature, and nature is God, so we must stop polluting the Earth. Everyone deserves a full stomach and a warm hug. We should never die alone. An angel watches over each one of us, keeping us from harm. Everything happens for the best, even death, as our own bodies become the flowers of the next generation.

"I, uh, brought this one with me," Rich said of his Cuebar. He was also wearing a T-shirt with the Cuebar logo on it.

Adrienne said, "Great. So now what are we supposed to do? We'll probably be arrested if we try to get back home." She glared at Dad.

"Actually, orders on the border are to shoot," said Captain Whiting. Dad glared at him. Not knowing what else to do, Whiting glared at Umer for a moment, but Umer's sunglasses made that unsatisfying, so he tuned to Musad, who had moved from behind the cash register to behind the hot dog warmer, and glared at him. Jake glared at Rich. Barry just put the bags of ice back in the freezer; this was going to take a while, like one of those horrible hour-long pre-meetings his old boss would have before the real, three-hour, meeting. And he had come to Weinbergia to escape.

Musad, his hand in a glove, took a large hot dog—one of those foot-long Qool Dogs that are really kind of gross because they're also like three inches around; too much meat—put it in a bun, and offered it to my father. He took it gingerly, not really thinking. His nervous system was doing all the work. The bloom of confidence in his chest that made him get up and tromp out of his own country was gone, and what replaced it was nothing. No fear, but no thought either. A hot dog was as good as a Cuebar until he bit into it and frowned.

"What?" Adrienne asked. Dad clenched his teeth and pulled from the hot dog a piece of paper, tightly rolled up.

"Hold this," he said of the hot dog to Adrienne, who wouldn't. Jake turned and did. Dad found the edge of the paper with his thumb and carefully unrolled it, then quietly read the peace treaty to himself. In the corner, Rich thought, *Yes!*

Geri's Generic God was all *yes*. There was no hesitation: yes yes yes yes yes. Flowers are beautiful. The universe is a large and wonderful place. There was no room for a Generic Devil or even any explanation for the bad things in the world, like all those people who have been killed by Daisy Cutter bombs, tortured in camps, beaten to death by their parents . . . well, those things just happen so that Geri can understand how precious life is. Daniel might have beaten me to death, or maybe *his new girlfriend would have*. If not beaten, then maybe I would have been locked in the bathroom and forced to drink from the toilet, or abandoned to the crabgrass on Weinbergia's eastern frontier, or maybe even sent over to the Cases', where they eat spaghetti out of a can.

That's what brought her back. Me, her precious Love Bug, face smeared with sauce too bright red to be tomato, sitting on a stool at the counter in the Case kitchen, holding an ice cream scoop over the rim of a huge cafeteria-grade can of "prefab" pasta. The glories of life and universe, debased by factory pasta. It was as she awoke that Mom realized that her entire life had been a fraud and a failure. She had never really lived, not since that day when she had enjoyed the cold dark waters of Lake Ronkonkoma for a few seconds too long. She needed to reconnect with nature, to reclaim her wild, primitive self, to transform herself from media figure of the moment ("I think my book might suck" was her first coherent thought upon awakening) and back into Woman. Mother. Eve.

Her head still throbbing as though she had just been awoken from an incomplete nap by a telemarketer phone call, my mother ran around the bedroom, dragging out her luggage and yanking her clothes out of the dresser and closets. It was time for us to move on again, but she wasn't packing for a trip. She was packing to burn.

"Five years . . . peace between Weinbergia and the entire Muslim world, as vouchsafed and guaranteed by the Islamic Republic of Qool Mart," Dad read aloud.

"Wait a minute," said Whiting, "these people don't speak for the Muslim world."

"Hyah," said Barry. "He's got a point there." Barry hoped making friends with Whiting would get him out of here alive, maybe even without a prison sentence.

Musad said, "Of course I speak for the Muslim world. You, man," he continued, pointing his chin at Barry. "You made it so."

"We have video," Richard said.

Musad reached up to the security monitor and punched a button. The real-time footage on the screen went black and then a moment later was replaced with the same scene, but daylight, with Musad and Barry, only the latter in other clothes, chatting.

Video Barry waved a copy of *Newsday* in Musad's face and, his voice tinny as a thought from both the mic and the fact that the playback was on the small security speakers, said, "Why did your people go crazy this time? Bombing our soldiers just for trying to protect *your* freedom to sell me this newspaper!"

"So, you don't want the newspaper?" Musad-on-tape asked.

It's always strange for me to watch video. I never liked sitcoms, and always hated cartoons, because I could never tell what the characters were thinking. Live shows aren't much better. Reading from a teleprompter doesn't involve any thinking at all, and bands and dancers and stuff are just constantly mentally counting one-two-three-one-two-three, like that. It's pretty unnerving. Now, Musad was just eerily confident in watching the playback, despite the armored personnel carriers rumbling down Route 25A, despite just being a little island in great big America. Barry was just confused, and starting to get real nervous. He thought of a movie, *The China Syndrome*, and how some guy in it is trying to do something and just gets shot ten times by a machine gun in less than a second. Dying is like exhaling and forgetting to inhale again. Just like that. It could happen. A blink that never ends. He sweated: the lip, the shoulderblades, the crease of his waist against the elastic of his boxers.

He's so gross.

On the video, a gray and fuzzy Barry flails his arms and dives for the jar of beef jerky. Musad pushes him away. Barry swings and falls far short. Umer darts out from the edges of the frame and ties Barry into a full nelson, then leads him, kicking and thrashing, off the bottom of the screen.

"Well, that's definitive," Adrienne said. She was just a suicide of resentment. *Go ahead*, summed it all up. *Just go ahead.*

"I want a better hot dog, Musad," my father said. "If you know what I mean."

Musad did, and handed Dad a Double Qool with Cheezy Stuff, the hot dog that comes with its own injected American, Swiss, or Pepper Jack cheese. It's also a thrilling eighteen inches long, to hold in all that cheesy goodness.

"Hey," said Jake, a nervous scribble of thought, "why don't you just break this one open and see if there's a better or longer-lasting treaty in it, instead of eating." My father just stared and took a very deliberate bite of the Double Qool, then another. He chewed slow too. Whiting huffed. Barry decided to walk to the corner of the store and put his back against the Big Brapp Frozen Frappucino machine. At least he wouldn't be shot from behind. Dad clenched his teeth and pulled another tightly rolled piece of paper from the center of the dog, where the cheese would have been.

The lights came on. My mother, loud as a volcano, declared, "Love Bug! We have to leave, right now!"

8

My mother wasn't crazy. Well, crazy is relative. It's like static on a radio; sometimes it is louder than the song. She was still thinking loud and rumbly, over the noise of her religious experience. So she was kind of crazy, I guess. No crazier than Dad, whose stoic hot dog munching was pretty much the sanest thing he could do in his situation. For Mom it was the same. Anything that got her away from all the media would probably be a good idea.

Even driving out into a country and finding a flat glacial boulder on which to pile most of our clothes, the laptop, her microwave oven, and some photo albums, to set them all on fire.

"Why the microwave?" I asked, because I knew that Mom wanted me to ask.

She clutched it to herself and said, "It's not a natural thing. The only meals that come out tasting anything like they should are meals designed to taste that way only when microwaved. So it's a fake reality disguised as a real imitation. And it takes us away from what we need to experience, what people have done for ten thousand years." She planted it atop a bag I'd opened. Clothes spilled out, but gave the microwave a little cushion to sink into. "Plus, I don't like the beep that goes off when the timer counts down to zero. That isn't natural either. It sounds almost but not quite like a bell."

She squirted lighter fluid over the mass in wild streaks, then stepped back and told me to step back too. She had a book of matches, but the first three didn't take thanks to a little breeze. The fourth stayed lit long enough for Mom to ignite the corner of the book itself. She threw it onto the pile and a web of small flames flared up. The clothes didn't burn that easily, nor did the luggage, but there was a fair amount of black smoke that stung and made me cough a lot. Geri breathed through her mouth hard, willing the fire to really flare up and consume everything. It didn't. The only really exciting bit was when the cord of the microwave melted a bit and almost fell off, but didn't.

"Get back in the car," she said, finally.

We drove without purpose for a long while, down roads so dark that the usual horizon glare from the clusters of gas stations and motels was swallowed by the night. Both of us had floaters in our eyes from staring at the fire, but there wasn't a lot of traffic so it was okay, except that we were running out of gas, and Mom, still on her religious high, was sure that we'd pull up, exhaust sputtering and clutch freezing, at exactly the place the universe wanted us to be.

I guess, by definition, she was right, since every action is a caused action and there is no such thing as free will. (It's true; I checked. Every little thing we do or think is a response and reaction to something else—minds are like the white ball in a game of pool.)

It was a Qool Mart.

The best part about Qool Marts is that time stands still. I guess it's true of any convenience store, really, at least the chain stores with the bright fluorescent lights and the prepackaged miniature versions of everything. I could stare at a tiny packet of Oreos for hours, marvel at the pre-made sandwiches and the Stew in a Bubble (it comes with a fork *and* a straw), and all the magazines with boobs, guns, and cars on the covers. And newspapers I've never seen anywhere else: *The Serbo-Croatian Siren*, *The National Bugle*, and *The Republican-Democrat Advocate* (that last one makes me smile). There's everything here, just not enough of it. There was even a live feed from the Qool Mart's internal network on the security monitor, which the staff was too busy watching to greet us when Mom and I walked in. The left half of the screen was security cam footage from Port Jameson, in fuzzy, elongated, black and white; the right half was in color, and featured Qool Mart CEO Rolland Hoyt standing in front of a featureless background painted with Qool Mart's distinctive reddish-brown color. He was speaking; no audio was being piped out of what he had just called a "renegade franchise."

". . . this renegade franchise will be isolated, its assets frozen, and its communication logs heavily scrutinized. The Qool Mart family has always held that"—he raised his hands and flicked his fingers to make them quotation marks—"'going independent' would cause harm to our brand, to our trademarks, to our trade secrets, and most importantly, to the mutually beneficial relationships Qool Mart Co. cultivates with its franchisees.

"To this end, we are insisting that the Qool Mart family pull together in this, the time of our greatest challenge. Please stay open, stay friendly, serve your customers as if they too were a part of your family . . . of our family. And if any franchisee has any information that could be useful in any way toward engendering a resolution to this crisis, please contact us via the internal network immediately. We'll also be combing through the records of all employees who may have a connection to the Port Jameson store, and would appreciate the full cooperation of all our franchisees and associates to facilitate this matter.

"And finally, we have ordered an air strike on the Port Jameson store. We'd like to make it absolutely clear that this is a private response. The US government is not a part of this operation, though it has allowed use of its air space for the event. Indeed, our insurer, Bell, Winston, and Associates, has taken care of all the incidentals, from selecting the contractors to the sale of ancillary rights for overseas markets. We will also be releasing a one-shot magazine commemorating the forthcoming tragedy, called *Freedom's Qool*, which will be our periodical upsell for November of this year.

"Peace be with you all, and good night and good service."

Randall Hoyt was moved off-screen by a wipe, and a black-and-white King Daniel eating a hot dog filled the screen. Mom's face burned cold, the way yours does when you almost fall down a long flight of steps, or when a car whizzes by too close. The connection to the god in her temporal lobe faltered for a moment, but then reasserted itself with all sorts of goodie-good chemicals. Everything was going to be okay. Nobody would really blow up a Qool Mart, least of all Qool Mart itself, and if it did, nobody in the store was going to be hurt. They'd get out somehow, or something would happen that would save the day. And gosh, she was right, because back at the store, Rich had just received the news about the imminent attack from Levellin Inc., the manufacturers of Stew in a Bubble, Cherry Bomb Cola, Sweet and Sour Soup Mix, and Cuebars. Levellin shares an insurer with Qool Mart, and someone at Levellin headquarters in England had just received a phone call asking for a "thumbnail guestimate on a going-present basis" about how much inventory might be lost if, say, a Qool Mart was taken out in one shot by an attack copter.

Pardon me, Richard heard in his earplug, *if it's not too much trouble, could you begin to wrap up programming this evening and bring the camera outside, and beyond the parking lot as well? Thank you very much. We're anticipating an imminent violent incident and we'd prefer that you're not hurt and our property not damaged. Thank you very much in advance.*

My mother snapped, "Stop staring, Herb!" Then she smiled, God's own child again. "You're such a little daydreamer. Been through so much. Why not see if they have an ice cream you like? Or an ice pop? Whatever's less sticky."

"Okay."

"Well, whatever you want!"

To the back of the store I went. Geri kept an eye on me and an eye on the screen, and saw Richard rush up to my father and knock a hot dog out of his hand. Arms started flailing, jaws dropped, Whiting tried to rush the counter and tackle Musad, but Umer jumped on his back, sending them both tilting over onto the display case. Lottery tickets fluttered like moths across the lens of the camera. Adrienne ran off screen toward the doors. Jake punched Richard in the side of the head, and Barry rushed into the middle of it all, trying to hold everyone apart. Then everyone seemed to turn on him. My mother couldn't watch anymore; all the slapping and bumping was damaging her brand new world-view.

I wasn't ready for any more of this either. Instead of the ice cream freezer I went to the stand-up fridge that held all the milk, opened the door, and held it open by using a big gallon jug as a doorstop. Then I took out all the other gallon containers, sat on the floor, and sort of wiggled my way under the bottom shelf. It was a tight squeeze, but I was able to turn around onto my stomach and pull the gallon jugs back in. The employees and my mother were so entranced with the screen, and then, with their own dumb conversation—"Say, are you on TV?" "Well, sometimes, but maybe you saw *USA Today* yesterday? I'm Geri Weinberg. You're probably thinking of the front-page article, but I have to say that all those nasty things I said I no longer agree with. You see, I've found G . . ."—that they didn't notice all the jostling or even my grunting. The door closed when I pulled that first jug into the cooler after me. Qool Mart uses those great big coolers that are loaded from the back end, not the entrance, so I was able to shift onto my side and stand up, then push open the back door to the unit with my butt. I was alone in the dusty, cold, storage/ loading area at the back of the store.

The best part was that once my mother noticed I was missing, she went so crazy that she had to be sedated. The cops were everywhere: running slow with their high beams on to see if I was walking down the shoulder of the highway, checking the little wooded areas between housing developments, knocking on doors. A few of them had even taken the two Qool Mart employees—white kids with pimples and that dumb haircut everyone has—back to the precinct for a beating, in case they were Satanists or child molesters and working with "the enemy."

Nobody bothered to check the storage area. I drank an orange-strawberry-banana juice from a little container that came with its own straw and pulp strainer, and waited. I had a Qool Mart all to myself, my own little nation for a change. Herbia.

9

In Herbia, I finally felt free. And also chilly. But I remembered hearing on TV once that in the Middle East, old Arab traders were said to drink piping hot tea under the desert sun so that their internal and external temperatures would equate, so I tried the same with some ice pops. It's good to be king. I promised myself that I'd never be extradited. I still wasn't happy, though.

There was one cop car idling outside the store, but the whole place was otherwise abandoned. I'm small enough to not be seen over the counters, and I knew exactly where the junior officer in the car would be looking, and when, so I was able to just walk around the corner, through the Employees Only door, and into the Qool Mart proper, to grab some sweatshirts to use as blankets, and a few comics and magazines to keep myself busy. I also grabbed a flashlight, and a fistful of candy bars. Then it was back to Herbia, and back to my meditations.

At the Port Jameson Qool Mart, things had not gone well. Adrienne was sitting on her butt, moaning, having tripped and fallen, her head hitting the edge of a newspaper rack. Jake's arms were wrapped around my father's belly, while Dad was trying to cough up yet another hot dog–based peace treaty. Richard was screaming that an attack was imminent and that something had to be done. Whiting and the two representatives of the Muslim Republic were wrapped up in one another's limbs, and it sort of fell to Barry to handle things. He had a genius stroke and called Weinbergia.

"Weinbergia," said Kelly on the other end of the phone.

"Is there anything about us on the news?" Barry asked.

"Lemme check," said Kelly. She shouted at the din behind her and sighed the words, "Commercial commercial reality show," before saying, "Ah! No, you're not. Even we're not."

"Uhm—"

"That's bad," Kelly explained. "They must be planning something. Uhm, let me call you back, okay?" Before Barry could say

"No, wait—" or offer his eternal love or to lead an escape, she hung up.

Then she decided to talk to me. *Herb?* I heard from nineteen hundred miles away. Kelly was walking up the steps, then pushing her way into my old room. It had become a mini-workshop, full of sawdust and solder—Dad had had the idea to make little garden gnomes with glowing red eyes, to sell as folk art over the Internet—but nobody was on shift at the moment.

Herb? she thought again. *Can you hear me?*

I'd never heard anyone address me directly telepathically before. Well, not and expect me to answer. Sometimes in school I'd pick up something like "Hey, dipshit! Don't take the last lime Jell-O," on somebody's mind. And I wouldn't, but I would "accidentally" poke my thumb into it instead while reaching for a pudding.

I don't know if you can "talk" back to me or anything, but I've read your little notebook . . . you know the one, you stopped keeping it a long time ago. You were eight, but you didn't write like an eight-year-old. You described how your parents were thinking, how you could hear people in your head, and you even knew what was on people's mind when they thought in other languages.

I figure you're either really creative, need some kind of mental help, or . . . you're telling the truth.

Can you hear me?

Now I had to scramble for the phone. Another pair of cops had pulled up to the Qool Mart parking lot too, having gotten tired of searching the highway for me. Plus, the Scrapple Apple Pies (pork and MacIntosh, it's like an Easter dinner and dessert in your mouth!) were unguarded. A combination of the easy instincts of the police and pure dumb luck brought the new pair of police into the store and off to different corners where they could see every inch of the shelf space at once.

I hope you can. Something bad is going to happen. Hahaha, I said "going to." Like things haven't been happening already for months now, years. Damn damn, Kel, shut up. He wrote about this sort of blather in his dia—Herb, can you just ignore this part? Delete. Off the record. God, if you can hear me, can you tell me what's going to happen? What should I do?

The police, two young guys whose thoughts were all coffee buzz cut by the natural soothing qualities of a Qool Mart, dawdled over the products, just as I had an hour or so before. They were grooving to logos and bug-eyed mascots, and the occasional whiff of coffee or cheese floating in the air-conditioned breeze, the way you might half-listen to the radio or a CD full of waterfalls to go to sleep. But in the back of their heads, there was a sharpness. Always ready, always watching. I couldn't leave Herbia. No free trade for me, I was trapped behind my own borders, surrounded by belligerents with popular, if incomprehensible, ideologies. They thought I hated them, but they were the ones who hated me. All of them. Even my mother Geri. Even Dad, King Daniel I of Weinbergia. Kids are such a burden, and never quite work out the way you want them to. We're like pets, or really nice cars—you want to show them off, take care of them, own them, get and give affection, but there is still that massive chain of obligation, one that is one-way. Kids don't rush into burning buildings or bust up meth labs for the sake of the police, that's for sure.

It was getting hard to hear Kelly too, because my mother had managed to find a TV camera to put herself in front of, and now a million people were praying for me. I decided to do a kid thing. I squeezed out the back of the cooler, into the storage area, found the circuit breaker box, and flipped the big switch. There was cursing and the sound of fruit pies hitting the floor and then the flashlights went on. The cops headed to the Employees Only door to find the box while I walked back around to the cold room and slipped out under the bottom shelf of the milk fridge to the main part of the Qool Mart, claimed a calling card and a disposable cell phone in the name of Herbia, and then left the store to make a few calls.

"Hello, may I speak with Kelly please?" I affected as deep a voice as I could, holding my chin against my collarbone and speaking through my nose.

"Hey, is this Herb? Where are you, man?" It was one of those smelly guys from Vermont who had recently emigrated.

"I'm right outside the Qool Mart. Can I speak with Kelly please?"

"Aw, that's wicked. You're back with your dad—" I knew he'd jump to that conclusion, and then be happy enough to obey a child. "Sure, let me find Kelly. So, how's it goin' over there? Get any Cuebars?"

"Plenty for everyone," I said. "Listen, could you do my dad one more favor?"

"Sure, anything."

"Go get the gnome and bring it inside."

"Uh, why?"

"State secret. Need-to-know basis. You don't need to do it if you don't want to. I bet Kelly'll do it. But find her first, and if you do want to do your duty, be sure to keep it a secret, even from Kelly."

"No sweat, li'l dude," he said, then he shouted for Kelly.

———

"Hi," said Kelly softly.

"Hi."

"So it's—"

"—true," I finished.

"Are you going to—"

"—finish your sentences every time, as proof? No. And red with white lace trim. And you came up with the idea from that old *Superman* movie. And yes, I do think it's a little dirty to make a kid think of an adult woman in her underwear."

"So, what should I do?"

"There's going to be a helicopter attack on the Qool Mart. I'm not sure what to do," I told her. "But if you want to leave Weinbergia, you're going to have a chance. I know a lot of the soldiers are redeploying themselves along Route 25A because Dad left, but there are still a few hanging around."

"Yeah . . ." she said, tentative.

"Well, there's going to be a distraction. You can probably run over to Tommy Case's house without anybody noticing."

And then, in the tinny distance I heard over the phone some distant yelping and thumps. A soldier had spotted Curtis, the guy from Vermont, making a move for the bomb, and shouted "Hey, he's grabbing the gnome!" and a half-dozen buck privates ran across the border and onto the lawn to tackle and beat him down.

"Thanks!" Kelly said, and she ran out the back door of Weinbergia, the cell phone of state still in hand. She didn't run to Mister Case's, though she was thinking that she would, so she could watch some TV and stretch out on a carpet and have a drink of water and talk to someone without another thirty people breathing down her neck and interrupting and chewing loudly and guffawing at just the wrong moments. But as Kelly crossed the lawn and turned the corner, and saw the yellow and blue glow of the Cases' TV through the bellied-out mesh of their back screen door, she choked on some bitterness in her throat, and ran toward Route 25A.

She wasn't stopped, and didn't even meet any military traffic, except for trucks and occasionally a small brace of soldiers hoppin' to it on foot away from the Qool Mart. Down Valley Street to the port of Port Jameson, and the ferry to Connecticut. Out to Riverhead or even the Hamptons. One guy, a sniper painted dark and covered in a netting strewn with leaves, lowered himself off the high branches of a tree, and waddled, almost bow-legged, across Kelly's path, crossed Route 25A, and disappeared into someone else's tree-heavy lawn.

Kelly ignored the sign reading CLOSED and rapped at the door. Adrienne looked at her, eyes wide and face pale except for the big egg yolk bump on her temple. *My friend,* Adrienne thought, *whose side is she on now?* Kelly was just happy to see that Adrienne had decided that a knot was better than a steaming crater with its own parking lot, and she pointed at the handles of the door, pantomiming her request to be let in.

"Hey, it's not soundproof or anything," Jake called out. Dad nodded to Kelly as grandiosely as a man with two hot dogs in each hand could, and Barry took it as a signal to remove the broom and let her in.

"You guys, there's gonna be—"

"—a raid!" Whiting called from the back of the store. He and Umer were huddled by the toys section, filling plastic rockets with a mix of liquid soap and lighter fluid. Kelly hadn't even smelled a thing till she saw the bottles. "A helicopter, probably. Doubt it'll be a Blackhawk or anything of recent vintage, if it's even American."

"I thought the US was attacking?"

"No," Adrienne said. "They're just *letting* it happen to us."

"I find your lack of faith . . . disturbing," Jake said to Adrienne.

"We should really just evacuate," Richard said. "Cuebar is very serious about this."

"We're being attacked by Cuebar?"

"No, by my own erstwhile business partners," said Musad. Like my father, he was looking grandiose.

"Got it!" Dad said, happy but with clenched teeth. He had another piece of paper between his lips. He handed off the remaining hot dogs to Barry, and unrolled the paper to read it. Another treaty. Peace, in perpetuity, between all of Islam (why not?) and Weinbergia and all affiliates, co-thinkers, and well-wishers.

"This one, I'll sign," said King Daniel.

"That treaty ain't worth the paper it's written on," said Whiting as he gathered up the last red plastic rocket. "Or the hot dog it came out of." Umer, his own arms full of the thin hand pumps that served to pressurize the water kids would fill the rockets with in more peaceful times, nudged him forward.

"You guys seemed to be working together okay," Dad pointed out.

"It's all our necks."

"Ours as well," said Musad. "Thus, the treaty." Whiting snorted and stomped up to the counter to grab a handful of matchbooks and Umer reached up to snag a small vial of Krazy Glue, then the pair walked through the Employees Only door to head to the roof and set up their anti-aircraft battery.

"Can that actually work?" Kelly asked.

Barry shrugged and said, through a mouthful of hot dog, "Well, apparently Omar's grandpa shot down an Apache with a rifle or something, once upon a time."

"Umer," said Musad.

"Whatever," said Barry.

Then came the heavy beating of a rotor twisting through the air.

———

Hey, Kelly thought to me. *I guess this was a dumb idea all along.* I was tempted to call her again, but I know she wanted a monologue, and that she wished I was able to foretell the future and not just read minds, but I can't. If I could, I wouldn't be in my own personal mess now, telling you all this, would I?

It's pretty different than what you heard about on the news, huh?

Anyway, Kelly thought *I don't want to cry. I know that if I look at Adrienne, I'll start to cry. We were just friends, you know. Not even all that close. We were bored at work, and just wanted to be, I dunno, famous or something. Important. Part of history, whatever you call it. Like you are, Herb.*

I feel so bad. I can't even look at her; she probably hates me for that too now. Kelly started crying. Barry moved, arms wide, to hug her, but she jerked away. Everyone stared. Jake shrugged. She ran to the Employees Only door and then up the stairs to the roof, where Umer, Whiting, and the two other employees (both named Mohammed, their name tags reading *Mel* and *Johnny*), who had climbed up the service ladder on the side of the pillbox building to man the spotlight, were setting up. Kelly couldn't see the helicopter, but it was getting close. She was giddy with fear, like that burst of cold sweat when the dentist stops smiling and goes, "hmm." Would the store fall to flaming pieces beneath her, leaving her standing in air for a moment that would feel eternal, until it ended in a yank into the fire? That was all she could think of. Standing around a bunch of convenience store workers whose great idea was to launch toys full of homemade napalm at a leased attack copter didn't frighten Kelly at all. It didn't even occur to her.

My mother, all she could think of was me. Me, and making sure that everyone else in the world was also thinking of me. Was I in the grip of some foreign power, like the Palauvians, or was a new country born around me in a windowless brown van with mud over the license plates . . . a van-shaped country with no age-of-consent laws?

"Herbie, my darling, my love, my life," my mother told talk show host August Hickey over a cracking telephone line. You probably remember it: Hickey woebegone and staring into his mug while a map of the world pulsed behind him. A still of my mother, in black and white, with her fingers tucked awkwardly under her chin; a shopping mall glamour shop stripped of color for purposes of dramatic import, in the corner. LITTLE PRINCE LOST scrolling horizontally across the bottom of your TV screen.

The copter was a white and red light in the sky.

"There it is, boys," Whiting said, the captain in him asserting himself. "Let's stagger the launches. Umer, you'll launch that green number in your hands there as a tracer, then Mel can hit it with a second battery. Johnny, you man the spotlight, try to dazzle 'em. Qool Mart will probably come in low and strafe first, try to scare us, so we have a shot. And if your volleys all fail, I'll use my rocket." He paused, purposefully, dramatically. "For the killing blow."

Mel said, "Oh-kay." Johnny was already busy cleaning moths out of the bowl of the spotlight. Umer just started pumping his rocket.

"I know you can hear me," my mother said to the world, hoping I'd overhear.

Oh, I could.

"I'm sure he can hear me, August."

August nodded, "I am too. We're all praying that your son is somewhere out there, where he can hear you."

"Herb, please, be very careful. And whoever out there has my son, my son, Herb, please, let him go, bring him back home to his mother. I love him so much. Herb has been through just so much recently. He doesn't have a father figure in his life, no male role models. He doesn't know how to survive on his own."

I did wish that I had snagged some jerky or something before leaving the Qool Mart; I just didn't think of it. But with my luck I probably would have been caught somehow, and then I'd have to bring it back and apologize to the store manager or maybe even to Randall Hoyt, who was planning on killing my father.

My father was on the verge of a religious experience of his own. Not just head injuries, but stress and nitrates cause religious experiences. Also, believing your own press releases. Dad had all that going on, and the sound of winged death ("winged death"—he actually *thinks* like that sometimes) right outside, so he flipped.

"Musad," he declared, arms thrown wide. "Barry, Jake! Embrace! We are changing the world forever, finally and peacefully."

"Oh, let me get this," Richard said, cam back in his hands, to his knees and then back up, trying to get a good angle. Musad put out his arms gladly, Jake laughed and offered one arm to remain heterosexual, and Barry sighed and patted all available backs, careful now to turn his face and avoid the camera.

"Adrienne, come on, join the crew," said my father. "They're afraid of us. The Army, the government, big business. We're a threat to them," Dad said. Once again, it was good to be king. "What do you call 'em, Musad, the Great Satan?"

"Nooo," said Musad. "Imperialists, I guess. Not every Muslim believes whatever some mullah in Iran says."

"This is ridiculous," Adrienne said. "I'm leaving."

Jake snorted. "You can't leave. They'll kill you."

Barry said, "Or lock you up in Gitmo and throw away the key."

"No," my father said. "She can go. We're all our own country now. She's safe. You can't imagine America continuing after this. I mean, everyone knows the jig is up. Things will never be the same!" He turned to the camera—it's one of those things people do when they have religious experiences, try to spread the word with the power of eye contact—and said, "Don't you think? Haven't things changed for you out there?" He glanced up, at Richard. "And you?"

"Well, I think we should leave."

"So why don't you go, Richard?" asked Jake.

"C'mon!" said Adrienne.

"I guess I just want to see how this all ends," Richard said. "It's almost like being a journalist or something."

"It's going to end with us all dying!" said Adrienne. "Mark my words—"

"—Oh relax," my father interrupted. "Nothing is going to happen."

Then three bodies flitted into view and hit the parking lot, hard.

My mother sobbed, half for me, half as a way to fill the air while thinking of what else to say to all of you out there in televisionland. Finally she said, "I don't know what else to say, August. I just feel that there is a lot of love out there in the world, and that love is the most powerful force in the universe, and I just hope that everyone prays for everything to turn out okay. I just want everything to be back to normal."

Deep in August Hickey's lizard mind, the old high school reporter who wished that someone would give him the nickname "Scoop" or at least take him seriously, stirred. Dare he ask a follow-up question, instead of just letting this inane woman go on about prayers and love and her snot-nosed brat son, who was probably already in a goddamn ditch somewhere like all these kids always end up being? (Hey!) The hell with it, why not?

"By 'back to normal,'" August asked, his tongue and lips no longer even used to the idea of responding to a statement with a question, "do you mean back on Long Island, with your husband? No more countries, no more nuclear crises, no more martial law or garden gnomes or any of that, just back where you were in September?"

Whiting stood triumphant. His shoulders ached, he may have pulled something, he thought, but it was an honest injury. And those Muslim bastards didn't even land on their heads, so it's not like he killed anybody.

"You killed them!" Kelly shouted. *Dead, dead, dead* burned into her brain to the beat of the approaching copter. It was almost soothing in a way; she was hollering only to be heard.

"Ah, they're fine," Whiting shouted back, dismissively waving a rocket. "Fine as those little bastards need to be. Now, let's get that spotlight ready; we'll signal for a pickup, leave the terrorists downstairs, and then my boys'll take care of them."

"We can't do that!"

"You wanna die with the rest of 'em? Go ahead—"

"—but the plan, the rockets."

Whiting tossed Kelly the rocket he'd been holding. "Plastic toys filled with lighter fluid and soap? Good luck, dear." He stomped past her to the spotlight on the other end of the roof, just as the wind of the copter hit the roof hard. The pilot turned on the copter's own floodlight and washed the roof blind.

"Hello!" said a voice, amplified and crackling. "Are either of you Qool Mart employees?" Then the greeting and question were repeated robotically in Arabic. Then in Farsi. In Urdu.

"Yes!" called out Whiting.

"No!" shouted Kelly.

"They're going to save us," Whiting hissed.

"They're gonna blow up the building, why would they save us?"

"Attention Qool Mart employees. Your employment has been as of this moment terminated by order of the Qool Mart board of directors. This means that your employee insurance has been cancelled. This decision may be appealed by submitting an appeal request within sixty days to the Global Arbitration and Mediation Association."

Again the statements were repeated with the weird microchip tinge of a computerized translation, and when the third translation was finished, the copter spun so that its side was parallel with the front of the store, the door slid open, and a man holding a rocket-propelled grenade launcher and wearing a traditional Qool Mart blazer—except no name tag and no little hat—poked out from the interior and took aim.

Kelly planted her feet, wound up, and threw the toy rocket into the wind. It clunked off the edge of the RPG launcher, split open, and spun liquid fire in an arc over the man's head and into the copter. The copter lurched and the computerized voice started again, but squealed hysterically like an old record being played at the wrong speed. The guy fell back and into the bright orange sheet of flame on the far wall of the helicopter, not thinking anything at all but "Whoa!" as he dropped the RPG launcher, which hit the parking lot, bounced hard once, twice, and then didn't go off. The copter, spewing white and black smoke, roared and tore upwards over the rooftops of Port Jameson.

Whiting stared at her, aghast. Kelly said, "Softball. Three-year varsity." Then she cracked her knuckles.

Things seemed to happen very quickly from inside the Qool Mart. Umer and the Mohammeds tumbled into view and lay on the ground, not altogether still. Wind from the helicopter's rotors picked up trash and sand and junk from the parking lot and painted the windows in brown and the flashy reds of newspaper coupon pages. The announcements were made.

"That's not a very good translation," Musad commented.

"Oh, the humanity," Richard said, bending down again and tilting his little camera to take a shot of the underbelly of the helicopter.

"Is there a basement?" asked Jake. "Another entrance somewhere?"

Barry and Adrienne looked toward my Dad, both of them like kids desperately sure that the big man in their life could solve any problem.

"History's on our side," he said.

"Does that mean you have a plan?" Barry asked.

Adrienne answered first. "No, it means that he doesn't care whether or not we die anymore!"

Dad only smiled. Then the copter flared, and the RPG launcher fell, and bounced. Everyone gasped, and even Dad twitched a bit. It bounced again. Barry felt his consciousness sliding down into the core of his spine. Then the launcher settled, and hadn't fired. Umer got on his knees and gave a thumbs-up. Then, from the back of the store, there was a yelp, and half a dozen sharp thuds, and a few more yelps.

Richard swung his camera, and the others all ran for the Employees Only door, from which the sound had come.

Musad held up a hand. They weren't employees. He opened the door and in the tiny vestibule where the door to the restroom was shut and the one to the roof was flung open lay Captain Whiting on his back, his face dipped in deep red blood and his nose smashed up against his face. Kelly walked down the steps and explained, "Tae Kwon Do. Six years."

Somehow my father decided that he was entirely responsible for all of this. Kelly didn't help when she walked up to King Daniel, spread her arms, and said, "I get it now. I really, really do. We can do anything we want, anything we need to. That's real freedom."

Kelly stopped thinking to me. She stopped thinking *of* me. And so did my dad.

My mother didn't know what to say, or even what to think. The last dregs of her religious experience melted away, leaving her at a total loss. The whole thing hit her at once: no fame, no God, no marriage, no child, a public spectacle and possibly even exposed to harmful amounts of radiation. That's her life. Geri's life, the girl with the big blonde wings in her high school yearbook, the former Realtor, the woman who likes to dip Double Stuf Oreos into her tea because it makes her feel like a kid and an adult at the same time.

Is Daniel having an affair? was the first coherent thought to emerge from the fog, even as Hickey was desperately asking follow-up after follow-up now, just to avoid doing something other than staring silently off into the distance. "Do you hate the people of Weinbergia? Have you found another man, like the tabloids say? What about Muslims, are they behind all of this, you think? Are you a Christian? What's the last thing you said to your son? What were you doing at a Qool Mart one hundred and ten miles away from your home tonight? Do you think your son is dead? What will you do if Herbert is dead?!"

My mother pictured me dead, face white, eyes wide and still like they were painted plastic, a bit of blood on the lip. Leaves and kicked up dirt everywhere around me, limbs bent exactly the wrong way at elbows and knees. Like the men named Mohammed in the parking lot, but without groaning, no movement, no dizzying replays of the world slipping out from under their feet and bonking them on the head. Like looking at a photo of myself, or a videotape, more than half blind because not only can I read any thoughts of myself, but there's nothing there at all, not a twitch or a spark of anything, just me, but no!

"NO!"
Except without even that no.

But that no is what you heard from me, the first time I shouted rather than listened, three days ago. I didn't know that I was able to transmit thoughts, to do anything other than eavesdrop on the world all at once.

As it turns out, I can. My nose starts bleeding, my head feels like two Mack trucks smacked into either side of it, I fall down, and I wake up starved and cold a day later when it rains on me. It took a couple of days to get the new ability under control; it was like bicycling with the training wheels off. I didn't want to clue my parents in to where I was, and I think I might have caused a couple of traffic accidents over on the highway just from thinking, "Shut up, shut up, SHUT UP!" but now I can do it. Telepathy is much easier now.

So.

So, here we all are then.

10

There are one or two things I know. Reading minds isn't the same as knowing everything, even though I can pick up a lot. Language isn't an obstacle, words are just wrapping paper—you know whether you get a hockey stick or a pair of socks for your birthday based on the shape of the toy or the box; it doesn't matter what design the paper is. But still, some things are unrecognizable. I don't know what the big sigma on some math equations is good for, or what epistemology is or how ambergris was turned into perfume or why Amish people stay Amish or anything like that.

I mean I know what people *think* about those things, when they think it, but that's all. Seeing the hockey stick and playing hockey are two different things.

But, like I said—like I've *been* saying, I know a few things. I said my Dad wasn't crazy when he founded Weinbergia, and it's true, he wasn't. He is *now*, but that's just another thing I know. I know that I need to grow up. It happens to almost everyone eventually; you look at your parents and you see their mistakes, or you bury them and go through their stuff afterwards and you see the gaps: the passport with no stamps on it, because they never made it overseas thanks to all the terror alerts and wars—or just because they liked dreaming on their couch with a coffee table full of pamphlets better.

Or other things. All over the world. The first time your goatherd father fell down while you watched and hurt himself and cried. When your mother cursed in front of you, and then slapped you across the face for being shocked that she'd said a bad word. The first time you go over to your piggy bank or little stash of money and find that there's less change there than there should be, then you smell the tobacco drifting through the screen windows facing the backyard. And you see this, and you grow up.

It happens. It just usually doesn't involve lots of foreign policy and talk shows and explosions.

You probably know the story. The Weinbergians raided a gas station for Cuebars—well, Richard had an expense account and just signed for them, but Kelly did wave the grenade launcher around—and pushed their way back home with the help of the RPG (Kelly said "ROTC" as she hefted it, but she was really just on a crazy brain chemistry high and had never been anywhere near a gun or anything like that before. She'd kicked a man in the face, and was now all-powerful.) The Army let them right back in, having already dismantled the gnome bomb, and replacing the statue exactly as it was before.

Dad guessed this would happen and wanted it to. He was tired of the stresses of living in Weinbergia in the nuclear shadow of his own plans. Commercial endorsements were a much better deal. The next day a squad of elite Special Operators burst into the kitchen, guns high on their shoulders, but Adrienne smiled at them and gestured toward the brand new stainless-steel three-door Kelvin Refrigertainment Center from which she had just retrieved an ice bag for the bump on her head. They lowered their guns and took down their face masks to smile and nod at one another. She opened the center door. The camera inside—it clicked on along with the little light—recorded their happy wonderment at the size of the fridge, the rotating cake tray, and the holographic smiley faces that floated over the plastic containers of veggies, sauces, and various leftovers, signaling freshness. One face had a flat-mouthed look . . . better eat that tortellini soon.

I'm sure you all saw that on TV. You might remember PFC Norris from that episode of *Law & Order* where he played that genius crack addict with Tourette's syndrome. (He got a haircut.) Richard got in good with a few casting directors in the city. Now Weinbergia is all about product placement—and interdictions of suspected Canadians, whom Dad keeps in the basement and pretends to torture. They're fed well, of course, and have their own TV and free access to the basement's half-bath, which actually puts them ahead of the Weinbergian citizens on the upper floors. But the poor things do have to put up with all sorts of questions about Canada whenever someone comes downstairs to get some rice or find a wrench. "Wait, what do you call those hats again? Tooks? I know you told me yesterday, but I forgot." "So, how do doctors make any money?" "Chocolate Twinkies? You're kidding!" That sort of thing.

And my mother? Well, today you got the blue ribbon in the mail. Yes, Geri had decided to reclaim the blue ribbon for herself, because hers are *light* blue, you know, for "boy," so you'd think of me, and pray for me, and then Geri's Generic God would be compelled to get off His holy duff and hand me over. Plus, all the companies that got to put their logos and offers for flashlight keychains and figurines—one of them is modeled after me at age five, except with huge ink blot eyes—loved the idea and paid some private eyes to find me, and some publicists to tell the TV that there were private eyes looking for me.

Even the Islamic Republic of Qool Mart Store No. 351 got into the act—it's a tax haven and makes meth out of cough syrup, then launders the money through a large commercial bank in the city. You know, for freedom's sake. And it keeps your mortgage rates low.

Needless to say, I'm leaving my parents, the Weinbergians, the cops, the army, the PIs, and anyone else who might come after me right now out of this little conversation. And yes, I know what you're thinking: what if someone else, one of us, tells? Well, go ahead and tell. Who do you think will be more open to the possibility that you're receiving a psychic message from me, complaining about my parents: my born-again-twice-a-day mother and her concussion, or the guy who made himself king of his own living room?

Or you could go to the authorities. You could even prove your claim by telling them that you know that the bomb was removed and replaced with a seemingly identical garden gnome during the Qool Mart Treaty crisis. Enjoy your trip to Cuba afterwards. Or, you could hear me out.

What I want to do is be home. This is not the same as going home, because you can never go home again. (See, I listen.) That's what my folks have taught me—Weinbergia is just America Junior now, a TV show with a flag, a tax shelter where at least they speak English and worry about showering often enough, so it's just like the US. My mother thinks the whole universe is watching out for her. God is the mom and dad who never gets mad, always does the right thing, and who can solve any problem, and make everything feel better.

You know, I never remember thinking that of my own folks. One of my earliest memories was of a hard fever, so hot it hurt to blink. Geri was hovering over me of course, with damp washcloths and plenty of juice and then ice packs and children's chewable aspirin that were so gross-tasting to me that I puked them up, so I was put in a cold bath with ice and the next round of tablets were melted into the orange juice and fed to me via tablespoon. She looked at me when I drank the stuff, smiled a thin paper smile, and told me that I was a good boy and that everything would be all right. And just as she said that, she thought—and this was the first thought I had ever heard, other than my own—that she had no idea what she was doing, was a horrible mother, and might end up killing this damn kid. She even entertained, for a second, the idea of just burying me in the group courtyard of the garden apartment complex in which we lived at the time, in case I did die, because she didn't want her own mother to find out if anything ever happened to me. It was just for a second, but she thought it, and she didn't utterly expel it from her mind afterwards, but used me in a hole as a way to distract herself from me on the couch. *"What would I tell Daniel?" "Good thing Herb isn't in school yet— only a few people will miss him." "Does Daniel love me enough to forgive me if something happened—to help dig?"*

So I always knew parents were faking it. Enough of you are anyway to make the whole world a conspiracy against children. You fall right into it after a certain age. One time, in kindergarten, we were on a class trip and my teacher, Mrs. Surgus, had some trouble controlling us. It was sunny, the bus had been full of fumes, and it had been a cold winter with a lot of slush but not too much snow, and this April afternoon felt like the first *real* day of spring. Nobody wanted to hold hands as we walked in double-file. We were all big, most of us had turned six, and hands were sticky and the breeze was so nice and there were lots of things to point at, even on the block between where the bus had let us out and the Port Jameson Museum, which featured harpoons, nets, and the actual desk where a judge once sat while he tried suspected witches.

But it was always a cold February day for Mrs. Surgus—yes, I see you out there still, and it's true, it's true, and what I'm about to say isn't the only secret of yours I know, *Eleanor*—so she decided to put a scare into us. She spotted a man in the window of a creaky old building with one of those haunted-house porches, he was a handyman who was fixing the place up a bit to sell, and pointed to him and said, "Behave, or that man'll get you!" and obligingly the man raised his arms, a long screwdriver in his right hand, and howled like an animal. They didn't know each other, it wasn't a plan. It was just two grown-ups acting in solidarity, because they know how important it is to keep kids terrified and obedient. I knew the truth in a way that the other kids could never imagine, and that made me more scared than any of them. You're either part of the conspiracy, or against the conspiracy.

I could tell stories like this all day, but twilight is coming and it's getting cold again. I just want to tell you something, then ask you a favor.

What I have to tell you: the world you're in is not the world you're from. There are two ways to grow up, and it's just that so far everyone's chosen the easy way—just get new parents and do what they tell you. All families are unhappy, but some—Saudi Arabia, Qool Mart, the Mormons, being "in sales"—are more abusive than others. But even unhappy families are made out of happy people. Nearly everyone has some kind of friend, and if you didn't before, you do now. Me! And if you don't like me, at least I'm a conversation starter. You have something to talk to your pretty neighbor or the guy who sits next to you on the bus or the woman in the next cell about.

Hey, are you hearing what I'm hearing?

Yeah! Freaky, huh?

God, I hope he's not messing up some brain surgeon's concentration right now.

Don't worry, I'm not. For some of you, this is just a daydream, or a smell like the doughnuts you ate as a kid, or a paperback novel, or the orange blobs you see when you squeeze your eyes shut, but you're all in this together. We're all in this together. Well, you all are. I'm going to grow up the *other* way. But I need your help.

Specifically, I need you to forget, just for a few minutes, everything you think you know about kids and travel and the dangers of the shoulder of the highway and the outstretched arm. I need you to anticipate my coming and do something other than shout at me, "Hey kid, get off my lawn!"

Because I'm going back to Weinbergia.

11

Lenora Cline-McGrath: "Life is a strange and wonderful place, full of the bittersweet and just plain bitter," my grandma always used to say. "But it's the second that makes the first taste better," and indeed, she was one hundred percent right. I like having my own country with Gary. We signed a separate peace treaty too, with about three hundred different countries. Have you seen treatyonline.org yet? It's very handy.

Politically, we argue all the time, but he's pretty open to being educated. He's a passionate man. Ever since the bomb, he's just gotten more passionate. We all have to help each other now, I guess. Of course, it was horrible, a tragedy, nothing will ever be the same, but you just have to keep on living. We're living just fine out here. We're very open now, even single-race couples can emigrate if they wish to, as long as they can pass our citizenship tests. We interview them and if they can get through it without saying "Some of my best friends are . . ." or "I grew up around . . ." then they're good.

We do get a fair amount of hate mail, it's true. But that's fine, live and let live. Have your opinion; have your ugly-ass stamps with your cracker grandfather on it, that's fine. We don't care. We're happy now. How many people can truly say that they're happy?

[laughs] Yeah, I know. Everyone is supposed to say that they're secretly happy now, right?

Roger Whiting: I was being debriefed, so that's why I'm alive today. We're lucky—damn sure that *I'm* lucky at least—that there was some concern that I'd turned, so I wasn't present in DC that day. Yeah, by debriefed I mean interrogated, but by interrogated I don't mean tortured or anything. They let me have a coffee, tissues, anything I wanted. About seventeen hours, all told, including the polygraph. It was fine. I'm just glad to be home. I'm still an American. Arizona is full of *normal* people, thank the Lord.

Richard Pazzaro: We were watching TV in the living room when it happened. First the gnome started falling over, then it fell over. Then came the light. That was pretty much it. I know we're not supposed to use the word ironic anymore, but it just seemed, you know, ironic to me that the bomb was being paraded around as some sort of trophy. It was like the Soviet Union or something, wasn't it? Well, they marched their own weapons through Red Square, not captured ones, but if they *had* captured an American nuke or something, I'm sure they would have shown it off.

Jesus Porter (former Secretary of Veteran Affairs): Yeah, we joked about it, my undersecretaries and I. Everyone after the Attorney General in the line of succession does. Even after 9/11, or so I was told. I was still in the private sector then. VA was never a "lesser" department, succession is based on the founding of the particular Cabinet departments.

I didn't return to Washington, but not because I was afraid. Never let it be said that I was afraid. Really, what was there to be afraid of? I was in Burlington, visiting my mother. The city had already "gone indie," as the kids say, but there was an open border and we weren't recognizing any microstates at the time, and really *nobody* was, not even their own so-called citizens. All the stores on Church Street still took American scrip, and that's really the decisive element of the existence of a state as far as I'm concerned. So I was there and I was fine with it, and security was fine with it, and the FBI was entirely fine with it.

I just didn't want to go back. I never wanted to be president. It struck me, walking through the streets after I'd heard, with people gathering around their car radios, others opening up their windows and bringing their TVs to the windowsills, just to let the people hear what was going on . . . there wasn't panic. There wasn't even much sadness, not once the estimated death counts were dialed down from forty-five thousand to six hundred. And the wind didn't blow the radiation into Virginia or the suburbs. Most of the people I met just seemed relieved, as if an obnoxious uncle had left and the unpleasant Christmas dinner was finally over. So I decided to stay here. I run a little juice stand three days a week. It's nice. I like working with people.

Mirella "Madusa" McAlister: I picked the kid up on the Kansas-Missouri border. He looked fine. Clean, well fed. I'd heard him. I didn't want to get into trouble, but I didn't want to get him into trouble either. Herb was a polite little man. No, I never wanted children; I barely had a mother of my own, so it wasn't my ovaries talking. We stopped outside Jefferson City for a potty break and next thing I know, I'm in Little Rock, and only then did I remember that he wasn't with me anymore.

Adam Indore: We tracked him for a while. SatMaps.com is really handy. You know, I'm sure. One time, I used it to find a key-chain that fell out of my pocket at Burning Man. I had spares of all the keys, of course, but the keychain was a limited edition that came as some swag if you bought a *The Stars My Destination* DVD boxed set on the first day, and I was on the line for three days to get it, so it had a lot of sentimental value. It was really lonely looking out there on the playa by itself. Anyway, I put out a call on all the listservs, and the next year someone snagged it for me and delivered it to Camp The But I Love Hims and Other Fake Band Names, which I was associated with that year. So it's a great tool, I highly recommend it.

Anyway, yeah, we were tracking him, and I was using this Tibetan technique I'd picked up at my dojo to blank out my mind so he wouldn't sense my endeavor, but I guess my roommate Todd—and he won't be my roommate anymore after the lease is up, that's for sure—gave it away because after that he'd constantly duck under doorways or walk under the canopy of trees on highway dividers.

Laurel Richards: The numanist community will never be the same.

Kelly Donnor: God, I wish I was famous for *just* fifteen minutes. The books, the PhD dissertations, the *cultists*, they just don't stop. Half of them have me set up as the Virgin Mary to Herb's Jesus, the rest want me to be Mary Magdalene. I used to argue with them, but there's no dissuading true believers. What Herb's message was, I mean, to the extent that he even had a message, is just this: "Grow up!" You're not supposed to be looking for a new mama and a new papa, especially when that new mama is me. Of course, true believers, like I said. How many murders has "Thou Shalt Not Kill" prevented? How many murders have true believers in "Thou Shalt Not Kill" precipitated? Yeah, that's my point.

No, I haven't kicked anyone in the face since that night. After the adrenaline wore off, I found out I tore a tendon. Thank God Weinbergia had a doctor. She was just out of her residency, and she really wanted to help the unfortunate. It was either us or India, and she wanted to be close to a mall. Isn't that a riot?

Herb hasn't talked directly and only to me since that night either, no. I miss him. I haven't talked to Adrienne either. I think she emigrated to Ocean Parkway in Brooklyn. Was she sleeping with Daniel? Ugh, I hope not.

Thomas Case: I don't give two craps. I didn't give two craps before, and I don't give two craps now. You know what "growing up" is? Growing up is getting a job; making sure your kids are fed, healthy, go to school; and minding your own business. I just want to live my life. Anything that helps is good. Anything that hurts is bad. I had a lot of civil rights, and they didn't help. I gave some up, it didn't help. My neighbor built a nuke, and that didn't help either, and neither did all those soldiers peeing on my driveway and leaving their cigarette butts everywhere.

The whole thing was just disgusting, I tell you. I don't bust my ass every day to come home to that. People should have some respect. That's growing up!

I want to see what these cooler-than-thou types are gonna do when the Mexicans come swarming over the border, or when there's a hurricane and nobody to fix up their little "country" homes after the flooding.

from topplethegnome.com: The "official account" of the events—to the extent that anything emerging from the Georgetown Rump can be considered "official"—of 10/19 is full of inconsistencies and even impossibilities, but the media is not interested in seeking out the truth. Take the following into account:

How does a nuclear bomb, even a small, home-brew bomb, manage to detonate after falling onto its side? This has never happened before in the history of the existence of nuclear weapons. Wouldn't the vibrations from the travel from New York to our nation's former capital have set it off? What about the fissionable material that traversed our nation's highways during the Cold War, and the third Gulf War, and the Sino-Sacramento incident?

Why wasn't the gnome secured? Why wasn't the gnome disarmed?

Why, for the first time in recent memory, was there a "parade of spoils" that left the president and so much of the cabinet vulnerable and out in the open?

What about video footage of the "first flash," which was also widely reported by witnesses?

What about "Weinberg Sympathy Syndrome?", the so-called mental disorder widely reported on in the days immediately before the detonation?

THE ANSWERS WILL SHOCK YOU!!

There is only one force on Earth capable of eliminating the federal government of the United States, and that is . . . the federal government of the United States. Remember that the government is huge, being both the single largest employer and the single largest spender of money in the world. Many layers of government exist "below" the figurehead president and his cabinet-level appointees; these civil servants have frequently been called "the permanent government" by social scientists and other legitimate scholars.

Also note:

Not one of the one hundred and nine Republican representatives or the forty-one senators were on the platform or dais at the time of the explosion. Why would they not be in attendance on that fateful day?

Not one member of the Supreme Court was in even Washington, DC, on 10/19.

The IRS, Federal Reserve, VA, Homeland Security, and

FEMA—all elements of the "permanent government"—had "off-capital" offices up and running within hours of the detonation . . . as if such an attack had been planned for in advance.

FACTS:

Approval ratings for the president were at a historic low of 21 percent on 10/17.

The government had "shut down" earlier that year due to contentious budget battles in Congress. Without news reports . . . would you have noticed?

Since the detonation and the subsequent secession trend, the Georgetown Rump government was able to withdraw billions from infrastructure, entitlement, law enforcement, and other federal projects. Much of this money has been poured into deficit and debt recovery, enriching foreign creditors with close connections to the various remaining federal departments.

Most of the "new countries" that have emerged in the wake of the Weinbergia secession and then post-10/19 retain American customs, language, tastes, and sometimes even our money. They have simply excluded themselves from both taxation and services, allowing a networked underground economy to emerge. A network that actually allows for a number of previously illegal activities to emerge unchecked . . . but for the profit of the Rump, which can now get away with those activities as well!

Think about it. Who has the motive, the means, and the opportunity to seemingly strike a "killing blow" against the American government? The answer is clear: the American government destroyed itself in a public and inexplicable way, in order to consolidate its power. The president and his "bully pulpit" are gone, and now only the pure bureaucratic force of apparatchiks— a bureaucracy much larger and more powerful than is needed to provide "services" to their so-called "citizens"—remains. The Gnomes of Zurich are AMERICAN and they have ALREADY WON!!

Ty Towns, Bargeland: We didn't pick him up, he just showed up, really. I'm not sure how he got onto the barge. Jedi Mind Trick or something? We have lots of dinghies, supplies coming on and off all the time. He could have snuck onto any of them. Smart kid. Little creepy, though. Funny how he stayed so clean; lots of people must have taken him in for a night or two, let him use the shower, get a good night's sleep on a guest dignitary bed.

Geraldine "Geri" Weinberg was unavailable for comment, on the advice of her lawyers and her spiritual adviser, TV personality Dr. Hamilton Crabb.

King Daniel I, Weinbergia: He came to the door, right after sunset one night. A few of the people in the living room were pretty spooked. We'd been following the news as best we could, of course, and lots of people were very helpful in reporting their encounters to us. I just wasn't sure what was going on—obviously, a lot of the information we'd received was false. People claimed he was dead, that he appeared before them in "ectoplasmic form" (whatever that is), that he was claiming to be the "Holy Grail" and a descendent of Jesus, or a Muslim. We had a big cork bulletin board in the rumpus room with all the sightings, to try and separate the wheat from the chaff.

I wanted to hug him, but my arms just felt heavy, like lead, and I couldn't move them from my sides. I wasn't afraid or anything; after all I'd been through in trying to get this country off the ground, I think the fear centers of my brain had burnt themselves out. But I couldn't move, and I knew he had something to do with it.

"Dad," he said, "just listen." And he talked for a while, about being a grown-up and what he thought it meant. It was kid stuff mostly, *Catcher In The Rye*–style preciousness, but he really thought he was on to something. Heh, I dunno. Maybe he was at that. Basically, I guess he just sees that when people are patriotic, when they care about a society that's greater than themselves, when people find what they have in common with others and form nations, that they're somehow pathological or neurotic to do so. He said that the solution to imaginary lines wasn't more imaginary lines. That "vertical formations" don't work, whether they're families or countries.

I wanted to tell him, "Hey, how far do you think you would have gotten if it wasn't for me making sure your little butt was wiped and there was food on the table?" but I couldn't say anything. I didn't like that, but then it occurred to me that I'd, and plenty of times, made him stand in a corner and be quiet while I lectured him about proper behavior. Is that how it feels? I guess I remember that queasy stomach feeling from when I was a kid too, but I got over it.

I was proud of him, though, because he thanked me. Lots of kids his age would fire back with "I never asked to be born!" or something as juvenile. He said he was very grateful to be raised by a man like me, by someone who "almost got it." I guess I've said I've never asked to be born American, eh? Yeah, he pointed that out to me, as if he could read my mind. But the final trick is to ask what you *were* born to be, and to be that thing.

Then he disappeared. No, he didn't run off, he disappeared. I realized then that after he was kidnapped, I'd really stopped thinking about him. Affairs of state got in the way. I missed him, but he was with his mother, and really, the border wasn't the best place for a child. My great-great grandmother sent her son to America long ago, so he'd be safe from the pogroms, so it was sort of the same thing . . . wasn't it?

12

Qool Marts are different now. There are a lot more weird things on the shelves, like homemade taffy from some old lady's country down the block. In another store, a few miles and two border stations away, it's all misshapen cookies with vanilla and chocolate frosting. One of the ones Rich and I stopped at on our whirlwind tour even had real stew, and benches to sit at, and corn bread. They took out the hot dog machines and microwaves and turned the front of the store into a picnic area. It's pretty nice, but uneven. Sometimes I miss being able to walk into any Qool Mart or McDonald's or whatever and being sure that every bite and every glance would be exactly the same. Sort of like bathrooms in the suburbs I've walked through.

Also, sometimes the new Qool Marts just throw rocks at the car when they see us coming.

We got some plastic sunglasses and ice cream sandwiches—a local brand where the sandwich part actually tastes like chocolate, maybe even too much like chocolate. But it beats the old industrial confection: an inert substance designed to have the peculiar texture and flavor of not-quite-right-but-inoffensive. Richard had the camera. We paid with exposure on our feed, except for the gas. A pile of various local monies did that trick.

In the car, Richard put the cam on the dash and said, as he said after every stop, "Well Herbie—where to?"

"I dunno," I said. "Canada?"

CIA World Factbook

Weinbergia

Background
The first of the modern "armed micronation" trend, Daniel Weinberg built a nuclear device in '19—and seceded from the United States. Open "borders" into the fledgling state and a custody case led to a tense standoff between Weinberg and the United States, which was resolved when the nuclear device was captured without incident. The device later accidentally detonated in Washington, DC.

Geography
Location: Divided lot on North Shore of Long Island.
Geographical Coordinates: 40 N 56 , 73 W 03 Area: 40' x 200'
Note: Includes home of 20' x 50'
Area Comparative: One third of one city block. (Washington, DC)
Land boundaries: *total*: 480' *border countries*: United States 480'
Coastline: —
Environment current issues: Lice infestation from "refugees."

People
Population: No indigenous inhabitants
Note: Approximately thirty-seven individuals, thirty-two of them American citizens, have taken up residence in Weinbergia and have renounced their citizenship. A UN observer (Palau) is also a long-term resident as of 1 December 20—.
Languages: English, "Weinbergian" pidgin

Government
Country name:

Conventional long form: The Kingdom of Weinbergia
Conventional short form: Weinbergia
Dependency status: A sovereign nation, in practice Weinbergia closely adheres to US laws and social mores.
Capital: Living room
Legal system: King is standing sovereign, with moral suasion and pseudo-consensus driven voice votes among population working as a *de facto* veto.
Executive branch:
Chief of state: King Daniel I, Weinbergia
Head of government: King Daniel I, Weinbergia
Elections: Issue ballots with voice votes, as needed.
Diplomatic representation in the US: None
Diplomatic representation from the US: None
Flag description: Several models of the flag, some parodic, have been offered. Most common is a dark blue field with an image of Daniel Weinberg at age twenty-three, with sideburns and sunglasses, in the center.

Economy
Economy overview: Economic activity is limited to funding extraordinary rendition, remittances from ideological cothinkers, "off the back" infusions from new immigrants, and intellectual property (book, reality programming, video game) based on Weinbergian "concept."

Communications
Radio broadcast stations: None. Uses podcast technology.
Television broadcast stations: None. Uses Internet connections to stream media.

Military
Military note: Weinbergia is no longer a nuclear power.

Under My Roof

I started getting political in college, when I got to meet people with a wide variety of opinions ranging from the anarchocapitalist to the Maoist, and when George H. W. Bush launched the invasion of Iraq. The months' long build-up to war was nerve-wracking, and the horror unleashed was made even worse for the fact that despite mass media on the ground, the war was all but universally depicted as a walk in the park. The US-led coalition easily pushed the occupying force out of Kuwait, met almost no resistance from Iraqi forces, thumped Saddam Hussein on the nose with a rolled-up newspaper, and then everything was fine. The mainstream anti-war movement had been shamed into prefacing every criticism of war with a ritual claim of "supporting our troops," and the main political discussion after the war had to do with whether or not Bush should have pushed Hussein out of power.

Even universities, supposedly a bastion of the radical left, were the home of "pro-troop" (read: pro-war) rallies. I protested where I could, argued to the extent I was able, and retreated into literature. I read Aristophanes—he was Greek, funny, and critical of war, just like someone I knew well—and became enamored with his play *Acharnians*. In it, a man sues Sparta for a personal peace and gets it, while the Athenians around him continue to wage war and suffer. Sounded good to me, especially since the people in my community had no taste for peace. I decided to work on a modern-dress version of the play, in which a normal family would build a nuclear device out of everyday items and declare their independence from the United States.

Under My Roof started out as a screenplay, though I got no further than one scene in which a man walking down a Long Island beach with a metal detector becomes the first unlucky casualty of a surface-to-surface missile launched by the submarine. The punchline was that in the moments before impact, the metal detector went crazy. It was still the 1990s, and I got heavily involved in anti-war and anti-occupation activism around the Balkans, Somalia, and Haiti, but again, the people around me were sick of peace and autonomy for all. "Humanitarian intervention" was the new pro-war-as-anti-war watchword.

After I published my first novel, *Move Under Ground*, to some success, I needed a follow-up. The first few thousand words of *Under My Roof* came easily, but then I stalled out and decided to instead upend my life and leave New York for the first time and move to California. That put me in an economic pit of debt that took me years to escape from, but it did inspire me to finish the book. But, perhaps unsurprisingly, New York publishing had no taste for anti-war sentiment. One editor, ultimately in the employ of professional war propagandist Rupert Murdoch, told my agent that she loved the book; she thought it would make a great YA or even middle-grade novel for boys, an underserved market. "But," she said, "instead of a nuclear bomb, can't the kid have a girlfriend or something?"

I ended up selling the book myself to my erstwhile employer, Soft Skull Press. While not as radical as it once was when it was run semi-legally out of a basement on the Lower East Side, Soft Skull was enthusiastic about the project, and even paid me a few bucks to finish it. Everything was going well. The cover design concepts were beautiful. Bookstore events were were announced.

Then Soft Skull's distributor went bankrupt. Soft Skull, which often borrowed money from the distributor to pay its printing bills, nearly went along with it. Instead of a copy-edit, *Under My Roof* got a once-over by an intern. Thanks to a missing scene break, the meaning of the end of the book was literally changed to something much darker and sadder than I ever intended. The great cover concepts were too expensive to actually produce, so instead the book got a stock photo of a cloud and a white band. My agent of the time described it as a cover more suited for "a breast cancer memoir" than a satire about nuclear war and nuclear families. The book stayed on a loading dock for a month, and the remainder of my advance wasn't paid for another eight months. I was lucky, in a way, as the book was printed but not distributed on time, so it wasn't considered an asset.

Despite the problems, the book got decent reviews, and also appeared in German and Italian. A review in the *San Diego Union-Tribune* not only called it "the great American suburban novel," it led, five years later, to a phone call from a San Diego–area maker of commercials and industrial films. He wanted to do a feature, and thought my book would be perfect, as most of the action is limited to a house and a nearby convenience store. Maybe the budget would be a million dollars. Maybe two million. I'd get several percent. We drew up an option agreement, and I wrote my first script for an extra pittance, and a promise of more money were it used.

For a long time, nothing happened. Eight months later, I heard back from the filmmaker. His wife had a new draft of my script, and they wanted me back in to write a third, happier version. As it turns out, I was better at writing my characters than someone else. So, I did it. Then, more months of waiting. More drafts were written without my input. My voicemail messages went unanswered, as did my emails. Then I received the fifth or sixth draft of the script for *Under My Roof: The Movie.*

The kid had a girlfriend.

By the ninth draft the girlfriend was gone, and another year had passed. The option was renewed, as was the silence. Then, one evening, I got an email. There was a draft that made everyone happy. Money was raised—around a quarter of a million bucks, of which I'd earn several percent. An IMDbPro page was created, casting calls went out, a poster was mocked up, and an official film Twitter account launched.

Then, for a long time, nothing. Casting a film is difficult on a quarter of a million bucks. Maybe the script wasn't so great after all; maybe it wasn't so funny when a real-life kid actually had to say the lines. Maybe the Obama presidency meant that the war-mad Bush years could be forgotten. Then, some test footage was shot of a certain practical effect.

Here's an interesting fact: a film option is an agreement that at some future date, a producer can purchase a screenplay, or an idea for a film. The option basically just takes it off the table for everyone else while the producer tries to raise money and line up talent. But an option is realized—that is, the idea is purchased—not when a film comes out, or even when it is completed, but when a single frame of film or a tiny bit of digital data is recorded.

The test footage counted. I got a check for several percent of a quarter of a million dollars!

And then, nothing. Unanswered email, unanswered Facebook messages, unanswered voicemails. For years.

To this very day.

But *Under My Roof* lives again, and just in time.

ACKNOWLEDGEMENTS

Who else is there to acknowledge in the final page of a short story collection, save the editors of the short stories? So thank you Sean Wallace, Sheila Williams, Brian Thornton, Jason Sizemore, Brian Slattery, Aaron French, Cameron Pierce, Ellen Datlow, John Joseph Adams, Neil Clarke, Shawn Garrett and Alex Hofelich (they're a team), and Richard Peabody. That's in no particular order, by the way.

Also, thanks to Richard Nash for *Under My Roof,* frequent first readers Carrie Laben and Molly Tanzer for their help on many of these stories, and Jacob, Jill, and Elizabeth from Tachyon for the book you are reading right now.

I'd also like to acknowledge the casual Facebook game Cookie Jam for getting me through many evenings of procrastination.

NICK MAMATAS is the author of several novels, including *Love is the Law*, *I Am Providence* and the forthcoming *Hexen Sabbath*. His short fiction has appeared in *Best American Mystery Stories*, *Year's Best Science Fiction & Fantasy*, and many other venues.

Nick is also an anthologist; his books include the Bram Stoker Award winner *Haunted Legends* (co-edited with Ellen Datlow), the Locus Award nominees *The Future is Japanese* and *Hanzai Japan* (both co-edited with Masumi Washington), and *Mixed Up* (co-edited with Molly Tanzer). His fiction and editorial work has been nominated for the Hugo, Locus, World Fantasy, Bram Stoker, Shirley Jackson, and International Horror Guild awards.

Nick lives in the San Francisco Bay Area.